THE FAT BADGER
SOCIETY

by

DAWN HARRIS

Cover image: Anne & Paul Cameron

Other books by Dawn Harris
"Letter From A Dead Man" (a Drusilla
Davanish Mystery)

Short Stories
"Dinosaur Island," a collection of historical,
mystery and romantic short stories

Reviews for "Letter From A Dead Man."
"Letter From a Dead Man" has a similar wit
to "Pride and Prejudice," and Harris holds up a
mirror to society in the sort of way that Austen
did."
Margot Kinberg, award winner reviewer of
mystery novels.

"A delightful murder mystery in an 18th
century setting." Historical Novel Society.

Website:- **www.dawnharris.co.uk**

To my husband, Geoff, for his unstinting support and encouragement, and to my author daughter, Anne Cameron, for her expert advice and help

CHAPTER 1

May 1794

I was in the garden, talking to the King, when two men came out of the trees and began to cross the lawn. One pushed a wheelbarrow, the other carried a hoe. I was staying at Ashton Grange with my aunt and uncle while the friends who owned the house were away, but these two men were not on the gardening staff, and I had never seen either of them before.

They were some thirty yards away, walking very slowly, their eyes fixed on the King. But far from gazing at him in wonder, as many people did, these two seemed surprisingly tense.

No-one else gave them more than a glance. The King had turned his attention to my aunt, while my uncle and our other guests, Mr Reevers and Mr East, both tall and athletic, were enjoying a joke with Jeffel, my butler, as he set out light refreshments on the garden table. A third guest, the usually reliable Mr Hamerton, had unaccountably failed to arrive.

I heard the King say to my aunt, 'Frankly Mrs Frère, I detest London. The Queen and I prefer to be here in Windsor. Tell me ma'am, is our town to your liking?'

I never did catch what Aunt Thirza said, for the man with the hoe suddenly threw it aside and stared at me.

'What the devil---' I muttered under my breath.

At which point Mr Reevers inquired, 'Is anything wrong, Lady Drusilla?'

'Those men —' I began, and instinctively taking a step in their direction, I demanded, 'Who are you? What are you doing here?'

The large gathering of sparrows in the trees stopped chattering, a dark cloud blotted out the sun, and just as a gust of cool air rippled through the garden, the two men turned their backs on us, reached into the wheelbarrow, and swung round again with pistols in their hands.

I gaped at them open-mouthed, and when they began to run towards us, Aunt Thirza gave an odd little groan and fainted. At the exact moment I yelled out to the King to get down on the ground, they fired the first shot, and someone bowled me over with such force my head struck the lawn with a resounding thump. A second later Mr. Reevers raced past and threw His Majesty King George 111 unceremoniously flat on his face, ignoring his voluble protests.

All I saw of the man shielding me was an arm in front of my face, but that was enough to tell me who it was, and removing a blade of grass from my mouth, I burst out, 'Don't be foolish, Jeffel. You'll get hurt.' He didn't answer, or move, but before I could protest further, two more shots were fired, and I wished fervently that we had stayed at home on the Isle of Wight. Or gone anywhere but Windsor. Or even that I had not met the King so often when out riding before breakfast. Then he would not have been here today, where he was an easy target for assassination.

Nor was I under any illusions as to the fate in store for the rest of us. These men would not leave live witnesses behind. And I hadn't made a Will.

Foolishly I'd thought that, at twenty-seven, I had plenty of time to decide who would inherit Westfleet Manor and the large fortune my father had left me.

I was shaking like a blancmange, but I forced myself to think sensibly. They meant to kill the King and had brought two pistols each. Three shots had been fired, which meant they had one left, and then they would have to re-load. My well-meaning butler having pinned me to the ground, I could do nothing, except grit my teeth and pray. But, instead of the single shot I'd expected, two were fired in quick succession, and so close to me I flinched.

Then Mr. East gave a shout of triumph. 'Got the b--- beggars.' He dashed past me towards the intruders and a moment later assured us, 'It's all right. They're both dead.'

It was our good fortune that, as Government agents, Mr. Reevers and Mr. East were accustomed to carrying pistols. The one I had brought in case of highwaymen on the road to Windsor, was locked in a drawer in the study.

I heard the King say to my uncle in a remarkably calm voice, 'Mr. Frère, allow me to help you to assist your wife indoors. This has been a nasty shock for her.'

Closing my eyes in relief that they were all unharmed, I urged my butler, 'Do budge, Jeffel. It's quite safe now.'

Only then did I notice blood on the grass beside my head. I hadn't been hit, which meant it was Jeffel's blood. So that was why he'd ignored my orders. Fear set my heart pounding again, and instinctively I called out to Mr Reevers, who hurried over at once.

He gently moved Jeffel and I got up onto my knees. My butler's eyes were shut, and only then did I see how unnaturally still he was.

'Oh no,' I whispered, catching my breath. Jeffel had been at Westfleet since before I was born, and looking up at Mr Reevers through a haze of tears, I mutely beseeched him to tell me that this kindly, cheerful man wasn't dead.

Mr Reevers reached out, took my hands and assisted me to my feet. I tried to speak, but couldn't swallow the lump in my throat. 'I'm so sorry, Lady Drusilla,' Mr. Reevers murmured, his expressive dark eyes full of compassion. 'He was a good and honourable man.'

Toby East offered hurried words of sympathy, and begged me to go indoors for my own safety. 'Those men may not have been alone. I've told the servants to stay inside until we've searched the grounds.' And he handed me a loaded pistol. 'In case you need it,' he said.

As I watched the two gentlemen rush off, I realised that if I hadn't invited them today, the King would now be dead. As I would be. And my aunt and uncle.

I watched until I lost sight of them in the small copse of trees bordering the garden. The grounds were not extensive, and the two gentleman were accustomed to dangerous situations, but that didn't stop me worrying about them. And one of them in particular.

It would have been sensible to go indoors, but I could not bring myself to leave Jeffel. It was then I heard someone running, and my heart began to race again. Giving my fair curls a firm shake, I lifted the pistol ready to fire, and was surprised at the steadiness of my hand. But it was only Mr. Hamerton, who should have arrived much earlier.

The unaccustomed exercise had turned his face bright red and left him gasping for breath, as he explained, 'I -- heard ---- shots.' A trifle on the plump side for thirty, his kind brown eyes widened in horror on seeing Jeffel, and they stood out on stalks when he looked past me to the two dead men on the lawn.

'The King?' he blurted out aghast.

'He's quite safe,' I assured him.

'Thank heaven. But your poor butler, Lady Drusilla.' He shook his head in disbelief and asked, 'How did it happen, ma'am? Who are those men?'

I explained briefly, and decided to take a closer look at the villains. He protested that it wasn't a proper sight for a lady, but followed when that failed to stop me. The fact was, I wanted to remember the faces of the men who had taken Jeffel's life.

They were both young, probably no more than twenty; muscular, with rough hands and filthy torn nails. Not farm labourers though; they didn't have the skin of people who spent their lives out of doors. Their clothes suggested they pursued a trade of some sort.

When I saw the gentlemen returning from their search, I closed my eyes in relief. No other intruders having been found, I returned the pistol Mr East had given me, and pointed out to Mr. Reevers that his right ear was bleeding. 'A bullet clipped it,' he said, dabbing at it with his handkerchief. 'I was lucky.'

'Yes,' I agreed, more thankful than I cared to admit. And looking at Jeffel again, wished with all my heart I had left him back at Westfleet.

Mr. East asked Mr. Hamerton why he'd arrived so late. 'You should have been here an hour ago.'

'I- I- I was unavoidably delayed.'

'How did that happen?'

'Well -- I -' he hesitated, glanced at me and fidgeted with the buttons on his dark brown coat, his face turning rather pink, contrasting vividly with his ginger hair. 'This is not the time or the place, I believe.'

Shrugging, Mr East began searching the bodies, finding nothing but a few coins. When he turned one man over I saw something on the ground, and picked it up. It was a small piece of stiff cardboard, triangular in shape, on which someone had painted a rather fat badger. Mr Reevers asked to look at it, and without a word, passed it to Mr East.

Observing the King coming out of the house, I walked up the garden to meet him. 'I came to tell you ma'am, that your aunt has gone to lie down upon her bed. I urged her to take some tea to steady her nerves.' I thanked him, and His Majesty, who suffered from poor eyesight, peered in the direction of the gentlemen, and asked who the third one was. 'I can't quite make him out.'

'It's Mr Hamerton, sir.'

'Ah, yes. The poor fellow who lost his wife in that dreadful accident.'

As we stood talking, two gardeners carried Jeffel's body indoors. Mr. Hamerton accompanied them, as I learnt later, to ensure Jeffel rested in a suitable place and with due respect. I was grateful for his thoughtfulness.

The King expressed his sorrow at my butler's death and when the other two gentlemen joined us, he said, 'Nasty business, this. I----'

'I beg your pardon sir,' Mr. East interrupted with barely suppressed urgency, 'but we should get you home at once. Those two men may not have been working alone.'

'What makes you say that?' retorted the King, frowning.

Stretching out his open palm, Mr. East showed him the small piece of cardboard I'd picked up. 'That's why, sir.'

Having carefully studied the painting of the fat badger, the King looked Mr East straight in the eye. 'Isn't that the kind of thing the French royalists use to identify themselves to each other?'

'Yes they do, sir. But other societies may use them too. Corresponding societies for----'

I broke in, 'The people demanding the vote for all working men?'

He turned to me, more serious than I had ever seen him. 'That's what they say they stand for, Lady Drusilla, but we have evidence that some are secretly planning to overthrow the monarchy and the government.' Addressing the King he said, 'Both men carried these tokens, sir. This wasn't a random attack by two madmen. They were attempting to start a French-style revolution.'

The French, having guillotined their King and Queen, along with much of the hated nobility and clergy, were now gripped in a reign of terror, where no-one's head was safe. Not aristocrats, lowly peasants, or even revolutionary leaders, for Danton himself had perished only last month.

Silently I cursed France for their revolution. And for declaring war on us last year. If they won that war, we would see tumbrils rumbling through English streets, guillotines set up in our market places, and innocent heads rolling into those gruesome baskets.

'The grounds are clear,' Mr. East went on, 'but if there are others watching the house, and they see you leave unharmed, they might try again before you reach home.' He ran a hand worriedly through his thick blond hair. 'I'll send for an escort-----'

'Soldiers? To protect me from the people of Windsor. Never. What would they think of me? What? What?' The King often ended his sentences in this way. 'You forget they are accustomed to me walking about the town.'

He and the Queen liked to talk to people in the streets, and enjoyed visiting the shops. I had seen the King myself, sitting in a book shop studying the latest publications. Pleasures they could not easily enjoy in London. The gentlemen protested vigorously, pointing out the dangers, but he only shook his head. 'No, I won't hide behind soldiers. I'll ride back as usual. And that's my final word.'

Mr Reevers tried another tack.' No-one would think it odd sir, if Toby and I rode with you.'

Still the King refused to budge, but admitted, 'I accept it would be better if no-one knew I had been here today. There will be an inquest and----.'

'With your permission sir,' Mr Reevers said, 'we will suggest the men were London thieves who, hearing the owners of Ashton Grange were away, thought the house was empty. They brought the wheelbarrow to carry off the goods, but panicked when they saw us and started shooting.'

The King gave this his careful consideration. 'That sounds an excellent idea. Keep me out of it if you can.

What?' Looking at Mr Reevers' ear, which was bleeding again, he told him to go indoors and get it seen to. 'Or the blood will ruin your coat,' he pointed out with a faint smile.

He did as he was bid, Mr East went to organise the removal of the two bodies, leaving me alone with the King. 'They are fine fellows, Lady Drusilla, only I do hate fuss,' he confided. 'I had enough of that after that poor mad woman tried to attack me with a knife a few years ago.' And he gave a weary sigh. 'Still, it would be sensible to take a pistol with me. What?'

'Indeed it would, sir. I have one in the house.'

Going back inside, I took the King into the study to collect the pistol. Leaving the door open, I was loading the firearm when I heard footsteps, and a moment later, Mr East said, 'Oh, there you are, Radleigh. I've been thinking. When the King leaves, if we follow at a discreet distance, we'll be on hand if anything goes wrong.'

'There'll be the devil to pay if he finds out.'

'Better that than a dead King. He's a brave man, Radleigh, but foolhardy.'

The King put a finger to his lips, warning me not to speak, an understanding twinkle in his eyes. As their voices faded into the distance, he said, 'They mean well, Lady Drusilla, but I believe those two men were alone.'

'Perhaps. Only you can't be sure, can you, sir?' He eyed me thoughtfully, but said nothing, and I went on, 'You would be dead now but for the quick thinking of Mr Reevers and Mr East.' He nodded slowly, knowing it to be true. 'If there are other assassins out there, and you are killed, the country will descend into chaos, and those who want a French-style revolution could seize power.'

Frowning, he stood gazing out the window for a minute or two, before admitting I was right. 'Tell Reevers and East they may accompany me. Hamerton too, if he wishes. Not that I think he'd be much use in a fight. Incidentally, why was he so late?'

'He said he was delayed, sir. I don't know why.'

'A gentleman shouldn't make an engagement if he cannot keep it.'

'I expect he had a good reason.'

'Make sure he has, ma'am. He tells me he's to be your guest when you return to the Isle of Wight, and you can't be expected to tolerate that sort of behaviour.' He picked up the loaded pistol and put it carefully into his coat pocket. 'I gather he's thinking of moving to the Island. Personally I cannot understand why anyone would want to leave Windsor.'

'Too many memories of his wife, I imagine, sir.'

'Ah, yes. Of course. I should have thought of that. What?'

Ten minutes later the King rode off, closely guarded by his three escorts. I went out to watch them go, and stayed outside listening long after they were out of sight, fearing I might hear the sound of gunfire.

My uncle came out to join me, and seeing me shiver, murmured, 'You're cold, Drusilla. Come inside.'

'It's not the cold, Uncle. If you must know, I'm frightened.'

'Frightened? That's not like you.'

'Isn't it? I shook like a blancmange waiting for that fourth shot. I regret to say more in fear of my own life than the King's.'

He took my hand and patted it. 'Self-preservation is a natural instinct. I wouldn't let it trouble you. Tell me what frightens you now, my dear.'

Wishing I had his calmness, I said, 'If Mr. East is right and those two men were part of a conspiracy to start a revolution, the others won't rest until the King is dead. What I fear, Uncle, is that today may only be the beginning.'

CHAPTER 2

Within the hour Mr. Hamerton kindly came back to tell us the King had reached the Queen's Lodge without incident. But it was four days before I saw Mr. Reevers again.

The newspapers were full of the arrests of leading reformers, including Hardy, the founder of the London Corresponding society, whose manners and dress were described, rather alarmingly, as resembling that of a French sans-culotte. But there was nothing about the assassination attempt and I was relieved to see it had not got out.

I was walking in the garden on that fourth day, roundly cursing Mr. Reevers for not sparing me half an hour to tell me what was really going on, when I suddenly saw him striding across the lawn in my direction. He was smartly turned out in a pale blue coat and fawn riding breeches, his jet black wavy hair neatly tied back, and I found myself wishing I had put on one of my new gowns instead of my old dark green one, which owed more to comfort than fashion.

Radleigh Reevers and I had met once as children, and not seen each other again until last summer, at the height of the Saxborough murders.*

Shortly after that he was sent back to France, not returning until last week when, quite by chance, I'd bumped into him in Windsor. On reaching me he bowed and held out his hand. As I took it his dark eyes searched mine in a manner that left me unaccountably breathless.

See "Letter From A Dead Man."

'I can't stay long,' he murmured softly, still holding my hand. I should have removed it, but for some reason I found that difficult. 'We still haven't identified those two would-be assassins, or found any other members of this Fat Badger Society.' The strain of the past few days so clear in his voice that I felt guilty at cursing him earlier.

I finally removed my hand from his and we strolled along a path between some flower beds. Being a mere shade under six feet in height, I met few men taller than me, but he was, by some three or four inches. Raising my eyes to his, I asked if escorting the King home after the assassination attempt had been as easy as Mr. Hamerton had suggested.

'It would have been if the King hadn't insisted on stopping to talk to people in the street.' Smiling, I shook my head at his foolish disregard for personal safety, yet at the same time I couldn't help admiring his courage. 'Toby was practically tearing his hair out.'

I agreed the King could be very stubborn, and went on, 'I read the newspaper reports about the arrest of those corresponding society leaders. Were they involved in the assassination plot?'

'We don't know yet. Still, the suspension of Habeas Corpus will allow plenty of time to interrogate them. Meanwhile, Mr. Pitt insists on the King being closely guarded.'

'The King won't like that.'

'He refused point blank,' he admitted with a reminiscent grin. 'Until Mr. Pitt reminded him that if he was assassinated the Prince of Wales would become King. Even he knows that would be disastrous.'

Thinking of the prince's expensive tastes and unfortunate choice of female companions, I sighed. 'It's a pity the prince is not like his father.' For no-one could ever accuse King George 111 of neglecting his duties.

Remembering Mr. Hamerton's odd behaviour on the day of the assassination, I asked if he knew why that gentleman had arrived late that afternoon.

'He *said* he mistook the time.'

'But you don't believe that?'

'No. He was far too uncomfortable for it to have been that simple.' And he inquired, 'Tell me, what is your opinion of Hamerton?'

That was easily answered. 'I find him most amiable. He's pleasant, good-natured, sensible, and very much the gentleman.'

He nodded slowly, considering what I'd said. 'Is he still to accompany you to Westfleet when you return?'

'Of course.' Aunt Thirza had invited him in my presence, and that of Mr. Reevers and other friends, leaving me no choice but to urge him to accept. It was as well, I thought, that I liked him.

'Forgive me, but when Mrs. Frère made the invitation you did not seem overly pleased.'

'Do not mince your words, Mr Reevers,' I said, trying not to laugh. 'The plain fact is, whenever my aunt behaves as if Westfleet belongs to her, which she frequently does, I find myself overwhelmed by an intense longing to boil her in oil.'

His eyes danced merrily, but he made no comment, merely asking, 'Are you still going to London next week?'

'We are. My aunt and uncle are looking forward to it.' We were to attend a ball in honour of their god-daughter. I ran a hand across a lavender bush, enjoying the delicious scent drifting into the air. 'My aunt's only fear is of being held up by highwaymen on Hounslow Heath.'

'You should be safe enough in daylight,' he said in some amusement. 'Is Hamerton going to the ball?'

'No, he's not joining us until the day after. He has some business to attend to.'

'Well, Toby and I may see you there. We have orders to return to London at once.'

I looked up at him. 'So you came to take your leave of us.'

'That's one of the reasons. I also have a message for you from Mr Pitt.'

'Mr. Pitt?' I repeated, turning to him in astonishment.

'Indeed. He would be much obliged if you would do him the honour of calling at Downing Street on Tuesday.'

I stared at him in disbelief. 'Mr Pitt wishes to meet me? But why?'

'He will explain on Tuesday,' he said with a faint smile.

'Do you know why?'

He inclined his head. 'But I have been forbidden to tell you. May I inform him you accept his invitation?'

Naturally I agreed. I could hardly ignore the commands of the first Lord of the Treasury, the highest and most important minister in the land. Even so, having never met Mr. Pitt I simply could not understand why he wanted to see me. It certainly did not occur to me that he was about to change my life.

Mr. Reevers must have known it, but did not warn me, nor did he refer to it again. Instead he inquired,

'When are you returning to the Island?'

'Next Friday.'

'Then Toby and I will be there before you.'

Again I reacted with surprise. 'You're going to Norton House?' This residence, some five or six miles from Westfleet, had been his home for the past year, ever since he had been forced to sell his family estate on the mainland to settle his deceased father's debts. He nodded and I looked at him, puzzled. 'Are you going on leave?'

'Well, we have been in France since early November. And England does have other agents.'

That was true, and they deserved a rest, yet I had the distinct feeling that he wasn't being entirely truthful. And I wondered why they were really going. But suspecting he would not, or could not, tell me, I asked instead if Mr. East had been with him in France.

'He was. I couldn't have wished for anyone better. But he didn't find it easy living there.'

'Oh?' I murmured suspiciously, observing his innocent look. 'Why was that?'

'He absolutely loathes garlic.'

I burst into laughter. 'Poor Mr. East.'

Reaching a garden seat he suggested we sat down, and immediately asked me about Jeffel's funeral. 'I should like to attend if I-----'

'That is good of you Mr. Reevers, but Jeffel told me that when his time came he wished to be laid to rest in Westfleet churchyard. It is all in hand. My uncle made the – the- arrangements,' I ended, suddenly choking up.

His eyes softened. 'You still blame yourself, don't you.'

'If I hadn't met the King, Jeffel would still be alive.' On the several occasions the King had called at Ashton Grange he'd invariably exchanged a few words with Jeffel. My butler, overawed at first, had soon learned to relax and enjoy these encounters.

'You couldn't have foreseen it would end in tragedy.'

'No, and I realise it is utterly pointless to regret what cannot be changed, but the fact is I do regret it.' Jeffel had saved my life without a thought for his own. And the guilt I felt was beyond bearing. Yet, I had no choice except to bear it. I would never forget it, I thought, no matter how long I lived. Jeffel had always been part of my life and I simply could not imagine Westfleet Manor without him.

After Mr. Reevers had gone I wandered round the garden thinking of my happy childhood, when Jeffel had given me piggyback rides round the hall on wet days, laughed at my silly jokes, and listened patiently to my childish chatter. And when my father died eighteen months ago his quiet good sense helped me through those dreadful dark days.

When I eventually went indoors I found Aunt Thirza writing to the friends who owned Ashton Grange, telling them of the supposed robbery and assuring them nothing had been stolen. She also enclosed the newspaper report of the inquest, in which the coroner praised Jeffel for his bravery in attempting to prevent a robbery, and commended Mr. Reevers and Mr. East for dealing speedily with the villains, thus avoiding further bloodshed.

Earlier that morning I had written a similar letter to my friend, Julia Tanfield, on the Island, asking her to read it out to the servants at Westfleet.

No highwayman accosted us on the journey to the capital early the following week, much to my aunt's relief. Mudd drove us skilfully through the busy streets to our hotel, and after an excellent meal we spent the afternoon resting, conserving our energies for the ball that evening and enjoying the letters we found awaiting us. My aunt and uncle's was from Lucie, their only child, now married to Giles Saxborough of Ledstone Place, which was situated some four miles from Westfleet. Mine was from Giles's mother, Marguerite, who was my godmother, now visiting Yorkshire with Lucie and Giles.

I sat chuckling as I read mine, for Marguerite wrote as she spoke and her letters were always a delight. Unashamedly indolent, she said and did precisely what she wanted, but there wasn't an ounce of malice in her, and I adored her.

Having read it twice, I put it in a drawer. Then I sat looking out the window of my bedchamber watching the activities in the bustling street below, and puzzling over why Mr. Pitt wished to see me at a time when he must be incredibly busy, what with the arrests of the reformers, the suspension of Habeas Corpus, and the war. What could he possibly want of me when we had never met? Mr. Reevers knew, but did not have permission to tell me, which meant it was not a social occasion.

I was to have met him last autumn, to hand over the French invasion plan that came to light at the time of the Saxboroughs murders. My aunt and uncle were to have escorted me and I'd also hoped to see something of Mr. Reevers in London, but an untimely bout of influenza made it impossible for me to go. Mr. Reevers had taken the plan himself, and had been sent back to France immediately afterwards. Fortunately the French had not carried out the invasion, so that wasn't what Mr. Pitt wanted to see me about.

Well, I told myself firmly, when I saw him tomorrow he would explain. But that did not help one iota; I wanted to know *now*. And I smiled to myself thinking of how my father used to tease me about my lack of patience. How right he was, I thought; I never could abide waiting.

It was only when I began to dress for the ball that I finally managed to put Mr. Pitt from my mind. I loved dancing and was eagerly looking forward to the evening. I wore a new gown in a shade of blue that brought a gleam of pleasure to my aunt's eyes when I joined her and my uncle in the drawing room.

'Did I not tell you that colour and style of gown would become your height and figure?'

I gave a carefree laugh. 'Indeed you did, Aunt. And I am most grateful.' I wore the simple pearl necklace I'd inherited from my mother, and my maid had piled my fair hair high on my head, allowing one or two curls to hang becomingly around my face. In many ways Gray was just as silly as most girls of twenty, but she had a natural ability with styling hair and an eye for what suited me. Skills I would lose when she married, as she undoubtedly would, for she was a pretty girl with large appealing brown eyes.

My uncle took my hands and holding me at arm's length, said affectionately, 'You remind me of your dear Mama.'

I knew from the portrait on my bedchamber wall that I resembled my mother, who died giving birth to my stillborn brother, when I was three. I had her hazel eyes and good complexion, but although my countenance was pleasing enough, not even my doting father ever suggested I had her beauty. And Aunt Thirza, my mother's only sister, was rather plain, but what she lacked in looks she made up for with sheer elegance.

Mudd drove us to the ball and with so many carriages arriving together, it was a few minutes before we could alight on that windy, rainy night. But it was well worth the wait. The ballroom itself was a picture of stylishness and good taste, the light from the magnificent chandeliers and hundreds of candles set off the elegant gowns and priceless jewellery to perfection.

The instant we walked in, some old friends of my aunt and uncle engaged them in conversation, and as I wandered off admiring the room, I caught sight of Mr Reevers and Mr. East.

Mr. East had his back to me, but Mr. Reevers saw me at once and drew his friend in the opposite direction, introducing him to a young lady I could not see clearly. Leaving them talking, he came straight over to me. He was immaculately turned out, his black wavy hair neatly in place for once, with no sign of a stray lock curling round an ear, as it often did.

'Lady Drusilla,' he murmured softly, taking in my ball gown at a glance. 'You look utterly charming. May I have the honour of taking you in to supper later?'

'I should be delighted,' I said formally, and asked in some amusement why he had quite deliberately got rid of Mr. East.

'Well, Toby was determined you would be *his* partner at supper, so it was necessary to distract him so that I could ask you first,' he explained with a wide grin. 'Fortunately there was a rather stout young lady with buck teeth I felt I ought to introduce him to.'

I stifled a chuckle. 'I thought he was your friend.'

'Yes, but in this situation I am at a distinct disadvantage. He's far too good looking.'

I laughed. 'That's true. When he called at Ashton Grange I swear every female servant in the house found an excuse to walk across the hall in order to gaze at him.' Mr. East was my own height, possessed laughing blue eyes, thick blond hair and immense charm. 'But he doesn't appear to favour any young lady in particular.'

'Not now, although there was someone.' Watching Mr. East leading out the stout young lady to dance, Mr. Reevers suggested we follow their example. 'But perhaps it would be wiser to join a different set.'

A little later, when Mr East learnt how he had been tricked, he threatened, 'I've a good mind to call you out for that, Radleigh.'

Mr. Reevers shook with laughter. 'Don't waste your time, Toby. I should choose swords.' As he was explaining to me that Mr. East was an excellent shot but hopeless at fencing, an acquaintance interrupted, wanting to introduce him to his wife.

He excused himself with a bow and Mr East, observing sets were forming for the next dance, had just asked me if I cared to join them, when a gentleman accidentally bumped into me, the room having become very crowded.

I turned to find myself gazing into the steely eyes of the Earl of Rotherton. 'Lady Drusilla,' he said, bowing formally. 'My apologies.' He was about to move away when he became aware of my companion, and sneered, 'So you're here, are you, East?'

Mr East did not reply. He looked right through Lord Rotherton as if he wasn't there, and to my astonishment, for he had impeccable manners, he abruptly turned and marched off.

CHAPTER 3

Rotherton, quickly losing sight of Mr. East in the crowded room, turned to me his cold eyes blazing with anger. 'I advise you to avoid that mongrel whippersnapper, ma'am. Can't have his sort marrying into the aristocracy. You know, he actually thought his money would make him acceptable to me as my son-in-law. He soon learned his mistake.'

I looked him up and down, not bothering to hide my dislike. 'Your daughter married Lord Troughton, I believe.' I'd met his daughter, his only child, once. A pretty girl, but shy and timid. Troughton was three times her age, his way of life left much to be desired, but his lineage was unimpeachable, his ancestors, like the Rothertons, having come over with William the Conqueror. And Troughton desperately needed an heir. The match had outraged London society.

'Yes. She saw sense in the end.'

'And died in childbirth.'

'Indeed, ma'am. But she did not disgrace the family name.'

I looked him straight in the eye. 'No,' I said slowly. '*She* did not, certainly.'

He did not mistake my meaning and I thought for a brief moment he meant to strike me. When his face reached a satisfying shade of puce, I turned on my heel and went off in search of Mr. East. He was standing in a corridor, apparently looking out at the torrential rain, and I persuaded him to come back into the ballroom, where I suggested we sat down.

After a moment or two he said hesitantly, 'You must be wondering at my rudeness, Lady Drusilla.'

'It is none of my concern, Mr East.'

'Even so, I should not have left you with that man.' The venom in those last two words sent a chill down my spine.

'I am perfectly capable of dealing with Rotherton.'

'I thought I could deal with him too, but when I began to take an interest in his daughter, he informed me he would never allow her to marry a man whose grandfather had been born in the gutter. Being fully conscious of his staggering debts, I reminded him that I possessed a considerable fortune, which I inherited from my grandfather,' he said in his self-deprecating manner. 'When I politely pointed out that breeding did not pay the bills, he chose to see that as an insult and sent me packing.'

The anguish in his eyes brought such a lump into my throat I hurriedly asked how his grandfather had made his fortune. He didn't answer at once and afraid he thought I was merely prying, I said, 'I'm sorry, I shouldn't have asked, and you are too polite to tell me to mind my own business.'

That brought a broad smile to his face. 'It's not a secret, ma'am. As a boy he ran errands for a lady who took a liking to him and taught him how to read and write. That enabled him to obtain a position as a clerk in a shipping firm. And eventually he ended up owning it. I'm not ashamed of him, Lady Drusilla. In fact I'm proud of what he achieved.'

'As you should be. He must have been a remarkable man. But Rotherton will always think he was right, even though by all accounts, his ancestor who came over with the Conqueror was a particularly nasty piece of work.'

'So I've heard, ma'am.' He took a deep breath. 'Still, it all happened long ago and I don't believe in living in the past. Unfortunately seeing Rotherton again brought it all back to me. Probably his daughter would have grown fat like her mother, and think of the disillusionment I would have suffered! Instead I shall always remember her as a sweet young girl.'

I didn't think it would be long before Mr East succumbed to another pretty face, and he would make the right woman an excellent husband. I liked him enormously myself. We took our places in a country dance a few minutes later, and he proved to be an expert dancer, very light on his feet. As was Mr Reevers, much to my surprise.

Despite returning home in the early hours I was up at the usual time in the morning, excited at the prospect of meeting Mr. Pitt. I still could not think of any reason why he would wish to see me, but eager to meet the man who had been running the country for eleven years, ever since he was twenty-four, I dressed with care in a new gown of soft green.

I had been to London several times with my father, and had seen number 10 Downing Street from the outside, but never imagined I would ever be invited beyond that spotless oak door with the lion's head knocker.

Mr. Reevers, who was to escort me, arrived in good time. Mudd drove us there and on being admitted into the house we were promptly escorted to a waiting room, before being taken, within a few minutes, into Mr. Pitt's study. He was a rather thin, tall gentleman with plain features, and I wondered how it must feel to be in charge of the most powerful government in the world.

A servant came in bearing a heavy tray of refreshments, and I accepted a little wine, while Mr Reevers took a glass of our host's favourite port. When the servant left the room Mr Pitt came straight to the point. 'No doubt, Lady Drusilla, you are wondering why I wished to see you.'

'Indeed I am, sir.'

'Then I won't keep you in suspense.' He took a sip of port, put his glass down and picked up a book from a nearby table. I saw at once that it was the book my father had written, "The History of the Isle of Wight." Published six months before his sudden death from a seizure, it had been very well-received. 'I thought it a fascinating book, Lady Drusilla, and I was most impressed with your achievements.'

'I'm glad you enjoyed it sir, but my father wrote the book,' I pointed out politely. 'I only helped with the research.'

'From what I've heard you are being too modest ma'am, but that is no bad thing. Over confidence can be dangerous. Mr Reevers said that when you came across a mystery that was difficult to unravel, it was your idea to write the known facts on a sheet of paper and fix it to the wall where it could always be seen.'

I glanced at Mr Reevers, curious to know why he should tell Mr Pitt such a thing. 'Yes, I did do that, sir. I thought it made sense.'

'Indeed.' He picked up a quill from his desk and absently twisted it in his fingers. 'May I inquire how long you worked on the book?'

'Some five or six years.'

'Did you enjoy it?'

'I did. Immensely.' In fact, I had never been happier.

That seemed to please him and he asked, 'Did you solve every puzzle you came across?'

'No, sir. Some things were simply not possible to resolve.'

'How did you feel about that?'

Smiling, I was forced to admit, 'To be truthful, I found it very frustrating. I like to get to the bottom of things.'

'Mr Reevers said that too. He also informed me you are highly perceptive, have a logical mind, and more brains than any other woman, and most men, of his acquaintance.'

His words brought a flush to my cheeks, and as Mr. Reevers' attention appeared to be concentrated on the contents of his glass, I could only express my bewilderment. 'I cannot imagine why he should say such a thing, sir.'

'No need to blush, ma'am. Mr Reevers knows what he's about, believe me. He feels skills of that nature should be put to good use. And he's quite right. Did you use the same methods when you solved the Saxborough murders last year?'

'Yes sir, I did.'

'I was sorry you were unable to bring the French invasion plan to Downing Street yourself, but Mr. Reevers was an excellent deputy.' I answered suitably and he crossed to the window, where he stood looking out as if thinking. Suddenly he said, 'Tell me, ma'am, do you like the Spring?'

'I believe there's something to be said in favour of all the seasons sir, although Spring is my favourite.'

He nodded. 'When the weather is fine, there's nothing to beat it. But my poor garden is in a sorry state after last night's heavy rain and strong winds.'

'I'm sure it will soon recover now the sun's out.'

He swung round at that. 'So you are an optimist.' I agreed that I was and that seemed to please him. 'What is your opinion of the French, ma'am? Do you believe we can beat those devils?'

'I do, sir. And we must, if our way of life is not to be lost for ever.'

He gave a sharp nod of approval, a fierce glint in his eyes. 'How long do you imagine it will take us?'

I stared at him, hardly knowing how to answer such a question. After a moment, I said, 'Surely sir, you must know that better than anyone.'

'Yes, yes,' he muttered a little testily. 'But I want to know what *you* think.'

I glanced at Mr Reevers, who sat grinning at me. Feeling a little nettled that he obviously knew what Mr Pitt was up to when I didn't, I decided that if the great man wanted my opinion, then he should have it.

'In that case sir, I think it may take quite some time. Possibly years. France may be in chaos with that revolutionary band of cut-throats running the country, but they are a proud nation, and I don't think they will be easily crushed.'

If I hadn't been so slow-witted, I would have realised he was making his own judgement of my character.

He inclined his head. 'An optimist, but one who faces facts. Good.' And he sighed. 'Well, I pray you are wrong, but I'm obliged to you for being so candid.' He sat down opposite me then, and it suddenly struck me that if I had not given a rational answer, he would have brought our meeting to an abrupt end. Instead he spoke for some considerable time of the war, and his worries over the current unrest in England, with people forming themselves into organised societies and demanding the vote for all working men.

'We have evidence that some corresponding societies want a French-style government here and are secretly arming themselves with pikes and pistols. Hence the need to suspend Habeas Corpus, much though I regret the necessity. After what happened at Ashton Grange it was thought wiser to arrest the worst of these agitators. England will be a safer place with them in prison. I promise you ma'am, while I live there will be no guillotines set up in our market squares, and no bloodthirsty revolutionaries strutting around Downing Street.'

'I'm very glad to hear it, sir. I think-----` I stopped, realising what I had been going to say was a criticism of him.

'Go on,' he urged, clearly reading my face. 'Say what you think.'

'It's just that we have been at war for over a year now and - what I'm trying to say is - if the people had a victory to celebrate there would be less unrest.'

He pursed his lips and I promptly made things a thousand times worse. 'Of course, victories don't come to order---` I said, floundering. When he didn't answer, I went on, 'I beg your pardon, I should not — `

'Not at all. You're quite right. I'm only too aware of it myself.' He refilled my wine glass. 'Still, there's more than one way to win a war, and everyone can play a part in it.' He leaned forward and fixed his eyes on mine. 'Are you willing to serve your country, Lady Drusilla? England needs people like you, if we are to beat the French. What do you say, ma'am?'

I stared at Mr. Pitt, utterly dumbfounded. Did he want me to go to France? To be a government agent? Unable to see how I was to do such a thing, I protested, 'But my French is unspeakably bad.'

He roared with laughter, insisting his own French left much to be desired. 'As for going to that Godforsaken country,' he went on, 'that kind of thing is best left to people like Mr Reevers. In any war, however, there is always an upsurge in spying. Traitors – Englishmen spying for the French are particularly difficult to root out. Yet, we must if we are to win this war.' He drank a little more port and put his glass down. 'These spies are infiltrating corresponding societies, instructing them in the way the French organised their revolution, recruiting no more than ten or twenty members in one place. It being easier to mobilise small numbers. We believe there is one such group on the Isle of Wight.'

'On the Island,' I echoed, stunned.

'The Island is a quiet backwater. Perfect for organising another attempt on the King's life without anyone being the wiser. Or so they believe.'

He refilled his glass, and asked softly, 'Tell me, do you think you could flush out a French spy?'

That made me gasp out loud. 'Me? But how----'

'I need people like you. People who are adept at seeking out the truth, and capable of making good judgements.' Leaning back in his chair he gazed at me, a hint of a smile hovering on his lips as he waited patiently for me to answer.

To give myself time to think, I reached for my glass and slowly sipped a little wine. 'I hardly know how to answer you sir,' I admitted eventually, twisting the half empty glass in my fingers. 'Would it mean moving to London?'

'No, nothing like that. We have agents here who smoke out most of those working for the French. But with a few – the cleverer spies – it's not easy to get to the truth. So we have to use more subtle methods, and these take time.' He leaned forward again, his eyes searching mine. 'Would you allow such a man to be a guest in your own home, possibly for many weeks?'

'At Westfleet?' I exclaimed, astonished. 'You want me to house a man who may be a French spy?' And, suddenly, I understand exactly what he wanted. 'You mean, to treat him as a guest and at the same time find out where his true allegiance lies?'

He inclined his head. 'Precisely. No man can watch what he says twenty-four hours a day for weeks on end. He's also more likely to relax in the company of a charming woman, such as yourself, and be far less guarded in his conversation.'

Mr Reevers, who had sat quietly listening for some time, reminded Mr Pitt, 'Perhaps Lady Drusilla should be warned that it may well be a little dangerous.'

'Ah yes, quite right. I should have mentioned that, ma'am. I'm sure you can see how a French spy might react if he knew you'd found him out.'

I could see exactly how it would be, I thought acidly, but as Mr Pitt clearly did not expect that prospect to weigh with me, I merely nodded as if it was of no great significance. Glancing across at Mr Reevers I saw his eyes were alight with amusement; not, I knew, from any desire to see me in danger, but because he understood precisely what I was thinking. Nevertheless, such considerations were soon swept away by the surge of excitement I felt at being involved in the struggle to beat the French.

I began to see how it could work. A man given a pretext for staying at Westfleet would have no idea what I was doing, nor would anyone else in my house. I would make my report to Mr Pitt, and if the man was a French spy, he would never suspect me, a mere woman, of having had any part in finding him out. And it might help, albeit in a very small way, to win this war.

Thus mollified, I turned to Mr Pitt and said, 'I'm very willing to try.'

'Good,' he beamed.

'But I might get it wrong. You do realise that.'

'They get it wrong in London too, on occasion,' he sighed. 'Although I'd be grateful if you didn't repeat that.'

In that kind of business mistakes must happen, I thought. Praying I would not add to them I asked how I was to go about inviting such a man to Westfleet without him suspecting he was being watched and appraised.

The two gentlemen exchanged glances, and when Mr. Pitt gave a slight nod, Mr Reevers said, 'In this instance that isn't a problem. The man whose loyalty is in question is Mr Hamerton.'

CHAPTER 4

'Mr. Hamerton?' I gasped. 'But – he's so --- so --- inoffensive.'

'Spies rarely appear sinister, ma'am,' Mr Pitt pointed out. 'Most seem remarkably ordinary.'

It only took a moment to see that made perfect sense. For, agents who drew attention to themselves would not last long. It was also stupid of me not to have realised that. I hoped it wouldn't make Mr. Pitt change his mind about employing me. 'But --- why do you suspect him?'

'Well, to start with ma'am, two years ago his wife was knocked down and killed by a carriage in the street.'

'Yes, Mr. Hamerton told me about that.'

'Did he also tell you the carriage was driven by a rich aristocrat, known for his arrogance and reckless driving?' I had to admit he had not. 'I regret to say a few members of the aristocracy use their influence to escape justice when ordinary mortals committing similar crimes are hanged, imprisoned or deported. The French nobility have paid for that kind of behaviour with their heads. It's impossible to say whether Mrs. Hamerton's death was a genuine accident. There were no witnesses and the driver insisted she walked straight out in front of him. But a week later he was found dead in a wood. He had been shot.'

I stared at him open-mouthed. 'Are you saying Mr. Hamerton murdered this man?'

He shrugged his shoulders. 'We don't know. But, on that particular night, he did not return home until after three. Hamerton told his butler he had been out studying moths.'

'Moths?' I repeated in scathing tones.

'Exactly so, ma'am, and that's not all. He was seen quite recently at a London Corresponding Society meeting. And yesterday we learned his sister is married to a Frenchman.'

I protested, 'That doesn't mean he's a spy. My aunt married a Frenchman.'

Mr Pitt smiled. 'So I understand. But this man is one of Robespierre's closest confidantes.'

I could not believe what he'd said. 'Mr. Hamerton's brother-in-law is close to Robespierre?' I repeated, convinced I'd misheard. Robespierre, the first deputy of the French Convention, was the most important and the most feared man in the whole of France.

'I'm afraid so. He isn't well known, preferring to remain in the background, but there is no question of a mistake. This comes from one of our most reliable agents. Nevertheless, that does not mean Hamerton is a traitor. As I'm sure you have read in the newspapers, my own sister's husband, Lord Stanhope, supports the French revolution.' He gave a long deep sigh of weariness. 'The misguided fellow has even taken to calling himself Citizen Stanhope. I am not responsible for his views, just as Mr. Hamerton cannot be blamed for the part his brother-in-law takes in the revolution.'

Still stunned, I said, 'Mr. Hamerton has never spoken of a sister.'

'I can't say as I blame him. I wish I need never mention my brother-in-law,' Mr. Pitt remarked acidly. 'But that is not all, I'm afraid.'

He raised an inquiring eyebrow at Mr. Reevers who

took the hint and explained, 'Lady Drusilla, that day at Ashton Grange when those two villains tried to kill the King, Mr Hamerton was very late in arriving. And he refused to say why. If he was involved in that plot, it may be that he expected to find the King dead.'

'What's more,' Mr. Pitt went on, 'our intelligence people have learned that an Englishman working for the French is expected on the Isle of Wight this month. He goes by the name of Mr. Brown, one of the pseudonyms the French use for their agents here, and we're told the French expect big things of him. Frankly, we don't know if Mr. Hamerton is Mr. Brown. And that's where you come in. What we need is proof. One way or the other. But, whoever this Mr. Brown is, he must be stopped, ma'am. And quickly. It's vital that we seize every member of this traitorous Fat Badger society, and to that end, Mr. Reevers and Mr. East will leave for the Island on Wednesday.'

So that was the real reason they were going to the Island. I was not surprised, for I could not believe they would agree to take leave during a crisis. But to everyone else, including Mr. Hamerton, they were simply spending a few weeks enjoying the summer at Norton House.

I asked, 'If I do learn anything, how am I to----'

'Pass the information to Mr. Reevers, ma'am. He'll send it to me by special messenger.' He thought for a moment. 'I believe that covers everything. Tell me, ma'am, when do you mean to return home?'

'On Friday.'

'I beg of you not to delay one moment longer than necessary.'

I promised I would not, and left Downing Street a

little later, still in a state of shock. As I told Mr Reevers, when Mudd drove us back to the hotel, I was flattered to be asked but afraid I might fail. 'If Mr. Hamerton is this Mr. Brown he might deceive me too.' The carriage suddenly stopped with a jolt, and Mudd, busily threading his way slowly through a mass of gigs, carts, carriages and riders, admonished an urchin who had run across in front of him.

'In our business there's always a chance of that, 'Mr Reevers said. 'But Mr Hamerton will be living at Westfleet. He'll sit at your dinner table, ride and talk with you, your family and friends. You cannot help but get to know him better and no man can guard his tongue every moment of the day. That is what Mr Pitt is counting on.'

Despite everything I had learnt about Mr. Hamerton I found it hard to believe this seemingly harmless man was working for the French. But if he was, and the Fat Badgers succeeded in killing the King, the French could launch an invasion, win the war, and set up guillotines in market places all over our beautiful land.

Just let them try, I thought. They would not find it easy. First they had to defeat the Army and the Navy, and even if they succeeded, the whole of England would rise up and fight to the last breath to preserve the country we knew and loved. Now I had my own small part to play, and I had one distinct advantage. For, what had not been said was that, as a woman, no-one would suspect me of working for the government.

Back at the hotel, discovering my aunt and uncle had gone out, I gave way to the excitement that had welled up inside me on the drive back to the hotel, dancing round and round our private sitting room until I ran out of breath and collapsed into a chair. To be given this chance was beyond anything I could have imagined, for women rarely had any influence in a war. And I wished, so much, that my father could have known.

I couldn't wait to get started, and when I got back to Westfleet I intended to write every fact I'd learnt today onto large sheets of paper and pin them to my workroom wall, so that all the evidence could be seen at a glance, as I had done when working with my father. When looking into a mysterious death involving Island families, we refused to condemn any man without cast-iron proof. This was what Mr. Pitt needed now. Evidence that proved either Mr. Hamerton's guilt, or his innocence. And it was my job to find it.

Determined nothing would be forgotten, I took a sheet of paper from the desk, wrote down everything Mr. Pitt had told me concerning Mr. Hamerton, and considered each fact one by one. Why had he arrived late at Ashton Grange on the day of the attempted assassination? Did his sister's husband being close to Robespierre have any real significance? But what puzzled me most was the murder of the aristocrat who'd knocked down Mrs. Hamerton. Or rather Mr. Hamerton's alibi. Had he really been out observing moths at that time of night? If he came in at three in the morning, having committed a murder, why come up with such a pitiful excuse?

Either it was the truth, or he had failed to think up an alibi beforehand, not expecting anyone to see him arriving home in the middle of the night. And why had he gone to a meeting of the London Corresponding Society? The opinion I'd gained of Mr. Hamerton during our short acquaintance, was that he rarely acted on impulse.

I was still thinking about it all when my aunt and uncle returned. Naturally they asked what Mr. Pitt had wanted, and thankfully, his interest in my father's book seemed to satisfy them. Fortunately, Aunt Thirza was more curious about the interior decoration and furnishings in Downing Street than in what Mr. Pitt had said.

She went on to talk about Mr. Hamerton, expressing her delight that he'd agreed to come back to Westfleet with us. It wasn't difficult to guess what she was leading up to, as she was forever trying to find me a husband. 'He may not be particularly handsome,' she said, with an encouraging smile, 'but he is good-tempered, sensible and genteel. His fortune is more than respectable, and he is only a very little shorter than you are.'

I burst out laughing. 'He's coming to the Island to decide if he wishes to live there, not to find a wife.'

'Well, there's nothing to stop him doing both.'

'Very true, but Mr Hamerton is not at all in my style, Aunt. He's perfectly pleasant, but I have no desire to marry him.'

My uncle winked at me and suggested to his wife, 'Drusilla might do better to consider Mr East, my dear. He's a very handsome fellow. Good natured too.'

My aunt retorted, 'Mr Hamerton has the kinder disposition. And that's most important in a marriage.'

'Well, there's a dilemma for you, Drusilla,' my uncle declared jovially. 'Your aunt wishes you to marry Mr Hamerton, and I favour Mr. East. Now, which is it to be?'

I laughed. 'I doubt I shall ever marry.' I had decided that years ago. The truth was I enjoyed being in control of my life, and my estates. If I married that would change. Westfleet and my estates would belong to my husband, as would my entire fortune. That was the law. And what man would allow me the freedom I enjoyed now? Domesticity was not for me. I liked children, but detested the small talk married woman indulged in.

'You must marry someone,' my aunt insisted.

'Why must I?'

She floundered. 'Well --- I mean ---- there's your estate----'

'I've looked after that since father died. And helped him with it since I was twelve.'

'What if something went seriously wrong?'

'I would deal with it.'

My uncle folded his arms, so clearly enjoying the situation that my aunt burst out, 'It's not funny, Charles. Drusilla is twenty-seven. She should have married years ago.'

'In my opinion, my dear,' he said, taking his life in his hands, 'Drusilla is very well able to decide for herself what she wants.'

'Oh – really,' she exploded. 'You are quite ---- impossible.'

'You mustn't worry about me,' I said, attempting to calm her down. For I knew she only had my best interests at heart.

'But I do worry, Drusilla.'

'Yes, I know, but I'm perfectly happy as I am.' She would never understand how I felt, and if she discovered I was working for Mr. Pitt it would terrify her. Even my easy-going uncle would be concerned for my safety, whereas I saw no real danger, for Mr. Hamerton could not possibly know what I was doing.

Later Mr. Reevers and Mr. East came to take their leave of us, as they were setting off for the Isle of Wight first thing in the morning. Talking over the events of the ball, Mr. East assured me I had been the most beautiful woman there.

'I would be flattered,' I said, tongue-in-cheek, 'if I hadn't overheard you saying much the same thing to that dark-haired beauty you danced with last night.'

'Did you?' Mr East was aghast. 'Are you quite sure?'

'Why – don't you remember?' I teased.

Mr Reevers, enjoying his friend's discomfort, announced, 'You must be slipping, Toby.'

'By heaven, you're right. I must be.' He humbly begged my forgiveness, then observing Mr. Reevers was still grinning, declared, 'At least I had the sense not to say it to that buck-toothed frosty-faced female you introduced me to.'

Amused, I intervened, 'You asked her to dance, though.'

'Didn't have much choice, did I? You should see my poor toes. They're black and blue. Just as well we don't have to walk to Portsmouth.'

At a glance from Mr. Reevers, Mr. East asked my aunt and uncle what they thought of the suspension of Habeas Corpus and the arrests of those involved in Corresponding Societies. Both began to talk at once, enabling Mr. Reevers to quietly draw me over to the window.

'You did that on purpose,' I accused.

He grinned at me. 'I needed to keep them occupied for a minute or two.'

'Did you indeed? I don't see why.'

'Don't you?' he murmured. 'I wanted to speak to you alone, of course.'

Words that made me catch my breath. 'You really are impossible.'

'I knew you would understand. It concerns Hamerton. Should you have good reason to believe he is this Mr. Brown the French expect so much of, you must get word to me or Toby at Norton House immediately. If he realises you have found him out he won't hesitate to kill you.' Lowering his voice even further, he urged, 'Whatever happens, please do not take any unnecessary risks.' I gave him the answer he sought, certain I would be able to keep my word. Quite forgetting, in that moment, that there are no certainties in life.

CHAPTER 5

Mr. Reevers looked as if he wished to say something more, but the arrival of Mr. Hamerton from Windsor prevented any further private conversation. Greetings were exchanged, Mr. Hamerton took a seat, accepted a glass of wine, and in answer to my aunt's concerned query, assured her he hadn't seen a sign of a highwayman on his journey. He was eager to hear all the details of the ball and when that subject had been exhausted, Mr. Reevers asked if he was looking forward to visiting the Isle of Wight.

'I am. Very much. When I was a boy we used to stay with a great aunt who lived near Cowes. Deaf as a post she was. Kept calling me Tom. Told her my name was John, but it didn't make a jot of difference. Couldn't hear me, you see. She was rolling in money by all accounts, and Mama said if I was polite and kind to her she might leave us some of it. She never did, of course.' Reminiscences that made us all smile.

I inquired, 'When were you last on the Island?'

'Oh, about twenty years ago. I liked it then, and when I married, my wife and I talked about visiting, with a view to moving there. But she was afraid of the sea crossing.' He was sitting immediately to my left and he turned to look at me, his brown eyes softening. 'Eventually she said that, with me at her side, she could brave anything. We planned to go after our child was born, but it wasn't to be. She died a few weeks later.'

'I am so very sorry, Mr Hamerton,' I murmured. A sentiment in which everyone joined.

'Thank you. You are all very kind.' He drank a little

wine and put his glass down on a table. 'The nobleman who drove the carriage that knocked her down came to see me the day after the accident. The poor man was greatly distressed. It seems my wife walked straight out in front of him, as if her mind was on something else. He said everything I would expect of such a gentleman. That was two years ago, but it seems like yesterday to me.'

No-one quite knew what to say and Mr Reevers broke the silence by asking if he still had relatives on the Island. Mr. Hamerton shook his head. 'Not now, unfortunately, but I should like to see if the place suits me. I have a feeling that it will.' Turning to me he asked about the arrangements for the journey. 'Do you wish me to ride or-------'

'I should prefer that, Mr. Hamerton,' Aunt Thirza broke in. 'An extra gentleman riding by the carriage will make any highwayman think twice about accosting us.' My aunt had an obsession regarding highwaymen.

'I shall be most happy to oblige, ma'am.' Glancing at the gentlemen he inquired, 'Talking of rogues, who were those two men who tried to assassinate the King?'

'We haven't been able to identify them yet,' Mr. East told him, and remarked in his pleasant way, 'Speaking of that day, why were you so late? I can't believe you mistook the time, and people do not generally keep the King waiting.'

I recalled Mr. Hamerton's embarrassment when asked that question on the day itself, but he answered easily enough now.

'Oh that.' Grimacing, he explained, 'Well, if you must know, I was assisting a lady in distress. Or so I thought. I always took the short cut along the bridleway when I walked to Ashton Grange, and I'd gone about half way when I came across a lady sitting on a log under a tree. She felt faint and shivery and begged me to help her, so naturally I took off my coat and put it round her shoulders.'

Mr East grinned. 'Pretty, was she?'

'Stunning,' he owned. 'She soon recovered and went on her way. But when I put my coat back on I realised the lady was not what she seemed. All my money had gone, and I went in search of a constable.'

'Did you lose much?' inquired Mr Reevers sympathetically.

'A considerable sum, I regret to say.' My uncle asked if he had found a constable. 'Not then. And, later, I decided not to bother. The woman had long gone. I should have explained at the time, but the fact is I felt such a fool.'

Aunt Thirza was full of sympathy and setting the conversation in another direction, asked if he had always lived in Windsor. He shook his head. 'I was brought up in Kensington.'

'But you have travelled, I'm sure.'

'Only on the Continent, ma'am. That experience made me thankful I was English, I can tell you. At least we can complain about our government without being arrested and guillotined.'

Mr. East eyed him lazily. 'True, but if these corresponding societies get their way that could happen here too.'

'If,' I said, 'something was done about the electoral system, the corresponding societies would have nothing to complain about. I mean, look what happens in Dittistone.' Dittistone was about four miles from Westfleet. 'It's a small place, yet it is represented by two members of parliament. And they are elected through the votes of just four people. Whereas towns like Manchester and Birmingham have no representation at all. And that cannot be right.'

A long and lively discussion ensued, and during a slight lull Mr. Reevers casually remarked, 'You haven't said much, Hamerton. What's your opinion on electoral reform? Are you in favour? Should every working man be given the vote?'

Taking a pretty enamelled snuff box from his pocket, Mr. Hamerton helped himself to a good pinch of the contents before answering. 'I agree something ought to be done, but in my view, this isn't the right time. It seems to me people don't want a lot of unrest when we're trying to beat the French.'

'Mr. Hamerton is right,' Aunt Thirza announced firmly.

'Don't know about that, ma'am. Might not be right. Just my opinion, that's all.'

Mr. Reevers and Mr. East left shortly afterwards and as we were going to the theatre that evening, we all hurried off to change for dinner.

Two days later we left for Portsmouth. Mudd drove our carriage, my uncle and Mr. Hamerton rode beside it, with the servants following in the second carriage. It was an uneventful trip, without any sign of highwaymen, which my aunt still feared despite my pointing out to her that the road to Portsmouth being a busy one, daylight robbery was rather unlikely.

I'd hoped for a peaceful journey, but we had barely

left Windsor when Aunt Thirza demanded to know what I was doing about finding a butler to replace Jeffel. 'I suppose you haven't even thought about it and----'

'I shall give Luffe a chance,' I said, for I had indeed thought about it.

'Luffe?' she exclaimed in scathing tones, dismissing the idea with a toss of her head. 'That's ridiculous. He's far too young. You need someone who knows the work.'

'He does know it.' I liked Robert Luffe. He had been at Westfleet for less than a year, assisting Jeffel. An intelligent young man of twenty-four, he had a pleasant manner, an upright bearing, spoke well, and was a fast learner.

'He makes mistakes,' she protested.

'But never the same one twice. In any case, my mind is made up.'

She grumbled that no-one ever took any notice of her, that the house would undoubtedly go to rack and ruin, and reminded me of several other occasions when I had ignored her advice, all of which would have turned out right if I'd only listened to her. My uncle and Mr. Hamerton, riding beside the carriage, missed it all, and I wished to heaven I was with them.

When she eventually ran out of complaints, I closed my eyes, pretending to doze, while I thought of what Mr. Pitt had said about Mr. Hamerton. Before that meeting I had seen nothing to object to in that kindly, inoffensive, slightly plump gentleman.

Indeed, Aunt Thirza's suggestion that he could protect us from highwaymen on the journey home had made me smile, for as the King had observed, no-one looked less like a bodyguard. Now I had to view him in quite a different light. Mr. Pitt said spies often appeared to be very ordinary. And I knew no-one more ordinary than Mr. Hamerton.

I was still excited at being given the opportunity to do something, however small, to help beat the French, but I realised it was unlikely to be easy. Mr. Pitt believed Mr. Hamerton would give himself away. But would he? No man could seem more innocuous than him, which meant that if he was a spy, he was also very clever. Someone who would watch what he said all the time. What if I made a mistake? What if he was a spy and I decided he wasn't?

This wasn't at all like assisting my father with his book. The people we had investigated then were long dead, and a blunder on my part put no-one in danger. But this was happening now and was a matter of life and death. It was vital I did not make a mistake.

On the journey home Mr. Hamerton assisted my aunt and myself in and out of carriages, quietly assuring we received good service at the inns where we stopped to eat, and to change horses. Still, I reminded myself, a French spy could be as polite as anyone else.

We reached the "George" Inn at Portsmouth around six, and after being shown to comfortable bedchambers, were soon enjoying an excellent dinner. At night, the noise of revellers and passing vehicles usually kept me awake, but the long journey over roads that left much to be desired, while my aunt droned on endlessly, had made me so tired I didn't hear a thing.

The boat for Cowes left early in the morning and a favourable wind made for a fast crossing. The sight of the Island's church spires rising from those beautiful green hills filled my heart with joy. Elation that intensified on arriving in Cowes, for we would soon be home. We hired two chaises, one for my aunt and Mr. Hamerton, who offered to escort her; the other for the servants. While my uncle and I hired riding horses, for I could not bear to be cooped up another minute.

Riding home, I revelled in the fresh sea air, the glory of the Downs, and finally in the magnificence of Westfleet Manor. The sight of that mellow stone, the oaks lining the drive, and the mullioned windows thrown open, filled me with a peace and contentment I never experienced anywhere else.

As we rode up to the house servants rushed out to greet us, their happy smiles turning to sadness as they expressed their great sorrow at Jeffel's death. I answered their questions as best I could, and told them I owed my life to Jeffel.

When I explained my aunt was returning by carriage with a guest who was to stay with us, and that they might be some time yet, cook, who had left her kitchen to welcome us, assured me, 'Don't you worry about that, my lady. I'll see everything is just as you like it.' And she hurried back to the kitchen, a broad smile on her face.

The other servants returned to their duties and I turned towards the open front door. From here I could see into the hall, and I hesitated. For, I was so accustomed to Jeffel being there when I came home, even if I had only been out for an hour or two.

My uncle took my arm and urged gruffly, 'Come on, my dear. Better to get it over with.' When we walked in, the sheer emptiness, the lack of Jeffel's cheerful, welcoming presence, brought a lump to my throat.

As I stood there, unable to speak, my housekeeper came bustling in, assuring me everything was in order. Which I did not doubt, for despite having just turned sixty, she had the energy of someone twenty years younger. 'Everyone was so shocked about Mr. Jeffel, my lady. Mrs Tanfield brought your letter over to Westfleet the very day it arrived.'

It was some five years since Richard Tanfield, a captain in the Royal Navy, had brought Julia back to the Island as his bride, and in that time she and I had become the greatest of friends. Richard owned Breighton House, just a mile from Westfleet, and I had known and liked him all my life. He and Julia were around my own age, and their son, Edward, almost three now, was my godson. It seemed a long time since I had written that letter, giving Julia the official version of what had happened to Jeffel.

My housekeeper went on, 'Mrs. Tanfield gathered everyone together, right down to the gardener's boys. No-one was missed. She read out your letter, just as you wanted. None of us could believe it. It must have been terrible for you, my lady.'

'I shall never forget it,' I agreed sadly.

'Poor Mr. Jeffel. It won't be the same without him.'

'No,' I sighed. 'It won't.'

'Mrs. Tanfield was that upset too. All concern for you, my lady, with never a thought for her own loss.'

I caught my breath in alarm. 'Whatever do you mean?'

'Of course, you won't know,' she said, not quite managing to hide her eagerness at being the one to impart this sad news. 'She told me herself there was no point writing when you were about to come home. She feels it deeply, my lady, as I'm sure I don't need to tell you. Such a likeable young gentleman too.'

My heart pounded with fear. I hadn't heard of any sea battles with the French, but men could be killed in small skirmishes too. 'Captain Tanfield – is he---'

'Oh no, my lady. Captain Tanfield is quite safe.' I closed my eyes in relief. 'He's at Breighton House. He--'

'At Breighton House?' I echoed puzzled, for he should have gone to sea early in May.

My uncle said, 'Didn't he sail with the Channel Fleet?'

'No, sir. He had an accident, but he's recovered now. In fact, he insisted on taking charge of Mr. Jeffel's funeral.'

'That was good of him,' my uncle said.

I looked at my housekeeper. 'Then who---'

'It's Mr. Septimus, my lady.' Julia's brother Septimus was an intelligent, studious, rather shy young man of twenty-one with strong beliefs. Poverty, and especially the sight of hungry children, distressed him deeply. When he finished his degree at Oxford he wanted to do something to alleviate such suffering. Then he'd caught the measles and when complications set in, Julia persuaded him to stay with her while he recovered, fitting out a small parlour as a study for him, putting in a desk, chair and bookshelves. I was so stunned I couldn't speak. 'It seems he fell over the cliff in the dark. They only buried him on Monday.'

I turned to my uncle, my own distress mirrored in his face. 'I must go to Julia at once.'

'Yes, of course, my dear. Don't worry, I'll see to everything here.' He put a comforting hand on my

shoulder. 'Poor Septimus,' he sighed. 'Such a nice young
man.'

I looked at my travel-stained riding habit. 'I must wash and change first.'

Somehow I remembered to tell my housekeeper about Mr. Hamerton, and she went off to have the yellow bedchamber prepared for him. Removing my hat, I left it on the hall table, ordered hot water to be taken up to my bedchamber, and sent a message to the stables for Orlando, my favourite horse, to be saddled. Hurrying upstairs I judged I had an hour or two before my aunt and Mr. Hamerton arrived.

Going into my bedchamber I was greeted by the delicious smell of newly polished furniture. While I waited for the hot water I wandered about the room touching all my familiar and most loved possessions, the portraits of my parents on the wall, the ormolu clock I'd brought back from Paris years ago, the first fossil I ever found on the beach, but my mind was on what Julia must be suffering. I thanked heaven that Richard was home to comfort her, and not at sea risking his life fighting the French.

Once I'd made myself more presentable, wishing my maid was here and not still on the road from Cowes, I ran downstairs, picked up my hat from the hall table, put it on and went outside. Orlando, the beautiful grey horse I adored, had been brought up to the house.

He gave a whinny of excited recognition and nuzzled my neck, no doubt expecting a long gallop across the Downs. 'Not today,' I sighed regretfully, making a great fuss of him, and said, as if he could understand, 'Tomorrow morning, I promise.'

Westfleet Manor was to the east of Westfleet village, and Breighton House to the west. Orlando made short work of the long steep hill up to the Tanfield residence, and I handed him over to the servant who came running out as I dismounted outside the main door. The butler, Wade, ushered me into the drawing room and I saw Julia's strained white face break into a faint smile. 'Drusilla. Oh, I am so glad to see you.'

'I came as soon as I heard about Septimus.' And I begged her to tell me how the accident had happened.

'It wasn't an accident, Drusilla,' she said, urging me to be seated. 'Septimus was murdered.'

CHAPTER 6

'Murdered?' I gasped, unable to believe what she was saying. For, who could possibly want to kill the kind, gentle, good-natured Septimus?

'He was found at the bottom of Hokewell cliff.' Julia, a tall attractive redhead with sparkling green eyes, sat with her hands tightly clasped in her lap. 'His horse was tied to a gate nearby and it looked as if he'd gone for a walk along the cliff top and either missed his footing, or a piece of cliff had given way under him.'

He wouldn't be the first to suffer that fate, I thought, with immense sadness, for the cliffs were notoriously treacherous. The pounding of the sea against sandstone and clay could dislodge quite large chunks of cliff, sending them tumbling down onto the sand below.

'The verdict at the inquest was "Death by Misadventure." But it wasn't an accident, Drusilla. I *know* it wasn't.'

When I asked why she was so certain, she said, 'He went to a meeting that night, and if he did stop for a walk afterwards, he would not have gone within ten yards of the cliff edge. Septimus was absolutely petrified of heights.' Her voice was breaking, and she stopped to calm herself, then said, 'But that's not all. For about two weeks before he died he was dreadfully jumpy and anxious, and so pre-occupied that sometimes he didn't hear when I spoke to him. As if his mind was on something else.'

'You asked him what was wrong?'

'I begged him to tell me,' she said in remembered despair. 'He said all was well. But he was lying. I know he was. If he was murdered Drusilla, I want his killer made to answer for it.'

'Have you spoken to Roach?' He was the constable at Dittistone.

'Yes, but he thought I was just being hysterical. To be fair I was rather overwrought at the time. Richard says I'm talking nonsense and I shouldn't bother you with it, but I've thought and thought and I know I'm right.' She took a deep breath. 'Will you help me find out who killed him?' I was so stunned by such a request, I didn't answer at once, and she beseeched, 'Please, Drusilla. You're the only one who knows how to go about it. Your father told me that you solved most of the mysteries he came across when he was writing his book.'

Whatever the truth of that, there was a huge difference between tracking down a live killer and uncovering the truth about one long dead. If Septimus had been murdered, his killer had nothing to lose by getting rid of anyone discovering his identity. A thought that made me shiver. Nevertheless I told Julia, 'I can try, but I may fail, or find it was really an accident after all.'

'I just want the truth, Drusilla.'

Glancing out of the window I saw young Edward playing with his nursemaid in the garden, and needing a moment to gather my thoughts together, I stood watching him, remarking on the amazing energy of my Godson. Turning back I noticed a bowl placed discreetly behind Julia's chair, and she, observing my puzzlement, explained, 'Edward is to have a brother or sister in November---'

I clapped my hands together in delight. 'That's wonderful news.'

'Yes, we are very pleased, but I regret to say I am suffering from sickness. It comes on me suddenly and at any time of the day, not just mornings. Hence the bowl. I have to be prepared. Dr Redding says it should pass soon, but I wish to heaven it would hurry up,' she ended, attempting to make light of the unpleasant time she was clearly enduring.

Before I could ask her anything more about Septimus, the door burst open and Edward came running in. 'Illa,' he cried in delight, his early attempt at my name having stuck. He held out his arms to me and I scooped him up and hugged him, burying my face in his soft curls as his chubby arms went round my neck. 'Illa --- I *missed* you.'

'I missed you too.'

'Come play ring-a-roses. Mama can't – she's sick and Papa's busy. Ple-a-se.'

I looked at Julia, who was watching with a contented smile, and she nodded. To her son, she said, 'Edward, I wish you would remember that it is *Aunt* Drusilla.'

'Yes, Mama,' he said carelessly as I set him down. Putting his hand in mine he urged, 'Come on, Illa.'

After an exhausting twenty minutes of dancing round in circles, chanting and falling down, I handed him over to his nursemaid again, and went back to Julia. She laughed as I sank thankfully into a chair. 'You don't have to play with him.'

'I know, but I enjoy it. Everything is incredibly simple to him.' And my life had suddenly become immensely complicated. Julia was so pale and drawn my heart went out to her. 'Tell me about Septimus,' I urged. 'You said he'd been to a meeting that night.'

'Yes, with a group of friends. He went every Tuesday.'

'Where was this?'

'At an inn, somewhere. He starting going soon after you left for Windsor and always went on horseback, so it wasn't in the village.'

'Did you meet any of these friends? Or hear their names?'

'No. He didn't talk about it at all, except to say it was a convivial gathering of like-minded people. And I didn't like to pry. I was just pleased to see him getting out and about again.'

'When did he start acting oddly? Was it after one of these meetings?'

She thought for a moment. 'No it wasn't. He missed a meeting on account of being invited out to dinner. Then, a few days later, he went to Newport to look for a book he particularly wanted. When he came home, it was obvious to me he'd suffered a severe shock. He said he'd fallen off his horse on the way home and hurt his back, but there wasn't a mark on his clothing. And – and he had this awful stricken look on his face.' Her bottom lip began to tremble. 'I – I can't get that look out of my mind. It haunts me day and night. The thing is, he knew this wretched sickness was getting me down, and that I was worried about Richard, and it's my belief he did not want to add to my troubles. If only I'd dragged the truth out of him, he might still be alive,' she ended on a sob.

I put my hand on her arm. 'You mustn't blame yourself, Julia. With hindsight we would all do some things differently.' If I had tackled those two would-be assassins sooner, Jeffel might still be alive. I felt so sorry for Julia. Normally optimistic and cheerful, she'd had to deal with the death of her brother, debilitating sickness, and Richard's accident. No wonder she was feeling low.

At that moment Richard walked into the room, dressed for riding. I greeted him affectionately, for I had always been fond of him. After thanking him for taking charge of Jeffel's funeral, I asked how he had come by the fading cuts and bruises on his face.

'I slipped,' he explained in the manner of someone weary of repeating the same tale, 'and fell headlong down a gangway shortly before the channel fleet was due to sail. I knocked myself out, so they took me ashore, and by the time I came round, the fleet had left without me.'

'You couldn't have gone,' Julia pointed out reasonably. 'You were unconscious.'

'Indeed,' he agreed shortly.

'You must be very disappointed,' I sympathised, remembering how his eyes had lit up every time he spoke of being involved in the search for the French fleet.

'Disappointed,' he repeated, saying the word slowly, his voice full of bitterness. 'That's one way of putting it, I suppose.' I looked at him in surprise. For Richard, normally blessed with a sunny nature, wasn't easily upset and believed in finding ways to overcome setbacks.

Julia sat beside him and laid her hand over his. 'It was an accident,' she reminded him tenderly. 'Such things happen.'

'I'd rather not discuss it any more, if you don't mind.' And he jumped up. 'I'll leave you two to talk. I only came to tell Julia I was going out.' As if realising how churlish he'd sounded, he attempted to make amends. 'Please forgive my foul mood, Drusilla. I am delighted to see you. Truly.'

As he shut the door behind him, Julia clearly felt the need to explain his odd behaviour. 'I was so thankful to have Richard here, safe and sound and I thought he'd soon get over his disappointment at not sailing with the fleet. They sent him home to recover properly, but he has remained --- well, as you saw-----'

'He wishes he was in the thick of it at sea.'

'Yes, but that's not what's on his mind, Drusilla. It's something else. He swears there's nothing bothering him, but I know there is. And w-what really worries me is he's behaving just like Septimus did before he died. He – he sits for ages, sometimes, just staring into space.' Her voice began to break up, and she quickly dabbed her eyes with a handkerchief. 'I'm frightened, Drusilla. Terrified I'll lose him too.'

I had never seen her in such low spirits before. She was so unlike the happy, spirited, lively Julia I knew, that, instinctively, I burst out, 'That will *not* happen.'

She looked at me, a watery smile trembling on her lips. 'Oh Drusilla, I *have* missed you. You always make me feel anything is possible.' Looking down at her hands, she confided her worst fears in a whisper, 'The thing is, Richard and I have always told each other everything, and if he won't tell me what's worrying him, it must be something really terrible.' She rallied a little, saying, 'He may not want to worry me while I'm suffering with this sickness. But he might confide in you. Would you speak to him?'

I promised to do so, although if he wouldn't tell Julia, I couldn't see him unburdening himself to me. Richard adored Julia, and would be in no doubt as to how worried she really was. Yet, he still refused to tell her. A fact that sent a cold chill of fear rippling down my spine, and I quickly changed the subject.

'About Septimus,' I said. 'Have you kept all his things?'

She nodded. 'I couldn't see anything being of use, but when you were helping your father I remember you saying that one insignificant fact had sometimes given you the key to the whole puzzle. So you'll find the study exactly as Septimus left it. Go and look if you like.'

When I stood up, she remained seated and I said, 'Aren't you coming?'

'Not yet. I regret to say I am feeling rather unwell again.'

At her insistence I left her and crossed the hall to the study. This rather dark, east-facing room, contained a desk, two chairs, an attractive fireplace, a bracket clock, and a bookcase holding the books Septimus had needed for his studies. The desk was bare except for a fine silver ink standish and a selection of quill pens.

It was here I hoped to find a clue to the identity of the friends he'd met every Tuesday. Letters, visiting cards, or some such thing. Emptying the desk drawers, I found a supply of writing paper, some excellent drawings of Edward watching a frog, which made me smile, and various small items including sealing wax, wafers for sealing letters, a penknife, some string, and sand to dry the ink on his letters.

The kind of things I expected to find, but there was nothing that told me who these friends were, nor were there letters of any kind, or any bills, which I thought decidedly odd. It was as if he'd deliberately put all his affairs in order. As if he knew his life was in danger. And the hairs on the back of my neck began to tingle.

I was about to put it all back when I caught sight of something wedged in the far corner of the top drawer. Pulling the drawer right out, I removed what proved to be a small piece of cardboard. It was triangular in shape, and in the centre, was a painting of a rather fat badger. A token, just like the ones found on the two assassins at Ashton Grange.

I held it in the palm of my left hand, and gazed at it stupefied, utterly unable to believe what I knew it must mean. For, how could Julia's studious brother have even the slightest connection with those murderers? The sequence of events on that awful day in Windsor raced through my mind. Septimus would never have become involved with such evil villains. He was a kind-hearted, amiable young man. Yet, he had a Fat Badger token, just as they had.

Hearing the door open I swung round to see Julia entering the room. She shut the door and leaned against it, looking decidedly pale. 'What's wrong, Drusilla? You're every bit as pasty-faced as I am.'

'It's nothing,' I blustered ineptly. 'I – er- caught my fingernail in the corner of the drawer.' And I began to rub it industriously, praying she wouldn't notice my hands were trembling.

She eyed me thoughtfully. 'You know Drusilla, you never could tell a lie.' I began to protest, but she cut me short. 'I'd like the truth, if you please. What did you find? I couldn't bear it if you starting hiding things from me too.'

'Julia,' I floundered, 'I-----'

'I shall worry far more if you don't tell me. And I do have a very vivid imagination.'

I gave a long deep sigh, knowing how true that was, yet I dreaded having to add to her troubles. She saw me trying to find some other way out and declared, 'The plain truth is best, I always find.' When I still didn't say anything, she inquired politely, 'Would it help if I sat down?'

Reluctantly I nodded and she did so. I moved the other chair beside her and seated myself, handing her the token. 'This was wedged in a corner of a drawer.'

She looked at it and then at me, obviously puzzled. 'But – what is it?'

'It's the kind of thing French royalists carry to identify themselves to each other. It's possible some corresponding societies use them too.'

She stared at me dumbfounded, as the implications of what I'd said sank in. 'When you say *some* corresponding society members, you mean those reformers I've read about in the newspapers. The ones who want England to go the way of France....' I didn't deny it and she burst out indignantly, 'If you are suggesting Septimus would betray England---'

'No, I'm quite certain he wouldn't.' And without thinking I said, 'The men who murdered Jeffel both carried a token just like this.'

She frowned in bewilderment. 'But they were burglars. You said so in your letter, and it was in "The Times" too. You cannot believe Septimus would be involved with burglars.' I groaned inwardly at my own stupidity. I wasn't accustomed to keeping secrets from Julia.

What use would I be to Mr. Pitt if I couldn't learn when to keep quiet? As I tried to think what to say, she burst out, 'Drusilla, what is going on? What is it you're not telling me?'

'Forgive me --- I can't say any more – I'm not allowed to.'

'Not allowed to? But why not? Who said you can't speak of it?'

'I can't tell you that either.'

She pressed her fingertips against her forehead trying to work it out. 'Was Jeffel shot by those men?' I nodded, and as I sought for an explanation she would accept, she asked, 'If these burglars thought the house was empty, why did they bring pistols?' When I didn't answer, she said, 'That's the wrong question, isn't it?' And her eyes narrowed. 'Oh, *now* I see. They weren't burglars, were they?' I stayed silent and she said, 'If they weren't burglars, why did they come to Ashton Grange? And why must it be kept quiet?' Baffled, she sat thinking and I tried changing the subject, but she was not so easily distracted. Nor did it take her long to work it out.

Suddenly she gave a small gasp of understanding. 'The King – that's what it was. He was there.' I had written to tell her how I'd met the King, and that he often called at the house. 'Those men came to kill him.'

'I didn't say that.'

'No, but that's what happened, isn't it?' Again I didn't answer, and she said, 'I can see from your face that I'm right.'

'For God's sake Julia, swear to me you won't repeat that to anyone. Not even to Richard. If the newspapers found out there had been an assassination attempt when these corresponding societies are causing so much unrest----'

'I won't tell a soul, I promise. Provided you tell me who said you mustn't speak of it. Was it the King?' I shook my head. 'It must have been Mr. Pitt then.' Again my face gave me away. 'Well, Septimus would never have been involved in a plot to murder the King. He wanted to change things for the better. He thought what was happening in France was unspeakable. He often told me so.'

He had said much the same to me too, and I believed him. 'He was a patriot. We both know that. I'll get to the bottom of it somehow, Julia.' I glanced at the clock on the mantel shelf and said, 'Oh heavens, is that really the time. I must go, I'm afraid. But I'd like to check Septimus's study again, and his bedchamber, if I may.'

'Yes, of course.'

'I must go to church in the morning, but I could come over in the afternoon.'

We agreed on a time and as she rang for her butler to see me out, I decided it would be sensible to mention Mr. Hamerton's arrival, if I could do it without her suspecting his visit was connected with what we had been talking about. The difficulty was she knew me so well that an absolute lie would never fool her, but fortunately I saw exactly how to do it, and in a way that would give her something else to think about apart from her own troubles. I waited until Wade came into the room, and as I got to my feet I said, 'Oh, by the way, we brought a guest back with us from Windsor. A gentleman who is thinking of moving to the Island.' I followed Wade to the door, and stopped just long enough to tell her, 'He's about thirty and a widower.'

Her face instantly brightened. 'You wretch. You could have told me before. Do you like him?' I laughed and went on my way without answering. Julia loved matchmaking and was always trying to marry me off. If such thoughts lightened her mood, even for a little while, so much the better.

As for Septimus, I believed what she'd told me. Julia was not given to exaggeration or making a fuss unnecessarily, and I was determined to find out how he'd died. One thing was clear, however, the Fat Badger corresponding society was already established on the Island, and probably had been all the time I was in Windsor, if not before. This society had failed to assassinate the King in Windsor, but they'd killed Jeffel, and probably Septimus too. And I swore, there and then, that I would not rest until every one of these murderers had been strung up on the gallows. If that included Mr. Hamerton, then so be it.

CHAPTER 7

When I reached Westfleet I learned my aunt and Mr. Hamerton had arrived from Cowes half an hour earlier. He, having now been conducted to his bedchamber, was changing for dinner. My aunt and uncle were on the point of going to change too when I walked into the drawing room. Naturally they wanted to hear what I'd learnt about Septimus, and why Richard was home. Shocked though they were over Septimus's death, they accepted the inquest verdict without question. After explaining about Richard's accident, I mentioned Julia was unwell, and told them why, knowing the news of the expected child would delight them both.

Over dinner we did not speak of the Tanfields, good manners demanding we did not discuss the problems of people with whom Mr. Hamerton was not yet acquainted. But we were not short of conversation. Mr. Hamerton said he'd looked at the newspaper while waiting for us to join him in the drawing room before dinner. 'It seems the elderly and infirm in France are no longer to be excused from the guillotine,' he declared in disgust as he cut into a slice of beef. 'Two women of almost eighty were executed the other day. If I could get my hands on those butchers on the Committee of Public Safety I would----' he stopped suddenly, his cheeks growing pink with embarrassment. 'I beg your pardon sir,' he said, addressing my uncle. 'I – I – should not speak of the French in that manner in your presence.'

'Why ever not? I agree with every word you said.'

'But – I understand you are French by birth.'

'True, but I grew up in England. My father was French, only he died when I was a baby, and my English mother took me back to London. Where I stayed until my French godfather left me his small estate in Normandy. We moved there some eighteen months before the storming of the Bastille.'

'But you returned to England when the revolution started?'

'Would that we had,' came the rueful response. 'Foolishly, we thought it would all blow over. I persuaded my wife and daughter to take refuge at Westfleet, while I stayed behind, convinced the revolutionaries would not trouble themselves with my small estate. We were not wealthy, and those who worked for me had plenty to eat and decent homes to live in. But, in the end, that made no difference. I was arrested, and my house burned to the ground.'

'Arrested?' Mr. Hamerton exclaimed in horror. 'But how – how did you get away, sir?'

'I was fortunate.' He hesitated and then said, 'I had been in prison for months when I was told I was being moved to Paris. Thousands are imprisoned there, and people of our class invariably end up climbing the steps to the guillotine. Knowing there would be no escape from a Paris prison, I wrote what I believed would be my last letter to my wife and daughter, and begged the prison governor to send it to them.'

'And did he?'

'Not him. He just laughed and tore it to shreds in front of me. The next morning a carriage came for me, I was handed over to two soldiers, who cursed me roundly, and said I had a fine head that would look better when Sanson, the executioner, held it aloft for the crowds to see. I know the road to Paris very well, but instead of taking that we turned north towards the coast. I assumed they were picking up another prisoner, but we didn't stop again until we reached a fishing village late that night, where I was put on a smuggling vessel going to the Isle of Wight.'

Mr. Hamerton stared at him in amazement. 'Who were these brave men, Mr. Frère?'

'One was my future son-in-law.'

'Giles Saxborough?'

My uncle nodded. 'I hadn't seen him since he was a boy and didn't recognise him. The other was a Frenchman.'

'By heavens sir, you had a lucky escape.'

'I know it, Mr. Hamerton. I am an extremely fortunate man. So you may say what you like about France.'

'Well, I don't approve of the revolution, Mr. Frère, although I believe the aristocracy brought it on themselves. The way they treated their workers was an absolute disgrace. No Englishman would allow children on his estate to starve.' He looked up from his dinner, a puzzled frown on his face. 'Yet, some people in this country still want a revolution. At all costs we must prevent that happening. When I think how close those two men came to assassinating the King at Ashton Grange, it makes my heart pound.'

We all expressed our heartfelt agreement, and later my aunt said to me, 'Mr. Hamerton expresses himself just as he ought, Drusilla. He is the perfect English gentleman.' She eyed me speculatively. 'You do like him, don't you?'

'I do,' I said. And I did. But I had no intention of letting that, or his fine words at the dinner table, get in the
way of finding out whether or not he was a French spy.

Mr. Hamerton joined us for church in the morning, and before going in we stopped by Septimus's grave, that being the first one we came to. Jeffel's was nearby, and I was thankful he had been laid to rest here as he'd wanted, but I made a solemn, and silent, promise to him, that Mr. Brown, whoever he was, would be brought to justice. And I went into the church my fists clenched in anger at the loss of those two fine men.

I hadn't expected Julia to attend the service in her delicate state, but Richard was not there either. Afterwards, out in the sunshine, I saw Mr. Reevers and Mr. East, but could do no more than exchange greetings with them before friends and acquaintances, understandably shocked by what had happened to Jeffel, came to offer their condolences. When I parted from the last of these kind people, I saw my aunt and uncle and Mr. Hamerton were talking to Mr. Upton, the parson, and a young man I hadn't met before. As I approached them, both gentlemen bowed, and Mr Upton begged to be allowed to introduce his nephew to me. 'Mr Sims, my sister's son,' he said proudly. 'Paying us a visit from London, ma'am.'

Mr Sims was of less than middle height and decidedly skinny. His dress was neat and sober, in keeping with his features. After exchanging the usual civilities I asked if he meant to make a long stay on the Island.

'A few weeks, ma'am.'

Aunt Thirza said, 'Mr Sims is recovering from an illness, Drusilla. His doctor advised sea air would be of benefit.'

I smiled encouragingly at the newcomer. 'Sea air is one thing the Island is not short of.'

Mr Upton gave his nephew a hearty slap on the back, making him stagger a little. 'Never fear, Lady Drusilla, we'll soon have him on his feet again. Fresh air, long walks and good cooking, that's what he needs. Frankly, he spends too much time with his head stuck in a book.' And he explained pompously, 'Francis is an academic. History is his subject, and chess his hobby. In fact he spends his evenings pitting his wits against another academic young man in Dittistone. It keeps him out very late. Sometimes,' he confided in a tone that suggested he was about to divulge something quite shocking, 'he doesn't get back until after eleven. Well, at the parsonage we are always in bed by ten. But, as he says, it would be too rude to expect his friend to stop in the middle of a game. So we have given Francis his own key. Not something we do lightly I assure you, but as my wife says, if we can't trust our own nephew who can we trust.'

'Indeed,' I murmured politely, relishing every word, wishing Mr. Reevers had not already left, knowing how much he too would enjoy this insight into life at the parsonage.

My uncle asked Mr. Sims which era in history was his favourite, and was told without hesitation, 'The Civil War. A most exciting time, when England was in great turmoil.'

'Much as France is now,' commented Mr. Hamerton, who had been listening politely.

Mr Sims looked as if he would say more but, as he drew breath, Mr Upton announced, 'I pride myself on knowing a thing or two about revolutions. Francis and I have already enjoyed some excellent discussions about France.'

His nephew said very little, merely agreeing. He seemed rather reserved and I could not decide whether that was due to a natural reticence or because Mr Upton gave him little chance to speak. For Mr Upton liked nothing better than to air his views, convinced that, whatever the circumstances, he always knew best.

Aunt Thirza remarked, 'Personally I've always been fascinated by the Tudors.'

Mr Upton wrinkled his nose. 'Not a great interest of mine, I must confess. Henry the Eighth was not a good man, but without him there would be no Church of England. Of course, when Mary succeeded him she tried turning the country Catholic again, but thankfully it didn't last.'

I glanced at Mr Sims, wondering how he would react to Mr Upton removing Henry's son, Edward the sixth, from the succession, and was rewarded with an answering gleam, but neither he nor I said a word. Mr Sims, I decided, had the measure of his uncle.

But my aunt would never allow such a mistake to pass without comment, and she politely pointed out that Edward had succeeded Henry.

'Oh no, ma'am. Edward died at a very young age. Am I not right, Francis?' Certain his nephew would back him up.

'He did die at fifteen, but-----'

Mr. Upton interrupted, 'There, what did I tell you, ma'am? Francis knows his history, believe me.'

When his uncle finished speaking Mr. Sims said, 'I'm afraid Mrs Frère is right----'

'Right? But----'

'Edward succeeded his father at nine, reigned for six years and died at fifteen.'

Mr Upton stared at him and thundered in disbelief, 'Are you *sure*?'

'I am.' And taking his watch from his pocket, said he rather thought it was time they returned to the parsonage. 'It won't do to be late for nuncheon, Uncle.'

I suppressed a smile, aware Mrs Upton was a stickler for meals being on time. As for Mr Sims, he was obviously accustomed to his uncle's mistakes, but I thought him rather calculating; a cold fish, as my father would have said.

That afternoon Mr. Hamerton accepted my aunt and uncle's offer to show him the full extent of the Westfleet gardens, enabling me to visit Julia as promised. But as I went up to my bedchamber to put on my hat, I saw Mr. Hamerton's valet walking down the drive, heading towards the village, giving me the perfect opportunity to search Mr. Hamerton's bedchamber. Quietly slipping into the room, I saw it was exceedingly neat and tidy, with nothing on the bedside cabinet except a small portrait of a lady I assumed to be his late wife. Inside the cabinet was a bible and a couple of books on moths and butterflies.

Searching for anything that might connect him to the Fat Badgers I discovered a box at the back of his closet. It wasn't locked and I opened it eagerly, my fingers trembling slightly. Inside were papers concerning financial matters, which to my surprise, showed he'd already sold his house in Windsor. And that his furniture had been moved into store on the day of the ball in London.

At the bottom of the box were two letters, written by his wife before their marriage. But nothing else, nor were there any hidden compartments in the box. I replaced everything exactly as I'd found it, and quietly left, feeling very disappointed.

I'd hoped to find a Fat Badger token, but I wasn't surprised that I had not. For, surely, no top enemy agent would be so foolish as to leave such a thing in his bedchamber. His lack of personal papers was surprising, however, for they bore no resemblance to the quantity I had accumulated over the years. As if he'd kept only what really mattered to him, and destroyed the rest. The one thing that was clear, was that he'd decided to move to the Island some time before he'd mentioned it to us.

But why had he not told us? I could not ask him, at least not in a direct way. It was, however, the first indication that he had something he wished to hide. As I was to discover, it was not to be the last.

I decided to walk to Julia's, it being only about a mile. I put on a hat with a wide brim to keep the sun out of my eyes, walked downstairs and told Luffe where I was going. And having decided his efforts so far showed he had the makings of a good butler, I offered him the position permanently.

'Me, my lady?' he said, touching the middle of his chest with his index finger in disbelief.

'Yes,' I smiled. 'Do you think you can do it?'

'Oh yes, my lady. I can do it all right. I just thought--'

'That's settled then.'

'Thank you, my lady,' he said, beaming from ear to ear. 'I won't let you down.'

'No, I don't think you will,' I assured him.

Aunt Thirza would not be pleased, but if she complained I would have to gently remind her, yet again, that Westfleet Manor belonged to me, and therefore the decision was mine alone. It was getting on for two years since she and Lucie arrived at Westfleet without warning, seeking refuge from the revolution in France. My father had been alive then and had welcomed them warmly, begging them to stay as long as they wished. I was happy for that arrangement to continue, for my uncle had not totally recovered from the months he'd spent in a French prison.

Fortunately, when they moved to France he'd left some funds in an English bank, but their circumstances were now considerably reduced. Although they could afford to buy a small house on the island, my aunt's strong sense of propriety required her, as she saw it, to remain at Westfleet until I married, so that I would not scandalise the Island by living on my own. A thought that still had me smiling as I left the Manor.

Heading towards the village I soon came to the row of neat cottages my father had built for the estate workers, and acknowledged a greeting from the landlord of "The Five Bells," who came out of the door as I passed.

'Good to see you home again, my lady.'

'It's good to be back, Barlow. How are your wife and children?'

'All in good health, my lady.'

Walking on I passed the duck pond, smiling at the antics of some ducklings, and waved to the children playing on the village green. Going up the hill on which the church stood, I hurried past the parsonage, unseen by the Uptons thankfully, for escaping from them without being rude was never easy, and then I took the right turn up the very steep hill that led to Breighton House.

Julia looked no better than she had the previous day, and I prayed her tiresome sickness would go soon. She sat in the garden while I searched the rooms Septimus had used. Finding nothing in his bedchamber I went down to his study and looked through his desk, books and other belongings. But there was no mention anywhere of the society he'd joined, or any names that might be connected. I sat at his desk and put my head in my hands in despair.

Then it struck me; there was a way of finding out who these Fat Badgers were. A way I should have thought of before.

CHAPTER 8

When I promised Julia I'd try to find out who had murdered Septimus, I knew I had to put my duty to Mr. Pitt first, never imagining that the two matters could be connected. Now it was obvious that discovering who'd killed Septimus would lead me to the other Fat Badgers, and to the identity of Mr. Brown himself.

Yet, to have any chance of success, I had to make sure no-one could guess what I was doing, and that presented me with certain difficulties. For, as a noblewoman, there were places on the Island I simply could not go without causing the kind of comment that would make it obvious what I was doing. I needed someone to assist me, someone who could go unnoticed where I could not. And the person most suited to that role was my groom, John Mudd.

Mudd had come to Westfleet at the age of fifteen, when I was three, and there was no servant I trusted more, nor one who was more loyal. He had always been totally devoted to my interests, and nothing had ever changed that, not even his brief marriage some fifteen years ago, or the loss of his wife and son in childbirth, and the dreadful months that followed. I had only been twelve at the time, too young to understand properly. But, conscious of his grief, I'd tried to find him a new wife by pointing out pretty young village girls to him, when we were out riding. He'd shaken his head, saying he'd never marry again. Nor had he.

After dinner I walked down to the stables and found him leaning on a rail watching my aunt's horse being put through its paces in the paddock. I stood talking to him about the horses for some time, as I frequently did. Then taking the Fat Badger token from my pocket I showed it to him. 'Have you ever seen anything like this before, John?'

Taking the token, he studied it carefully before returning it to me. 'No, my lady, I haven't.'

'Mr Reevers says this may be used by members of a corresponding society as a means of identification.'

'A corresponding society?' he repeated in surprise. 'I've read about them in the newspapers, my lady.' My father had taught Mudd to read years ago, and our newspapers were passed on to him after we had finished with them. He'd told me once that he thought it wonderful that he, a simple groom, could read about the most important people in the land. How the King and his family had spent the day, and what Mr Pitt had said in Parliament. Since then, in Windsor, he'd met the King several times, and had told me, in unaccustomed awe, that it had made him very proud.

He went on, 'Those gentlemen arrested in London — didn't they belong to corresponding societies?'

'I believe so.'

'I thought they just wanted working men to have the vote.'

'Indeed,' I murmured dryly.

'Are they really planning to start a revolution like the Frenchies, my lady?'

'Mr Pitt has evidence that some societies are arming themselves with pikes and muskets.' There wasn't a soul in England who hadn't heard how the severed heads of the aristocracy were paraded through the streets of Paris on pikes.

Mudd shuddered. 'I can't believe that kind of thing will happen here, my lady. The very thought of that guillotine makes me go cold.'

I looked at him in amusement. 'I'm the one who will have cause to worry about the guillotine if there's a revolution in England, not you.'

'No-one wants that kind of thing here, my lady.'

'I hope you're right,' I said feelingly. 'The thing is John, Mr Ford had one of these tokens in his desk.'

'Mrs Tanfield's brother,' he exclaimed in a shocked voice. 'A fine young gentleman like Mr. Septimus? Surely he wasn't a revolutionary?'

'No, I'm quite certain he wasn't. But he did want to change the way we elect our members of parliament. He thought that with the right people in parliament, more could be done to prevent poverty and hunger.'

'That's a different thing altogether, my lady.' He spoke with such approval I asked if he wished he had the vote. 'I do, my lady. But it will be a long time before that happens.'

'Not so long, I fear, John, as it will be before *I* am allowed to,' I pointed out dryly.

He opened his mouth to protest, thought for a moment, then realised I was right. 'Seems to me, my lady, there's a lot that needs changing. But in a peaceable manner.'

'There's nothing very peaceable about a society that murders one of its own members.'

'Murdered?' he gasped. 'Mr. Septimus?'

'I'm afraid so.' I explained that I was determined to find the culprits and asked if he was willing to help me, pointing out that it was no part of his duties to assist me with anything that was likely to be dangerous. But he brushed that aside as if it was of no importance, promising to help in any way he could. I told him everything, including how terrified Septimus was of heights, about his agitated behaviour before he died, and how he'd put all his affairs in order. For he could not assist me without such knowledge.

'I want the names of the other members of the society he joined. If I knew which inn they met at, the innkeeper should be able to help.'

He nodded and stood frowning. Then, quite suddenly, his eyes widened, as if he'd remembered something. 'May I see that token again, my lady?' I handed it to him and he said thoughtfully, 'The Pig and Whistle in Luckton used to be called The Fat Badger. They changed the name about ten years ago.'

'Are you sure?'

'Yes, my lady. My father - er, what I mean is, it's an inn used by smugglers.' Mudd's father had been involved with smuggling for years, and despite his increasing years, probably still was. 'I've heard him talk of it, my lady. Sometimes he forgets and uses the old name.'

I could hardly believe my good fortune. If this was the right inn then I would soon have the names of these Fat Badgers. Eagerly I said, 'We'll call in there tomorrow, John.'

He looked at me in alarm. 'But a place like that will be full of smugglers.'

'Not if we go early in the morning, surely?'

'My lady, I could go----'

'Thank you John, but no. I must do this myself.'

'His lordship would never have approved, my lady.' My father had been dead for a year and a half now, yet Mudd had still not quite got out of the habit of being guided by what he believed my father would have thought.

'I must speak to the innkeeper, John. And that is what I mean to do.' He still hesitated and I did what I could to put his mind at rest. 'Don't worry, I shan't go into the inn without you.'

Mr. Hamerton, who had dined at Norton House with Mr. Reevers and Mr. East, returned later, saying the gentlemen had very kindly offered to show him around our part of the Island the following morning. He was full of praise for the wonderful views he had seen that day from the Downs, and was eager to get started in the morning.

The two gentlemen duly arrived soon after breakfast, when I had meant to tell Mr. Reevers about Septimus's Fat Badger token, and that he'd probably been murdered. But I had no opportunity to do so, and seeing no great urgency I decided to wait until after I had visited the inn. In truth, the idea of handing him the names of the members of the Fat Badger Corresponding Society – on a plate, so to speak -- was immensely appealing.

The three gentlemen were about to leave when Richard Tanfield was ushered into the drawing room. Mr. Hamerton took one look at that blue-eyed, rugged figure, and gasped out loud. For one moment Richard seemed equally dumbstruck, then he put down the book he was carrying and shook Mr. Hamerton's hand warmly. 'I don't understand why you are here, but I'm delighted to see you again.'

Still bewildered, Mr. Hamerton blurted out, 'What are you doing on the Isle of Wight?'

'I live here. About a mile away, in fact.'

Mr. Hamerton's jaw dropped for a second time. 'I thought you said you lived in Ireland.'

'Ireland?' Richard repeated incredulously. 'I spoke of the Island, not Ireland.' Like all of us, Richard often referred to the Isle of Wight as "the Island," and once this was explained both men began to laugh uproariously at the misunderstanding.

'I take it you two know each other,' I teased in amusement.

Richard said, 'Well, in truth, we have only met once. In London a few weeks ago.' And turning to Mr. Hamerton again, asked him to dine at Breighton House later that day, an invitation that was eagerly accepted. Richard then recollected his reason for calling, picked up the book he'd brought and handed it to my aunt. 'Julia asked me to return it, ma'am. And to tell you how much she enjoyed it.'

I smiled to myself aware that, unable to visit herself, she'd sent Richard to find out about our guest from Windsor. Thinking back, I realised I hadn't mentioned his name. I wondered how they had met, for Richard did not belong to any London clubs and I assumed had only been there for a day or two at most. Chance meetings did occur, yet the kind of rapport they clearly enjoyed rarely came about in five minutes. A fact that left me feeling a little uneasy.

Once the gentlemen had gone I left the house as if setting out on my usual morning ride, correctly accompanied by Mudd. Heading east we made our way up onto Luckton Down, the village itself being some seven or eight miles distant. As I'd expected the inn was perfectly respectable, indeed I was sure Septimus would not have ventured into a disreputable one.

After tethering the horses, Mudd pushed open the oak door, and I walked inside to a newly swept floor, and the tang of fresh sea air coming in through wide open windows, which was rapidly removing the smell of stale beer and tobacco. As I had hoped, there were no customers at that time of the day, and when Mudd called for the innkeeper, he appeared almost at once.

His mouth fell open when he saw me. 'Your ladyship,' he gasped, for in this part of the Island everyone knew who I was, even if I did not know them. But he soon recovered and confirmed that Mr. Septimus Ford and his friends had indeed met here. I explained Septimus's sister wished to contact those friends and said with an encouraging smile, 'If you would be good enough to furnish me with their names, she would be most grateful.'

'I wish I could help you, my lady, but Mr Ford was the only gentleman I spoke to. After his accident I got a message saying there wouldn't be any more meetings. All I can tell you is, they used my upstairs room, and had a light supper at nine. Mr Ford arranged it, and paid promptly. A proper young gentleman he was.'

'Yes, indeed,' I agreed. 'Well – could you describe these other gentlemen?'

He ran a hand round his chin. 'Like I said, Mr Ford arranged things, and I hardly noticed the others. I'm usually run off my feet at that time of night.'

'I see,' I said, trying to keep the despair out of my voice. 'Can you tell me if they all rode here?'He lifted his shoulders a little, his face expressing distress at being unable to assist me. 'I really don't know, my lady.'

'You must know which horses were in the stables, surely?'

'Well – there was Mr Ford's, of course.' He scratched his head as if thinking. 'Now I come to think of it, Jim did mention another horse that was bang up to the mark.'

'Jim?' I lifted an eyebrow in query.

'My ostler.' His expression lightened. 'He'll remember. If you'd like to wait here, I'll----'

'No, I'll come with you. I should like to speak to Jim myself.'

'Just as you like, my lady.' He led the way out the back door and round to the stables.

The inn was a respectable size for a small village, and he told me that most of his regular customers lived in Luckton itself, but he kept a horse and a gig, both of which could be hired out. 'I can take a dozen horses here,' he said proudly. 'And I've two rooms for visitors to the Island, and my upstairs room for customers wanting to meet in private, like poor Mr Ford.'

I nodded, showing no more than polite interest, as I suspected most customers hiring the private room were smugglers. Those who ran the gangs probably stabled horses here, using the inn to give out orders. Smuggling was a part of Island life and while I did not buy smuggled goods myself, many otherwise respectable people did.

Mudd and I followed the innkeeper to the stables, where Jim was inspecting a rather worn bridle. On seeing me, he put the bridle down, and touched his forelock. The innkeeper explained I was inquiring about the gentlemen who used to meet in the upstairs room on Tuesday nights.

'Yes,' I said, smiling at him. 'If they came every week, you will have known their horses.'

He nodded eagerly. 'There was Mr Ford's bay mare. And another gentleman had a lively looking chestnut.`

I took a deep breath. 'Can you tell me the name of the second gentleman?' Jim's brow furrowed in thought, followed after a long interval by a statement that he disremembered ever being told. Sighing inwardly, I asked, 'What did this gentleman look like?'

Jim's brow furrowed even deeper, and then he shook his head. 'It's horses I remember, not faces.'

'Well, was he tall?'

Jim hesitated. 'I don't think so, my lady.'

'All right, Jim,' I said kindly, for it was useless to expect him to recall what had not been of interest to him. 'Tell me, were there any other horses on those Tuesday nights?'

'Yes, but they weren't up to much. Three or four tired old nags, that's all.'

'Would you recognise the horses again?'

Removing his cap he scratched his bald head. 'The chestnut, I would. But not the others.'

'When did you last see the chestnut? Was it before or after Mr Ford had his accident?'

'Before,' he said without hesitation.

'You're sure of that?'

'Yes, my lady. I remember in particular because Mr Ford and this other gentleman wanted to talk in private, and they gave me a guinea to warn them if anyone came near the stables.'

I thanked him myself with a guinea, and on going back into the inn, I asked the innkeeper, 'You said the group always had supper?'

'Yes, my lady.'

'Who took the food into them?'

'Betsy Reid, my lady.'

'She might remember something.' If she had seen these same men every week, she must know what they looked like, and might even know their names. Eagerly, I said, 'I'd like to speak to her, if you would tell me where----'

'I only wish it was possible, my lady. But she died two days ago.'

'Died?' I repeated, as if such a thing was impossible.

'Yes, my lady. She was as right as rain first thing, but dead by nightfall. In terrible agony, she was. Dr. Redding said he'd seen it before on occasion. Some problem with the stomach.'

There wasn't much to be said after that. I paid the innkeeper well for his trouble, and urged, 'If you or Jim remember anything else, I'd like to know at once. Anything at all, even if it seems unimportant.'

'I'll do that, my lady, with pleasure,' he beamed, jingling the coins in his hand.

What did I have to go on, I thought, as Mudd and I rode off up the narrow street. A gentleman, who owned a lively chestnut horse, had stopped coming to the meetings shortly before Septimus Ford had died.

'What do we do now, my lady?' Mudd asked, breaking into my thoughts.

'I wish I knew,' I sighed. There had to be a way of finding out who these people were. There had to be. I had been so sure the innkeeper would know and that I would be able to hand the names to Mr. Reevers that very day. I shook my head at my own foolishness, for I should have known better. When helping father with his book, a few problems had been quite easy to resolve, but many had not, and we had totally failed to get to the bottom of a few. I had not forgotten that, but tended to remember the ones I had solved. And I had the distinct feeling that nothing in this business was going to be easy.

CHAPTER 9

I did not know what to do next, and that preyed on my mind for the rest of the day. That night, after snuffing out my bedside candle, I left the bed curtains pulled back. A shaft of moonlight shone through a small gap where the window curtains did not quite meet, illuminating the portrait of my father on the wall. And I wondered what he would do in this situation. I lay awake going through what little I knew, without finding an answer.

Going into the workroom in the morning, I sat at my father's old desk praying for inspiration. I ran my hand over the wood, thinking of him sitting here, and smiling at the memory of how he loved to hide things in the secret drawers, of which there were three.

Suddenly I banged my fist on the desk, making the pens jump. The desk Septimus used was very similar and about as old, having been made for Richard's grandfather, John Tanfield, who'd built Breighton House sixty years ago. Could that have a secret drawer too? Well I would soon find out. I rang for Luffe and told him to send a message to the stables for Orlando to be saddled at once and brought up to the house.

When I arrived at Breighton House Julia was sitting on the terrace. 'You're early,' she said, smiling. I did not ask how she was, for the bowl was still in its place. Instead I spoke of Mr. Hamerton and the incredible co-incidence of his having met Richard in London recently.

'Yes, isn't it amazing? But I'm so pleased he did,

Drusilla. It has cheered Richard no end, and Mr. Hamerton seems a most amiable gentleman. I saw at once why Richard liked him. And no-one could have been kinder when I had to make a hasty exit from the dinner table yesterday.' I commiserated with her and then, unable to contain myself another second, asked if I might take another look at Septimus's desk. Surprised that I wanted to see it a third time, and observing the excited sparkle in my eyes, she demanded to be told what had happened.

'It's probably nothing-----'

'But------?'

'Does the desk have a secret drawer?'

'Not that I know of. But by all means look. If you don't mind my leaving you to it.'

It took a long time, but I found it in the end. A small, cleverly concealed button released another drawer. Inside was a journal, with the name Septimus Ford inscribed on the front.

Sitting down, I opened it and soon discovered why Septimus had hidden it, and why he hadn't wanted Julia to read it. When I finally reached the end, I was trembling, for there was no doubt now that Septimus had been murdered. And if those who had committed that foul deed found out that I knew, they would kill me too.

I read it through again, slowly, to be sure I hadn't missed anything important. Written in a clear firm hand, it began, with much enthusiasm, on the Friday after we had left for Windsor.

Bumped into George in Newport. He told me he'd joined a new society on the Island, whose aim is to see that every working man has the right to vote. To my mind this is the only way ahead if we are to improve matters for the poorer classes. He asked if I wished to go along, for he is as keen on reform as I am, this being our chance to do something about it. George says, if I join, there would be eight members.

March18th.

Went to the meeting at the Pig & Whistle in Luckton. We had the upstairs room to ourselves and we came away later feeling very elated. There are many corresponding societies around the country now, and most want to bring about change in a peaceful way, which is our aim too. Neither George nor I would consider any form of violence, and societies can achieve so much more than a mere individual. We're to be called the Fat Badger Corresponding Society, after the original name of the Luckton inn. We were all given a small cardboard token, portraying a fat badger, so we can identify ourselves to other members when new groups are set up. It seems we are the first on the Island. George and I were the only gentlemen present, but the other men seem perfectly respectable.

Mr. John Brown, who set up the Society, is a gentleman living on the mainland. George believes he's involved with the London societies. Unfortunately Mr Brown was unable to attend our meeting, but insists we use pseudonyms so that we treat each other as equals in what is a common cause. These were decided by drawing names out of a hat, that seeming the fairest way.

The person who told us about Mr Brown, is to be Mr Silver, which amused us, as he is rather swarthy in appearance, and a great bear-like individual. George is now Mr Jade, and I am Mr Gold. A rather nervous ginger-haired individual, a clerk by the look of him, is to be Mr Pearl. A bespectacled tradesman of about forty has become Mr Garnet, and his friend is Mr Emerald. One member, a Mr Ruby, could not be there tonight. Mr Silver emphasised that the society was deadly serious about changing the electoral system, and anyone who thought it an excuse for a convivial evening should leave now. I liked his enthusiasm and feel that when working men have the vote, something will be done at last to improve the lot of those less fortunate than ourselves.

Entries for the next several Tuesdays recorded his attendance at the meetings, suggestions for achieving their aims, and what the other corresponding societies around the country were doing. Mr Brown, who still had not appeared, was in correspondence with these societies with the aim of holding a big convention in London in the summer. Septimus wrote that, with so many people wanting to change the system, the government could not go on ignoring them. Then, on the last Tuesday in April, everything turned into a horror that made me shudder.

I didn't go to last night's meeting as I was dining out, but George went. He said it had gone well, with everyone very excited at the prospect of the summer convention in London. When it broke up around ten, his mind was so full of it all that it wasn't until he reached the stables that he realised he'd forgotten something. Going back up the stairs to the meeting room, he saw the door was slightly ajar, and was about to push it open when he overheard Mr Silver telling Mr Ruby, a man neither of us liked, that Mr Brown wanted everything in place by the end of July. And that Mr Brown himself would be on the Island some weeks beforehand to organise things.

George thought they were discussing the big London convention, but what they said next made it clear they were planning something quite different. Something so dreadful that George's voice shook when he repeated what he'd heard.

It has shaken me so badly I can barely write for the trembling of my hand. The truth is we have been thoroughly taken in, and our presence tolerated merely to give their meetings the appearance of respectability, for it is not electoral reform that Mr Brown and Mr Silver want, but revolution.

George tried to creep back down the stairs, but in his haste he slipped and they heard him. He told them at once that neither he nor I would have anything to do with such an abomination as they planned to carry out. At which he was advised we were in too deeply to get out now, and if we informed on them, Julia and Edward, and George's wife and four children, would be put up against a wall and shot one by one in front of us. George did not doubt they meant it. Then Mr Silver said, if he was caught, he would say the whole scheme was my idea, because everyone knew how keen I was to change parliament, and we would be arrested and hanged too, for no-one would believe we were not involved.

Yet, it is our duty to prevent this terrible thing from happening. George was beginning to despair until I reminded him we had until the end of July, some three months, in which to find out the real names of these people, and Mr Brown too, if we could. As soon as we have them we will go and see Mr Pitt himself.

On Tuesday, we mean to attend the meeting as usual, and let Mr Silver believe his threat has worked. This way the families will be safe. After the meeting we intend to follow Mr Silver home and discover his true identity. Mr Silver thinks he has frightened us off, yet the day will come, not too far away I pray, when he will find out how wrong he is. I can't help but wish that next Tuesday wasn't almost a week away.

The next entry, for the following Sunday, was written in a decidedly shaky hand.

George is dead. I heard of it at church this morning. He was walking by the river yesterday evening, a habit of his, when it is believed he tripped and fell in. George couldn't swim. I am certain he was pushed. Murdered. But I intend to continue with the plan we devised. Alone.

Monday's entry read:-

Julia knows there is something worrying me, but I dare not tell her the truth. This is one burden I must bear alone. I am determined to stop those fiends carrying out their dreadful plan; at the same time I must not put her life, Edward's, and her unborn child, at risk.

Wednesday

I watched the inn last night and saw Mr Silver ride in on that poor horse of his. How it bears his weight I do not know. All the others arrived, and I waited two hours for them to leave again. Mr Silver was the last, and I followed him through Luckton and up onto the Downs. At which point it began to rain so heavily that, in the darkness, I lost sight of him.

The following Tuesday.

I must get this information to Mr Pitt, and risk it implicating me now, for there is no time to be lost. I do not doubt that I am to be next. I suppose George and I were needed at first to make the society look respectable. I see now why they asked me to deal with the innkeeper, for while he did not object to smugglers, he spat on the ground in disgust at the very mention of the French, Robespierre and his gang of revolutionary cut-throats. Having served our purpose, we are expendable. Tonight I will follow Mr Silver home.

This was the last entry and I closed the journal with a sigh. For I did not believe George's wife and children, or Julia and Edward, and her unborn child, had ever been in danger. Such an outrage would have had the whole Island snapping at the heels of the Fat Badgers, destroying both the society and Mr Brown's plans for revolution. The threat was simply a means of stopping Septimus and George talking, until suitable 'accidents' could be arranged.

At that moment Julia came into the room, and she spotted the journal at once. 'I haven't seen that before. Where did you find it?' Looking up at me, she quickly realised the answer. 'So there was a secret drawer after all.'

'There was.' And I showed her how it worked.

Her astonishment quickly gave way to fear, realising why he had hidden it. 'Septimus didn't want me to see it,' she whispered.

I agreed he had not, wishing with all my heart that I could avoid adding to her troubles, but I'd given her my word I would tell her if I discovered how Septimus had died, and I couldn't go back on it now. 'He did join a corresponding society.'

She clutched at the desk for support, hurriedly sat down, and groaned, 'Oh no---'

'His intentions were of the highest,' I told her, for many honourable men wanted to change the way Members of Parliament were chosen. Mr. Pitt himself had tried in '85 but failed. If he'd succeeded, we might have avoided fanatics screaming about sticking the heads of the King, Mr. Pitt and other ministers on Temple Bar. 'Septimus believed he would be campaigning for working men to be given the vote. When he found out the society planned to start a French-style revolution in England, he refused to go along with them and they ---'

'Murdered him,' she said, her voice trembling.

I nodded, for it was better that she knew before reading the journal. I handed it to her, and as she read what her brother had written, her face turned even paler. When she'd finished she gripped the journal tightly with both hands and said, 'This Mr Brown – he was the one who had Septimus murdered.'

'I believe so.'

'Septimus said they're planning to assassinate the King later in the summer. He didn't know there was to be an earlier attempt at Windsor.'

'No, I'm sure he didn't.' This puzzled me too. If this assassination had been carefully planned for late summer, why send two incompetent men to kill the King in May? And why only two? It didn't make sense. Still, as I suggested to Julia, there could be other reasons.

'Perhaps Mr. Brown didn't send them. They may have wanted to steal the glory, as they saw it, of starting the revolution.' This did seem the most likely explanation. 'On the other hand the society might have several plans for assassinating the King. If one fails, they try the next.' That was also a possibility, and one I found rather more worrying.

'They won't give up then?' When I shook my head, she sighed, 'Poor Septimus. All he ever wanted was to do some good in this world.' She stood up and walked to the window, saying in a muffled voice, 'I see now why he couldn't tell me. It wasn't only my life and Edward's he had to consider, there was his friend George's family as well. Those fiends murdered George too.'

'Almost certainly. Did Septimus ever speak about him?'

'No. Never. I've no idea who he is. Or rather was,' she ended sadly.

In his journal, Septimus had written that the Fat Badgers meant to murder the King, his family, Mr. Pitt and important government ministers. The very thing Mr Pitt most feared; not out of concern for himself, but for England.

Yet I saw one glimmer of hope. Mr Brown wanted his barbarous scheme in place by the end of July. And in August, as everyone knew, the King usually took his family to Weymouth for several weeks. They stayed at Gloucester Lodge, a pleasant residence on the sea front, where they enjoyed sea bathing, using the new bathing machines. Mr Pitt and top ministers visited the King here, offering the perfect opportunity to assassinate the most important men in England.

Julia said, 'The journal does help, doesn't it, Drusilla? Septimus described the other members of the society. And told us Mr Brown is a gentleman.'

'Who will arrive on the Island this summer.'

'It's almost June now,' she pointed out in alarm. 'He could be here already.'

'I think that's quite likely.' Unable to warn her Mr. Hamerton might be involved, I impressed upon her the importance of not telling anyone else about the journal.

'What – not even Richard?'

If he became well acquainted with Mr. Hamerton, as he showed every sign of doing, I dare not take such a chance. 'The fewer people who know about it the better. If only you and I know, then it can't get out.' She was still a little uncertain and I pointed out reasonably, 'It only takes one careless word, and if the Fat Badgers found out how much we knew, all our lives would be in danger. Yours, Edward's, the baby's, Richard's----'

Her eyes grew round with fear. 'I won't say a word, I promise.' I wished there was something I could say that would help her cope with the horror of it all, but there were no such words. In truth there was only one way I could help her. I had to find Septimus's killer. I prayed I would not let her down.

It wasn't difficult to see why Septimus and George had been encouraged to join the society. Septimus, serious-minded and mature, had been chosen to deal with the innkeeper to give the appearance that this was simply a convivial meeting of gentlemen. To ensure that no constable or magistrate would go poking into their affairs.

Julia was quite happy for me to take the journal home to make a copy of the appropriate entries for myself, and I intended to do another to send to Mr Pitt, by the special messenger Mr Reevers used. Before I left she reminded me of my promise to speak to Richard, which I did at once, although I was not hopeful of finding out what was troubling him.

He was walking in the garden, deep in thought. When I caught up with him he forced a smile. 'Oh, it's you, Drusilla.'

'You might sound a little more enthusiastic,' I teased.

'I'm always pleased to see you,' he responded mechanically, instead of making a joke of it, as he would have done normally.

I left it at that, and as his facial injuries had almost faded, commented that things seemed to be improving for him now. 'Improving?' he repeated in scathing tones. 'I think not.'

Puzzled, I pointed out, 'But your face is virtually free of bruises.'

'Oh I see. My bruises. Yes, they are disappearing at last.' And before I could ask what he thought I'd meant, he hurried on, 'I only wish Julia could get rid of this awful sickness. She's still suffering badly, I fear. Although she makes very little of it.'

'Indeed.'

He half grinned. 'Unlike me. Go on, say it.'

'As if I would be so cruel,' I smiled. Then went on more seriously, 'But you are not your usual self, Richard. Julia believes you're in some kind of trouble. And, frankly, so do I.'

'Nonsense,' he retorted abruptly. 'It's just that I should be at sea, and I'm not.' Reaching a garden seat he suggested we sat down, and muttered, 'Although, I may never go back – who knows.'

I was so stunned I could barely speak. 'But – you love the sea. You've told me so often.'

He gave a shrug. 'Life changes.' I'd never heard him sound so despondent.

'How has it changed, Richard?'

He gazed at a red admiral resting on a nearby wall, and I guessed he'd let slip more than he'd meant to. Then he said what he thought would satisfy me. 'I see now how Julia suffers when I'm at sea. Never knowing from one minute to the next whether I'm alive or dead.'

'Has she complained?'

His lips curled into a wry grimace. 'Julia? Not her. Not one word of reproach for the agony I put her through.'

'Have you told her?'

He looked across at me in sudden alarm. 'Told her what?'

'That you might never return to sea, of course.'

Any doubts I'd had about whether he had something to hide were swept away by the relief I saw in his eyes. No, I haven't. You won't say anything to her, will you Drusilla? Nothing is - er – well -- settled.'

'I won't say a word,' I promised, and rose to my feet. 'I must go. Oh I almost forgot, Richard do you know any of the people Septimus used to meet on a Tuesday evening?'

'Me? No. He didn't mention them to me.' The old Richard would have asked why I wanted to know, but instead he changed the subject, inquiring after my aunt and uncle.

I told Julia I'd failed to learn a thing, and rode home trying to fathom out what trouble Richard could be in, and why he thought he might never return to sea. Julia said he was acting like her brother had done before his death. But if Richard had been involved with the Fat Badger Corresponding Society, Septimus would have noted it in his journal. To my mind, Richard wasn't just deeply troubled, he was also bitter, angry, and possibly a little scared.

CHAPTER 10

When I reached Westfleet, Luffe told me Mr. Hamerton had gone to Newport. This was only his third day on the Island and I had not seen much of him yet. But, once he'd settled in and relaxed, I would have a better chance of assessing what kind of a man he was. Other agents on the Island, organised by Mr. Reevers and Mr. East, watched his movements whenever he left Westfleet, although I had not seen anyone hanging about near the house. Still, agents had to be unobtrusive, and I prayed Mr. Hamerton wouldn't realise he was being followed.

I told Luffe I was going into the workroom and did not wish to be disturbed. This was the room my father had used for his hobbies, part of the east wing and the extensive additions my father had made to Westfleet on his marriage. It was here I had helped him solve some of the puzzles he encountered in writing his history of the Island. Where, as I'd told Mr. Pitt, we had written the relevant facts on large sheets of paper, and fixed these to the walls, where they could be seen at a glance. As I planned to do with the facts concerning Mr Hamerton.

For it was vital that I missed nothing, but if I suddenly started to spend a good deal of time in the workroom, my aunt and uncle would guess I was trying to solve some new mystery, and demand to know what it was. I could see no answer to the problem, except to use the workroom when they were out, or had retired to bed.

I copied out the relevant passages of the journal for Mr. Pitt, making another for myself so that I could return the journal to Julia. The earlier entries, about normal life, would mean so much to her. Then I went to look for my uncle. I found him reading in the library, and explaining I needed to speak to Mr. Reevers on a private matter, I asked if he would be kind enough to escort me to Norton House.

He eyed me thoughtfully but agreed readily enough, and said, 'I was hoping for a chance to browse through his library again.'

I laughed. 'I wish everyone was as understanding as you, Uncle.'

'If you speak to Mr Reevers out in the garden that would satisfy your aunt's sense of propriety, I think.' The library overlooked the garden. 'I would be able to say, quite truthfully, that you never went out of my sight.'

On reaching Norton House we saw Mr Reevers sitting reading on the terrace in the sun. The house, built some eighty years previously, had a very long garden running down to the beach, and as my uncle was aware, it also sported an extensive library. Thus, while I talked to Mr. Reevers on the terrace my uncle went off to enjoy himself browsing through the books.

Mr. Reevers folded the papers he had been reading and told me, 'Toby's out checking on newcomers to the Island. As he says, it would be foolish to assume Hamerton is Mr. Brown when we have no actual evidence.'

'Are there many gentlemen newly arrived here?'

'Three that we know of.' When I refused his offer of refreshments he sat back in his chair, his eyes searching my face and said, 'I am delighted to see you at any time, but your expression suggests you have news for me.'

He was smiling at me in a manner that set my heart racing, and reminding myself severely why I was here, I lowered my eyes and tried to behave like the sensible woman I'd always believed myself to be. 'Julia Tanfield believes her brother was murdered.'

His eyebrows shot up. 'Does she indeed?'

'And I think she's right.'

His lazy eyes were suddenly alert. 'What makes you say that?'

'The journal I found in a secret drawer of his desk.' I handed him the copy I'd made, and he rifled through the pages to see how long it was, before putting the sheets on the table beside him. 'I should like you to read it now,' I urged. 'If you would be so good.'

His lips began to twitch at my impatience. 'My nurse taught me that reading in the presence of a lady was impolite.'

'In this instance I beg you to forget such considerations.'

He heaved a sigh. 'Must I?' And murmured softly, 'I would much rather look at you.'

The faintest of flushes coloured my cheeks. 'Mr. Reevers, I'm sure I don't need to point out there are any number of much prettier women than----'

'Yes, but none with a tenth of your intelligence.'

'In that case, oblige me by reading those pages.'

'I fail to see what can be so urgent. Or even how it concerns me at all. Surely you should inform the local constable or ------'

'This is why it concerns you,' I broke in impatiently,

handing him the token I'd found in Septimus's desk. 'Septimus belonged to the same corresponding society as those two assassins. And this journal,' I said, handing him the sheets again, 'says they mean to kill the King, his family, Mr. Pitt and important Government ministers all on the same day. And we have very little time in which to prevent it.'

Unable to sit still while he was reading, I got up and walked about the terrace. Even the sight of a thrush perched on a nearby wall, seemingly watching us, failed to distract me. The instant he finished reading I returned to my seat. He still held the pages in his hand and when he glanced up at me, something in his expression made me blurt out, 'What is it?'

'Yesterday I had a message from Mr Pitt informing me it is believed Mr. Brown was recruited very recently. Which would certainly fit with Hamerton. Pitt says the French are expecting something really big from him.'

'Nothing is more important to the French than revolution,' I said more calmly than I felt.

'Indeed,' he agreed absently, and sat staring into space.

Watching him, I wondered how he and Mr. East coped with the knowledge that Mr. Pitt relied on them to capture Mr. Brown and every member of the Fat Badger society on the Island. Relied on them, in fact, to prevent a revolution. Knowing that, if they failed, England would be changed for ever. Coming out of his reverie, he reached out and took my hands in his. 'My dear girl, you must take the greatest care. If it is Hamerton, he'll be more dangerous than any man you have ever met. If you offer the slightest hint that you so much as suspect him, he will kill you without a single qualm.'

I caught my breath, knowing he was right, yet whatever the cost, I had to discover whether Mr. Hamerton was guilty, or innocent. For if their plot succeeded, demagogues like Robespierre would strut about on English soil, dictating whose head would be next to roll from the guillotine into those grotesque baskets.

Thanks to Septimus's journal we knew Mr Brown wanted everything ready by the end of July. When Mr. Pitt received the copy I'd made, he would take every possible measure to ensure the safety of the King and top government ministers. Measures Mr Brown would be unaware of, as he couldn't know Septimus had kept a journal. Thoughts I clung to gratefully, for they gave me hope. It was, therefore, vital that Mr. Hamerton did not find out about the journal. I was never more thankful that Julia had promised not to tell a soul about it, not even Richard.

I was afraid I would find it difficult to conduct an amiable conversation with Mr. Hamerton so soon after reading the journal, but it was easier than I'd expected.

'I spent the morning in Newport,' he told us over dinner. 'And this afternoon I bought a house.'

We all stared at him in astonishment. 'A house?' I echoed.

He nodded and told us, with great enthusiasm, 'It's exactly what I'm looking for. The owner, Mr. Bush, died recently but his widow kindly showed me round.'

My aunt looked up from her large portion of apple pie. 'Where is this house exactly?'

'On the outskirts of Dittistone. Quite isolated, but on a hill overlooking the sea.'

'Oh, yes I remember,' I said. 'Mr. and Mrs. Bush moved down from London a year ago.'

'Well, Mrs. Bush is returning to London. The climate doesn't agree with her, whereas I find the sea air and lovely countryside suits me very well, and the house couldn't be better.'

That pleased my aunt, but my uncle said, 'Are you sure it's wise to make that kind of decision so quickly?' We had got back to Westfleet late on Saturday, and today was only Tuesday.

'I'm quite sure, Mr. Frère. I have only been on the Island for three days, but already I feel I could happily spend the rest of my life here.' He hesitated as if uncertain how to continue. 'The house won't be available until the first of July. I thought of moving to an inn ----'

'Nonsense,' I insisted, my aunt and uncle quickly adding their protests to mine. 'You are welcome to stay here as long as you want.'

A shy smile hovered on his lips. 'You really are most kind. I should like to stay, if you are quite sure----'

'I am.' I was astonished at the speed with which he was buying a house, for he seemed far from impulsive in all other ways. Yet, if he was a French agent, an isolated house on the Isle of Wight, where no-one would see who visited him, or what he did, was ideal for planning a revolution. It also meant that if he moved in on the first of July, I had precisely four weeks in which to find out if he was Mr. Brown. I prayed it would be enough.

In the morning I started my search for Septimus's friend George, convinced it would be easy enough to find his grave. As a gentleman, he was bound to have a gravestone, and surely there couldn't be many Georges of the right age who had died in early May. Remembering that Septimus had bumped into him in Newport, I hoped that was where George had lived, and where his grave would be. Once I learned his surname I could approach his wife, with every chance of discovering who else belonged to the Fat Badger society.

I explained the situation to Mudd on the way, relating what was in the journal, watching his growing horror as I told him what this society planned to do.

'No-one I know wants to go the way of the French, my lady.'

'Most people don't, John, I agree. But if these men kill the King I fear that those who do want a revolution will ensure that it happens.' Even so I rode into Newport full of hope. If we could find out who else was in this society, we still had time to stop them.

After a day spent searching cemeteries and church records, my optimism had disappeared, for those named George who had died in Newport at that time were old men or children. As we left for home Mudd, seeing my despair, suggested, 'Perhaps the gentleman lived in a village near Newport, my lady.'

'Let's hope so, John. We'll try again tomorrow.'

Riding back across the Downs we stopped to give the horses a rest, and I noticed two riders on a lower path, riding side by side, deep in conversation. They were going away from us and were not aware of our presence. We could not hear what they were talking about, but I recognised one as being Mr. Sims, the parson's nephew. Watching them disappear into the distance I said to Mudd, 'That older, larger gentlemen – isn't that Mr. Young?'

'Yes, my lady.'

'My father said he made his money from smuggling.'

'That was on the mainland, my lady. It must be nearly thirty years since he came to the Island. He's quite respectable now.'

This was true. His money had made him acceptable to many, including the impoverished but genteel family in Dittistone, into which he'd married. A widower now, he had a daughter of about eighteen, took a great interest in politics and was known to have a fondness for gambling. 'What business could Mr. Sims possibly have with such a man?'

But Mudd did not know either, and I smiled to myself thinking of what the Uptons would say if they could see their nephew now. To them gambling was the worst of sins.

'As we're talking of smugglers, my lady-------..'

He hesitated and I encouraged, 'What is it, John?'

'It's just that I saw Mr. Hamerton talking to smugglers at Blackgang.' I turned to him in horror, for some of the Island's most notorious smuggling gangs were to be found at Blackgang. 'I thought I should mention it, my lady, what with Mr. Hamerton coming from Windsor and not knowing the ways of Island smugglers.'

'When was this?'

'Sunday morning, my lady. I was exercising his lordship's horse, and came back by Blackgang.' I should have sold my father's horse but could not bring myself to part with him. 'I was so pleased to be home I was up very early, eager for a good long ride. That not being so easy in Windsor,' he added in his matter of fact manner. 'No-one else was about when I left, so I think Mr. Hamerton must have saddled his horse himself.'

I'd told Mudd about Septimus, but he knew nothing of Mr. Hamerton, as Mr. Pitt had forbidden me to tell anyone. Yet if Mudd was to assist me, he needed to know it all. Besides, as a servant he could hear or see things that I might not. As he had at Blackgang. Unless I told him what to look out for, he couldn't help. And I had absolute faith in Mudd's discretion, aware that not one word of what I was about to tell him would ever pass his lips.

John Mudd had taught me to ride, and in doing so had passed on his love of horses to me. He had never been over protective, nor was he now, although I was conscious that, since my father's death, he had, in his own quiet way, kept a more watchful eye on me. He would see that what I was doing was dangerous, but I did not believe he would fuss about it.

Up here there was no-one about, except a shepherd some distance ahead, looking after the flocks of sheep that roamed the Downs. Thus, I told him about John Hamerton and added, 'Mr Reevers and Mr. East are the only other people who know.' He nodded, as if that was what he'd expected, and I pointed out, 'If you help me with this your life could be in danger too. If you would prefer to have nothing to do with it, I shall quite understand.'

He spluttered with indignation, 'As if I would ever do such a thing, my lady.'

He remained so clearly affronted that I quickly explained, 'I wanted you to have the choice, John. I didn't mean to offend you. And it's no good saying you're not, because after twenty-four years it's not something you can hide from me.'

His face broke into a reluctant grin. 'The fact is, my lady, I thought you'd know I'd never let you down.'

'I do. But there's a difference between not letting me down, and putting your own life at risk.'

'Not to me there isn't, my lady,' he chided respectfully. The very fact that he had fallen back into chastising me, much as he had when I was a child, told me how much I had upset him, and it took me a few minutes to rectify the situation. Which I did by reminding him of some of the scrapes he'd rescued me from when I was young.

He made no comment on my involvement in such matters, suggesting he did not disapprove. If he had, he would have said so, if only by remarking my father would not have liked it. As he did not do this, I knew I could count on him to assist me in every possible way.

I suspected too that he already had some idea of what was going on, as when Mr Reevers had escorted me to Downing Street to meet Mr. Pitt, Mudd had driven us there and back.

Afterwards, in the carriage, I had talked freely about what Mr. Pitt had wanted, and I felt sure he must have heard some of the conversation, despite the streets noises going on all around us. The lack of surprise when I explained I had to report back on Mr. Hamerton certainly suggested that he had. But all I said was, 'It would be unwise to assume Mr. Hamerton is Mr. Brown. It may be some other gentleman who has recently arrived on the Island.' He nodded and I went on, 'The only other gentleman I've seen is Mr Sims. Do you know of anyone else?'

He thought for a few moments and then shook his head. 'No, my lady, I don't.'

I urged him to keep his eyes and ears open. 'These Fat Badgers killed Jeffel. And pushed Mrs Tanfield's brother over the cliff. I won't rest, John, not until every one of those fiends is either dead, or awaiting the scaffold.'

That evening, after my aunt and uncle had gone to bed, Mr. Hamerton said he had a letter to write, and I was able to go into my workroom. Here I spent some time studying the journal again, in case I'd missed anything. I also checked the chart I'd made for Mr. Hamerton, and I was sitting in my chair thinking about him when I saw a light in the garden.

A glance at the clock showed me it was already well past midnight. The light was clearly coming from a lantern, and taking the pistol I kept in the drawer of my desk, I walked quietly towards the nearest side door and went outside.

CHAPTER 11

It was a still night, but the lantern was swinging at head height, and as it did so, the light shone on the face of the man holding it. I put the pistol back into my pocket and walked towards him. 'Mr. Hamerton, whatever are you doing?' I asked pleasantly.

He uttered a gasp of surprise. 'Lady Drusilla. You startled me, ma'am.' He pointed at the moths fluttering around the lantern. 'Moths are such pretty things.'

I thought of his wife, and the fact that the aristocrat who'd knocked her down had been murdered. On the night of that murder, Mr. Hamerton explained his absence from home by saying he had been out watching moths. 'Indeed they are,' I agreed with a smile. 'I'm afraid that when I saw the lantern bobbing about I thought you were a burglar.'

I heard his sharp intake of breath. 'I do beg your pardon, ma'am. I shouldn't have come out here without telling you, but I thought everyone had retired for the night. And I was eager to see if Island moths were different from those in Windsor.'

Standing by his side I watched the moths fluttering around the lantern, with Mr. Hamerton telling me the names of those we saw. 'Such attractive colours, don't you think?'

'Indeed.' Though, frankly, I thought them rather ugly. 'Do you have a large collection?'

He arched his brows at me. 'I don't collect them, ma'am. I just observe and keep a record of those I see. I couldn't bear to kill them. They don't harm anyone, and they have a short enough life as it is. The same goes for butterflies.'

'I enjoy watching butterflies myself. Unfortunately, so does the kitchen cat.'

'Ah well, that's nature. I like cats too, and thankfully enough butterflies survive to give us pleasure.'

'Well, I shan't worry in future when I see lanterns bobbing about in the garden.'

He drew his brows together into a deep frown. 'Forgive me ma'am, but I do think you were unwise to come out here alone. What if I had been a burglar?'

I decided not to mention I had a pistol with me. 'I'm not afraid of burglars, Mr. Hamerton.'

'I don't wish to frighten you, ma'am, but villains set on robbery tend to carry firearms and cudgels. It makes no difference to them who they hurt, when robbery will see them hang anyway. No-one likes to lose their silver, ma'am, but it is not worth dying for. I beg you not to take such a risk again.'

Assuring him I would not, I said I would go in now. 'It's becoming a little chilly.'

He bowed. 'Of course, ma'am. Don't worry, I will lock the door when I come in.'

Back in the workroom, I snuffed out the candles as if retiring for the night. Then I went out of the house by a rear door, taking the key with me. Mr. Hamerton had been less than twenty yards from the road, and might easily meet someone under the pretext of watching moths.

I walked up the hill at the side of the house, and on this moonlit night, I was able to watch him for some time, but no-one else appeared. I was about to go in when I heard a horseman coming down the lane on the far side of the hill, and I ran to a good vantage point. In the moonlight I recognised the slight figure of Mr. Sims, riding a horse belonging to Mr. Upton. I smiled to myself, for the Uptons believed he came home at about eleven, and it was well after one now. As I wondered what they would say about him coming back at such a time, I saw Mr. Hamerton walk into the house. And after a few minutes I followed.

In the morning, I was seated at my desk in the workroom, thinking about Mr. Hamerton, when my aunt stormed in. 'There you are, Drusilla,' she pronounced, as if I had been deliberately hiding from her. 'I've been looking for you everywhere.'

The moment the door opened I had picked up a quill pen as if I was writing a letter. Annoyed at being interrupted, I answered somewhat testily, 'What is it, Aunt?'

'Luffe has still not attended to the music room door.' I stifled a groan, remembering she had complained about it yesterday. 'I told you Luffe wasn't a suitable---'

'I haven't spoken to Luffe yet,' I broke in.

'Well, really-----' she muttered huffily, having been deprived of a scapegoat. 'I should be obliged if you would speak to him immediately.'

'Yes, I will do so presently,' I promised. 'I'm rather busy at the moment.'

Having opened her mouth twice and shut it again without finding suitable words to express her disgust, she took herself off grumbling that writing a letter was clearly of more importance to me than her comfort.

I tried concentrating on my notes on Mr. Hamerton, but it was no good. Knowing I would never have any peace until I had dealt with my aunt's complaint, I rang for Luffe. When he came in, I directed him to look at the music room door, adding with a weary smile, 'Mrs. Frère is of the opinion that it has developed a squeak.'

Luffe had been at Westfleet long enough to know my aunt's constant complaints irritated me intensely. Now it was his job to deal with them, I couldn't help comparing him with Jeffel who, aware I detested living in an atmosphere of discontent, had always done everything possible to keep the peace. Luffe simply did not have Jeffel's experience, but he did his best, and in all fairness, I could not expect more than that. 'Very good, my lady,' he said. 'It probably needs a drop of oil. I'll see to it at once.'

I thanked him, and decided I would go for a ride instead, where no-one would interrupt my thoughts. I went on my own, which I did on occasion; at twenty-seven I couldn't see the need for a groom to accompany me every time. It was still quite early, and I loved to ride at this time of the day, for it blew the cobwebs away and I felt much better for it.

Riding into Manor Lane, I turned right, heading for the Downs, as I did most mornings. On reaching the top, I set off at a gallop, but soon had to slow down when I ran into the mist that often developed in this part of the Island. I rode on, eventually turning towards the coast, as I frequently did, meaning to go home by way of the cliff top that ran from Dittistone, at one end of the bay, to Hokewell village at the other, a distance of some four or five miles.

Dittistone relied a good deal on fishing, and while it was not the size of some of the larger towns on the Island, it was certainly the largest place in the west, boasting a constable, a doctor, and two members of Parliament.

Here the tangy scent of the sea drifted in on a faint breeze. Gulls screamed overhead, but Orlando being used to their noise, ignored them. On the way back, having clarified my thoughts on Mr. Hamerton as far as was possible, I decided to visit one of my tenants who lived about a mile this side of Hokewell. My estate was small enough for me to look after myself, and I enjoyed doing so. I knew every child by name and recorded the details of each tenant, his family and birth dates of his children in a special book, which I kept in the library.

By the time I left that particular farm, the mist had begun to lift a little, giving occasional glimpses of the sea as I headed for the cliff top again. A few dense patches remained, however, one of which I saw just ahead of me when I turned in the direction of Hokewell. It was as I approached it that I heard someone shouting for help.

My father's warning that I tended to leap straight into a situation without thinking, did fleetingly cross my mind, but I quickly dismissed it, for it sounded to me as if someone was in desperate trouble. I rode Orlando quietly into the gloom of the mist, and was immediately confronted by two men, standing no more than ten yards away, pointing heavy flintlock pistols at me. One man was rather thin and weedy, the other, a decidedly burly individual, yelled at me to dismount.

Ignoring their threats, I instantly urged Orlando into a canter, riding straight at them, wishing I'd had the sense to bring my own pistols with me. The thin one threw himself out of Orlando's path, but the burlier man failed to move quickly enough and I bowled him over. His firearm went off as he hit the ground, and seeing him sprawled out flat, groaning in agony, I turned Orlando to face the weedy individual, who was already getting to his feet. I raised my riding whip ready to lash out at him, but before I could do so he fired a shot into the air so close to Orlando's ear it startled him. Orlando rose onto his hind legs, and my efforts to get at this man having left me somewhat unbalanced in the saddle, I was instantly unseated, hitting the ground with an impact that took my breath away.

Winded, I saw to my horror that I was very close to the edge of the cliff. As I scrambled to my feet, the thin man put the empty pistol into his pocket and started to run towards me, his face twisted with evil intent. Rapidly gathering speed, he suddenly thrust out his arms in a manner that made his intentions all too clear. He meant to push me over the cliff.

The drop was some forty feet here, the crumbling clay and sandstone sloping down to a sandy beach. At high tide, waves smashed against the cliff, and anything, or anyone in the water along with it. Fortunately the tide was out, but I doubted I would survive a fall from that height straight down onto the sand, and even if my fall was broken by hitting the outward slope of the cliff, it was likely to result in some nasty injuries. A fate I intended to avoid. I stood quite still, held my nerve, and at the very last second, threw myself sideways out of his reach. As I'd hoped, sheer momentum carried him straight over the cliff top.

He yelled something I didn't understand, and I watched him strike the edge of a ledge before plummeting onto the firm sand. I waited a moment to see if he got up, but he didn't move. The burly villain however, was struggling onto his feet, and I had just started to push myself up from the grass cliff top when a man appeared by my side. All I saw of him at first was a pair of highly polished brown riding boots. Boots I recognised. Hurriedly rising to my knees I found myself looking down the barrel of a gun.

'M-Mr. Hamerton?' I whispered shakily.

I tried to get to my feet but he ordered abruptly, 'Stay where you are.' This was no longer the jovial inoffensive gentleman I knew, this was a different man altogether.

Before I could utter another word, I heard someone running and Mr. Hamerton took in his breath sharply. 'Keep quite still, ma'am,' he muttered, his closeness making me aware of how tense he was.

The slight figure of Mr. Sims emerged from the mist. He stopped when he saw us and demanded, 'What's going on here?'

Mr. Hamerton gave a deep sigh. 'You are beset by rescuers, ma'am,' he murmured. And putting the pistol in his pocket he reached down to assist me to my feet, once more the smiling, cheerful man I knew. 'It's quite safe now. When that burly ruffian saw I was carrying a pistol, he rode off in a great hurry. What he couldn't know, ma'am, was that it wasn't loaded.' He took a handkerchief from his pocket and mopped his brow. 'Brought me out in a sweat, I don't mind admitting. I mean, if it had come to a fight he would have made mincemeat of me. And when I saw someone running out of the mist, I feared it was another of those scoundrels.' And he turned to Mr. Sims. 'I was exceedingly thankful when I saw it was you, sir, I can tell you.'

I expressed my gratitude to them, and learnt they had both been alerted by the shots. Mr. Hamerton had left his horse some way back, not wanting to charge into the mist, he said. Mr. Sims, who carried a book, had been looking for a spot out of the mist in which to read. 'There is very little peace to be had at the parsonage,' he explained.

I sympathised with him, and Mr. Hamerton, who was looking over the cliff at the weedy man stretched out on the sand, said, 'At least we'll catch one of those devils.'

But the man on the beach was dead. He was about my own age, with the weatherbeaten face of a sailor. He'd struck his head on a large rock at the bottom of the cliff, and as we all stood on the firm sand looking down at him, I confessed, 'Well, I cannot say I am sorry.'

'No, indeed,' Mr. Sims agreed.

Mr. Hamerton gave a shudder. 'It could so easily have been you lying there, Lady Drusilla.'

'That had occurred to me,' I murmured.

With a sudden exclamation he pointed at something on a ledge near the bottom of the cliff, some twenty yards away. 'Look, ma'am. Isn't that a pistol?'

'It must have come out of his pocket when he fell,' I said, going across to pick it up.

When I turned back Mr. Hamerton was kneeling beside the man's body, going through his pockets. He looked up at me and said, 'I hoped there might be something to identify him, but there's nothing here except some powder and shot.' These he laid beside the body.

'Isn't there any money?' I asked in surprise, expecting he would have a few coins on him.'

'Nothing at all.' He stood up and brushed the sand off his riding breeches. 'No doubt that was why they decided to rob you.'

Mr. Sims agreed and advised, 'The local constable ought to be informed, ma'am.'

I nodded. 'Yes, I'll attend to that.'

Mr. Sims offered to stay by the body until the constable came, but I assured him that wasn't necessary. 'I'll send a groom,' I said, aware that Mr. Reevers and Mr. East would want to see the body before the constable had it taken away.

Mr. Hamerton insisted on seeing me safely home and hurried off to collect his horse. Mr. Sims went on his way, and I walked back up the path to the cliff top, where Orlando was quietly grazing. As I went towards him I saw something on the ground. Picking it up I was not surprised to see it was a Fat Badger token. Guessing it had fallen from the weedy man's clothes when he threw himself out of Orlando's path, I put it in my pocket and took a careful look around, but there was nothing else.

Mr. Hamerton escorted me home, showing the kind of concern for my welfare that I had come to expect of him during our short acquaintance. By now the mist had completely disappeared, revealing dull grey skies. On arriving back at Westfleet I hurriedly dismounted, handed Orlando over to a servant and directed him to send Mudd to me at once. I went into the library and wrote a note to Mr. Reevers, giving the bare details of the attack, explaining where the body was, and that I had not yet informed the constable.

When Mudd appeared I sealed the note with a wafer and gave it to him to deliver. 'If Mr. Reevers is not there, Mr. East will do.'

'Very good, my lady.' I told him briefly what had happened. Watching the horror growing on his face I was not surprised when he reproved, 'You shouldn't have gone out alone, my lady.'

'No, I shouldn't. I shan't do so again, John.' His look of unqualified relief made me smile. He never fussed normally, but he was right, I had been very foolish.

Learning from Luffe that my aunt and uncle had gone out ten minutes earlier for a walk on the Downs, I took the opportunity to go into the workroom and note down the details of the attack. It was already difficult to find time to do what I needed here, aware that if I stayed too long, and too often, my aunt and uncle would guess I was trying to solve some new mystery and demand to know what it was. Mr. Pitt had forbidden me to tell them about Mr. Hamerton, and so far I had used the workroom when they were out, or had retired to bed. This being far from a desirable solution, the problem nagged at the back of my mind.

I took the Fat Badger token from my pocket and compared it with the one I'd found in Septimus's desk drawer. They were the same, except that Septimus's was much cleaner. The card was good, strong stuff, and of the highest quality. Not the sort of thing the two villains on the cliff top seemed likely to be able to afford. Which, again, pointed to a highly organised society.

From the window I could see the pond, and I stood watching the kitchen cat pawing at the water. Amused at her efforts to catch one of the goldfish, I decided that if she succeeded she deserved her prize. My father couldn't have chosen a better situation for his workroom, for apart from the antics around the pond, I loved to watch the blackbirds rushing in and out the shrubs. In summer the wonderful scent of lavender wafted in through the open windows on the slightest breeze, and every time I had entered the room in these past few weeks, the sheer peace to be found here seeped into my bones. But it hadn't always been like that.

After my father's death I'd avoided the room for months, for everything in it reminded me of him in a way that didn't happen in other rooms. This being where he was at his happiest, working on the hobbies that fired his enthusiasm. Even now, I often had a sense of his presence, which I realised was not helped by the fact that I had changed nothing. But I could not see a better arrangement of the room than the one we had so carefully chosen. A long working table ran down the middle of the room, and our two desks still faced each other by the middle window to gain the best of the light. I had meant to have one taken out, but found it useful to have a choice of where to sit when the sun got into my eyes.

All my life I'd loved the smell of the old books in here, and the faint tang of the sea emanating from the cabinets displaying father's collection of fossils. In the mornings, with the sun streaming into the east facing room, to me it was the perfect place for deep thought.

The cat, having failed to catch anything, wandered off to a quiet spot in the bushes, curled up and went to sleep. Smiling, I turned away from the window, and taking a fresh sheet of paper from a drawer, settled to the task of writing down what had happened during the attack on the cliff top.

I was so engrossed I failed to notice it had come on to rain, consequently I was rather taken aback when the workroom door opened and my uncle walked in. Foolishly, I tried to cover up what I was writing, and his eyebrows arched in surprise. I blushed and made things very much worse by muttering fatuously, 'I thought you were out.'

He indicated the rain pattering against the window and walked over to me. 'You look like a schoolgirl caught out in some misdemeanour. I'm sorry if I've disturbed you.'

'It's all right, Uncle.'

Sitting down opposite me, he studied my face and then quietly inquired, 'May I know what you are doing?'

CHAPTER 12

I hesitated, but only for a moment, for I suddenly realised my uncle could help me solve the problem of working in here without anyone asking questions. 'If you wish. I'm trying to find out what happened to Septimus.' Uncle Charles was a man I could confide in, and the simplest solution was to let him deal with my aunt when she demanded to know why I spent so much time in the workroom. As she undoubtedly would. 'Julia thinks he was murdered. Although I would rather you did not repeat that to anyone.'

He eyed me thoughtfully for a moment or two. 'And you do too, don't you, or you wouldn't go to all this trouble.'

I felt my lips twitching. 'Uncle, you know me far too well. It's a good thing I can trust you.'

'Ye-e-e-s,' he said slowly, and casting a glance at the locked shutter on the other section of the wall, which covered all that I knew of Mr. Hamerton, he inquired, 'May I be permitted to know what you are hiding there?'

Meeting his eyes, I said at once, 'I'm sorry, but I'm not at liberty to tell you.'

'I see,' he said slowly. 'Is it to do with Septimus?' When I shook my head he said casually, 'So there was more to your visit to Mr. Pitt than you told us. It doesn't surprise me; I thought you were holding something back at the time.'

I sought for an answer that would satisfy him, and failed. 'Did you,' I mumbled awkwardly.

The alarm in my voice amused him. 'I thought it odd

that Mr. Pitt had time to speak to you about your father's book when he was dealing with the suspension of Habeas Corpus and the arrests of leading reformers in the corresponding societies. Don't worry, I haven't mentioned it to your aunt, but if you ever need help I will do all I can.' In some relief, I thanked him, and he urged, 'You will be careful, won't you, Drusilla?'

'Of course I will,' I promised, thankful he could not possibly guess the truth. 'Uncle, I need an excuse to work in here without my aunt asking awkward questions.'

He considered for a minute or two. 'I'll tell her you are working on a book, but don't want to speak about it until you know whether you can do it properly. Will that do? Does it give you enough time?'

'Yes, it does,' I said thankfully. 'How clever you are, Uncle.'

'Flatterer.' I laughed and he asked, 'Who else knows about this?'

'Only Mr. Reevers and Mr. East.'

He smiled at me in an enigmatic way. 'I see,' he murmured. 'Am I right in thinking you particularly don't want Mr Hamerton inquiring into what you are doing?' I looked across at him, but didn't answer, aware I had underestimated his intelligence. A gleam of humour lit his eyes. 'So my role is simply to fob people off.'

'Please----' I begged affectionately.

He left me to it then, and I almost called him back to tell him about the cliff top attack, but decided to wait until he and my aunt were together, so I would only have to explain it once.

Mr. Reevers arrived soon after and I received him in

the library. The instant Luffe shut the door behind him I demanded eagerly, 'Did you see the body?'

'Yes, but the constable was already there, so I couldn't examine the man. Not that I think it would have helped.'

'How on earth did the constable find out?' I asked in exasperation, indicating he should take a seat. 'I didn't tell him.'

'Apparently Mr. Sims bumped into him on his way back to the parsonage, and thought to save you the trouble of contacting him. I'm afraid the constable didn't recognise the man.'

'A pity,' I sighed, but I wasn't that surprised. I explained in detail what had happened on the cliff top, and took the Fat Badger token from my pocket. 'I found this on the ground.'

I gave him the token and he fingered it thoughtfully. 'When exactly did Mr. Hamerton appear?'

'After the thin man fell over the cliff and the other one was still groaning on the ground.'

A smile played around the corners of his lips. 'I do wish I'd been there to see that. '

'I wish you had too. Particularly when I thought Mr. Hamerton was going to shoot me.'

He considered for a moment. 'Yes, I see. The other two had failed, and you think he came to----'

'Finish me off? That's exactly what I thought. Later, after Mr. Sims arrived, he told me the pistol he carried wasn't loaded.' Mr. Reevers did not comment and I went on, 'I think I know why the constable didn't recognise the dead man. I'm almost sure he was French.'

'What makes you say that?'

'He shouted something as he fell. I think it was an oath of some sort------'

'More than likely,' he grinned. 'If I fell over a cliff, I'm sure I would—'

'No doubt, but what I mean is, if it had been an English oath I would have recognised it.'

'*Would* you?' he inquired innocently, failing to quite control the twitching around the corners of his mouth. 'I must say ma'am, I am deeply shocked. Tell me, how many English oaths do you actually know?'

I couldn't help laughing. 'That isn't what I meant, as you know very well. I-----'

'But my dear girl, you said-----'

'Will you please be serious, Mr Reevers?' I begged rather unsteadily. 'The man spoke in a language that wasn't English. I think it was French, but I can't be sure.'

In a tone of polite inquiry, he ventured, 'Would you like me to repeat some French oaths? Just to see if you recognise them, I mean?'

I choked back the laughter rising in my throat. 'I would not.'

Taking out his handkerchief he mopped his brow in mock relief. 'Thank heavens for that.'

'I wish you would be sensible,' I chided. 'This is a serious matter.'

'Indeed it is,' he said, leaning back in his chair. But he was still smiling.

'I think the burly individual was Mr. Silver. The description in Septimus's journal fits him.'

'Does it indeed. Now that is interesting.'

'I'm so glad you think so,' I retorted in acid tones. 'Personally I found the whole episode rather frightening.'

His eyes softened. 'You dealt with them admirably, but I don't understand why they attacked you. Spies normally avoid drawing attention to themselves. Their job involves a good deal of listening, watching, and reporting back. Mostly no-one knows they are there, which is why they are so difficult to find.'

'Is that what you do in France?'

'I try to, yes.' He gazed at the cardboard symbol again, pursing his lips. 'We know the French are infiltrating the corresponding societies. Even so, I don't understand why they would want to------'

He stopped, but I finished it for him. 'Kill me? That is what they meant to do, isn't it?'

'Indeed,' he said, lowering his eyes. 'They must have had a very compelling reason for attacking you. Something vital to their cause.' He was right, but it was to be a long time before I found out what that reason was.

Later, when I told my aunt and uncle about the attack, I let them think the dead man had simply fallen over the cliff by accident; even so they still reacted with horror. My uncle went rather pale while Aunt Thirza scolded me for going out without a groom.

'It was very foolish of me,' I agreed. 'I won't do so again.'

That took the wind out of her sails, but she still went on at length about how she'd warned me time and again not to ride alone. 'But you never take any notice.'

'Well, I'm taking notice now. You were right and I was wrong.'

Considerably mollified, she declared, 'In that case we'll say no more about it.' And she immediately launched into a long tirade of things I ought to do, but did not. Eventually she ran out of my misdemeanours and went off to write a letter to her daughter, Lucie. Once the door had closed, my uncle, who looked more than a little troubled, asked, 'What are you not telling us, Drusilla?'

'Uncle,' I protested. 'I----' I stopped, for he was looking at me from under his brows in a way that told me he knew I was about to lie to him, and I saw that it would hurt him if I did. And I was far too fond of him to do that. 'Oh, very well, but not a word to Aunt Thirza. Or anyone else for that matter.'

I told him how the man had really fallen over the cliff, which turned his cheeks even whiter, but all he said was, 'You won't go out without Mudd in future, will you?'

'I give you my word I won't. Nor will I go without a loaded pistol.'

A faint smile flickered across his lips. 'I can't help wishing my dear, that Mr. Pitt had asked someone else to do whatever it is you are doing.'

'I don't,' I assured him cheerfully. 'It's the most fascinating thing I have ever done.'

'And the most dangerous.'

That was true, and while I did not actually enjoy that part of it, neither did it give me nightmares, but before I could say any of this, Luffe came into the room with a letter that had arrived by hand. 'The groom is waiting for a reply, my lady.'

It was from Julia. Her sickness had passed as suddenly as Dr. Redding had promised, and I was invited to an informal nuncheon party the day after next. Delighted, I wrote a quick note of acceptance. The groom had barely gone when Luffe came in again with another letter.

'My goodness,' my uncle said. 'We are popular today. Who's this one from, Luffe?'

'The parsonage, sir.' And informing us the groom had already gone, he left the room.

I opened the letter and groaned. 'The Uptons are holding one of their musical evenings on Saturday. We are all invited.'

Even my uncle heaved a sigh, having endured their gatherings before. 'Well, we have no real choice but to go. I expect your aunt will enjoy it.'

'She'll be the only one who does.'

'Come now, Drusilla, that is a little uncharitable.'

'Possibly,' I admitted with a faint smile. 'But it is also the truth.'

In the morning I wrote a reluctant acceptance to the Uptons, and then went for a ride along the cliff top, accompanied by Mudd. As we neared Hokewell I saw Mr Sims sitting on the cliff edge reading what looked like a very thick academic book. I stopped to exchange a few words, and although he spoke perfectly politely, I did not miss the initial irritation on his face at being interrupted.

'A beautiful day, Mr Sims,' I said.

'Indeed,' he agreed, while holding a finger in the place he'd reached in the book.

'I hope the Island air is improving your health.'

'I believe so, ma'am.'

When he didn't elaborate I inquired, 'I trust your illness wasn't of a serious nature.'

'Nothing more than a recurring fever, ma'am. But my strength is returning now.'

'Well, I won't stay chattering. I expect you came up here for some peace.'

He inclined his head. 'The parsonage is never quiet, ma'am. And I like to read every day.'

I went on my way, puzzled that he'd come to the Uptons to recuperate, when he must have known that life with his uncle would be anything but quiet, for the dratted man never stopped talking. And I wondered why he had really come to the Island. Not to recover from illness, that was certain. For, he appeared to be in excellent health. Whatever his real reason was, he was clearly prepared to put up with the shortcomings at the parsonage.

Leaving him, I rode along to Dittistone and then up onto the Downs. At the top I came to a halt, enjoying the peace and beauty of the hills all around me. I dismounted and handed Orlando's reins to Mudd. 'I'll walk for a while, John.'

I strolled along the hillside, the warm breeze in my face, while Mudd followed slowly on horseback, leading Orlando. Nothing disturbed me here except the bleating of the sheep, the shrieking gulls and the occasional snort from Orlando. Way below in the wide bay, the breakers continued to crash onto the sand and rush to the foot of the cliffs. Out at sea the breeze filled the sails of the ships making their way along the island's west coast.

I needed to think carefully about the cliff top attack. I still felt a trifle shaky, for Mr. Silver and his companion had obviously meant to kill me. They could easily have shot me, yet the pistol had been fired into the air instead. Clearly they had orders to make my death look like an accident. If I had gone over the cliff, and the fall had failed to kill me, I felt certain they would have remedied the matter instantly with a convenient rock. I had indeed been very fortunate to escape with my life.

But why did they want me out of the way? Mr. Reevers believed they must have had a compelling reason to risk drawing attention to themselves. Yet, I couldn't see that I'd learnt anything of vital importance. I only wished I had.

And then there was the co-incidence of Mr. Hamerton turning up, pointing a gun at me, when one man was dead and the other lay groaning on the ground. Would he have shot me if Mr. Sims hadn't appeared? He'd said the pistol wasn't loaded, but was that true? Since then he had behaved perfectly normally. I had, of course, thanked him for intervening.

I was also very concerned about the fast growing friendship between Mr. Hamerton and Richard. It did seem to have made Richard a little happier, which pleased Julia, but it was obvious his troubles had not gone away.

Deciding I'd walked long enough, I climbed back into the saddle and rode along with Mudd at walking pace, discussing the Fat Badger situation with him. 'It seems to me we're getting nowhere. We don't know if Mr. Hamerton is involved with the society, or where they are meeting now, or what he wanted from the smugglers at Blackgang.'

'Well, my lady, I could ask my father if he can find out.' Mudd's father probably knew every smuggler in this part of the Island. 'It might not be easy. There's a lot of rivalry between the gangs.'

The men at Blackgang were notorious for their violence, and I urged, 'He's not to put himself in any danger, John. I don't want him getting hurt.'

'He won't do that, my lady. He's a wily old devil. If he can help, he will.'

'In that case, I would be grateful if you would speak to him.' I suggested he went that afternoon and stayed as long as was necessary. 'I shan't go out again today.'

It was a lovely sunny day and when I arrived home to find a letter from my godmother awaiting me, I took it out into the garden to read. Sitting on the seat near the pond, I broke the seal, smiling in anticipation, for her letters were always a delight. And I was soon chuckling over her description of her travels through Yorkshire.

I read it twice, then put it in my pocket and strolled down through the colourful flower beds to the walled garden, where I saw Mr. Hamerton sitting in an arbour, reading. Hearing me approach he looked up, and instantly got to his feet.

I smiled at him. 'Don't let me disturb you, Mr. Hamerton.' Assuring me I was doing nothing of the sort, he asked if I had recovered from yesterday's dreadful attack. 'I think so,' I said, seating myself in the arbour. Watching the bees going in and out of some nearby foxgloves, I commented, 'Aren't they fascinating? They never seem to stop working.'

Sitting beside me he said, 'I've been watching them too. And the butterflies.'

'I suppose it's a bit early in the day for moths.'

'Some do come out in daylight,' he informed me in his quiet way, and spreading his arms to encompass everything around us, commented, 'I must say ma'am,

I do admire your walled garden. I mean to have one when I move.'

'With flowers that attract moths and butterflies?'

'Exactly so, ma'am,' he answered with enthusiasm.

'Have you definitely settled on the house in Dittistone?'

'I have. It is exactly what I want.' And told me he'd bought the contents of the wine cellar too, as poor Mrs. Bush no longer had a use for it. He went on talking about the house until I managed to move the conversation around to Richard, determined to discover if he knew what was worrying him.

'Richard is very kindly teaching me to sail,' he said. 'And I've already seen a yacht that would suit me perfectly.'

'You have been busy,' I declared pleasantly. 'First a house and now a yacht.'

'No point in wasting time, ma'am. One never knows how much of it one has left.'

'Indeed not,' I agreed, reminded of yesterday's attack. 'You are very wise to take advantage of Richard being at home. I imagine he'll be back at sea before long.'

His hesitation was so slight I wouldn't have noticed it if I hadn't been watching for any hint that Richard had confided in him. 'Yes,' he said. 'I suppose he will.' He pointed out a reddish moth on a stone. 'Look at that pretty cinnabar, Lady Drusilla ----'

'Mr. Hamerton,' I cut in, taking the direct approach. 'Do you know what's troubling Richard?'

CHAPTER 13

Mr. Hamerton's eyebrows shot up in surprise, and he avoided my gaze, a reaction that confirmed my belief Richard was in serious trouble. And that he knew very well what it was. If he hadn't known, he would have been puzzled, or concerned, or both, not guarded as he was now. But he covered it well. 'I do know he wishes he was at sea fighting the French.'

I had already learnt that Mr. Hamerton kept his emotions under strict control at all times, and never spoke without thinking. Thus, I responded, 'I'm sure you're right. Richard has always loved the sea.'

'As I am beginning to as well, ma'am.' His relief, that I did not pursue the matter, was barely perceptible, except again I was watching for it. He said, 'When I was a boy I rather fancied myself as a pirate.' I laughed dutifully, aware he was trying to lead the conversation away from Richard, and he went on, 'I would have been hopeless. I'm a poor shot, I can't fence, and I'm useless at fisticuffs.'

We sat talking for some time about the horrors going on in France in the name of liberty, of the war, and the corresponding societies, but at no time did he say anything out of place. I was about to get up and leave him when he said, 'Lady Drusilla, might I ask a small favour?'

'Of course.'

'I've started to hire servants for my new house, including a first class groom. A man called Bridge. His last employer died a short time ago, which has left him without a job and a home. As I don't move into my new house until the first of July, I wondered if it would be possible to house Bridge here until then. He could look after my horse and make himself useful about the stables.' I assured him it would be no trouble at all, there being plenty of room in the grooms' quarters. Thanking me he said, 'Would it be convenient for him to arrive today?'

'By all means,' I agreed easily.

'I'm going sailing this afternoon and could call on him on my way. I really am most grateful, ma'am.'

I left him to his book and went back indoors, more worried than I cared to admit. Richard refused to tell Julia or myself about his problems, yet he'd taken Mr. Hamerton into his confidence. A man he'd only known for a few days. If Mr. Hamerton was Mr. Brown, I was afraid Richard could become caught up with the Fat Badgers. He wasn't easily influenced, but he was extremely vulnerable right now, and Richard had always had a reckless streak.

That afternoon I was out in the garden when I saw a man walking towards the stables, and guessed from his attire that he was Mr. Hamerton's new groom. I went to meet him and on reaching me he touched his forelock. 'I'm Bridge, my lady. Mr. Hamerton said it was----'

'Yes, it's quite all right.' He was about forty, smart and clean, with a ready smile, and I casually asked who his last employer had been.

'Mr. Jenkins, my lady. Over at Newchurch. He lived at Hill House, down Field Lane.'

'Mr. Jenkins,' I mused thoughtfully. 'I don't think I know the gentleman.'

'He died a few weeks ago, my lady. Very sad it was, him being so young and with a family too. He fell in the river and drowned. I'd only just started work there and Mrs. Jenkins couldn't keep me on. There wasn't enough for me to do.'

I stared at him, unable to believe what I was hearing. Newchurch was only about five miles from Newport. Not daring to hope, I repeated, 'Mr. Jenkins drowned, you said.'

'Yes, my lady.'

When Mr. Hamerton told me Bridge's previous employer had died, I'd assumed him to be a much older gentleman. But if he was young------- 'Tell me, what horse did he ride?'

He blinked, understandably a little bewildered. 'His favourite was a lively chestnut. Very fond of it he was.'

Barely able to breath, I asked, 'Was your master a Mr. *George* Jenkins?'

'Why – yes. Did you know him after all, my lady?'

'No, but a friend of mine did.'

I asked one or two more questions, but learned nothing more. After getting one of the other grooms to show Bridge his quarters, I walked back towards the house in a state of jubilation. Certain, that at long last, I'd found Septimus's friend, George. Reaching the south lawn I had a sudden urge to cartwheel across it as I had as a child, and laughed to myself, thinking of what my aunt would say should she see me doing any such thing.

I considered going to see Mrs Jenkins that instant, taking another groom with me. But quickly dismissed the idea. I preferred to take Mudd, and tomorrow morning would do as well. Surely, I thought, Mrs. Jenkins must know at least one of these Fat Badgers. I could hardly wait for tomorrow to come.

Going into the workroom I was about to write down what Bridge had told me when my aunt suddenly stormed in, slamming the door behind her. 'There you are, Drusilla,' she remonstrated. 'I've been looking everywhere for you.'

I sighed, for although Aunt Thirza and I got on reasonably well much of the time, there were too many occasions like this one. Occasions I could do without. 'Luffe always knows where I am.'

She sniffed. 'He was nowhere to be seen. You don't realise what goes on in this house. The servants do just what they like, they're rude and refuse to obey orders, and----'

'Who wouldn't obey an order?' I cut in, for whenever she carried on in such a way, it was always one particular servant who had upset her.

'Granger. I ordered him to cut down the tree outside my bedchamber window, and he refused point blank.'

'Cut down the tree?' I repeated in disbelief.

'That wretched bird woke me at daybreak again. I didn't get a wink of sleep after that. It can sing somewhere else. I told Granger I'd have him dismissed for insolence but----'

That was the moment I lost my temper. I was so excited to have found George Jenkins, but still desperately anxious about many other things. I didn't know if Mr. Hamerton was Mr. Brown, or how we were to stop the Fat Badgers attempting to assassinate the King in August, I was worried sick about Richard and his friendship with Mr. Hamerton, and I did not want to go to the Uptons on Saturday. And my aunt was making a fuss about a mere blackbird.

I brought my fist down onto the desk in front of me with such a bang she jumped. 'You did what?' She blinked at me in surprise, as if she had every right to have my servants dismissed. 'Granger is the best head gardener on the Island, and he knows better than to cut down one of my trees without my permission.'

She had been angry before, but my furious reaction made her splutter, 'How dare you speak to me like that.'

'Like what, Aunt?' Ice dripped off every clipped syllable, for I was so enraged I could cheerfully have thrown the ink standish at her.

'As if I was of less consequence that a mere servant. I won't have it.'

'And I won't have you upsetting *my* servants. This is my house, Aunt. Something you forget when it suits you. I give the orders here, and I will not have a tree I am particularly fond of, cut down. If a blackbird chooses to perch on one of the branches and sing its heart out at five in the morning, then in my opinion, you should enjoy the treat. That is my last word. Now, you must excuse me, I am rather busy.'

She didn't move, but stood staring at me, her bosom heaving with righteous indignation, as she tried to think of a hurtful response. It didn't take her long to find one. 'You forget we are under no obligation to remain at Westfleet. We could just as easily leave.'

I shrugged. 'Leave if you wish, Aunt.'

'And who would act as chaperone?'

'I doubt I should bother with one,' I said airily, deliberately saying what I knew would shock her, for I was still boiling with anger.

'You'd set the whole Island talking.'

'More than likely, but I shan't care for that.'

'I believe you would do it too. Well, I shall tell Charles we are leaving.' Swinging round on her heel, she stormed out of the room in far more of a fury than when she had entered it.

Trembling with rage, I muttered one very rude word out loud, for I had promised myself time and again that I would not let Aunt Thirza provoke me into behaving in this undignified way. Thankfully, I could never stay angry for long, and within a few minutes I admitted to myself, somewhat ruefully, that if my uncle had complained of losing sleep because of this blackbird, I would have ordered Granger to cut down the tree at once. As I might also have done if my aunt had asked in a reasonable manner.

I knew too that I would have to make the peace, for she would not, and as I sat gazing out of the window wishing there was some other way, I saw my uncle riding up the drive. I gave a long deep sigh, for I knew exactly what would happen now. Aunt Thirza would pour out the whole sorry episode to him, and after he had calmed her down, he would seek me out. I hated to see my uncle upset, as I knew he would be. And, sure enough, about half an hour later, he poked his head round the door and asked quietly, 'Is it safe to come in?'

I laughed. 'I think so. I've had all traces of blood removed.' He sat down beside me, and I admitted to him what I would not to my aunt. 'I'm sorry, Uncle. I lost my temper.'

'I know.' He patted my hand in his understanding way. 'Do you want us to leave, Drusilla?'

'Of course I don't,' I murmured a little indistinctly,

swallowing the lump rising in my throat. 'That wasn't my suggestion.'

He nodded. 'I didn't think it was.' And he went on in his thoughtful way, 'I'm aware your aunt infuriates you at times Drusilla, but she doesn't mean half of what she says. She's run her own house for so long, it's hard for her not to interfere here, especially as you're so much younger. But I've made her promise she won't do so in future.'

I gazed at him in astonishment. 'How did you manage that?'

Chuckling, he said, 'I shan't tell you.'

'Do you think she will keep to it?'

'I hope so. At least for a time. She did admit to me that perhaps she had over-reacted, but don't tell her I told you.'

I smiled at him affectionately. 'How is it you never lose your temper with anyone?'

'Well, I tend to think it's a waste of time,' he said with a grin. How right he was, I thought. And once again, I swore I would keep calm the next time my aunt riled me.

Her admission, through my uncle, that she might have over-reacted was the nearest to an apology I would ever get, and poor Granger would never get one, for she wouldn't admit a fault to a mere servant. Whereas I, being anxious not to lose the best gardener on the Island, wasted no time in informing him, without criticising my aunt, that he'd acted quite properly, and all such orders were to be verified with me first.

'That's what I thought, my lady,' he said righteously. Not unnaturally he was a little ruffled by the experience and I spent half an hour walking round the garden with him praising his efforts, leaving him in a much happier frame of mind.

I was heading back to the house when I saw Mr. Reevers making his way towards me. He was smartly dressed in riding breeches and a pale blue coat, and my heart leapt at the sight of him. 'I was passing and couldn't resist calling in to see you,' he murmured. 'I thought you would wish to know that the agent following Hamerton when you were attacked, lost sight of him in the mist. Toby was absolutely furious.'

It was a pity, but as I said, such things happened. 'In all fairness the mist was very thick in places.' Suggesting we sit on a nearby garden seat, I asked, 'How is Mr. East? I haven't seen him lately.'

His eyes began to dance. 'That, I suspect, is entirely due to a certain Miss Charlotte Adams.'

'Really?' The name wasn't familiar to me. 'I don't---

'I doubt you'll know her. The family has only been here two weeks. They have taken a house near Newport for the summer and we met them at a party a few days ago. She's a lively dark-haired beauty of nineteen and Toby couldn't take his eyes off her.'

'Oh, I am pleased,' I said happily.

'So am I. That business with the Rothertons affected him badly at the time.'

Recalling how Mr. East had cut Lord Rotherton dead at the ball in London, I asked, 'Does Miss Adams return his interest, do you think?'

He gave a hearty chuckle. 'Judging by the way she was smiling up at him when they were dancing I think there will be wedding bells before the year is out.'

'What about her father – does he approve?'

'It appears so.'

'It seems to be a day for good news,' I said, and told him about Bridge and Mrs Jenkins. 'I'll call on her tomorrow morning.' And added, 'When I think of the time I wasted searching for Septimus's friend George, and in the end I found him by sheer chance.'

'That often happens, believe me. I only wish Toby and I could report some similar success, but our efforts have produced nothing of any significance so far.'

We talked about Mrs. Jenkins in hopeful tones, then I told him how anxious I was about Richard. To which he merely raised his eyebrows at me, murmuring a trifle absently, 'Oh?'

Nettled by his lack of interest, I declared, 'It may not seem important to you, but it is to me.'

His eyes gleamed appreciatively. 'Whatever affects you is of concern to me.' I looked up at him, uncertain how to answer, and he said softly, 'I thought you knew that.'

There was a glow in his eyes I could not mistake, and being rather confused about my own feelings, I said nothing, and he went on, his voice retaining that caressing note, 'Tell me why you are concerned about Richard.'

'Well, for a start, Mr. Hamerton knows what's worrying him.' I explained about the slight hesitation and guarded reaction when I asked Mr. Hamerton if he knew what the problem was. 'Why has Richard confided in a man he hardly knows?' A question that only deepened the frown on Mr. Reevers' brow. 'And why hasn't he been given a ship now he's fit enough to return to sea? Surely the Navy needs every experienced officer it can get in this war?'

'I would have thought so.'

'You see, I've known Richard all my life and when he has a problem he does his best to resolve it. He never sits back and does nothing, as he seems to be doing now. Which makes me think it's not possible for him to resolve himself. That the solution lies in the hands of other-----' I stopped, seeing my groom riding towards the stables. 'Mudd's back,' I said in surprise.

'Shouldn't he be?'

'I did say I wouldn't need him until this evening.'

'Perhaps he was bored.'

I smiled rather absently, as Mudd, having seen us, quickly dismounted, handed his horse to a stable boy to attend to, and hurried in our direction. When he reached us his eyes were full of excitement. 'What is it, John?'I asked eagerly.

CHAPTER 14

Mudd said, 'My father already knew why Mr. Hamerton spoke to the Blackgang smugglers, my lady. It seems the gentleman wanted someone to take a letter to France. To Paris, my lady.'

'Did he, by God?' exclaimed Mr. Reevers. 'Were any of them willing?'

'My father didn't know, sir.' Mudd's answers to our other questions soon made it clear that was all his father could tell us. 'He wouldn't have let on to anyone but you, my lady.'

'Tell him I'm very much obliged, John,' I said sincerely.

He went back to his duties then, and I asked Mr. Reevers, 'If Mr. Hamerton is Mr. Brown, and he wanted a letter taken to Paris, why didn't he send one of the Fat Badgers?'

'Perhaps none of them speak French. He couldn't send anyone who didn't. Whereas smugglers often know enough to get by, and they make perfect spies. They are used to dangerous situations, accustomed to keeping their mouths shut, and most will do anything for money. We use them and so do the French. But, whatever the reason, the plain fact is an innocent man does not communicate with the enemy in secret.'

'No,' I said thoughtfully. 'I suppose not.'

'You sound doubtful.'

I gave a little shrug. 'You can't condemn him on that alone.' I would not have done so when helping my father. 'Everything we have against Mr. Hamerton is circumstantial. We don't have any actual proof.'

'Aren't you forgetting that business on the cliff top?'

'No, but he may have genuinely come to my rescue.'

'Is that what you really think?'

I hesitated, not knowing what I really believed. 'I think it is possible. And in every other respect he appears to be a truly patriotic Englishman.'

He broke into an indulgent smile. 'In France, I curse the English as easily as any Frenchman. No-one could doubt my allegiance to the revolution, believe me.'

Watching a moth land on a nearby stone, I mused over Mr. Hamerton's interest in these delicate creatures, for it seemed so out of character for a French spy. But, I reasoned, even murderers might have a gentle side. 'He hasn't betrayed himself in any way at Westfleet. Not even one careless word.'

'That doesn't surprise me. Top agents are extremely difficult to outwit. But you're quite right. We can't arrest him without proof that will stand up in court. And, as Hamerton will be well aware, no smuggler would ever admit taking a letter to Paris. Still, he's bound to slip up at some point, and when he does, we must be ready for him.'

I walked with him the short distance to the stables, and as we said goodbye, he murmured, 'May I have the pleasure of driving you to Mrs. Tanfield's party tomorrow?'

'Thank you. I should like that.'

Getting onto his horse he smiled. 'So shall I.' And he rode off down the drive.

Needing time to think, I decided to go for a walk. Fluffy white clouds scudded across the sky, driven on a brisk wind, but I have always loved the feel of the wind blowing through my hair, and rarely bothered with a hat on solitary walks. Much to the disgust of my aunt.

I climbed the steep path at the back of the orchard and on reaching the top, strolled along the Downs, barely aware of the sheep, the view, or the birds, my mind fixed on the problem of Mr. Hamerton. He was the perfect guest, easy to please, and he possessed excellent manners. He spoke of the bloodthirsty revolution raging in France with convincing loathing, appeared to disapprove of corresponding societies, and had seemed horrified at the assassination attempt in Windsor. But, as my father used to say, when gathering evidence for his book, most people were much what they seemed, but a few were not. And it wasn't always easy to tell which was which.

His interest in moths took him outside at night, but only into the garden, for I had watched him on several occasions now. Yet, he'd pointed a firearm at me during the cliff top attack when I'd got rid of one of my attackers and floored the other. And he'd asked Blackgang smugglers to take a letter to Paris. Incidents I thought about for a considerable time.

Wandering slowly back, worrying about his rapidly growing friendship with Richard Tanfield, I sat for a moment on the seat placed close to the top of the steep path. From this beautiful spot, the whole of my property was laid out below and I could see everything that was going on. I loved this view, as my father had before me, and I often wondered if those who had lived at Westfleet before us, had come here to think about their problems.

I hated to see Richard in such distress. He had been much more cheerful since Mr. Hamerton's arrival, and was now teaching that gentleman how to sail. But a brief conversation I'd had with him yesterday told me his troubles had not gone away. I'd asked if he'd heard from the Admiralty yet, and he drew in his breath sharply, demanding in a rough, abrupt manner, what the devil I meant by that.

Puzzled I said, 'Only that they might have given you a ship. I mean they must need experienced naval officers in this war.'

'Oh I see. Well, I haven't heard a thing.'

The bitterness in his voice alarmed me so much, I begged, 'Richard --- I wish you would tell me what's wrong.'

'What good would that do?'

'You might feel better for talking about it.' He shook his head at me but didn't answer. If he wouldn't even admit he'd confided in Mr. Hamerton, I knew I was wasting my time, but I tried again. 'And it might stop me worrying about you.'

'You think so?' And he gave way to a brittle laugh. 'No, Drusilla, it would not. I realise you mean well, but there's only one way to resolve this.....matter. And resolve it I will.'

'Whatever do you mean?' I asked, full of apprehension, having caught a glimpse of recklessness in his eyes. Again he didn't answer and I urged, 'Promise you won't do anything rash.'

'I don't have any choice, Drusilla. Death or glory, that's me,' he ended jokily.

I walked back down the hill thinking about the Fat Badgers, for so far Mr. Reevers and Mr. East had failed to find any trace of them on the Island. This highly organised group clearly knew how to keep their members and activities well hidden. Yet, things must go wrong on occasion, even for them.

The following morning, straight after breakfast, I set off for Newchurch, accompanied by Mudd. Still scarcely able to believe that in the space of a few hours we had finally learnt the surname of Septimus's friend George, and what Mr. Hamerton wanted with the Blackgang smugglers.

On reaching the village, a boy directed me to the Jenkins residence, an attractive stone house down a quiet lane. When I knocked on the door, however, the butler informed me Mrs Jenkins and her children were staying on the mainland with her brother, who had recently moved from London to Hampshire.

'We expect them back tomorrow. If the weather remains fair, that is,' he ended gloomily, casting an eye out the window at the scudding clouds.

I groaned inwardly at the prospect of waiting another couple of days to find out what Mrs Jenkins knew about the Fat Badgers. I've always detested having to wait when I'm eager to get on with things. The fact that there was nothing I could do, except leave a message, only made it worse. Trying not to show my impatience, I allowed the butler to usher me into a pleasant library, to a desk with an excellent selection of writing materials. Sitting down, I considered how much I should say in my note, and settled for explaining I was interested in any information she had about the corresponding society to which her husband had belonged.

Having sealed the note with a delicate wafer, I stood up, and turning towards the door, I caught sight of a pretty blue and white bowl in a recess. Going over to take a closer look, I saw the words "Liberty" and "John Wilkes 1768" on the side. And I smiled; Mr Jenkins, it seemed, had not been averse to proclaiming his views to the world.

The butler promised to give Mrs Jenkins the note the instant she returned from the mainland, and we rode down the lane to the nearby churchyard, where Mudd looked after the horses while I found what I had been searching for. A new headstone, with a simple inscription. *In sacred memory of George Jenkins, who departed this life on May 3rd 1794, aged 28 years.*

There was nothing to be done but ride home again, and I enjoyed a good long gallop before returning to Westfleet in time to change for Julia's nuncheon party. Mr. Hamerton left before me, explaining he and Richard meant to sail to Windsor soon and needed to discuss arrangements for the trip. 'I must settle my affairs there, and I hope to improve my sailing abilities at the same time.'

'That sounds an excellent idea.' And I asked if he meant to sell his house in Windsor.

'Well, actually ma'am, I've done that already.' I reacted with as much surprise as I could muster, having seen the document of sale when I searched his bedchamber. 'Once I'd decided to move, I saw no point in waiting,' he explained. 'After I've attended to these last few legal matters I shall find myself an attorney on the Island.'

'When do you mean to go to Windsor?'

'Next week. Then I shall settle down to my new life on this beautiful island.'

Mr. Reevers arrived a trifle early, and on the short drive to Breighton House I told him about Mrs. Jenkins being away. 'These things happen,' he said in a matter-of-fact voice.

We were nearing the church at the time, and seeing Mr. Upton walking towards us, I cursed under my breath. 'I beg your pardon,' my companion murmured, his eyes dancing. 'I didn't quite catch what you said, ma'am. But if, as I believe, you expressed a desire to avoid the parson, nothing could be easier. We will simply drive past as if he wasn't there.'

I choked back a laugh. 'Do be serious. We cannot do that.' But, on reaching the parson, I called out to him, 'Good morning, Mr. Upton. I'm sorry we can't stop. We're late already.'

Driving on, Mr. Reevers said, 'There, you see how easy it was. You lied most convincingly. We are a good ten minutes early.'

I felt decidedly warm, despite the lightness of my summery blue gown and wide-brimmed matching hat, and on arriving at the house we saw Julia was sensibly sitting in a shady part of the terrace. She was talking to Richard and Mr. East, and I was delighted to see some colour in her cheeks again. As we exchanged the usual civilities, Edward came running from the garden to greet me, well scrubbed and smartly dressed in a sailor suit Julia had made for him.

'Illa,' he beamed happily, as I gave him a hug.

'Don't let him plague you,' Julia urged, as she begged Mr. Reevers to be seated.

Edward clearly understood the word, for he looked affronted. 'I don't plague Illa. She *likes* me. Don't you,' he insisted, tucking his chubby little hand into mine.

'Indeed I do,' I admitted, laughing.

'We got kittens,' he confided, and tugged at my hand, eager to show me.

When we began to walk off Julia glanced over her shoulder and begged, 'Be good now, Edward. And do try to stay clean for once.'

Once we were out of Julia's hearing, he announced proudly, 'I'm *never* good.' As I smothered a giggle he spotted the mother cat walking through a bed of roses. Letting go of my hand, he crashed headlong through the bushes after her. Catching his sleeve on a thorn, he simply wrenched off the offending branch, and I heard the ominous sound of tearing material. Realising what he'd done, he turned round and looked at me. 'Oops,' he said and broke into an angelic smile.

It was impossible not to laugh. Life, to Edward, was sublimely uncomplicated, and in that moment, I envied him. If only, I thought, unmasking Mr Brown was as simple.

After admiring four tiny adorable kittens, I took Edward back, apologising to Julia for the torn shirt. 'I was too late to stop him, I'm afraid.'

'Oh – Edward,' she groaned despairingly. And informing me the gentlemen had gone to look at the horses, she suggested a stroll in the gardens.

Edward ran ahead of us chasing butterflies, and I said, 'Are you truly better now, Julia?'

'I am. It was absolutely amazing. I woke up the other morning feeling perfectly well. Incredibly the sickness had gone.'

Edward, who was some distance in front, suddenly stopped and stamped his tiny foot vigorously on something in his path, pronouncing with loathing,

'Nother blasted snail. Dratted things,' in an almost perfect imitation of Wilson, Julia's head gardener.

Greatly amused, I inspected the squashed snail, praised Edward for his prompt action and ruffled his curls. Edward, spotting Wilson working in the garden, charged off to demonstrate how he'd dispatched the snail, and the gardener threw back his head, laughing heartily.

Julia, although amused, commented rather dryly, 'I must tell Wilson to mind his language in front of Edward if my son is not to put us all to the blush.'

Having promised to tell her if I discovered the name of Septimus's friend George, I took the opportunity to do so now. 'Poor man,' she sighed. 'A wife and four children too. I pray she knows these other men, Drusilla. You will tell me when you hear from her, won't you?'

Again I promised to do so, and once she'd collected her thoughts she began to speak of the delights awaiting us for nuncheon, and added, 'Oh, by the way, I've invited Mr. Sims too. It's time we all became properly acquainted with him.'

'Do you like him?'

She wrinkled her nose. 'I'm not sure. He's an odd creature. But I am very taken with Mr. East.'

'So is my godmother. In my last letter I told her how handsome and charming he is, and this morning I had a reply saying he sounded the very man for me.'

Julia went off into a peal of laughter. 'That is so like her. The thing is, do *you* like him?'

I pretended to consider the matter. 'I find him most agreeable.'

She turned to me, her eyes wide with curiosity. 'Don't tell me you've finally met a man you really like?'

'Oh, I think everyone must like Mr. East,' I said deliberately.

'Don't be so provoking. You know what I mean.'

'I've only known him three weeks, Julia.'

'I knew I wanted to marry Richard after three hours.'

I teased, 'I'm surprised it took you that long.'

She giggled, but said, 'Drusilla, I know you keep saying you won't ever marry, but at least give Toby East a chance. Mr Reevers too, although he's not as handsome as Mr. East.'

'Perhaps I should discount him, then,' I mused tongue-in-cheek, hoping this would put her off the idea that I had any particular interest in Mr Reevers.

She fixed her intelligent green eyes on mine, and I saw that I hadn't fooled her for a moment. 'I always thought you rather liked him.'

'Did you? But if his looks are inferior would I be wise to consider him?' I inquired teasingly. 'In any case, my aunt favours Mr. Hamerton.'

'Does she? I don't think he'd suit you, Drusilla.'

'There is Mr. Sims......... '

'He looks as if a breath of wind would bowl him over.'

'Appearances can be deceptive,' I pointed out.

'I can see I'm wasting my time,' she remarked in her good-natured way. 'I suppose I won't really know what you think until I receive an invitation to your wedding.'

'Should I ever decide to marry, I will tell you well before that,' I promised with a smile.

Edward was taken back to his nursery, and soon after Mr. Sims arrived Julia invited us to partake of the veritable feast laid out on the terrace table. Over the meal, Mr. East mentioned a report he'd seen in the newspaper of two reformers who'd tried to escape from the Tower.

Julia commented, 'Yes, I saw that. Thank heaven they were discovered in time.'

'That man who helped them,' Mr. Hamerton said, 'must have belonged to a corresponding society too. Is it as bad as Mr. Pitt seems to think? Are these societies really making pikes and teaching people to use firearms in order to start a revolution?'

Mr. East said casually, 'So it seems. But how many will follow them? That's the question.'

Picking up his glass of wine, Mr. Hamerton said, 'I see no sign of ordinary people wanting a revolution. Quite the reverse. No sensible Englishman wants to go the way of France.'

'Very true,' Mr. Reevers commented. 'But the few who do want revolution are organised. As they were in France. When their leaders spoke of liberty, not surprisingly everyone was for it. But liberty has ceased to exist in France now.'

Mr. Sims reminded us, 'People will follow anyone offering freedom. Look at John Wilkes. Thirty years ago the favourite cry of London mobs was Wilkes and Liberty.' Mr. Wilkes, now an elderly gentleman, had a villa on the Isle of Wight, which he visited on occasion.

'I met him once,' Julia remarked.

'Did you?' I said, surprised. 'What did you think of him?'

Her eyes sparkled mischievously. 'I rather liked him.

His dreadful squint didn't inhibit him at all. He flirted with me outrageously, and he's nearly old enough to be my grandfather.'

Opening his pretty enamelled snuff box, Mr. Hamerton murmured, 'He is a good fellow in many ways, but his reputation with the ladies is, I regret to say, lamentable.'

'Indeed,' Richard agreed darkly.

'Nevertheless,' Julia pointed out, 'he did try to change the way Members of Parliament were chosen. Frankly it's time we got rid of these rotten boroughs. If two members can be returned to parliament through the votes of only four electors, as they are in Dittistone, it's no wonder corresponding societies are springing up everywhere.'

'I do believe my wife is as much a firebrand as John Wilkes,' Richard remarked light-heartedly. He seemed cheerful enough on the surface, but his eyes still had that haunted look.

Julia smiled at him indulgently. 'Well, I don't think it's right.'

'Neither do I,' I said.

Julia eyed me curiously. 'I thought you'd be against changing the system, Drusilla.'

'Did you?' I made a slight grimace. 'Frankly, I think women should be allowed to vote. I wish I was able to. Don't you?'

Mr Sims broke in, 'Forgive me for speaking plainly ma'am, but that is ridiculous.'

'Why?' Julia demanded indignantly.

'Women don't understand politics.'

'What nonsense,' I spluttered, almost incoherent with anger, for I well knew that most men did think that, believing they were superior to women.

Julia was even angrier. 'I know a great deal about such matters, and so does Drusilla.'

'I don't doubt it,' Mr. Sims said in the patronising manner so reminiscent of his uncle. 'But you are very much the exception. Most women are incapable of making a judgement, and look to their husbands to show them how to think on such matters.'

'I don't,' Julia snapped.

Richard grinned. 'I can vouch for that.'

We all laughed but Julia had clearly taken a dislike to Mr. Sims, and said in barely concealed irritation, 'I don't agree with corresponding societies resorting to violence, but their demands are sensible. The ballot should be secret, and working men ought to have the vote. It was what Septimus wanted. And I've heard you say the same yourself, Richard.'

'That's true,' he agreed, toying absently with his half empty glass of wine.

Mr. East casually asked him, 'Have you ever been to a corresponding society meeting?'

Richard drained the remainder of his wine and slamming the glass down on the table, answered in defiance, 'As a matter of fact I have.'

Julia gasped,' Oh no – Richard ----'

'Don't worry, my love. Once was enough.' He began refilling his glass. 'It was after I had been to the Admiralty the other week. I was walking through the streets when I came across the coffee house where the London corresponding society happened to be holding a meeting. So I went in to see what went on.' And indicating Mr. Hamerton, he said, 'In fact, that's where we met.'

CHAPTER 15

Amid exclamations of disbelief, Mr. Reevers quietly asked, 'Are you a member of the society, Hamerton?'

'God forbid,' came the good-humoured response. 'But an acquaintance of mine is, and he persuaded me to go. He said I ought not to criticise corresponding societies without seeing for myself what they did. I can't say as I was impressed. A lot of rabble-rousers if you ask me. Kept calling each other "citizen" as they do in France. I don't mind admitting it sent shivers up and down my spine. Frankly, I was heartily thankful when the government had the good sense to arrest the leaders. Perhaps now we will be able to sleep more easily in our beds. Still I'm glad I went or I wouldn't have met Richard.'

Julia beamed happily at him. 'Friendships can start in the oddest way, and we're so pleased you are moving to the Island.'

When she asked if he was leaving any family behind in Windsor, he said sadly, 'Not now.'

An answer that made her even more curious. 'No brothers or sisters?'

'I do have a sister, but she married unwisely and I haven't seen her for many years.'

'You must miss her,' I said.

'I do. We used to be very close.' He did not mention that her husband was French and close to Robespierre, but then who would want to make such an admission?

Julia asked, 'Does she live far away?'

'About two hundred miles.' But he did not say that included crossing the English channel.

'I prefer friends to relatives,' Mr. Sims remarked coldly. 'At least you can choose them.'

Julia and I had to bite our lips firmly. As she said later, when I was leaving, 'Poor Mr. Sims. Almost any friend would be preferable to a relative such as Mr. Upton.'

Laughing, I agreed. 'Last Sunday at church his sermon rambled on for half an hour, and I disagreed with every word. He will insist it is our duty to meekly bear every trial God sends us without a word of complaint. On the way out I asked after his health. As I'd expected, he immediately began to grumble about his boils, so I reminded him of the subject of his sermon. For once, he was speechless.'

'Oh, Drusilla,' she giggled, 'I wish I'd been there. But you are being a little hard on him.'

'Well, the man's impossible.'

Mr. East, catching that last sentence as he and Mr. Reevers came to take their leave of Julia, remarked jocularly, 'Lady Drusilla is talking about you again, Radleigh.'

Julia laughed and said, 'We were speaking of Mr. Upton.'

'Ah, the worthy parson,' Mr. East said. 'Who rides like a demented wasp and can bore a person to death in ten seconds.' Which apt description made us both smile.

In the morning Mr. Hamerton took us to see his new house. 'You must come, it stands in a splendid situation with a wonderful view of the sea.'

Mudd drove us, and we sat back in the open carriage, enjoying the sunshine on this hot early June day. The road up to the house was extremely steep, but as Mr. Hamerton said, the view at the top was worth the effort. Aunt Thirza being in the best of moods, exerted herself to be pleasant to Mr. Hamerton, to whom she had taken a decided fancy. We all genuinely admired the house, although my aunt thought it a little isolated.

'Oh, I shan't mind that,' he responded heartily. 'It suits my needs perfectly. And I've already made so many friends on the Island I don't think I shall ever be lonely.'

In fact, the spot was so isolated that only those visiting his house would venture that far. Making it the perfect place in which to plan a revolution, and to gather the Fat Badgers together in secret. Mr. Hamerton, far from impulsive in other ways, had seen and bought the house in an afternoon. But then August, the month of the planned assassination, was only seven weeks away.

The only other residence in the road, a hundred yards down the hill, belonged to Mr. Young, the reformed smuggling chief. Passing this abode on the way back, I saw Mr. Sims being admitted into the house. He didn't see us, and my aunt was too busy talking to Mr. Hamerton to notice, but if the Uptons heard their nephew went to Dittistone, not to see his academic friend, but a man who hosted gambling parties, they would be horrified.

On arriving home my aunt and uncle took a stroll in the garden, Mr. Hamerton rode off to see Richard, and I went into my workroom. I had barely sat down at my desk when a note arrived from Mrs. Jenkins inviting me to call on her the following afternoon, if convenient.

I wrote an acceptance which Luffe gave to the waiting groom, and minutes later Luffe came in again to tell me Julia had called and was awaiting me in the drawing room. I was about to put the note from Mrs Jenkins into a drawer when I was distracted by a butterfly coming in through the open window. I managed to catch it eventually, and not recognising it, puzzled over what its common name was. Mr. Hamerton would know, but he'd gone out.

Putting the butterfly outside again, I crossed the hall to join Julia, just as Luffe opened the door to two more visitors, Mr. Reevers and Mr. East. Once we were all settled in the drawing room, I enquired after Edward, and Julia told us all in some amusement, 'He wants to go sailing with Richard and Mr. Hamerton, but of course he's far too young yet.'

'And too fond of falling in water,' Mr. Reevers remarked. 'From what I hear.'

Julia laughed. 'There'll be no sailing until he's grown out of that, I promise you.'

'Better teach him to swim,' advised Mr. East.

Julia agreed that would be wise. 'But Richard's rather busy at present planning this trip to Windsor with Mr. Hamerton. And I'm afraid it means they will miss the Uptons' party.'

I sighed. 'I wish I had such a good excuse.'

'It may not be as tedious as you think,' Julia said cheerfully. And turning to Mr. East asked, 'Will we see you there?'

He drawled, 'I expect to have a prior engagement.'

'Whatever do you mean?' she responded, amused. 'Do you have another commitment?'

'No. But I'll think of something.'

Mr. Reevers murmured, 'The beautiful Miss Adams will provide you with an excuse.'

'Quite possibly,' he agreed with a grin.

Julia said, 'Well, I shall go. After being unable to accept any invitation for weeks, even an evening at the Uptons will be a treat. And if Richard's not here, I'll walk down the hill.'

'You will do no such thing,' I protested. 'We'll pick you up. Aunt Thirza will insist on using the carriage. And that is what Richard would wish you to do too.'

Aware that was true she accepted gracefully, and Mr. East urged, 'While these Fat Badgers are at large ma'am, I beg you not to venture out alone. We still don't know who these traitors are or where they are hiding.'

'Well,' I said, 'I may learn something tomorrow afternoon when I call on Mrs. Jenkins.' And I explained about the note I'd received.

'Oh, it would be wonderful if she knew their names,' Julia breathed, clasping her hands together tightly, almost in prayer. 'She must know something, surely. I tell you frankly, if I could get my hands on the men who killed Septimus, I'd willingly execute them myself.'

'And I would help you,' I declared, thinking of Jeffel.

'No doubt Mrs Jenkins feels the same,' Mr. East murmured in understanding.

We speculated on what she might know, and the hope that her evidence would lead to the arrests we longed for. When Julia had gone we discussed the difficulty of finding evidence against Mr. Hamerton. 'According to our agents,' Mr. Reevers told me, 'he hasn't met anyone outside your own circle of friends.

Apart from the Blackgang smugglers of course, but that was before we'd had a chance to organise our men.'

Mr. East mused, 'I wonder if they did take that letter to Paris for him? And, more importantly, has he received a reply?'

'He hasn't, as far as I know,' I said. 'Luffe has orders to bring me all the letters first, no matter how they are delivered.'

He nodded in approval and said thoughtfully, 'It may be too soon for a reply yet. But when it comes, Lady Drusilla, we must get our hands on it. Just think ma'am, a letter from the enemy. No question of that not standing up in court. We could arrest him at once.'

I smiled at his enthusiasm. 'If only it was that easy. Regrettably, in my experience, it rarely is.' And I asked, 'That odd reason he gave for arriving late on that day in Windsor, was he being truthful, do you think?'

Mr. East took in his breath and let it out slowly through his teeth. 'Who knows? But no other man was waylaid and robbed by a beautiful woman in Windsor, on that day or any other. Nor were there any witnesses, and no-one else saw this woman in the town.'

'But why would he make up such an elaborate lie?' Mr. East gave a shrug and I said, 'The other thing that puzzles me about that assassination attempt is that they appear to have planned for failure.'

Mr. Reevers looked across at me, his eyes narrowing. 'What do you mean exactly?'

'Well, if they really wanted to murder the King, why send only two men? If they had sent half a dozen, the King would be dead, as would we all. We know from Septimus's journal there were eight men in the society on the Island. In Windsor there may well be many more.'

'Perhaps,' Mr. Reevers suggested, 'those two wanted the glory of starting the revolution and went against their orders.'

'All organisations have members who think they can do things better,' Mr. East murmured in agreement.

I lifted my shoulders a little. 'I suppose that must be it.'

'But you don't believe that, do you, Lady Drusilla?' Mr. East said, smiling.

'No, I don't. Yet I cannot give you a sensible reason why not.'

Mr. Reevers pointed out, 'Don't forget, they only failed because Toby shot them.' That was true, yet some instinct warned me we had not got to the bottom of it. Why had those men tried to kill the King in May, when Septimus's journal said Mr. Brown wanted everything ready by the end of July? If I found the answer to that, I believed the rest would fall into place.

When the gentlemen took their leave, they promised to call the following day to see what I'd learnt from Mrs. Jenkins. And I returned to the workroom, thinking about what had been said. But when I sat down at my desk I realised it was not quite as I had left it. Instinctively I jumped up and checked the wall charts, but the shutters that covered them were still locked and did not appear to have been tampered with. I rang for Luffe at once, and when he came in, I asked when the room had been cleaned today.

'Before you came down to breakfast, my lady.'

'You're quite sure?'

'Yes, my lady.' And he asked, 'Is something wrong?'

'Someone has been in here while I was with my visitors, Luffe. The standish has been moved.' I indicated the note from Mrs Jenkins. 'This letter too.'

The furrow immediately disappeared from his brow. 'I think I can explain, my lady. It seems Mr. Hamerton came back while you were in the drawing room. Mr. Tanfield was with him, and I gather they went into the library. I didn't realise they were in the house until I crossed the hall and saw Mr. Tanfield coming out of the workroom carrying the ink standish. He said they'd run out of ink. I showed him the cupboard in the library where the spare ink is kept and put the standish back myself.'

'I see,' I said. 'That explains it then.' And I quickly made a joke of it. 'For a minute I thought we'd had burglars.'

The following afternoon I arrived in good time for my appointment with Mrs Jenkins, eager to discover what she knew about the Fat Badger society. Dismounting I gave Orlando an affectionate pat before handing him over to Mudd, who led him off to the stables. When I knocked on the door, the butler invited me into the hall before saying, 'I regret to inform you, ma'am, that Mrs Jenkins received word this morning that her brother was seriously ill. She left for the mainland within the hour.'

'Within the hour?' I repeated, taken aback.

'In order to catch the tide at Cowes.'

'Oh, I see. Did she say when she might be back?'

'She expects to be away all summer.'

'All summer?' I groaned. 'But what about her children?'

'She took them with her.'

I stared at him, puzzled. 'Into a house where there's illness?'

'Mrs Jenkins is very fond of her children, ma'am.' To me that was an excellent reason for not taking them, but perhaps the illness was not infectious.

'Did she leave a message for me?' The note I'd left when I first called, explained I was looking for information regarding the corresponding society her husband had joined. Illness had made her rush off, yet good manners required her to leave a note, and this she had done. But it was just a hurried scrawl expressing her regret at not being able to keep our appointment. She made no mention of the Fat Badgers.

When I asked the butler for her address, so that I could write to her, he informed me rather pompously, 'I regret ma'am, that my orders are not to disclose her direction to anyone.' I stared at him in surprise and wondered if a few coins would liberate his tongue. But he must have read my mind, for he said, quite deliberately, 'I have been in my present position for twenty years ma'am, and there is no way in which I can assist you.' He then bowed and opened the front door for me.

I gave every appearance of accepting the situation and smiled. 'Would you be good enough to tell me how Mrs Jenkins heard about her brother?'

'He sent a messenger, ma'am.'

'Did you see him?'

'No, ma'am. Mrs. Jenkins met him when she was walking to the village.'

'Oh, I see.' I thanked him and turned as if to leave. Then, quite suddenly, I stopped and looked him straight in the eye, for he was almost my own height. 'When she came in, was she *very* frightened?' His eyebrows shot up in such alarm I knew I had hit the nail on the head. 'I'm sorry,' I said, 'but I had to know.'

I made my way slowly back to the stables, certain that a message from her brother, however serious, would not terrify her. But one from the Fat Badgers was a very different matter. They were experts in fear, and I did not doubt they were behind this. They were afraid of what she might know, and wanted her off the Island before I could speak to her. She had responded to their threats by leaving instantly. I wished she hadn't gone, but in my heart I could not blame her.

Riding back down the lane with Mudd, I explained what had happened, and he told me he'd learnt from one of the grooms that the brother was a Mr Jones who had moved to Hampshire from London about a month ago. 'He wasn't sure where in Hampshire, my lady. He thought Winchester, or Warsash, or something like that. I'm afraid it doesn't help much.'

'No,' I sighed. For how could I expect to find a gentleman with such a common name, residing somewhere in Hampshire, probably in a place beginning with a W.

Mrs Jenkins might have helped me find the Fat Badgers, and now that wouldn't happen. And I rode home in despair. The instant I got back I spoke to Bridge, but he didn't know where the brother lived either. Going into the library, I wrote a note to Julia explaining Mrs. Jenkins had been called away suddenly due to illness in her family, and sent Mudd to deliver it. There was no point worrying her unnecessarily.

Somehow Mr. Brown had learned of my appointment and put a stop to it, fearing what Mrs Jenkins might reveal. But how did he know of our meeting? The answer that came to me was so terrifying my hands began to shake. Before I could compose myself, Luffe opened the library door to announce Mr. Reevers and Mr. East. Mr.

Reevers took one look at me and sat by my side. 'My dear girl, what's wrong? You're as white as a sheet. Tell me this instant. Did you see Mrs. Jenkins?'

Shaking my head I explained what had happened. 'She was frightened off by Mr. Brown.'

'Frightened off?' Mr. East repeated in alarm. 'That means he was aware of your meeting, ma'am. But how? Who else knew of it?'

I glanced up at him, unable to hide the despair threatening to overwhelm me. 'Mudd, of course. Julia----' And I hesitated.

He urged, 'No-one else?'

'I can't be sure. The note Mrs. Jenkins wrote making the arrangement – well, I foolishly left it on my desk in the workroom. Luffe said Mr. Hamerton returned to the house while we were all talking this morning. Richard was with him, and they went into the library where, a little later, they ran out of ink. There's spare ink in the library cupboard, but Mr. Hamerton didn't know that --- and---'

'He looked for some in your workroom?' Mr. Reevers supplied.

N-no. Not Mr. Hamerton. R-Richard.......' And my bottom lip began to tremble.

CHAPTER 16

Mr. Reevers took my hands in his, murmuring softly. 'It may not be as bad as you fear.'

'But if it is ---- if he's involved ----- Julia would never recover.' I could not bear to think of it. It would be preferable if Richard was killed in battle. Better a dead hero than a traitor. And I withdrew my hands from his.

'He must have told Hamerton about the note,' Mr. East surmised.

'But that doesn't mean Richard is mixed up with the Fat Badgers,' Mr. Reevers reasoned in his calm way. 'Perhaps Richard mentioned the note when they were talking about George Jenkins, or Septimus's journal, or----'

I broke in, 'Richard doesn't know Septimus left a journal.'

Mr. Reevers looked at me in surprise. 'Didn't Julia tell him?'

'She swears she hasn't told anyone, not even Richard, and I believe her. And the note from Mrs. Jenkins reads like any ordinary arrangement between acquaintances.'

Neither of the gentlemen spoke for a few moments, then Mr. East commented, 'Hamerton spends most of his time with Richard Tanfield.'

I forced myself to say, 'Richard is seriously troubled about something, and Mr. Hamerton knows what it is. But why would he confide in someone he only met a few weeks ago?' Mr. East shook his head, unable to answer. 'And tomorrow they sail to Windsor on the noon tide.'

The two gentlemen exchanged significant looks, and as if answering his friend's unspoken thoughts, Mr. East said, 'You're right, we're running out of time. Are they really going to Windsor do you think, Radleigh?''

'Well, there's only one way to find out.' And taking a coin from his pocket, he commented in jocular fashion, 'I'll toss you for it, Toby. Sailing should be most pleasant at this time of the year. But one of us must stay here.' He threw the coin upwards, caught it, Mr. East guessed correctly and chose to remain on the Island. 'Miss Adams will be pleased,' Mr. Reevers informed his grinning friend.

'You mean to follow them?' I asked in surprise. 'Won't that be rather difficult?'

'It will,' Mr. Reevers agreed. 'But it will be worth it if we find out what Hamerton is up to.' He didn't add that, if Mr. Hamerton was up to something, then Richard must know what it was. I wished too that it was Mr. East who would be away for a week, instead of Mr. Reevers.

A wish I did not expect to be granted, yet incredibly it was, as I learnt when Mr. East called again just after breakfast. 'Radleigh fell off his horse last night and hurt his neck. Which means I shall be going sailing after all.'

He looked so dejected I couldn't help teasing, 'Poor Miss Adams.'

'We were to attend a ball in Newport tomorrow too,' he sighed.

'I feel sure Miss Adams will find someone to take your place.'

'That, Lady Drusilla, is what I'm afraid of.'

'She may miss you as much as you will miss her,' I pointed out kindly.

'I hope you are right.' And he got to his feet. 'I must go if I'm to leave at noon.'

My aunt and uncle were two of the few people who knew Mr. Reevers was a government agent, and when they came down to breakfast, I told them about his accident. 'I think we ought to call on him this morning, especially as Mr. East will be away for a few----'

My aunt interrupted, 'I can't today. I promised to visit Mrs Woodford.' Turning to my uncle, she directed, 'Charles, you can go with Drusilla.'

'Why, thank you, my dear.' His tone of voice made Aunt Thirza glance at him a trifle suspiciously, but he merely said that he had been wondering what to do this morning, which almost made me choke. He looked at me, his eyes twinkling merrily. ' Your aunt has spoken, Drusilla. And you're right, we must make sure Mr Reevers is looking after himself.'

Before we left I spent some time deciding what I should do next, for I was making little progress with the task Mr. Pitt had given me. Yet, I could do nothing about Mr. Hamerton, or Richard, while they were away, and I tried, not very successfully, to put them out of my mind. I was, however, happier knowing Mr. East would be watching what they did.

I'd so hoped Mrs Jenkins would be able to name at least one Fat Badger, but her hasty departure had dashed that chance. Yet there had to be a way of finding them. There simply had to be. If only, I thought, I could discover where they were meeting now. Yet, I could not make inquiries at every inn on the Island with a private room for hire, without creating a great stir. Mr. Reevers and Mr. East could do so, but being gentlemen, might not learn the truth either. Whereas no-one would take any notice if Mudd made a casual inquiry.

Many inns did not have such a room, but it would not be an easy search for the Island was about twenty-three miles across at its widest point, and some thirteen from Cowes in the north to St Catherine's point in the south. Newport was the largest of the towns, only there were any number of villages, some with few inhabitants, others with several hundred, and most had an inn. Even Westfleet, tiny though it was, boasted one inn, the "Five Bells," and had done for some two hundred years.

Mudd was very willing, and there being no point in hanging about, he left later that same morning. Shortly afterwards a servant brought a message from Mrs Woodford, my aunt's gossipy friend, cancelling this morning's arrangement as she had sprained her ankle. But my aunt insisted on going to her friend at once, and being genuinely fond of Mrs Woodford, spent much of her time during the ensuing days at that lady's pleasant home in Dittistone.

My uncle said that, with my aunt being so busy, a visit to Norton House would enable him to take advantage of Mr. Reevers' kind offer to use the library there. 'He has a wonderful selection of books, and I can browse without anyone interrupting me.'

'Mr Reevers might offer to keep you company.'

'Not when you are with me, he won't.' Detecting a decided twinkle in his eye, I laughed. Charles Frère did not miss much. The truth was I wanted to go, and he knew it.

When we arrived at Norton House Mr Reevers was sitting on the terrace, and rose slowly to his feet to greet us, trying not to move his head more than was necessary. Once he had assured us he was being well looked after and merely needed to rest, my uncle inquired if he might browse through the library, as Mr. Reevers had kindly offered. Quickly assured that he was very welcome to do so, Mr. Reevers saw him comfortably settled in the library before returning to the terrace.

When I asked how he'd fallen off his horse, he said, 'It was dark and I didn't see the rabbit hole.' I couldn't help smiling for he was an excellent rider. 'You might show a little more sympathy,' he complained, tongue-in-cheek. 'I can't turn my neck. Still, I must be thankful that it didn't happen when I was in France.'

'What difference does that make?' I asked innocently, taken in by his bland expression.

His eyes gleamed. 'My dear girl, a spy must be able to look over his shoulder, you know.' I choked with laughter, and shook my head at him. Such interludes made a welcome change from the worries hanging over us, and although I couldn't know it then, this was the beginning of one of the happiest times of my life.

Mr. Reevers suggested a stroll in the gardens, and as we walked down the terrace steps to the flat parklands beyond, I told him my uncle had been given a golden opportunity to indulge himself and he meant to make the most of it. Matching my step to his unusually slow pace, I explained about Mrs Woodford's sprained ankle. A tale that made him laugh.

'I must say,' I chided in mocking tones, 'I am rather shocked that you find the misfortune of others amusing.'

'Oh, I wasn't laughing at poor Mrs Woodford. Only at the speed with which your uncle turned the situation to his advantage.'

'Well, it is kind of you to let him use the library.'

'Not at all. I like your uncle.' His eyes began to dance wickedly. 'Now, if it had been that cold-blooded Francis Sims, I would have informed him I never let anyone touch my books.'

Reaching the wooden bench under the next tree, he courteously waited while I seated myself, before sinking down beside me in some relief, holding his neck as he did so. The seat being a small one, we sat no more than six inches apart; a fact I found deeply disturbing. I thought he had not noticed how close we were, but then he turned to look at me and what I saw in his eyes took my breath away. The slightest encouragement from me now and he would take me in his arms. The thought of it set my heart thumping alarmingly, yet I hesitated. This was one thing I did not intend to rush into.

Deciding it would be wise to talk of ordinary matters, I told him of Mudd's expedition. 'I imagine it will take some days,' I said, explaining why I thought he might succeed where the rest of us would fail. 'But it's the only thing I could think of.'

He listened, the faintest of smiles on his lips. 'It's certainly worth trying.' His mind, however, seemed to be on something else, and when I foolishly asked what he was thinking about, he turned to me with a sigh. 'I was wishing this wretched war was over. That my life was my own again. That I could-----' he stopped in mid-sentence, as if he'd said too much.

'You'd like to spend more time here?' For although Norton House was not a large residence it had a comfortable homely feel to it.

He gazed at me, his dark eyes suddenly unfathomable. 'Something like that, yes.'

I thought of what his life as a government agent must be like. The danger, hardship and boredom. 'What is it really like in France? I only know what I read in the newspapers.'

'Don't let's talk about that.' He reached over, took my hand in his and studied it carefully. 'You have such elegant fingers. Long and slim. Perfect for playing the piano.' He looked across at me. 'Do you play?'

'Very badly,' I whispered a little hoarsely, for my senses were racing. Things were going too fast for me. There was nothing I wanted more at that moment than to be kissed, but it also meant I was agreeing to marriage, and I was not ready to take that irrevocable step. Thus I pulled my hand away and said with a good deal of constraint, 'We should go back now.'

'Naturally I would if I could,' he murmured in a caressing voice. 'But you must forgive me, I don't think I can move.'

I eyed him with suspicion. 'You walked this far. Surely----'

'Well, I suppose it might be possible,' he said doubtfully. 'If you allowed me to lean on you a little.' I deliberately raised shocked eyebrows at him and his eyes gleamed wickedly. 'Only for support, of course. In the manner of a nurse helping an invalid. I would summon a servant, but there isn't anyone in sight. You couldn't be so cruel as to refuse to assist me.'

At which point a tall young man effortlessly pushing a wheelbarrow full of logs came into view, and I burst out laughing.

Mr Reevers held up his hands in surrender, but as we walked slowly back to the house, he suggested that, in the days ahead, we should make good use of the free time created by my aunt's desire to look after her friend. 'Your uncle can browse through the library as long as he wants, and it will enable us to discuss the Fat Badgers without being interrupted.'

I did not argue, and the halcyon days that followed passed in the same delightful way. Each morning my uncle and I rode to Norton House, stayed to nuncheon, and reached home just before my aunt returned to dress for dinner. Luckily for us, Mrs Woodford's progress was slow. Mr Reevers and I talked of Mr. Hamerton, the Fat Badgers, my very real worries over Richard, of our favourite books and places, and much else besides, laughing and sometimes disagreeing, but never tiring of each other's company.

Just to be with him was a deep joy. I woke every morning in a state of blissful anticipation, thinking of the hours I was to spend in his company, while my uncle browsed through the library to his heart's content. Sometimes bringing out a book to read in the garden, always in sight of us, but never within hearing. Whether that was for his benefit, or ours, I was not sure.

Every day I left for home in a kind of a glow, wishing I could have stayed longer, yet knowing I could do it all again tomorrow. Throughout these glorious days, even the sun shone on us. And I went about with a happy smile on my face, refusing to think of where it might lead, being far too busy revelling in the present. As for Mr Reevers, his eyes lit up the instant he saw me, and I was more than content for things to go on as they were.

Whenever a thought of the future entered my head, I dismissed it quickly, determined for the present to treat him as a friend whose company and conversation I enjoyed, and who laughed at the same things as I did. Which was how I felt about Giles Saxborough, my godmother's son, who was indeed a valued friend. Only it wasn't the same with Mr Reevers, not by a long way, and I knew it. But I pushed that thought to the back of my mind, content in my happy dream, telling myself I was simply using this time to get to know him better.

I was free to do as I wished while Mr. Hamerton and Richard were away, safe in the knowledge that Mr. East would be watching them. If only, I thought, Mudd could find out where the Fat Badgers were meeting now, the rest would surely be easy.

Meanwhile I was able to relax and think of other things. Occasionally other visitors called when I was there, and I found myself resenting this interference. I wanted to be alone with Mr. Reevers, but I did not allow myself to dwell on what that meant, for I had never been as happy as I was now. Only when he took my hand did I become more reserved.

I did not realise my happiness showed, until I called on Julia one fine evening, and she demanded inquisitively, 'What have you been up to, Drusilla? You're positively blooming.'

'It must be the fresh air and sunshine we've had lately.'

'It has been lovely, hasn't it? Edward is quite brown. But no amount of sunshine puts that kind of glow into a woman's eyes.' I instantly thought of Mr Reevers and foolishly blushed, which made Julia laugh, but she did not pursue the matter.

In those few short days I almost forgot the worries hanging over us, but like all such idylls it had to end. On the day Mr. Reevers was able to ride again, Mrs. Woodford started to get about, and my uncle had an engagement in Cowes, so we did not go to Norton House.

When Aunt Thirza left to call on Mrs. Woodford to see how she'd fared after her first short outing, I went into my workroom, but a few minutes later Luffe informed me Mr. Reevers was here. I smiled, delighted I was to see him today after all. 'I'll receive him here, Luffe.'

He looked surprised, as well he might, for I had never invited any visitor into my workroom before. He did as I bid, and Mr. Reevers walked in saying, 'I am honoured. Though I don't think Luffe approved.'

'That's because I've told him never to usher anyone in here. Not even Julia.'

'Then I am doubly honoured,' he said, looking around the room with great interest.

I showed him my father's collection of fossils, a copy of the book he'd written, which I kept on the extensive bookshelves, and finally lifted the shutters from my charts. He looked at what I'd written and I explained, 'I only write the actual facts here. Nothing else. Speculation only confuses things.'

He stood with his hands behind his back reading what was on the charts. 'Yes, I see what you mean. It's very clear. And concise.'

'And nothing is forgotten.' He looked at the charts for so long I asked if anything was wrong, and he turned to face me with a reluctance I found puzzling, until he removed a letter from his pocket. Handing it to me, he said, 'Mr. Pitt sent this for you by his messenger.'

I took it, seeing from his face that it was bad news. 'You know what's in it, don't you?'

He nodded and advised kindly, 'It would be better if you sat down.'

CHAPTER 17

'Why do I need to sit down? Have I made some dreadful mistake?'

'No, it's nothing like that. I can only suggest that you read it.'

So I sat down, broke the wafer and did as he'd asked.

My dear Lady Drusilla,

I am much obliged to you for the copy of Septimus Ford's journal, an invaluable piece of evidence. I am also most grateful for your assistance in the matter of discovering whether or not Mr. Hamerton is a traitor.

As I am sure you will realise, in such cases we check on friends and acquaintances of the man in question. This, of course, takes time, and our checks on him were not complete when we spoke in London. This has since been remedied, and as a result I must warn you of a gentleman Mr. Hamerton met a few weeks ago. They were seen together at a London Corresponding Society meeting, and it would concern us greatly should their friendship continue on the Isle of Wight.

This gentleman must be known to you, as he lives in your part of the Island. His name is Richard Tanfield, a Captain in the Navy. Who, I am informed by the Admiralty, may soon be court-martialled for cowardice in the face of the enemy, and for disobeying a direct order.

'Wh-a-a-t?' I burst out, staring at those awful words in sickening shock. 'It can't be true. It can't. Richard's no coward. In fact, I swear he enjoys taking risks.' Mr. Reevers did not speak and I read what little remained, which was merely a polite reminder of the urgency of the situation. I sat clutching the letter tightly in my hand, refusing to believe what it said.

Yet, thinking of Richard's behaviour of late, I knew it

was true, for it explained everything. I'd believed that whatever was worrying him was something he couldn't solve himself, that the power to do so lay in the hands of other people, or an authority. Such as the Admiralty. Which meant it was something serious, but I never imagined he was fighting for his very life.

'No wonder he wouldn't tell me. Or Julia.' Numb with shock, I forced myself to face the worst possible outcome. 'What if he's found guilty.......?' I whispered. 'Admiral Byng was shot for cowardice.'

'That was nearly forty years ago.' He didn't say it couldn't happen to Richard, for we both knew that it could. Drawing up a chair beside me he took my trembling hands in his. 'But, much more recently, Admiral Keppel was acquitted.'

I nodded, grasping at hope. 'I remember my father talking of it, when I was about twelve.'

'There's every chance Richard will be acquitted too.'

'You can't know that. And what if he's not? How will Julia ever endure it?' He shook his head, aware as I was, that she would never be the same again. And that the disgrace would hang over Edward all his life.

'I cannot bear to think of it,' I said, removing my hands from his. 'That's why he said he might never go back to sea. No wonder he's in such black despair. A fine upstanding man like him, who would lay down his life for King and country, to have the principles he'd always believed in shot to pieces by this absurd accusation. He must have left the Admiralty that day shaken to the very core of his being, his whole world turned upside down by men of power and influence. That's why he went to that London corresponding society meeting---'

'On impulse, you mean? Well, I can see that, but when he'd calmed down and had time to reflect, do you really imagine he would betray England?'

I shook my head from side to side several times. 'No, I don't. Not Richard.'

He watched my face as thoughts raced through my mind. 'But you're not *quite* sure, are you?'

Looking up I saw only understanding in his eyes. 'The thing is, Richard detests injustice, and to be a victim of it himself will be beyond bearing to him. He relishes danger and hates being confined in any way. I don't know what he might do in this situation.' And I admitted reluctantly, 'He can be rather reckless at times. But I see why he wouldn't tell Julia in her delicate situation, and he dare not tell me in case I let it slip out to her by accident. What really worries me is that he chose to confide in Mr. Hamerton.'

After he had gone I went for a long ride across the Downs, accompanied by a groom. I did not believe Richard was guilty, not for a second. Yet, to be accused of disobeying a direct order was an extremely grave matter. And a charge of cowardice would shame any man. Innocent or guilty. To my mind, he was acting like a man who knew himself to be innocent, but expected to be found guilty. I was terrified that, because of that belief, he'd lost all sense of reason and allowed himself to become embroiled in Mr. Hamerton's schemes.

I returned home without any real recollection of where I had ridden, nor could I think what I should do next. I'd wanted to know what was worrying Richard, thinking I could perhaps help him in some way. Well, now I did know, and there was nothing I could do, nothing at all. Except worry. It made me even more anxious about his association with Mr. Hamerton. And I prayed Mr. East would be able to keep Richard out of trouble.

When I walked into the hall my uncle came rushing out of the drawing room, urging me to join him that instant. I had never felt less like talking, but I was too fond of my uncle to refuse. Mr. Pitt's letter had plunged me into despair, but life had to go on. So I went in, shut the door, and turned to find him beaming from ear to ear.

'I heard some tremendous news in Cowes,' he proclaimed exuberantly. 'The whole town was making merry. People were dancing in the streets and----'.

'Yes, but what has actually happened?' I begged, forcing a smile.

He rubbed his hands together with glee. 'Lord Howe's Channel Fleet has trounced the French Navy. It's a great victory, Drusilla.'

Overwhelmed with joy at hearing such wonderful news I grabbed my uncle's hands, and we whirled madly round in a circle until we were both dizzy. Finally, laughing and half crying at the same time, we collapsed into the nearest chairs. When he had regained his breath, he said, 'Your aunt's at Mrs. Woodford's and I've kept this to myself for a whole hour. I asked Luffe so often if you'd returned yet, he thought I'd gone mad.'

'You could have told him the good news,' I teased.

'What, and have him give the game away the instant you came through the door? I wanted to tell you myself. The word is that one of Howe's officers, Sir

Roger Curtis, left Falmouth two days ago with dispatches for London. Details are a bit hazy yet, but it's thought two French ships were sunk, and Howe should arrive in Portsmouth in a day or two with the six ships they   captured. Six prize ships, Drusilla. Just think of it. '

I wiped a tear from my eyes. 'I am thinking of it. I can hardly believe it. A victory at last.' England had never needed one more than it did now. 'It will give us all heart,' I declared happily. 'And no-one more than Mr Pitt. The port will flow freely tonight.'

'Think of the prize money for the crews too.' Everyone on board would receive a share in accordance with regulations. 'It's crippled the French Navy and I--'

'Oh heavens,' I cut in suddenly. 'Richard------'

That brought him up sharply. 'Yes, thank God he wasn't with the fleet.'

For battles were not won without loss of life. While the rest of us rejoiced, for some families it meant only grief and pain. At least Julia didn't have that to contend with.

Everywhere I went during the following days there was great rejoicing over Howe's victory, and it lifted my own spirits to the point where I felt anything was possible. Even that the Admiralty would come to its senses and realise Richard was innocent. And if Mudd found out where the Fat Badgers were meeting now, arresting them would be simple.

But Mudd efforts proved to be fruitless and my heart sank again. For, as Mr. Pitt had politely reminded me, time was running out fast. Soon Mr. Hamerton and Richard would return, and Mr. East would tell us if Mr.

Hamerton really had gone to Windsor to settle his affairs. I wanted to know, yet I was afraid of the truth. Afraid, most of all, for Julia.

Within hours of Mudd's return, Mr. Reevers was ushered into the drawing room. I was greatly surprised to see Mr. East with him, for Richard and Mr. Hamerton were still away. One look at their faces told me things had not gone well. Once they were seated, Mr. East admitted at once, 'I'm afraid I made a mull of the whole thing, Lady Drusilla. I followed the yacht for a day, observing from a considerable distance. When they anchored for the night, so did I, but when I woke at daybreak they had gone. I went on to Windsor, but the yacht wasn't there, nor could I find them in the town. And I gather they are still away.'

'Yes,' I said. I found it difficult to speak. We did not have one shred of evidence that could be presented in court to prove Mr. Hamerton was Mr. Brown, we had no idea where the Fat Badgers were meeting, and Mr. East had failed to discover the purpose of the yachting trip. The only good news was Howe's victory over the French.

Before they left I reminded them it was the Uptons party that evening, and Mr. East said, 'I shan't be going, I'm afraid.'

'Visiting Miss Adams, no doubt,' Mr. Reevers suggested good-humouredly.

'Possibly.' And he grinned.

When their horses were brought up to the house, I walked out with them. As Mr. East climbed onto his horse, Mr. Reevers asked me, 'Are you going to this wretched party?'

'I must, I suppose.'

'In that case, so will I.'

I laughed. 'And if I had said I wasn't going?'

'I'd cry off.'

'I am flattered,' I said demurely.

'My dear girl, you cannot imagine I would go otherwise.'

That evening I dressed with more care than was usual for visiting the parsonage, and my new gown of deep red, with delicate silver trimming, gained my aunt's unstinting praise.

'The Uptons,' my uncle declared, emphasising the name teasingly, 'will be bowled over.'

Before Aunt Thirza could ask what he meant, Luffe came to inform me the carriage was at the door. Mudd drove us sedately to Breighton House, where we collected Julia, who looked her best in a gown of the softest green, and a few minutes later the Uptons greeted us in their usual overpowering manner. Several other guests had already arrived, but Mr. Reevers was not among them. He was the last to appear and the expression in his eyes when he saw me made the colour rise rapidly in my cheeks.

The party itself was every bit as insipid as I'd expected, but I tried to enjoy it for my aunt's sake. Only there wasn't even a tasty supper to look forward to, for as my father used to say, the local blacksmith could shoe horses with the pastry made by the Uptons' cook.

There was much rejoicing over Howe's victory, with Mr. Upton pronouncing his views on this, and every other subject, as if he was still in the pulpit. Even so,

Howe's great victory had given us all hope that we would soon win the war.

A mood of optimism that was dampened by Mr. Upton informing us we were in for a real treat tonight as his wife was to sing for us. He accompanied her on the piano, without ever quite keeping up with her. When she occasionally hit a right note, Mr. Reevers glanced across at me, slowly lifting an eyebrow, and I had to bite my lip most firmly.

After three such ballads my uncle quickly intervened, suggesting Julia should sing for us, which she did in her clear, strong voice, with my aunt's accompaniment. Her singing was greeted with great enthusiasm, but she steadfastly insisted two songs were enough, and proposed, 'Perhaps Lady Drusilla and Mr. Reevers would delight us with a duet.'

I suspected she knew exactly how things stood between myself and Mr. Reevers, and before I knew it I was standing beside him at the piano. He chose a simple song and had a good baritone voice.

'I didn't know you could sing,' I murmured to him as we sat down afterwards.

'I enjoy it.'

'So do I, and I do at least sing in tune, but I don't have Julia's range or ability.'

'At least you know your limitations,' he murmured. 'Unlike the Uptons.'

I stifled the chuckle rising in my throat, for both Mr. and Mrs. Upton clearly believed their performance to be superior to the rest of us.

But Francis Sims, when applied to, refused to take part. 'I cannot sing or play.'

Mr. Reevers whispered, 'It must run in the family.'

I choked, quickly turning it into a cough as Mrs. Upton urged her nephew, 'A poem, then.'

He shook his head. 'I don't like poetry.'

'Don't like poetry,' she echoed in amazement. 'But surely----'

He looked round at us all. 'Forgive me, but I am not at all artistic.'

I found myself in sympathy with him, and as I said to him before we left, to be pressed to do what one has no talent for is most disagreeable. 'People with that kind of ability don't always understand why everyone can't do what comes so easily to them.'

A slight smile crossed his features. 'Indeed, ma'am. Much, I admit, as I expect others to know every king and queen since William the Conqueror. But few do.' He didn't actually glance in the direction of Mr. Upton, but we both knew to whom he was referring. And I found myself warming to Mr. Sims a little; perhaps he was more human than I'd first thought.

The evening lifted my spirits more than I thought possible, more due to the presence of Mr. Reevers than anything else. On the way home, we dropped Julia off at Breighton House, and as Mudd drove slowly down the steep hill back towards the village, my uncle asked in a puzzled voice, 'Why does Mrs. Upton insist on singing when she has no voice?'

Before anyone could answer, the horses squealed in fright, the carriage came to an abrupt halt, and the door burst open to reveal a masked man pointing a pistol directly at us. 'Get out,' he snarled in a deep, uncouth voice, 'or I'll shoot!'

And my aunt, who had always feared being held up by highwaymen, promptly fainted.

CHAPTER 18

Aunt Thirza's fear of highwaymen, pronounced when travelling on the mainland, had lessened on the Isle of Wight, but had never quite gone away. In fainting she cracked her head on a sharp edge on the side of the carriage, and began to bleed profusely. As my uncle cradled her in his arms, using his handkerchief to stem the bleeding, I turned my fury on the man responsible. 'Now look what you've done!'

'Never mind them,' he sneered, levelling the pistol at me. 'You're the one I want. Get out.'

I was too angry to be frightened, but those words made me shudder. He showed no interest in my aunt's valuable diamond necklace or my own gold bracelet, which told me he was no ordinary highwayman. I was the one he wanted, he'd said. His eyes, cold and menacing, watched me in the manner of a cat stalking a mouse. And, in that moment, I knew he intended to kill me.

'Hurry up,' he growled, waving the firearm to indicate where I was to stand. He wanted me outside the carriage to be sure of firing a fatal shot. The Fat Badgers, having failed to get rid of me on the cliff top, did not mean to fail again. Since then I had not gone out alone, certain I was safe when with other people. And I still had no idea what they thought I knew.

Much of the sky was covered in high cloud, with occasional glimpses of moonlight, and in one of these I saw another man, on horseback, holding Mudd at gunpoint. Mudd could not help me, but I did not intend to go tamely to my death. I rose to my feet, swaying, as if I too was about to swoon. Lurching against the side of the coach, I grabbed the loaded carriage pistol my aunt insisted on keeping in the holster. The highwayman stood back to allow me to get out, and didn't see what I was doing. Still feigning faintness, I passed a hand across my eyes, begging him not to take my gold bracelet. 'My father gave it to me,' I whimpered.

A sharp cry from his accomplice to 'Get on with it!' made him grab my left arm in an attempt to yank me outside, causing his gun to be momentarily directed away from me. And that's when I shot him.

He dropped like a stone, crumpling up on the carriage steps, the pistol landing at my feet. Grabbing it I fired at the other man before he realised what was happening. The bullet must have struck his arm for he dropped his own gun with an agonised howl, and digging his heels into the flanks of his horse, he rode off at speed into the woods. Instantly Mudd reached for the weapon he always carried and fired at the rapidly disappearing villain.

'I don't think I hit him, my lady,' he called out regretfully. I wasn't surprised, there were too many trees in the way, for they came right to the edge of the road at this particular point. Jumping down, Mudd dragged the masked man away from the steps, announcing with satisfaction, 'He's dead, my lady.' Removing the mask, Mudd closed those cold callous eyes. Then he searched the man's pockets, finding some coins and the now familiar Fat Badger token.

Thankful to see my aunt was coming round, I said to my uncle, 'I'll be back in a moment.' He looked up at me and I told him one man was dead and his accomplice had ridden off.

'There may be others, Drusilla. Do be careful, my dear.'

Alighting from the carriage, I looked at the man I'd killed. I felt no remorse; his friends had murdered Jeffel and Septimus and I was glad I'd shot him. I would kill them all if I could. Mudd told me he hadn't seen the men until they charged out of the wood, when the noise and suddenness of it all had caused the horses to rear up. He hesitated, then said, 'They were waiting for us, my lady.'

'Yes, they were.' Hearing a movement, I swung round on my heel, praying there were no others, but it was only my uncle descending from the carriage.

'Are you both all right?' he asked me anxiously.

Reassuring him, I said, 'The other man escaped, but not before I put a bullet in his arm.' And I asked in concern, 'How is Aunt Thirza?'

'Still rather dazed, but well enough to insist I help you.'

The moon having gone behind a cloud, I used one of the carriage lanterns to take a proper look at the man. He was about thirty, and thin-faced with a deep scar running from just under his right eye down to his chin. None of us recognised him, but I knew who the other man was. It was Mr. Silver. Described in Septimus's journal as a great bear of a man, he was the one who'd got away after attacking me on the cliff top. And I gave an involuntary shiver.

My uncle put his hand on my arm. 'It's only natural to feel a little shaky, my dear. You were very brave. But if you don't mind, I'd like to get your aunt home.'

'Yes, of course,' I said at once.

Mudd dragged the body under a tree by the roadside before driving us the short distance back to Westfleet. Aunt Thirza was still distressed, but managed to say, 'It's as well for us all that I insisted on having a firearm in the carriage.'

'It is indeed, Aunt. I am very grateful to you.' And I was. Her obsession had saved my life.

'You thought I was making a fuss about nothing.'

'I did,' I admitted. 'But I was wrong.'

Thus mollified she said rather smugly, 'Perhaps you will listen to me in future.'

'It was Drusilla who saved our lives,' my uncle reminded her gently.

'Yes, but she couldn't have done so if the pistol hadn't been in the carriage.'

'Very true, Aunt,' I agreed smiling, quickly moving on to say, 'When we reach Westfleet I shall collect one of the other grooms and----'

'What on earth for?' she demanded.

'Well, we can't leave the body where it is. Imagine if Julia and Edward were to see it in the morning.' Her eyes widened in horror and I said, 'I'll speak to Mr. Upton and have it taken into the church.'

At which she clutched my hand and begged, 'Don't go, Drusilla. That other man might come back.'

'Not with a bullet in his arm, he won't.'

My uncle said, 'I'll come with you.'

I assured him kindly that it wasn't necessary. He took some persuading but, as I pointed out, my aunt needed him. By the time we reached Westfleet he had reluctantly agreed, provided I reloaded the pistols and took a couple of lanterns. I went into the house with my aunt and uncle, while Mudd fetched one of the stronger grooms to help with the body.

Luffe greeted us with the news that Mr. Hamerton had returned earlier in the evening and retired to his bedchamber before ten, saying the sea air had made him extremely tired. If he was back, then so was Richard, and I thought how happy Julia must have been to find him at home when she went indoors after the party. But, remembering Pitt's letter, I wondered how long such happiness would last. I did not believe Richard was guilty, and nor would she, but that did not mean a court martial would acquit him. Innocent men had been executed before.

My uncle helped to reload the firearms, and heading back to Breighton Hill I stopped at the parsonage first. Mudd accompanied me down the dark path, leaving the other groom to look after the horses. There wasn't a light to be seen in the house, and Mudd hammered on the door three times before Mr Upton put his head out of an upstairs window.

'What is it?' he demanded testily.

'I am sorry to disturb you Mr Upton but----'

'Lady Drusilla?' he exclaimed, astonished. 'Is that you?'

'It is,' I asserted.

'I thought you'd gone home long since.'

Ignoring this, I urged, 'I need your assistance, Mr. Upton. Would you be so good as to come down, please?'

'At this time of night? Why, in a few minutes it will be the Lord's Day, and I-----.'

'It is a matter of some urgency.'

'Very well,' he said wearily. 'I will be with you directly.'

He left the window open and I heard Mrs Upton demanding to be told what was going on. In some irritation he responded, 'I don't know, my dear. It's Lady Drusilla-----'

'Lady Drusilla?' she echoed in disbelief. 'What the devil does she want at this hour?'

'Language, my dear,' the parson scolded.

'I'll say what I like in my own house. She left well before eleven. Why on earth has she come back?' I couldn't hear his answer, but Mrs. Upton promptly announced, 'I'd better come with you. We must pray that nothing dreadful has occurred at Westfleet,' she ended, speaking in the tone of one who hoped quite the opposite.

Despite everything we had gone through, I had to bite my lip to stop myself laughing. I murmured to Mudd, 'I suppose you heard all that, John?'

'Y-yes, my lady,' he said, trying to control his voice.

'Well, for heaven's sake keep a straight face, or I shall be lost.'

At which moment the door opened to reveal Mr Upton in his dressing gown and nightcap, holding a lighted candle aloft. 'It really is you, Lady Drusilla.'

Behind him, Mrs Upton peered out at us. 'And Mudd too.'

'Naturally,' I replied in my most prudish voice. And quickly explained what had happened.

'I'm sorry you had such a nasty experience,' he sympathised. 'But I fail to see what it has to do with me.'

'A man is dead, Mr Upton, and we cannot leave him in the road for some child to find in the morning.'

'Well no, but----'

'The church is the only suitable place.'

He frowned. 'Well, this is most irregular, I must say.'

'Can you suggest an alternative?'

He could not, of course, and promised to get dressed and go across to the church. But when Mudd drove us to the place where we had left the dead man, the body had gone. Stunned, I turned to Mudd. 'This is the right spot, isn't it?'

'Yes, my lady.' Fetching a lantern he shone the light onto something under the tree. 'Look, there's his hat.'

'So it is,' I said. 'You're sure he was dead?' He had certainly looked it to me, but in the darkness I might have been mistaken.

'Yes, my lady. The bullet went right through his heart.'

'Really? I hadn't realised.' I had been remarkably lucky with my shot. Mudd looked for the man's horse but it had gone. 'So there was a third man. You didn't see anyone else?'

'No, my lady.'

It being too dark to see anything in the woods I decided to come back in the morning. Stopping at the church, I found Mr. Upton impatiently pacing up and down. When I told him the body had disappeared he burst out angrily, 'Do you mean I've been dragged from my bed in the middle of the night on a wild goose chase?' I apologised, of course, but he carried on, 'Our little party went on long past my usual bedtime, Lady Drusilla. And I have to be up early, it being Sunday.'

'I do beg your pardon, but I didn't know someone was going to remove the body.'

Having done what I could to mollify him, I went home to find my uncle waiting anxiously, reminding me of how Jeffel used to wait up until I came in at night, no matter how often I told him it wasn't necessary. And I sighed. Life would never be quite the same again without Jeffel, and I meant to see that every one of those Fat Badgers paid for his death with their lives. As two of them already had. The man tonight and the one who fell over the cliff.

When I told my uncle the body had vanished, he was naturally astonished. 'Someone must have been waiting in the trees,' he said. 'Thank the Lord none of us thought to look there.'

I couldn't have agreed more, and I was immensely thankful we were all safe now. 'The local constable must be informed,' I said, thinking out loud. 'I'd better write a note.' I went into the library, settled myself at a table, wrote a brief description of the incident, explaining the body had since disappeared, presumably removed by an accomplice. I left the note in the hall for Luffe, instructing him to see a groom delivered it first thing in the morning.

With so many unanswered questions racing through my mind, I lay awake for a long time, going over all that had happened. 'You're the one I want,' the scar-faced man had said, deep menace in his eyes. But why? Why did the Fat Badgers want to kill me? Who had removed the body? And why had they done so? They hadn't worried about the man who fell over the cliff. Was that because he was French, and not known to anyone locally? If that was the case, then this man, if identified, would lead us to the others.

But why didn't the third man show himself? Was he afraid of being seen? If so, it meant we would have recognised him. Which kept me even wider awake.

If we had seen him, we would now have the cast-iron evidence we so desperately needed. The kind my father and I insisted on, before declaring any long-dead dubious character guilty of a crime. That was how we had worked, and it was that kind of certainty I needed now.

I breakfasted early and was buttering my second piece of toast when Mr. Hamerton walked into the room, greeting me in his usual cheerful manner. I asked if he'd slept well and he assured me he had. 'Nine hours, without stirring. And I feel greatly refreshed by it. Sea air is very tiring, although we didn't spend as much time at sea as I'd hoped.'

I looked up at him and smiled. 'Why was that?'

'Well, progress was so slow on the first day,' he said, filling his plate with substantial portions of ham and eggs, 'we set off really early the next morning. But there was so little wind we eventually put into Shoreham, hired horses and rode to Windsor. Which I'm glad we did as my business took three days to settle. Still it's finished with now,' he ended happily.

'You must be eager to move into your new house.'

'I am, ma'am. But I am also most grateful for the warm welcome I've received at Westfleet. You have all been very kind.' Cutting into a slice of ham, he asked how things had gone on in his absence, speaking as if he did not expect much to have changed. When I told him of the highwaymen, he gazed at me in disbelief. 'Highwaymen? Here on the Island?'

'I'm afraid so.' He listened in horror as I related the tale. 'My aunt suffered a nasty cut on the head, but otherwise we escaped unhurt.'

He sat there, his breakfast untouched, shaking his head from side to side as if unable to believe what he was hearing. I explained about the body disappearing, which again seemed to stagger him. 'There must have been an accomplice waiting in the woods.'

'Indeed. I'm going back to take another look. We couldn't see anything last night.'

'Is that wise, ma'am?' When I said, wise or not, I was going, he offered to accompany me.

'Thank you, but it's not necessary. I shall have Mudd with me. But you could explain to my aunt and uncle where I've gone, if you would be so good.'

On reaching the place where we had been held up, we looped the reins of our horses round suitable branches, and began to search the area. And I soon found what I was looking for. In a clearing about forty yards from the road, there were some fresh footprints and hoof marks intermingled in the soft ground. But despite a thorough search of the area, there wasn't a single clear cut footprint that could be used as evidence.

We were just about to leave when I saw the stocky, ginger-haired local constable hurrying up the hill to make his own search. 'Good morning, Roach,' I said, and lost no time in telling him exactly what had happened last night. 'The man had a scar running from the top of his right cheek down to his chin. Do you know anyone on the Island with a scar like that?'

CHAPTER 19

Roach took off his hat and scratched his head in thought. 'No, my lady, I don't. And I wouldn't forget a scar like that.' I had difficulty in hiding my disappointment, having expected Roach to know the man's identity. 'He must have come over from the mainland.'

'Very likely,' I sighed.

When I arrived home Mr. Hamerton was in the garden reading, but I did not disturb him. Instead I went into the drawing room, to find Mr. Reevers and Mr. East with my uncle. They, I soon learned, had called on their way to church to reassure themselves we were all safe.

'That is kind of you,' I said. Sitting near my uncle I asked him how my aunt was this morning.

'Feeling a little better, but I've persuaded her to rest quietly today. Perhaps you would be kind enough to accompany me to morning service, Drusilla?' I agreed at once, to please my uncle, for he was the kindest of men and would do anything for me.

Mr. Reevers said, 'I hear Mudd shot one of the highwaymen.'

'Who told you that?' I exclaimed in surprise.

'It's all round the village.'

My uncle said, 'Well, the village has got it wrong. It was Drusilla.'

'You shot him, Lady Drusilla?' Mr. East queried, his eyebrows shooting up.

'I did. It seemed the best thing to do at the time.'

That made him chuckle. 'It's a pity you don't speak French, ma'am, we could do with you in France.'

'I like my comforts too much I fear, Mr. East. Besides a woman of my height would be easily remembered.'

'You wouldn't care to stoop a little, I suppose?'

I couldn't help laughing. 'A tall hunch-backed woman might be even more noticeable.' And before he could think of a suitable answer, I glanced at the clock and said, 'You will have to excuse me, I'm afraid. If I'm going to church I must change at once.'

Mr. Hamerton joined us for the short walk to the church, and it being a hot day I took a parasol. After the service, with the news of the highwaymen on everyone's lips, my uncle was surrounded by people inquiring after my aunt.

Julia stopped to talk to Mr East, while Richard and Mr. Hamerton were soon in animated conversation, enabling Mr. Reevers to draw me a little apart from the others. The sun having gone in, I did not open my parasol.

'Tell me exactly what happened last night,' he urged. I did so, including the fact that the scar-faced man had said I was the one they wanted. He drew in his breath sharply. 'If I'd known I was putting you in that much danger I would never have suggested to Pitt that-----'

'I would still have tried to find out who killed Jeffel and Septimus.'

A faint smile touched his lips. 'Yes, I believe you would.'

'The other man was definitely Mr. Silver.'

People were beginning to come within earshot and he said, 'We can't talk here. Tell me instead what you thought of Mr. Upton's sermon.' The disquiet was still in his eyes, but the slight twitch at the corner of his lips told me his own opinion. To find a man who shared my enjoyment of the absurd was an absolute joy.

'If you wish,' I said, nodding to a passing acquaintance. Mr. Upton's overlong sermon was a lecture on the need to show consideration for others, and included a snide remark about not calling on decent God-fearing people after they had retired for the night. Referring to this, I said, 'Frankly, if he considered my feelings, he would never call on me ever again.'

His eyes were brimming with laughter, and I went on, 'As for giving thanks for Howe's great victory over the French fleet, I am exceedingly happy to do so, but I do wish Mr. Upton didn't make it sound as if he had personally arranged it with the Almighty.'

'Perhaps he thinks he did.'

I gave a gurgle of approval. 'He seems to think God is always on our side. What will he say if France gains a victory?'

'He will think of something,' he murmured.

'Pompous little man.'

Glancing over my head, he murmured, 'Pompous or not, he's heading this way.' I cursed under my breath and saw Mr Reevers press his lips firmly together.

Turning to face the parson, I civilly apologised again for the inconvenience I had caused him only a few hours earlier. He nodded in a manner that suggested he'd expected nothing less, and began speaking as if he was still in the pulpit. 'Nevertheless, I fear it is my duty to advise you there is a lot of talk in the village about your conduct last night.'

I took a very deep breath. 'I am not interested in tittle-tattle, Mr. Upton. And if, as you say, the whole village is talking about the highwaymen, then I know who to blame. I told no-one except you and Mrs. Upton.'

This neither embarrassed nor stopped him. 'You can't keep that sort of thing quiet, ma'am.'

'Not if the parsonage knows of it,' I retorted.

But I should have saved my breath, for he carried on as if I had not spoken. 'It was most unwise of you to go gallivanting about the countryside at midnight without a chaperone.'

Mr Reevers choked, which I ignored. 'Mr. Upton,' I hissed between my teeth. 'What I do is no concern of yours and if----'

'Please let me finish, ma'am. Mudd is to be commended for shooting that highwayman, but as for yourself, the rules of propriety must be observed at all times. A lady should never concern herself with the removal of a dead body. '

'For your information Mr. Upton, Mudd did not shoot the highwayman. I did.'

His prim brows rose in utter disbelief. 'No lady could bring herself to do such a thing. Mudd is obviously responsible,' he announced in the manner of a man who always knows best. 'Everyone says so.'

'Indeed,' I retorted in a quelling voice, unconsciously tapping my closed parasol against the side of my shoe. 'You would be well advised not to listen to gossip, Mr Upton. There is rarely any truth in it. And none at all in this instance.' Swinging round on my heel, I walked off down the path, leaving him standing.

Mr Reevers followed me, murmuring under his breath, 'Masterly. I thought you were going to hit him over the head with your parasol.'

'Serve him right if I had,' I fumed, as we stopped outside the gate to wait for my uncle. 'Insufferable man.'

'Well, that's taught me one thing,' he commented in a colourless tone.

I eyed him with suspicion. 'What might that be?'

'Never to make you angry when you're carrying a blunt instrument.'

I struggled with myself for several seconds, but the sheer merriment in his eyes soon had me laughing. Calming down, my conscience began to bother me a little. 'My father would not have approved of my behaviour. He taught me to be polite to people of inferior status.'

'I shouldn't worry on that score. Mr Upton does not consider himself to be inferior to anyone. Except perhaps to the Lord himself, and I wouldn't be too sure of that.' Smiling I shook my head at him and he casually inquired, 'Are you acquainted with anyone high up in the church?'

'Why?' I asked, full of misgiving, having observed the muscle twitching in his cheek.

'If you were, you could have Mr Upton moved to some obscure parish in the wilds of Northumberland.'

'Don't tempt me.'

Mrs Upton came gushing up then, eager to introduce Mr. Reevers to an acquaintance. Whereupon Mr. Sims claimed my attention. 'My uncle told me what happened last night, ma'am. It must have been most frightening.' The words he used were appropriate, but concern for my well-being was quite absent from his voice.

'It was not pleasant,' I agreed. 'I trust I didn't wake you when I knocked on the parsonage door last night.'

'Not at all, ma'am.'

'No doubt you are a deep sleeper,' I said, wishing my uncle would hurry up so that we could go home.

'It's not that, ma'am. The fact is I had gone out for a walk, to look at the stars. But this business with the highwayman's body is most odd. What can have happened to it?'

'Someone took it away, Mr. Sims. Someone who was out late.' And I asked, 'I don't suppose you saw anyone when you were studying the stars?'

He shook his head. 'Regrettably I did not, ma'am.' It was only later that I remembered high cloud had covered most of the sky, and that it hadn't been possible to see the stars.

The highwayman's body was never found and I did not expect that it ever would be. Mr. Brown had removed the body before it could be identified, because it would lead us to him and all the Fat Badgers.

It wasn't until Wednesday that my uncle decided Aunt Thirza had recovered sufficiently from her ordeal to benefit from a drive in the sunshine. When she came into the drawing room dressed in her favourite dove grey, I observed, 'You're looking very fetching, Aunt.'

My uncle grinned. 'That's what I said. It seems,' he admitted, winking at me, 'I should have realised the gown was new.'

Laughing, I shook my head at him, for he loved to tease my aunt, but she knew him too well to rise to the bait. Instead she turned to me and said, 'I trust the carriage has been thoroughly cleaned since that dreadful incident the other night.' Calmly I assured her it had, and she demanded, 'Who is to drive us? Not that spotty youth we had last time. I----'

'No. Ware will drive.'

She sniffed. 'He's a slowcoach.'

As I drew in my breath, my uncle intervened. 'Ware seems eminently suitable to me, my dear.'

He spoke firmly, and she rarely argued with him, accepting his decisions in a way she would never accept mine. 'Very well, Charles. If you say so.'

'I do.'

Luffe came in to say the carriage was at the door, and that Mr. East had called to see me. I directed Luffe to show him in, and my aunt and uncle stayed to greet him. He asked if I'd care to go for a ride, and when I accepted my aunt ordered in her peremptory way, 'You will take Mudd with you, Drusilla.'

'Of course,' I said, humouring her.

Half an hour later Mr. East and I, correctly accompanied by Mudd, were enjoying a good long gallop across the Downs. 'By heavens, ma'am,' he said, when we eventually stopped, 'I have never seen a lady ride as well as you do.'

I laughed. 'Flatterer. I feel sure you would prefer to be riding with Miss Adams.'

Grinning, he didn't deny it. 'Actually, if you don't consider it an imposition, I should value your advice. About Miss Adams I mean.'

A bee buzzing round Orlando made him shake his head and I ran my hand down his neck, murmuring a few calming words, before asking casually, 'What kind of advice?'

'Well, the thing is, I'll probably be sent back to France once we've caught these wretched Fat Badgers, and I---'

'You believe we will catch them?'

'I do, ma'am. Even if we can't pin Hamerton down before he moves to his new house, we will once he's living there. No doubt he chose it because it offers the perfect meeting place for his gang of murderers, but keeping watch on an isolated house is very easy. When they are in gaol and I'm ordered back to France.......' He hesitated briefly, then the words tumbled out in a rush of embarrassment, bringing a faint flush to his cheeks. 'In short ma'am, ought I to make Miss Adams an offer under those circumstances?'

I didn't answer at once and he said, 'Forgive me if I am being a little impertinent, but I suspect you may soon be faced with the same difficulty ----' I dismissed that with a wave of the hand, but he only grinned at me. 'Your view, as a woman, might help me decide. You see, if we married and then I went back to France ---- well, the thought of causing her so much anguish---- you understand, I'm sure.' He brushed a stray hair from his eyes. 'Yet, if I don't speak, I may lose her altogether. She's not short of suitors.'

Miss Adams, I thought, was a very lucky woman. Not every man would show such concern for a wife's feelings. I said, 'I believe in living for the day, Mr. East. Julia says the same. If Miss Adams returns your feelings, not being married won't stop her worrying.'

He gazed at me for some seconds, as if he hadn't considered that. 'Yes, I see what you mean. I'm very much obliged to you, ma'am.'

I smiled at him. 'I hope I shall soon be wishing you happy.'

'So do I,' he declared ardently.

We were still riding at a walking pace when we saw two riders crossing our path some distance ahead, and he muttered, 'Why does Mr. Sims spend so much time with a rascal like Mr. Young? '

'Rascal, Mr. East?' I teased. 'Mr. Young is a respected member of the community.'

'So I'm told, ma'am. Nevertheless, Mr. Upton would be horrified if he knew.'

'Undoubtedly. But I have no intention of telling him.'

'Very wise,' he agreed. 'Still I trust Mr. Sims knows what he's doing. Young is not a man I would like to cross. Or be in debt to.'

'No, indeed. It's to be hoped Mr. Sims has more sense.'

Mr. East's veiled suggestion that I might soon be in a similar situation to Miss Adams came into my mind the following morning when I saw Mr. Reevers riding up to the house. Colour rushed into my cheeks, but luckily my uncle, who was reading the newspaper while waiting for my aunt to change before they went for a walk, didn't notice. Thankfully it had subsided by the time Luffe showed Mr. Reevers into the drawing room. After chatting for a few minutes my uncle said, 'Would you excuse me while I see what's keeping my dear wife.'

He shut the door carefully behind him and Mr. Reevers chuckled softly. 'Do you think he realised he was leaving you without a chaperone?'

'You could have warned him,' I suggested, unconcerned.

He got up and sitting beside me on the sofa, murmured in a caressing tone, 'From my point of view that seems rather foolish.'

I raised my eyes to his and what I saw left me decidedly breathless. Which was why, I told myself later, I behaved like an innocent girl just out of the schoolroom, whispering, 'Why is that?'

He took my left hand and held it between his own hands. 'You must know there is nothing I want more than to be alone with you.' I did know it, and in that moment, it was what I wanted too. If I said the right words now, he would make me an offer of marriage. But I hesitated, and he murmured, 'What is it, Drusilla? What bothers you? You cannot be unaware of my feelings. And I thought that you-----'

'The thing is,' I broke in quickly, 'I'm not sure I want to be married.'

He looked at me from under raised brows, a faint smile twisting his lips. 'My dearest love, there can be no *other* option.'

That made me gasp. Glancing up at him, I saw his eyes were alight with laughter and I instantly admonished, 'You know perfectly well I didn't mean---'

'I should hope not,' he said, affecting a prim tone. 'For one thing, your aunt would never allow it.'

A vision of Aunt Thirza's outrage, should she be informed of such a situation, set me chuckling, dispelling any awkwardness I felt. Even so, I had spoken the absolute truth. I wasn't sure I wanted to be married. And I was just about to explain my reasons, when Luffe came in and announced, 'Mrs Tanfield, my lady.'

Julia took one look at us and insisted light-heartedly, 'Tell me at once if I should go away.'

Rising to his feet, Mr. Reevers bowed and assured her, 'Not at all, ma'am. I am always delighted to see you.'

'You are most gallant, if a little untruthful, I fear. At least on this occasion.' He placed a chair for her, which she accepted, and began to talk about Mr. Hamerton's new house, asking Mr. Reevers if he had seen it.

'I've not yet had that pleasure,' he said, sitting opposite me again.

'You must go. The hill it sits on offers splendid views of the Solent. Richard is so pleased he'll be living nearby. They have become the greatest of friends.'

'So I have observed,' he said in his pleasant way.

My aunt and uncle looked in briefly, but when they left for their walk, Mr. Reevers took his leave. Julia turned to me and asked, 'Has he made you an offer, Drusilla?' I smiled and shook my head. 'Then he was about to, and I came in at the wrong moment. I am so sorry. Why didn't you tell me to go away? I would have done in your place.'

I laughed. 'Yes, you would. But the truth is, I haven't made up my mind yet.'

She looked at me askance. 'Drusilla, it is obvious to me that you are in love, so ---'

'But it would change my life completely and----'

'Well, of course it would,' she said, gurgling with laughter. 'Being with the man you love is wonderful. I can recommend it.'

'Yes, I thought you would,' I teased. 'My difficulty is I enjoy being independent. I like looking after my estates, and my fortune. And if I marry----'

'It would all belong to your husband,' she said thoughtfully. For, that was the law. 'Could you not agree to decide things together? Richard and I do so.'

'Possibly. But it isn't only that. I'm not suited to a life of domesticity.' She wrinkled her brow, knowing it to be true. 'I detest sewing, and those matronly conversations about recipes, illness, or problems with servants, bore me to death. As far as I'm concerned Dr Redding deals with illness, I take good care to see my servants are happy, and cook is responsible for meals. What is there to talk about?' Julia gave way to a peal of mirth. 'It's not funny, Julia. I have no real accomplishments to talk about either. I can't draw or paint---'

'You play the piano.'

'Not very well.'

'And you can sing.'

'My voice is tolerable I suppose.' And I did enjoy it. 'But I was at my happiest helping father with his book. I loved solving the mysteries we came across, and it's what I do best. Now I'm trying to find out who killed Septimus. And what man would allow his wife to continue with such work?' Even she could not answer that; yet, if I accepted an offer of marriage from Mr. Reevers I had to resolve these difficulties.

That evening my aunt and uncle retired at ten as usual, and after they had gone, I went into the workroom to go through everything that had happened since the Fat Badgers held up our carriage. The first chance I'd had to do so. The servants had gone to bed, and Mr. Hamerton, who was outside observing moths, came in well before midnight and went up the stairs.

Thankful I would not be disturbed, I concentrated on trying to work out why the Fat Badgers were so desperate to get rid of me. 'You're the one I want,' that dreadful man had said. But what did I know that was so important? And I went through every tiny detail I'd written on my charts, without finding any answer.

I started to yawn and, glancing at the clock, saw it wanted only ten minutes to one. Deciding it was time I went to bed, I lit my bedroom candle from one in the workroom, snuffed out the rest, and had just opened the door quietly, not wanting to wake anyone, when I heard a creak on the stairs. I took no notice at first, as stairs often creak for no apparent reason, then almost at once it happened again, louder this time. Someone was creeping down to the hall. Putting my bedroom candle down well inside the workroom so that the light could not be seen, I stood in the dark doorway, and saw a man tiptoeing across to the drawing room, carrying a pair of shoes. A slightly plump gentleman of average height.

He opened the door and went in. Hearing him unlatch a window, I stole across the hall just in time to see him climbing out. I waited a moment, then went in and realised anyone giving the window a cursory glance would think it was closed, when in fact it was open an inch. But where, I asked myself, could Mr. Hamerton be going at such a time on this warm June night?

CHAPTER 20

Without stopping to think, I rushed back into the workroom and unlocked the drawer where I kept a pair of small pistols. Father had taught me how to shoot, and quickly loading them, I put one in each pocket. Snuffing out the candle, I unlocked the outside workroom door. This led into the garden, and was the door I had used late at night as a young girl, when Giles Saxborough and I sneaked out to watch the smugglers.

Slipping the key into another pocket, I ran quietly round to the front of the house, in time to see Mr. Hamerton walking on the grass verge beside the drive, intent on making no sound. Once he was out of sight, I lifted my skirts a trifle and raced after him, ignoring thoughts of what my aunt, uncle, Mudd, and even Julia would say if they knew I was following a gentleman who clearly did not want anyone to know what he was doing. A gentlemen who, if he was the French agent, Mr. Brown, was very dangerous indeed.

Clouds moved slowly across the sky, allowing only brief glimpses of moonlight, but one of these enabled me to see Mr. Hamerton was heading towards Westfleet village. Passing the duck pond and village green, he went up the hill into the churchyard, and headed straight for the church. I waited by the lych-gate, hidden by overhanging branches of trees. He stopped outside the entrance porch and looked all around. Satisfied no-one was watching, he went into the church, the ancient oak door creaking when he opened it, and again as he shut it.

The moon had disappeared and if I was to recognise whoever he was meeting, I had to get closer. Trees ringed the perimeter of the churchyard, and keeping to the darkest areas, I soon reached them. Then, climbing up the rising ground that led to the church itself, I headed for a tree ten yards from the door, and hid behind it. From here I would have a good view of anyone coming out of the church.

I had only been there a few minutes when I heard a faint rustling noise nearby. I hadn't seen anyone else in the churchyard, and had taken great care not to be seen myself. Praying the noise was the wind rustling through the trees, I carefully looked around. At first I saw nothing, yet every instinct told me I was not alone, and I took a firm grip on the pistols I'd brought with me.

The moon emerged briefly from behind a cloud, allowing me a glimpse of a tall man standing under a tree in the lane on the other side of the church. Close by were two horses. So, whoever Mr. Hamerton had come to meet was already in the church.

If only I could hear what they were saying. The church had a secret entrance, used by smugglers when hiding their goods, but I had no idea where it was. Nor did the local Riding Officer, who could often be seen poking around the building. I suspected Mr. Upton knew, for he was very partial to brandy and the parsonage never ran short of it. A few minutes later the church door creaked loudly and someone came out. Even in the dark I recognised him. It was that great bear of a man, Mr. Silver.

I fingered the pistols, itching to use them but, fortunately, common sense prevailed. If I killed him, the other Fat Badgers would leave the Island and carry on elsewhere without him, and we would have no idea where they were. Nor did I have any indisputable evidence that Mr. Hamerton was Mr. Brown, as I hadn't heard a single word they had said in the church, and therefore could not swear they had been plotting a revolution.

Mr. Silver strode round to the waiting horses, the two men rode off, and I could not stop them. If I'd brought Orlando I could have followed them, and discovered where Mr. Silver lived. Without Orlando, I could do nothing.

When Mr. Hamerton emerged from the church, he headed back to Westfleet, and I was about to follow when I heard a horse approaching. Had Mr. Silver come back? Had he forgotten something? Hurrying over to the lane I saw the rider was Mr. Sims. He dismounted and quietly led his horse round the back of the parsonage to the stables.

What on earth was he doing out at this time of night? Not studying the stars, for there were none to be seen. I guessed he'd been visiting Mr. Young, and again I wondered why he'd really come to the Island. He showed no sign of his supposed recurring fever, but puzzled though I was, I couldn't waste time thinking about him. I had far more important matters on my mind.

I half expected Mr. Hamerton to act differently in the morning, but he was his usual cheerful self. Announcing, when I inquired, that he had slept very well, and was up early in order to go sailing with

Richard. The thought of Richard's friendship with this man sent ice cold shudders of fear through me.

It was vital that I told Mr Reevers about the meeting at the church as soon as I could, but I couldn't go to Norton House without my uncle, and he had not yet come down to breakfast. Trying to curb my impatience, I went into the workroom and wrote down the facts concerning that meeting, and sat thinking about it for some time, but as I used the charts for facts alone I did not add anything further.

Mr. Hamerton left the house a few minutes before my uncle came downstairs, and the morning was well advanced by the time we arrived at Norton House. Here Mr. Reevers told us Mr. East had gone to call on Miss Adams, and I wondered if he'd made her an offer. Deciding when the time was right couldn't be easy when he'd only known her a few weeks.

My uncle soon went off to the library to return the books he'd finished with, and to borrow some more, at which point Mr. Reevers suggested that we took a stroll in the garden. Which, finally, gave me the chance to tell him about Mr. Hamerton's meeting with Mr. Silver. His bushy black eyebrows drew together into a frown. 'Our man watching the house hasn't reported this.'

'He probably didn't see him,' I said. 'There was very little moon.'

'Or he fell asleep. Well, there can be no doubt now that Hamerton is Mr. Brown, even if we can't actually prove it yet. But I'd like to know how Hamerton and Silver arranged that meeting. Our agents say Hamerton has done nothing untoward.'

'Luffe and Mudd have strict orders that any message Mr. Hamerton wants delivered must be brought to me first.'

He nodded, as if he'd expected that. 'Mudd will understand why, but Luffe must have thought it odd.'

Remembering the puzzled look on Luffe's face, I laughed. 'Yes, but he didn't ask questions. Jeffel ---' I stopped and took a deep breath, for I still found it hard to talk about him, 'Jeffel would have asked.'

'You still miss him, don't you?' he murmured softly.

His words made me choke up, but I managed to say, 'The house seems so empty without him. I – I can't remember a time when he wasn't there. My father and I relied on him a great deal. As I still do with Mudd.' The thought of Westfleet without Mudd made me shiver. 'No-one could ever take Mudd's place.'

'No. He is the best of good fellows.'

Reaching the beach at the end of the garden we saw Mr. East riding back towards the house, but he was too far away for us to gauge his mood. We stood watching the waves rippling gently onto the shore, and the boats going about their business in the Solent, and as we turned back towards the house I talked again of Mr. Hamerton's meeting. 'If I'd taken a horse and followed Mr. Silver, I might have learnt where he lived and-----'

'And got your head blown off in the process. Men like him know instinctively when they're being followed. It was fortunate Hamerton didn't see you either.'

'I took good care to ensure he didn't.' Even so, honesty forced me to admit I had acted hastily. As I told him, given time to make plans, I considered every eventuality carefully. But when something unexpected happened, forcing me to respond at once, I tended to react instinctively, without stopping to consider if it was dangerous. And I owned, somewhat contritely, 'I know exactly what you are thinking. I should have taken Mudd with me.'

His expression softened. 'You know, you are a constant delight to me. Few women would admit to such a fault. But then, my dearest girl, you are quite unlike any other woman I have ever met.'

'That is a compliment any woman would be grateful to receive,' I said demurely, trying to make light of it.

A wicked gleam came into his eyes. 'Grateful enough for us to renew the conversation so rudely interrupted by Julia?'

A gurgle of laughter broke in my throat, and I smiled up at him, all my resolve not to marry weakened by his nearness. In that moment the prospect of spending the rest of my life with him seemed infinitely desirable. For I could no longer deny my feelings for him. The more I saw of him, the more I wanted to be with him. A day without his presence was a dull day, no matter how much the sun shone. When we were with other people, and something amused me, I knew that if I looked across at him, his eyes would be laughing too.

The truth was, I loved him. It was useless to pretend otherwise. I longed to feel his strong arms round me, yet to rush into marriage would be foolish. Thus, when I spoke it was of Julia's untimely interruption. 'I thought you were going to wring her neck,' I teased light-heartedly.

His eyes rested on me in a most disturbing way, as if he had read all my thoughts, but he merely said, 'Not

Julia. I happen to like her. Now, if it had been your aunt------'

I laughed and he stopped, leaning against the far side of a large oak, where we couldn't be seen from the house. Taking my hands in his, he murmured softly, 'Now before we are interrupted again---'

'Too late, I'm afraid,' I said, having caught a glimpse of a tall, handsome figure heading in our direction. 'Mr. East is coming this way.'

He turned round and when his friend reached us Mr. Reevers urged. 'Do go away, Toby.'

Taking in the situation at a glance, Mr. East grinned. 'Sorry, Radleigh. This can't wait. A letter has just come from Pitt and he wants an immediate reply.'

With a sigh Mr. Reevers demanded, 'What does he want exactly?'

'He asks if we have enough evidence yet to arrest Hamerton.'

'Well,' he drawled, 'Lady Drusilla saw him with Mr. Silver last night.'

'What?' Mr. East gasped, his eyes alight with hope. 'Are you quite sure, ma'am?'

Mr. Reevers arched a mocking eyebrow at him and turned to me. 'I beg you to forgive him for doubting you. An hour in the company of Miss Adams has addled what few brains he possesses.'

Grinning, Mr. East begged my pardon and when, at his request, I explained what had happened, he agreed it would be foolish to arrest Mr. Hamerton now. 'The others would go ahead on their own, and we need Hamerton to lead us to them.'

'You deal with Pitt then, Toby.'

'That's not all he wants, Radleigh.'

Mr. Reevers gave a grimace. 'And there's Mr. Frère coming out now.' He turned to me. 'I wish I didn't have to go, but I must.'

I smiled. 'Of course you must.'

Returning my smile, his eyes told me everything I could ever want to know. 'Tomorrow then,' he said. 'At Westfleet.' And my heart hammered in happy anticipation.

Riding home with my uncle I glowed with happiness, for nothing would stop Mr. Reevers calling on me tomorrow to make me an offer of marriage. I saw now that he was the only one who would truly understand the concerns I'd had about accepting that offer, and with understanding, those concerns could be resolved. Indeed, must be resolved, for I knew in my heart I would never be truly happy again without him. And for the first time I understood exactly how Julia felt about Richard.

There were two letters awaiting me when I arrived home. The handwriting on one I'd seen before, but couldn't think where; the other was from Marguerite Saxborough, my godmother. That brought a smile to my face, for her letters were always a joy. Saving that for later, to enjoy in the quiet of my bedchamber, I slipped out the side door, sat on a garden seat and on opening the other one saw, to my astonishment, that it was from Mrs Jenkins.

It was ten days since she'd left the Island so hurriedly, hours before we were to meet, and I'd given up all hope of learning anything about the Fat Badgers from her. I thought of the courage it must have taken to write to me when the fiends who had murdered her husband George were still threatening her life and those of her children. But it wasn't until I'd finished reading her letter that I realised how incredibly brave she really was.

CHAPTER 21

Mrs. Jenkins did not include her direction on her letter, but I soon saw why.

My dear Lady Drusilla,

I must beg your pardon for leaving the Island so hurriedly after I had promised to meet you. You must think it very rude of me, even though that was not my intention. My friends and the servants believe I am attending my sick brother, but the truth is very different.

On that particular morning a burly fearsome looking individual stopped me as I walked down the lane to the village and said that, if I wanted to keep my children alive I must not speak to anyone about the society George had belonged to, and I was to leave immediately for my brother's house at Wickham and stay there all summer. He said if I doubted they would carry out such a threat, then I should know they had thrown George into the river, and when he managed to scramble to the bank despite not being able to swim, they held him under the water until he drowned.

I cannot bear to think of it, Lady Drusilla. George was a kindly man who would always help anyone in trouble. Yet I could not ignore such a threat to our four dear children.

How that man knew of our meeting I do not know, for I did not mention it to anyone. I left the house that very morning and went straight to my brother, but I was too frightened to stay there. Those murderers knew where we were, and I was terrified they might still harm my children. So the next morning, an hour before dawn, I left for the place where I am now. No-one knows my direction, not even my brother.

You wished to speak to me about the society George belonged to, and throughout that long journey I tried to recall what he had said, but I remember very little, except that he was full of enthusiasm at first. Then one night he came home and said he couldn't understand why one man, a Mr Ruby, had been allowed to join the society. I remember it particularly because of the odd name. George said this man had a deep scar all the way down one side of his face and spoke the kind of slang used by criminals.

The last meeting he attended he returned white-faced, but explained that, after leaving the meeting, he realised he'd forgotten his gloves and had gone back for them. Then, on his way out again he'd slipped and fallen down the stairs. And it had left him feeling rather shaky. I accepted that at the time, having no reason to disbelieve him, but now I am certain he made that up to stop me worrying.

I was determined to write, once we were safely ensconced in this place, for I want the men who killed George to be caught. I only wish I could be more helpful.

She ended in the usual manner, her grief still clear in her handwriting. Shocked and horrified by what I had read, and the sheer terror she had endured, my heart went out to her. Told of that vile murder and suffering those unimaginable threats, she had taken her children and fled for their safety. And who could blame her? It was what anyone would have done.

Hearing a rustling noise, I looked up to see three sparrows had landed on a nearby bush. The kitchen cat, who had been dozing in the shade, was now wide awake, crouching low on the ground, ears flattened, watching the chattering birds and waiting her chance to pounce. In much the same way, I thought, as Mr Brown was holding back until the right moment.

One of the sparrows foolishly flew down to a lower branch, the cat leapt at the bird, caught it firmly, and promptly shot through the garden and was soon out of sight. That was a death I could not prevent, and it made me think of the thousands of people who would die if Mr Brown was not stopped. A thought that sent an icy shiver right through me.

But, Mrs. Jenkins had been far more helpful than she'd realised. Her assurance that she had not told anyone of our arrangement to meet that afternoon set my mind racing. I considered who else had known of it. Obviously Mr. Reevers, Mr. East and Mudd, and lastly, Julia. But she had not spoken to anyone, not even Richard, about anything connected with her brother's death. Yet, Mrs. Jenkins had made the arrangement one day, and Mr. Silver had known of it by the following morning. Fearful of what Mrs Jenkins might say, he'd sent her scurrying off to the mainland within the hour. And the day I accidentally left the note from Mrs Jenkins on my desk, Richard had gone into my workroom, looking for ink. I got up, and walking over to the walled garden, leant against the sun-warmed brickwork and closed my eyes, but the fear of what his having seen the note could mean, refused to go away.

The other puzzle on my mind was the question Mr. Reevers had posed. How had Mr. Silver and Mr. Hamerton arranged that meeting in the church? His every movement away from Westfleet was watched, which suggested he had been contacted here. Yet, how could a message reach him here when all letters arriving or departing were brought to me first?

The only time he was outside alone in the evening was when he was studying moths. He never stayed out more than an hour, and I was ready to swear he didn't leave the grounds. I had watched him so often I knew exactly what he did. He started his perambulations by putting lanterns on the seat built round one of the big oak trees lining the drive near the entrance. Picturing that in my mind, it came to me in a flash that he always used the same tree. Which happened to be the one nearest the road.

As Mr. Hamerton was still out sailing with Richard, I wandered over to this particular oak. Walking round it, I trailed my hand on the bark, as I had as a child, remembering this was the tree with a small hollow where I used to hide my treasures. In those days I had reached it by standing on the seat, unseen from the house, as the hollow faced away from the building. The tree had grown considerably since that time, of course, but I soon found the hollow, obscured by a branch and filled with old leaves.

Curious, I stood on the seat to take a good look inside and saw it was much deeper than was apparent from a cursory glance. Eagerly I scooped out the leaves, but there was nothing underneath. Yet it made the perfect hiding place, being fairly close to the road. On a dark night Mr Silver could have easily slipped a message into the hollow without being seen.

Going indoors to dress for dinner, I met my aunt coming out of the drawing room. 'There you are Drusilla. I wish to speak to you, if you please.' Her tone did not bode well, and I wondered what had happened to annoy her now. Joining her and my uncle in the drawing room I asked what was wrong.

'I think you should know what happened yesterday.'

'Oh come now, my dear,' my uncle broke in. 'I thought we'd agreed it was unnecessary to bother Drusilla with anything so trivial.'

'It is not trivial to me Charles,' she announced huffily. 'I wanted Mudd to drive me to Yarmouth and he refused. He said-----'

'Thirza, he did no such thing. He explained it all to me most respectfully. Drusilla's orders prevented him from doing as you wished, but he arranged for one of the other grooms to take his place. And you said yourself that you were quite happy with----'

'That is not the point.' She turned to me. 'I want to know what is going on, Drusilla. Why couldn't Mudd drive me?'

'Because I need him here at Westfleet in case I decide to go out.'

'I am glad you have regained your sense of propriety but, surely, any groom would do.'

'No. It has to be Mudd.'

She sniffed. 'Why? One groom is as good as another.' I shook my head at her, for she would never understand. 'It never does to hobnob with servants, Drusilla.'

'I do not hobnob, as you put it, Aunt. Mudd has been at Westfleet for as long as I can remember. He's intelligent, utterly dependable, and he knows how I like things to be done.'

'Well, you cannot say the same thing about Luffe,' she said, and went on at length, giving me her opinion of him. 'He's not up to the job, Drusilla. Jeffel had his faults, but Luffe is worse. His shoes squeak, he often fails to do what I ask at once, and he broke a wine glass yesterday,' she ended, ticking off the complaints on her fingers.

On and on she went, until I lost patience and snapped, 'Well, I am quite happy with him.' I hoped that would put an end to it, but she barely drew breath, with the result that I didn't have time to read Marguerite's letter before dinner.

During the meal Mr. Hamerton amused us with his tale of how he'd made a paper boat for Edward, and my godson had promptly sunk it by putting a large stone in it. After dinner, he went for a walk in the garden, while I joined my aunt and uncle in the drawing room for an hour, before going into the library to read Marguerite's letter.

I sat in a comfortable chair by one of the big windows, smiling in anticipation as I broke the seal. This letter had come from London, where she, Giles and Lucie were to spend a few weeks after their trip to Yorkshire.

My dearest Drusilla,

It is such a joy to be in London after Yorkshire. The countryside in the north is very pretty, but to my mind one hill looks very like another, and try as I might I could not see what was so exciting about watching water fall from a great height. In London I am enjoying myself immensely, visiting old friends and going to balls, parties and the theatre. But, last night, at the opera, I learned something that I fear will cause you pain.

I had hoped, for your sake, that it was just gossip, but Giles says the story I have to tell you is true, and that Mr Reevers told him of it himself. He does not believe Mr Reevers behaved in an ungentlemanly manner, and says there is no need to repeat it to you, but I cannot agree. I believe you should have the opportunity to judge for yourself.

I hate to be the bearer of such tidings, for it is clear to me that you are greatly attracted to Mr Reevers. Still it is better that you should be aware of the truth. I'm afraid he is nothing but a fortune hunter, Drusilla.

You probably won't have heard of Sophie Wood, as the family live in a quiet way in Derbyshire. She is the only child of doting, wealthy parents, who wanted her to find true happiness in marriage, as they had done themselves. A pretty, sunny-natured, intelligent girl, she had difficulty in finding the right man as far too many were only after her fortune.

Then two years ago, when she was twenty-one, she met Mr Reevers, who made himself so agreeable to her that she fell headlong in love with him. After a suitable time Mr Reevers made her an offer, but Sophie's father already had his measure, and sent him packing.

It is clear that Mr Reevers exerts himself wondrously to captivate a woman when there is a fortune at stake, so please take care what you are about, Drusilla.

I beg of you not to mention this to Giles, as he is of the opinion you are very well able to make your own decisions. And, of course, Mr Reevers is a good friend of his. I wish with all my heart that I could have spared you such.....

The click of the door handle made me look up and I saw Mr. Hamerton entering the room. Folding the letter as swiftly as my trembling fingers would allow, I slipped it into the deep pocket of my gown.

'Am I disturbing you, Lady Drusilla?' he inquired. I tried to speak, but my mouth was too dry, and I could only shake my head at him. He gazed at me for a moment. 'Are you feeling quite the thing? You look awfully pale, you know.'

I forced a smile, and finally managed to make my mouth work. 'I'm quite well, thank you. I - I expect it's this gray gown I'm wearing. It always makes me look rather white in the face. I don't know why I bought it, really.'

His features relaxed at once. 'That explains it then.'

And sitting down opposite me, he went on, 'I wanted to ask your advice.'

'By all means,' I said, clasping my hands tightly in my lap to stop them trembling. As he began to talk I felt as if none of this was really happening to me, as if I was watching myself from afar. I wished he would go away and leave me alone, for I had this wretched lump in my throat and no amount of swallowing made it disappear.

In the beginning I had feared Mr Reevers was more interested in my fortune than in me. But it wasn't long before I came to believe that the expression in his eyes when he looked at me was genuine. The conviction that he truly cared for me had grown steadily over these past weeks, to the point where it seemed as certain as the arrival of the morning light. Yet, in her letter, Marguerite wrote that Mr Reevers had admitted to Giles that he'd pursued Sophie because of her fortune. Was that all I meant to him too? Had I really fallen into the same trap? I could not bear to think of it. And, quite suddenly, I felt sick.

Mr. Hamerton's voice intruded into my thoughts. 'Well, that's it in a nutshell, ma'am.'

Only then did I realise I hadn't heard a word he'd said, and I tried hard to pull myself together. 'I'm sorry Mr. Hamerton, would you go over it again, please.'

He looked at me in concern. 'I fear you are not well, ma'am. I should not have troubled you.'

I tried to smile. 'I have a headache, that's all.'

'I knew there was something. Can I get you anything?'

'Thank you, but no. What was it you wanted to see me about?'

'Nothing that won't keep for another day. Merely advice about furnishing my new house.'

At that moment my aunt and uncle came into the room, and conversation became more general. Somehow I got through the evening without anyone commenting that I wasn't myself. When my aunt and uncle retired for the night at ten, I went up to my own bedchamber feeling very tired. After my maid had brushed my hair, I sent her off to bed. The instant she closed the door behind her, I took out Marguerite's letter and read it through to the end, but there was nothing of importance after the point where I had been interrupted.

I tried telling myself I'd had a lucky escape, that I had been fortunate to discover the truth about Mr Reevers before I threw caution to the winds and accepted an offer from him. As I had been about to do. I could not allow my fortune and Westfleet to pass into his hands, unless I was certain he cared for me for myself. Marriage with affection on both sides might not always be easy, but without it what would my life become?

At least I had found out in time, and I reminded myself that he, at thirty-one, had learnt how to make himself agreeable to any woman. He must, I thought miserably, be a very good actor. Tears threatened, but I brushed them away, determined he would not make me cry.

Pain did not last for ever, I told myself, and until it went away I would simply have to bear it. Until then I intended to keep a proper distance between us. Having made this sensible decision, I tried to put him out of my mind, but I could not stop thinking about everything that had passed between us since we'd renewed our friendship in Windsor. Nor could I forget the expression in his eyes when he looked at me, the caress in his voice when we were alone, and the joy at finding a man who laughed at the same things as I did. Yet, it seemed now, that he had meant none of it. And I did not know how I was to bear such heartache.

CHAPTER 22

I was in the workroom the following morning, gazing unseeingly at the garden, when Luffe came in to inform me Mr Reevers wished to see me. He'd promised to call, and knowing my aunt and uncle often took a stroll in the hour before nuncheon, he'd deliberately waited until then. But this morning, with storm clouds gathering in the west, they had gone out earlier, and I expected them back at any minute. I looked out the window hoping to see them returning, anything to put off what I knew would be a painful ordeal, but there wasn't a sign of them, and I forced myself to say, 'Show him into the drawing room, if you please, Luffe.'

'The drawing room, my lady?' he repeated in surprise, for after their morning stroll my aunt and uncle invariably repaired to that room. Luffe's reaction told me that even he knew how things were between Mr Reevers and myself. Or how they had been.

I nodded. 'I will be there directly.'

It took all my courage to face him. For, along with the heartache, there was anger too. Anger that he had taken me in. Yet, I was determined not to let him be aware of it; at all costs to maintain my dignity in front of him. Therefore I lifted my chin, reminded myself that he was only interested in my fortune, and went to join him.

When I entered the room his eyes alighted on me with an expression that almost made me throw caution to the winds. How could he look at me in such a way if he was only interested in my fortune? Yet, Sophie Wood had believed he loved her. He came towards me with hands outstretched. 'At last,' he declared, beaming. 'I have waited far too long for this moment.'

Unconsciously I took a step backwards. 'My aunt and uncle will be back any minute.' The ice in my voice was clear even to my own ears.

He dropped his hands and stared at me in a puzzled fashion. 'What's wrong, Drusilla?'

I shook my head. 'Nothing is wrong. Why should there be?'

'Something has distressed you. And not a small thing either. What ....'

'You are mistaken, sir.'

He reached out and took my hands in his, refusing to release them when I tried to pull them away. 'I am very sure I am not.' He gave me a long searching look. 'Have I offended you in some way? If so, I beg you to tell me.'

I knew I ought to tell him, but I was afraid of losing control. I could not bear him to see he had reduced me to tears. In that moment I could not think beyond the need to maintain some kind of dignity.

Thankfully the door opened then, forcing Mr Reevers to let go of my hands, and I quickly put several feet between us, as my aunt and uncle entered the room. The four of us sat talking of the weather and other innocuous subjects, but my uncle kept looking at me in a way that told me he knew something was wrong. And I wished with all my heart that I could learn to school my features. Shortly afterwards Mr Reevers took his leave, but not before he'd tried to persuade me to walk with him in the garden; a suggestion I quickly rebuffed.

That short interview made it very plain that I must not see him alone again. If I did he would ask the same questions, and how could I tell him that I knew he was only making up to me on account of my fortune?

It didn't occur to me then that I had on several occasions used precisely those words to rid myself of some man's unwanted attentions. The difference was I hadn't cared one jot for any of them, and although I wished I didn't care for Mr Reevers, the truth was that I did. If I accused him of only being interested in my fortune, he would deny it. Yet, last year, when we barely knew each other, he'd told me he'd sold his family home in order to pay his deceased father's debts, but hoped to find an alternative way to recoup those losses. I had never forgotten it. The easiest way to regain a fortune was to find a rich wife, and I had so nearly fallen into the trap.

I'd hoped he would realise now that I had no intention of being used as a means of solving his financial problems, but just after eight the following morning I saw him riding up to the house. Unable to sleep the previous night, I had risen early and breakfasted at seven. Since then only Mr. Hamerton had appeared downstairs, and he was in the breakfast room. Thus I went straight into the hall, where Luffe was about to open the door.

'Luffe, inform Mr Reevers I am not at home, if you please.'

I saw the surprise in his eyes, but he answered without hesitation. 'Very good, my lady.'

'Tell him I will be out all day.'

'Yes, my lady.'

I went into the workroom, but had barely picked up my pen when Luffe came into the room and shut the door. I raised my brows at him. 'Is something wrong?'

'It's Mr Reevers, my lady. I informed him you were not at home—' He hesitated, as if uncertain how to continue.

'Go on,' I urged.

'He said he would wait, my lady.'

'Wait?' I exploded in exasperation.

'Yes, my lady. He said he wished to see you on a matter of importance.'

'Did he, indeed?' And I drummed my fingers on the table.

'I believe,' Luffe warned in a respectful manner, 'Mr. Hamerton has almost finished breakfast.'

I threw my pen onto the desk. 'Where have you put him?'

'In the library, my lady.'

'Tell him - no - I'll see him myself.' I was a little more in command of myself today, and saw the sense of not putting it off again.

When I opened the door into the library Mr Reevers was standing looking out the window at the garden. He turned at once and smiled, his eyes softening. 'Looks like thunder, don't you think?' He indicated the heavy black clouds overhead, and spoke in a bantering way of the risk of his being struck by lightning on the way home.

I interrupted icily, 'Mr Reevers, I am very busy this morning. What is it that you want?'

He dropped his mocking tone and taking a letter from his pocket, handed it to me. 'It's from Mr Pitt. He asked me to deliver it with all possible speed.'

Breaking the seal, I stood where I was and read the letter.

My dear Lady Drusilla,

First, I must assure you most sincerely that I do not attach any blame to you, Mr Reevers or Mr. East for the lack of success in finding evidence to prove whether or not Hamerton is the French agent known as Mr Brown. These agents can be notoriously hard to pin down, but I feel sure you will agree that, if Mr. Hamerton is to be arrested, we must do so before the King goes to Weymouth in August. Keeping the King safe for weeks on end in that town cannot be totally guaranteed. A day is easily achieved, a week perhaps. But after that, with the best will in the world, guards can become slack if everything is going on much as usual.

In the beginning we did not flood the Isle of Wight with agents, fearing that if this group realised we knew they were on the Island, they would simply disappear one night, and we might never find them again. But time is running short, ma'am, and we must reconsider how best to gain the evidence we need, and flush out every member of this traitorous society.

To that end, I wish you to meet Mr Dundas, His Majesty's principal secretary of state for the Home department. He will be in Portsmouth next week throughout the celebrations for Howe's great triumph over the French. Mr Reevers will inform you which day has been decided upon; he and Mr East are also to attend the meeting, when Mr Dundas will make a decision based on the information gathered so far. It may mean putting large numbers of agents on the Island after all, but that is for Mr Dundas to decide.

I understand from Mr. Reevers that Richard Tanfield, who we believe to be involved with Mr. Hamerton, is well known to you all. Nevertheless, I am certain I can rely on you to set friendship aside and do what is right. Indeed, England's very survival may depend on it.

I am greatly obliged to you for your co-operation and courage in this business. I have reports on Mr. Hamerton from Mr. Reevers and Mr. East, but I would be grateful for your opinion too. The messenger will bring it to me at once, and I must strongly emphasise the need for haste now.

He ended with the usual pleasantries, and when I had finished reading I folded the letter and asked Mr. Reevers if he knew was in it. 'I do,' he said.

'Must I go to Portsmouth? Leaving the Island for a week when there is so little time to find these Fat Badgers doesn't seem wise to me.'

'Nor does ignoring an order from the man running the country. I have never done so myself. It always seemed a trifle ill-advised, and I doubt a spell in the Tower of London would appeal to you.'

A gentle smile played on his lips, a smile I had seen so many times before that I almost smiled back. Instead I turned away, put the letter into my pocket and said I hadn't thought of it like that, and naturally I would go. 'I will write to the "George" today and bespeak rooms. I'm sure my uncle will escort me.'

'I doubt you'll find rooms at the "George." The messenger tells me there's not a bed to be had in Portsmouth under twenty guineas a night while the celebrations are on. But a friend of mine has a house that would suit you very well, and he'll be in London that week. I'll ask him, but please don't mention it to anyone or the poor fellow will be besieged with offers.'

I gave him my promise and hurriedly lowered my eyes, for he was looking at me in a way that turned my knees to water. And I babbled, 'Where will you and Mr. East be staying?'

'At Government House. Mr. Pitt has arranged rooms

for us.'

'You must be highly thought of.'

'With Pitt, quite possibly. I wish it was the same with you.'

'Yes, I'm sure you do,' I retorted, unable to keep the bitterness out of my voice.

Instantly he moved closer and begged, 'For pity's sake Drusilla, tell me what I've done.'

I brushed that aside with a dismissive gesture. 'I'm afraid you must excuse me. I have to write that report Mr. Pitt wants on Mr. Hamerton.'

I went to reach for the bell pull for Luffe to see him out, but he was there before me, standing in the way. 'You knew I meant to make you an offer yesterday, and your demeanour the day before led me to believe I could expect a favourable response. I've spent half the night racking my brains trying to recall what I could have said or done since then to cause you to put this brick wall between us, and I cannot think of a thing. Even a condemned man knows what crime he is accused of. Am I not at least entitled to that courtesy?'

We were standing only a foot or so apart, and although I knew he did not truly care for me, I saw only pain and bafflement in his eyes. And despite everything I had learnt, my feelings for him were such that I longed, even now, to feel his arms around me. I told myself that would pass, and it would be easier once he realised he had no chance with me. Taking a deep breath I said in a suffocating voice, 'Very well Mr Reevers. If you must know, I------'

He was interrupted by Mr. Hamerton entering the room. 'I thought I saw you riding up to the house, Mr. Reevers. There's something I----'

Mr Reevers spoke with an intensity I had never heard before. 'Later, if you please. Lady Drusilla and I are discussing an urgent private matter.'

Mr. Hamerton looked from Mr Reevers to me and back again. 'Yes, of course. I do beg your pardon. Later, then.' But as he headed for the door, my uncle entered the room, and I heard Mr Reevers groan.

My uncle smiled benevolently at us all. 'Goodness, everyone is about very early today.'

Pulling himself together, Mr Reevers explained why he had called at such a time. 'Howe's great naval victory over the French is to be celebrated in Portsmouth next week. The King and Queen, and other members of the Royal Family will be there, along with ministers----'

'Is Mr Pitt going?' I asked.

His eyes rested on me with an expression that almost undid me. 'Probably not. Affairs of state are rather critical at present. But Dundas, Chatham and some others will attend, and----'

'Dundas and Chatham, eh?' my uncle said. 'I met them when we lived in London. Pleasant fellows. They used to call Pitt's elder brother the late Chatham, I remember --- as he was never on time for anything.'

'They still do,' Mr Reevers said. 'He has a great brain but finds it more restful not to use it.'

My uncle chuckled. 'Yes, so I've heard. Still, as First Sea Lord he must use it now, surely. And Dundas is an able minister.'

'The Home department suits him,' Mr Reevers agreed. 'He's very involved too with the secret committee whose job it is to report on the corresponding societies.'

'Is there to be a review of the fleet?' Mr. Hamerton inquired with interest.

'I believe so,' Mr Reevers responded. 'And a big celebration dinner with Howe, the ministers, admirals, captains, and local dignitaries. The King is staying four days.'

'In that case,' my uncle said, turning to me, 'shall we go over and join in the fun, Drusilla? I'm sure your aunt will want to go.'

'That's an excellent idea, Uncle.' I was grateful not to have to find an excuse for going to Portsmouth, but he gazed at me for a long moment, his eyes narrowing in concern. It was never easy to fool my uncle, he always saw what my aunt did not, and he knew I was upset.

When my aunt joined us, eager to learn what all the fuss was about, she needed no persuasion to go to Portsmouth. With so many of us gathered in the library, Mr Reevers gave up all further attempts to speak to me alone. Instead, he asked Mr. Hamerton what he had wanted to speak to him about earlier, and was told, 'I'm planning a dinner party shortly after I move into my new house. I should very much like you and Mr. East to be there.'

An invitation Mr. Reevers accepted, saying all that was proper. A little later I watched him ride off until he was out of sight, conscious only of what might have been, and discovered I'd dug my fingernails into the palms so deeply, I'd drawn blood. As I gazed at my hands tears slowly trickling down my cheeks. How was I going to stop my heart leaping at the sight of him? Marguerite's letter ought to have made that easy, but it had not.

I reminded myself I didn't want to marry, that it was

better this way, and I would remain in control of Westfleet and my own life. But, that prospect, once so vitally important, no longer had the same appeal, somehow. In desperation I told myself how much I loathed, hated and despised him. The difficulty with that was, I did not know how I was going to live without him.

CHAPTER 23

I went back into the workroom to write the report Mr. Pitt urgently wanted on Mr. Hamerton. His belief that Mr. Hamerton would relax at Westfleet had proved sound, for I was sure he had. But, as Mr. Pitt had said in his letter, time was running out. August, the month the King usually went to Weymouth, was barely five weeks away. And a decision had to made. If Mr. Hamerton was to be arrested, the information I gave Mr. Pitt had to be absolutely correct.

I wrote down my opinion of his character, the manner in which he had conducted himself at Westfleet, and every tiny detail I had discovered about him. In conversation he had not put a foot wrong. He spoke, and sounded, like any other patriotic English gentleman who, above all things, wanted to see England triumph over France. Some of his actions, however, seemed far from innocent. He'd asked Blackgang smugglers to take a letter to Paris, I thought he was going to shoot me when he appeared on the cliff top after I was attacked, and he'd met Mr. Silver at Westfleet church in the dead of night.

I studied the wall chart I'd made in his name, showing the details that were not in question. John Hamerton was a widower, whose sister's husband was close to Robespierre. His wife had been knocked down in the street, and the aristocrat responsible was later murdered. He'd attended a London Corresponding Society meeting, and arrived late in Windsor just after the assassination attempt on the King. Those were the facts, and facts did not lie.

Beside his chart was the information Mr. Pitt had given me on Mr Brown. This traitor, spying for the French, had set up the Fat Badger Corresponding Society in order to start a French-style revolution in England. To which I'd added that Septimus believed Mr Brown was an English gentleman living in London. I expected such a man to appear to be patriotic, to know France well, and to speak their language fluently. As Mr. Hamerton did.

Twice these fanatics had tried to kill me. First on the cliff top, and then during an apparent highway robbery. And I still did not know why they wanted me dead. Septimus, and George Jenkins, who joined the group believing their aim was peaceful electoral reform, were murdered in cold blood when they refused to be involved in assassination. And Mrs. Jenkins, fearing for the lives of her children, had fled to the mainland.

I studied every piece of evidence I had, reading Septimus's journal again, and the letters from Mr. Pitt and Mrs. Jenkins. But if the proof was there I could not see it. There being nothing more I could add, I read it through carefully, and signed it. If only I'd found something that would stand up in a court of law; something that would prove beyond doubt whether or not John Hamerton was Mr. Brown. That was what Mr. Pitt desperately needed, and as I'd failed to find it, I could not expect him to offer me another chance to work for him now. What with that, and the situation with Mr Reevers, I was at a very low ebb.

The report had to go via the special messenger, and I made up my mind to deliver it to Mr Reevers myself. He'd promised to collect it the following morning, but I knew he would find some means of speaking to me alone. As he would do if I took it to Norton House escorted by my uncle. I had too much to do to allow myself to be distracted again; my own problems must wait, and I decided to go to Norton House alone.

Of course, if it ever got out that I had called on a gentleman without an escort, local society would be outraged. Aunt Thirza and Mr Upton would not hold back in their condemnation, while even Julia and my uncle would be shocked at such forwardness. Tongues would wag for months. Yet, unable to see any other way, I had to risk the scandal.

Naturally I would not enter the house, so there was nothing anyone could object to, and I intended to leave Westfleet under the pretence of going for a ride. My aunt had gone to see Mrs. Woodford, my uncle was engrossed in a book in the library, and I'd sent Mudd on an errand to Newport. No-one could possibly know where I was going.

Thus, I sealed the letter, wrapped it in some oilcloth in case it rained, which judging by the darkening sky looked all too likely. Then I strolled down to the stables, had Orlando saddled and rode off towards Norton House.

Stopping at the top of the Down to watch a frigate sailing out to sea, I glanced up at the sky, grimacing at the heavy black clouds racing in from the west. I felt the first spots of rain half a mile from Norton House. Spots that rapidly turned into a torrent, and I arrived at the house drenched to the skin. The sun came out again as I slipped from the saddle, and hanging on to the reins, I knocked on the door, which was promptly opened by the butler.

Finch had been butler at Norton House since I was a child, and I knew him well from the time when the house was occupied by other members of the Saxborough family. 'Good morning, Finch,' I said cheerfully. 'I trust you are well.'

'Yes, thank you, my lady.'

'And Mrs. Finch?' She was the housekeeper.

He looked around for my escort, and seeing none, eyed me suspiciously. 'She's well enough, my lady.'

'I'm glad to hear it,' I said, and inquired in a cheerful unconcerned manner, 'Is Mr Reevers at home?'

He hesitated. 'Well, he is, my lady, but-----'

'In that case be good enough to ask him if he'd step outside. I shan't keep him above a minute.' Ignoring the reproach in Finch's eyes I urged, 'Do hurry, Finch. I'm very wet.'

Grumbling that he didn't know what the world was coming to, he turned and walked off. Mr Reevers soon came striding out, his brow a trifle furrowed. 'Good God, you're absolutely soaked. I wish I could ask you inside to dry off, but I suppose it wouldn't do. Mrs Finch doesn't miss a thing.' And he cast a swift glance behind him, as if expecting the housekeeper to appear. When he saw she wasn't in sight, he mopped his brow with a handkerchief in mock relief, and it was all I could do not to laugh.

Forcibly reminding myself he was only interested in my fortune, I gave him my report saying in my primmest voice, 'I find I have to go out tomorrow morning, and I wanted to hand this to you myself.'

Thanking me, he promised the messenger would take it to Mr Pitt straightaway, and inquired, 'Tell me, are you in the habit of visiting a gentleman's residence alone?'

'Only when it rains.' He gave an appreciative chuckle and I said, 'I really must go.'

I used the mounting block to get back onto Orlando and he murmured, 'Yes, I suppose you better had. I wish I could believe you hadn't planned it this way. When we are in Portsmouth I mean to hold one conversation with you in a situation that won't ruin your reputation, and where we won't be interrupted.'

Unable to trust myself to speak, I headed back down the drive, all too conscious that he was still watching me. On reaching the Downs, I rode Orlando hard, uncaring of the showers, and cursing the fact that I had ever set eyes on Radleigh Reevers. Uncaring too that I had promised my aunt never to venture out alone again.

In the morning, eager to be out of the house in case Mr Reevers called, I set off after breakfast to visit my tenants, to ensure all was well before I left for Portsmouth. There was a new baby to admire, and a wedding in the offing, but no urgent problems, and I came home with a smile on my face. I enjoyed looking after my small estate, and back at Westfleet, I went into the library to add the name of the new baby in the book where I kept the details of all my tenants. Only to find my uncle entertaining Mr. Reevers and Mr. East. They rose and bowed as I entered and relieved that Mr. Reevers had not come here alone, I greeted them in a relaxed manner. There being no sign of my aunt I asked my uncle if she had gone out.

He shook his head. 'I'm afraid she's feeling under the weather and has decided to stay in bed.' My heart sank, for if she was unwell and could not go to Portsmouth, my uncle would not leave her, and I could not go without a proper chaperone. 'Don't worry,' he said, correctly interpreting my fears. 'It's just a cold. But I hope you don't want the servants to do anything in particular at the moment.'

'Why?' I asked, puzzled.

'Well, I'm afraid your aunt is keeping them very busy,' he informed me with a chuckle. 'After breakfast she fancied a hot lemon drink, then a glass of water, her favourite shawl, her spectacles, and a window had to be opened. Now she has everyone searching for a book she swears she's left in the blue salon, but which cannot be found.'

'Oh dear,' I smiled, thankfully aware it meant she was not really ill. But one problem was soon solved, when Luffe came in a few minutes later with the book, informing my uncle he'd found it in the music room. Thanking Luffe, my uncle said if we would excuse him he would return it to her now.

Once he'd shut the door, Mr. East explained the reason for their visit. 'We thought it sensible to have a discussion about Hamerton before we go to Portsmouth, ma'am. In case we've missed anything that would give us the proof we need.'

'Well, if there is proof,' I said with a sigh, 'I haven't been able to find it. And I don't think Mr. Hamerton has met Mr. Silver since he went to the churchyard that night. Sometimes he's out late observing the moths, but that's all.' I was not sleeping well and had no difficulty staying awake until one o'clock, but I was not going to admit that in front of Mr. Reevers.

'We have a man watching the church,' Mr. Reevers said. 'But he's seen nothing. Except Mr. Sims arriving home late most nights. I wonder what keeps him out until one or two in the morning?'

I gave a shrug of indifference, for as Mr. East rightly said it was Mr. Hamerton we had to concentrate on. We went through all the facts again, but it didn't help, and Mr. Reevers said, 'The only thing we are certain of, is that the assassination is set for August.'

'We wouldn't know that,' Mr. East commented, 'if you hadn't found Septimus's journal, ma'am. The sad thing is, if George Jenkins hadn't gone back into the inn to collect his gloves that night, he wouldn't have overheard what Mr. Brown's aim really was, and he and Septimus would still be alive. And with their help every member of that murderous society would be under arrest by now.' He suddenly crashed his right fist into his left palm. 'We must settle this business before August. We absolutely must.'

'What I still don't understand,' I said, referring to the question that had puzzled me from the beginning, 'is that, if this assassination attempt has been planned for August all along, why did they try to kill the King in Windsor? It doesn't make any sense.'

Mr. Reevers lifted his shoulders a little. 'In my experience revolutionaries are rarely guided by sense and logic.'

'They certainly aren't in France,' I muttered, thinking of those poor souls being guillotined for complaining about the price of bread, or that life was better under the King. And I asked if they knew the exact date the King would set out for Weymouth.

'We should find out in Portsmouth,' Mr. East said. 'Everything that can be done to guard him in Weymouth will be done. You can be very sure of that.'

My uncle came back into the room then, informing me I was barred from entering my aunt's bedchamber, as she didn't want me to catch her cold. 'Don't feel too badly about it, Drusilla. I have been barred too.' I laughed and he said, 'Still, she informs me she will be quite all right by Wednesday.' I prayed he was right. Whatever happened, I had to keep my appointment with Mr Dundas, the Minister of the Home Department.

Mr. Reevers made no attempt to speak to me alone, no doubt aware I would refuse. Tomorrow they were leaving for Portsmouth, a day ahead of us. There he would insist on being told why my feelings for him had changed. And that would be the end of it all, I thought miserably.

After dinner my uncle and I enjoyed an excellent game of chess, then I went for a stroll outside. On my way out, Luffe informed me Richard had called to see Mr. Hamerton and that they were in the garden. I nodded and took the opportunity to tell him I was very pleased with the way he was handling his new job. I saw the relief in his eyes. 'Thank you, my lady.'

I wandered along the paths through the flower beds, admiring the spectacular display of foxgloves, and the sight of a beautiful sunset. Reaching the walled garden, I was about to open the gate to go in when I heard Richard and Mr. Hamerton talking. I guessed they were sitting on the seat situated near to the gate. Not wanting to interrupt them, and needing to be on my own, I was about to go off in another direction when I heard Richard ask, 'So we are to go ahead in August as planned?'

'Yes, it's all set,' Mr. Hamerton answered. 'The letter

Silver brought back from Paris says that date fits in perfectly with Robespierre's plans.'

'Good. Well, you can count on me.' I stuffed my fingers into my mouth to stop myself crying out in protest.

'Are you sure, Richard? You have much more to lose than me. Julia, Edward and----'

'I am very sure. It's the only thing to do while this wretched government remains in power. The sooner it is overthrown the better.'

'If we're caught it means execution.'

'As it will if I'm court-martialled for cowardice and found guilty. That's judicial murder too,' Richard sneered bitterly. 'So where's the difference?'

'You may not be court-martialled.'

'Oh, I will be, believe me. But not until the autumn, I'm told. Time enough for us to do what we both believe to be right. I shall rid England of that wretched tyrant, or die in the attempt.' I heard sounds of movement and Richard said, 'I'd better go or Julia will wonder what has become of me.'

I was terrified they would come out of the gate and see me, but thankfully they walked off towards the house, talking about the yacht Mr. Hamerton had now bought. I leant against the outside wall, grateful for its solid support, as the conversation I'd heard echoed relentlessly over and over in my mind. Closing my eyes, I thought of the unendurable strain Richard had been under recently. Threatened with a court martial on a charge of cowardice and failing to obey a direct order, yet unable to do anything about it, except wait, for week after week. No man should suffer such torture.

Richard knew himself to be innocent, yet expected to be found guilty. A verdict that almost certainly meant execution - judicial murder, he'd called it – and Richard hated injustice with a fierce passion. To him, matters were either right or wrong; he didn't believe in half measures.

A coward would have run away, or left the country to escape justice. Richard, however, had stayed to face it. He was not a coward, but these charges had made him lose faith in everything he'd ever believed in. Clearly he saw no way out. Yet, I would have sworn he'd die rather than turn to the French, for he was fiercely patriotic. But Mr. Hamerton had talked of going ahead in August, and Richard of ridding England of 'that wretched tyrant.' Tyrant was a term the French had used for Louis XV1, even as he climbed the steps to the guillotine. And I put my head in my hands and groaned.

Mr. Pitt had wanted me to find out if Mr. Hamerton was a French agent, and in doing so, I had discovered what I could not bear to be true. And, having learnt of it, I had no choice but to inform Mr. Pitt. No choice at all. For England's very survival was at stake.

CHAPTER 24

Richard and Mr. Hamerton were sailing to Portsmouth on the morning tide. Mr. Reevers and Mr. East, who were to keep watch on them on the mainland, were also leaving tomorrow. It was getting dark, and I went back indoors, intending to go into the workroom to write down what I'd overheard. But when I walked into the hall my uncle came out of the drawing room.

'Ah, there you are Drusilla,' he beamed, and begged me to join him. Shutting the door behind us, he said, 'Mr. Reevers stopped by briefly to confirm the arrangements for our stay in Portsmouth. He did ask for you, but I had no idea where you were, and he was in a hurry.'

'Was Mr. East with him?'

'No. He's gone to take his leave of Miss. Adams,' he replied with a grin. 'Your aunt confidently predicts wedding bells.'

I smiled. 'More than likely.' But, afraid my uncle would ask if I had wedding plans too, I quickly changed the subject, inquiring where we were to stay in Portsmouth.

He told me the address and said, 'The gentleman who owns the house asks only that we don't speak of the arrangement. Apparently he has already turned down several requests from other friends and acquaintances, and wishes to avoid the embarrassment of these people hearing of it. He is in London on business this week and says his servants will look after us. There will be room for the three of us, as well as Mr. Hamerton and Richard.'

'Do they know?' I asked as casually as I could.

'Indeed they do. They both accepted eagerly, preferring to sleep in a house rather than on the yacht. And the house is in the perfect position for watching the procession on Friday.'

'What procession is that?'

The lack of interest in my voice made him ask, 'Drusilla, is something wrong?'

'Oh, I'm just rather tired, that's all.' And I said brightly, 'Tell me about this procession.'

He gave me a searching look, but did as I asked. 'Well, the King is to hold a levee at Government House to honour those brave officers involved in Howe's great Naval Victory. The top government ministers, local nobility, dignitaries and others will also attend. He will drive from the Dockyard through the streets so that the people can see him. And we will have a grand view of it all from an upstairs room in the house itself.'

'That sounds most agreeable.'

He broke into a smile. 'I was sure you would think so.'

'If we are still able to go to Portsmouth,' I said, thinking of Aunt Thirza.

He lifted his shoulders a little. 'Your aunt is determined to do so.'

'How is she today?'

'She was still sneezing when I was allowed a glimpse of her from the doorway this morning, but she informed me that would stop by this afternoon, when she intended to get up.'

That made me laugh. 'I hope she's right.' And that my uncle doesn't catch it, I thought. For no-one else could escort me on this trip, and I had to go, no matter what happened.

We talked for so long about the arrangements and Howe's victory, that I never did go back to the workroom. Overwhelmed by tiredness, heartache and distress, I went up to bed, where unable to stop myself going over what I'd overheard, I tossed and turned until I eventually fell asleep through sheer exhaustion.

Mr. Hamerton had already left when I went down to breakfast. Once I'd eaten and dealt with the usual household matters, I went for a ride, accompanied by Mudd. It was a lovely morning with the Island looking at its very best. I rode across Hokewell Down to Dittistone and onto Hodes Down, from where I had a perfect view of the boats going about their business in the Solent, while the sunshine and delicious smell of the tangy sea air began to restore just a little of my usual optimism.

I rode back along the cliff top and knowing that I must call on Julia before going to Portsmouth, no matter how much I dreaded it, I made my way up Breighton hill. As Mudd led Orlando off to the stables, I saw Julia on the terrace, and when I joined her, she said a little wistfully, 'I wish I could see the celebrations too. But Richard is right, it would be unwise in my present situation. And I wouldn't want to leave Edward for so long.'

'There will be other occasions,' I sympathised.

We were still talking of Howe's great victory when she suddenly asked in great concern, 'What's wrong, Drusilla? It's obvious something has upset you.'

If only, I thought, I could learn to hide my feelings, for she knew me too well to be taken in by any explanation that did not justify the devastation she obviously saw. I could not, and would not, tell her what I'd heard Richard say. Nor could I bear to think what his involvement with Mr. Hamerton's schemes would do to those I loved so dearly. I quickly shrugged it off by saying, 'Nothing of any consequence. Do let us talk of----'

'Not until you tell me what's happened. The last time I saw that look on your face was when your dear father died.' Unable to speak, I dismissed that with a wave of my hand, but it didn't stop her. 'Have you quarrelled with Mr Reevers?'

'Mr Reevers means nothing to me.' I tried to keep the bitterness out of my voice and failed miserably. In the end I said what I knew would satisfy her. 'If you must know---- I have discovered he is a - a - fortune hunter,' I said, barely able to utter those ugly words. And I told her about my godmother's letter.

'I see,' she said in a hollow voice. And suggested hopefully, 'She might be mistaken.'

'She said Giles admitted it was true.'

Julia gazed down at her hands for a moment or two, for she knew as well as I did, that fact settled the matter. 'What does Mr Reevers say?'

'I haven't spoken to him about it,' I whispered in a suffocating voice.

'But, surely,' she protested, 'you ought to give him a chance to put his side.'

'He would only deny it.' I took a deep breath. 'I could not bear to marry and then find that he – he – did not care for me.' I saw the distress in her eyes and went on bleakly, 'I shall never marry now. I've made up my mind once and for all. Life will go on and I will get over it.' And desperate to talk of something else, I told her I'd also had a letter from Mrs. Jenkins.

Accepting the change of subject with obvious reluctance, she asked, 'Is she back on the Island now?'

'No. She won't return until these villains are caught.'

'Very sensible,' she said in approval. 'In fact I was saying to Mr. East only the other day that if Edward's life was threatened, I would do absolutely anything to safeguard him. Anything at all. But he believes Mrs. Jenkins and her children will be perfectly safe in Wickham with her brother, because she's done exactly what those wretched murderers told her to do.'

'I'm sure he's right,' I agreed rather absently, our discussion about Mr. Reevers having left my emotions in utter turmoil again.

Julia asked what else was in the letter. 'Did she know anything about the Fat Badgers?'

'A little. The man I shot was Mr. Ruby. She described that dreadful scar down his cheek and said her husband hadn't liked him because he spoke the kind of language criminals used.'

'Well, if he killed Septimus I'm glad he's dead. I wish they all were.' She went on talking about her brother, and knowing how much she missed him, I tried to put Mr. Reevers from my mind. After a while I steered the conversation onto Edward and she made me laugh with the tale of how she'd watched him following a frog, imitating its movement and croaking.

Back at Westfleet, Aunt Thirza joined us for the midday meal, when I learned she had also come down to breakfast. Apart from a red and rather sore nose, she seemed much better.

'I haven't sneezed since yesterday afternoon,' she

told me, 'and I am feeling very much more the thing.' In fact she was so much her old self again that when she complained the kitchen cat had left two dead birds on the doorstep, that Luffe's shoes still squeaked, and the small print in "The Times" had become impossible to read, I merely smiled. For it meant she was back to normal and our trip could go ahead.

'Charles, I should like to go out for a drive this afternoon,' she declared, picking out an orange from the selection of fruit.

'Are you sure you're well enough,' he asked anxiously.

'It was just a cold, which has gone,' she informed him. 'I am quite recovered now.'

The carriage was ordered and after watching them bowl down the drive, I spoke to Gray, my maid, instructing her on what to pack for the visit to Portsmouth. Which, with our uncertain climate meant taking clothes suitable for the heat, cold and rain. Tomorrow we planned to ride to Cowes, stay overnight, leave the horses at the stables until our return, and set off early Wednesday morning for Portsmouth.

With that settled I intended to go into the workroom, knowing I must write down what I'd overheard yesterday evening, no matter how hard I found it. But as I walked across the hall I saw Luffe admit Mr. Upton and Mr. Sims into the house. I cursed under my breath, for I had no choice but to invite them into the drawing room, where I learned they had come to inquire after my aunt's health.

Mr Upton said, 'We would have called before, but I couldn't risk Francis catching a cold. He's still very vulnerable, you know. The last thing he needs is a setback.'

Mr Sims protested, 'I am much better now, Uncle. I don't think a cold would hurt me.'

'Well, perhaps not. But we can't take any chances. Am I not right, Lady Drusilla?'

'In my view you cannot be too careful,' I agreed, aware that it wasn't concern for his nephew that had stopped him calling at Westfleet, but fear of catching the cold himself. I hoped that worry would shorten his visit, but he could never speak of illness without detailing all his own ailments, and those of his wife. Having listened politely to the state of the boils on his neck, and the suffering Mrs Upton was obliged to endure because of her chilblains, I was seriously considering pretending to sneeze, when he said it was time they were leaving.

'I told Francis we mustn't stay long,' Mr Upton announced piously. 'But we couldn't let you go off to Portsmouth without wishing you well on your trip.'

I thanked him courteously and when I rang for Luffe to see them out, Mr. Sims said, 'As a matter of fact Lady Drusilla, I expect to be in Portsmouth myself. My friend in Dittistone is eager to see the celebrations and wishes me to accompany him.'

Mr. Upton frowned in disapproval. 'I thought we'd agreed that would be most unwise in your state of health.'

'I have already accepted his invitation,' he said pleasantly. 'As for my health, I have never felt better. Which I am sure is entirely due to the fresh air on this lovely island.'

Watching them leave, I wondered who Mr. Sims was

really going to Portsmouth with, and wished I could be at the parsonage when they heard of his association with Mr. Young. But I didn't dwell on it, having far more serious matters to think about. Crossing the hall to the workroom I told Luffe I was not to be disturbed until it was time to dress for dinner.

First I did what was hardest for me. On Mr. Hamerton's chart I wrote down the conversation I'd overheard between him and Richard, and sat absently tapping my pen on the desk, going over it all.

I thought too about a couple of other remarks made in conversation recently that had puzzled me. And going back to Mr. Hamerton's wall chart I carefully checked those remarks with the evidence I had already written down.

Then I walked over to the window and stood watching the trees swaying in the breeze, considering all these facts for a very long time. For, at long last, I began to see what had really happened, and how it all fitted together. From the start everything had pointed to Mr. Hamerton being Mr. Brown. But father had taught me never to make assumptions, always to keep an open mind, until I found conclusive evidence, one way or the other.

When researching for his book, naturally we came across a few crimes over the centuries. Of those where we found proof, most obvious suspects were every bit as evil as they had appeared. But one or two were completely innocent. Two days ago, writing my report for Mr. Pitt, I had not been absolutely sure which Mr. Hamerton was.

But what I had heard since then left me in no doubt. I'd needed conclusive proof and now I was sure I had it. I saw why the Fat Badgers had made that assassination attempt in Windsor, why Mr. Hamerton had arrived late that day, and how blatantly he had lied about losing touch with his sister.

When Mr. Pitt asked me to find out whether or not Mr. Hamerton was Mr. Brown, he'd said no spy could watch what he said all the time. And he was right.

Now I had the vital evidence Mr. Pitt desperately needed, but I couldn't send it to him because his special messenger was in Portsmouth with Mr. Reevers and Mr. East. Besides he'd given Mr. Dundas the task of deciding what to do next about the Fat Badgers, therefore it made sense to hand him the information when I reached Portsmouth.

Knowing I dare not waste any more time, I took a sheet of writing paper, picked up my pen, dipped it in the ink, and wrote those crucial words. For, I also saw why there would be a third attempt on my life. The unpalatable truth, which I had to face, was that I might not be so lucky next time.

I finished it in good time to dress for dinner, then decided to make two copies for myself. One I would leave where it could easily be found. But, in case that got into the wrong hands, I would hide the other one, making sure Mudd knew where it was. Aware of the need for haste, it was hard to concentrate on anything else over dinner, but I tried to take an interest when I learnt my aunt and uncle had visited Ledstone Place on their afternoon drive. 'Your aunt insisted on going. I'm not quite sure why,' he said, winking at me.

Aunt Thirza clicked her tongue. 'I went Charles, as you very well know, to make sure the house is being kept in good order. Lucie and Giles will be back soon.'

'Not for three weeks, surely?' Their daughter had been away for three months, and I knew how much they both missed her.

'Yes, but in my experience Drusilla, servants become slovenly unless someone keeps them up to the mark.'

'Doesn't Giles's steward see to all that?'

She sniffed. 'A man doesn't look at a house in the same way as a woman.'

I was tempted to ask if she'd found any dust or dirt, but thought better of it. For, I had already detected a tone of criticism in her voice that did not bode well for me, and sure enough, the instant the servants left the room she fired the first broadside.

'Mrs. Finch was visiting her sister at Ledstone today,' she began in an ominous voice. The housekeeper at Norton House often visited her sister, who was housekeeper at Ledstone. 'She informed me you called on Mr Reevers the other day without an escort of any kind. Not even a groom.' I did not answer. 'She felt I should give you a hint that such behaviour was not at all the thing. As if you didn't know that perfectly well. Whatever possessed you, Drusilla?'

'I cannot see what there is to fuss about. I didn't go inside.'

'I should hope not,' she said in a shocked voice. 'But Mrs Finch said you were soaked to the skin, and----'

'I got caught in a heavy downpour.'

'All the more reason to go straight home. I am told your clothes were clinging to you.'

'Wet clothes usually do, Aunt.' My uncle choked, quickly turning it into a cough, but my aunt was not fooled. 'It is not funny, Charles. This could ruin Drusilla's reputation.'

At which point my patience deserted me. 'Oh, for heaven's sake, Aunt.'

'Reputations have been lost for less.'

'I am twenty-seven. Not a young girl.'

'Let me tell you, you'll never get a husband if you go on like that.'

'I don't want a husband.' And unaccountably I felt the sting of tears in my eyes. Reaching for my glass, I drained the contents and the moment passed. 'I shall never marry, Aunt.'

'Well, I cannot imagine what made you go to Norton House. But if that's the sort of behaviour Mr. Reevers encourages,' Aunt Thirza sniffed, 'the sooner he goes back to London the better.' Words that almost overset me. I longed for him to go out of my life, yet dreaded it at the same time.

After dinner I slipped into the workroom, made the two copies of my report, putting one with my other important documents, and the second in the most obscure of the three secret drawers in my father's desk. Then I took a stroll round the garden in the fading light.

Approaching the stables I decided to acquaint Mudd with the details of what was in my report, and where to find it. Then I remembered, as he was accompanying us to Portsmouth tomorrow, I'd given him permission to visit his father this evening. Still, I thought, the morning would do as well. With Mr. Hamerton in Portsmouth, I was safe enough tonight.

I was so tired I fell asleep almost at once and did not wake until Gray drew the curtains back at seven. I got up at once, for this afternoon we were going to Cowes, staying overnight, in order to sail on the early tide for

Portsmouth, and I had a great deal to do first. As I walked downstairs I saw Fisher, one of the grooms, talking agitatedly to Luffe.

'Is something wrong?' I demanded at once.

Fisher turned to me. 'It's Mudd, my lady. His bed hasn't been slept in. And his horse came back to the stables ten minutes ago.'

I stared at him, too shocked to speak, realising at once that if Mudd had suffered an accident on his way home last night, his horse would have come back hours ago. Which meant someone had kept his horse overnight and deliberately released it this morning. Someone who wanted me to know Mudd had disappeared. And that it wasn't an accident.

CHAPTER 25

I had expected the Fat Badgers to make another attempt on my life, but never imagined they would do anything like this. I'd warned Mudd that assisting me could be dangerous but, in truth, I thought that, as a servant, he would be safe enough.

Fisher stood waiting for orders, and pulling myself together I told him, 'Mudd is out there somewhere and I intend to find him. I want every man who can ride to be ready in ten minutes. I'll come down to the stables then and organise the search.'

'Very good, my lady. Will you be coming with us?'

'Not until I have seen Mudd's father.' I was not looking forward to that. He had every right to expect his son to be safe at Westfleet Manor.

Fisher ran off to the stables and Luffe asked if I meant to have breakfast first. I shook my head. 'I couldn't eat a thing.'

'He might have taken a tumble and been injured, my lady.'

I wanted to believe that myself, but I knew it wasn't true for, as I told Luffe, 'If he had, his horse would have come back last night.' They had deliberately kept the horse back until this morning so I would know who was behind it and what they had done. They wanted me to look for him, which meant this was probably a trap.

Mr. Hamerton had, of course, been here last night when the abduction had taken place. But he'd stayed with the Tanfields overnight, as he and Richard were leaving for Portsmouth on the early morning tide. And they would be well on their way now.

My uncle, hearing sounds of great activity, soon joined me. When he learnt what had happened he insisted on coming with me to see Mudd's father, for which I was most grateful.

'It's a pity Mr. Reevers and Mr. East aren't here,' he said, putting a comforting hand on my arm. 'But don't despair, my dear. Mudd may still be alive.'

The compassion in his voice made me choke up. 'If they've murdered him too I don't know how I shall ever bear it. I'll never forgive myself ---- never.'

He went to tell my aunt what we were doing, and to change into riding clothes, while I hurried down to the stables to organise the grooms. I sent them in pairs to search the Downs between here and where Mudd's father lived at Dittistone, and along the cliff top to check the beach. I told them where I would be if they found Mudd, or had news of him. Otherwise I would meet them later at Dittistone Bay.

My uncle and I were soon ready to leave. He brought a pair of duelling pistols with him and the discovery that my mild-mannered, kindly uncle actually owned such weapons made me forget my fears for a brief moment. 'When did you ever fight a duel?'

'Oh, I haven't. But, when we married, your aunt insisted I should be prepared, in case I was ever called out.'

I shook my head at him in amused disbelief. 'You wouldn't have gone.'

'No, you're right, I wouldn't. I've always thought it a ridiculous way to settle an argument. But don't tell her that. I would hate her to think I was a coward.'

'As if she would,' I protested. 'As if anyone would.' How could they, when he'd stayed in France while the revolution raged around him, and later spent months in a French prison?

When we reached the cottage where Mudd's father lived, we found him outside tending his vegetable patch. I dismounted and handed Orlando's reins to my uncle, who waited by the gate. Mudd senior saw from my face that something was very wrong, and I sat with him on the small bench that leant against the cottage wall, gently explaining what little I knew. Then I asked, 'What time did John leave you last night?'

His hands shook as he said, 'It was before ten, my lady. He rode off towards the Downs, same as usual. I watched him go.' He turned to me, fear in his eyes. 'What can have become of him?'

I didn't know how to answer him. He was an old man now and my groom was his only son. All I could do was to assure him, 'Every groom at Westfleet is out looking for him. I'll speak to the constable and then join the search myself. I promise you we'll find him.' I prayed it was a promise I could keep. And that he would be alive.

'I'm grateful, my lady.' Tears misted his eyes. 'I'll get my friends to help too.'

Most of his friends were smugglers and I encouraged, 'That's an excellent idea.' Smugglers frequently knew what was going on, and if they didn't, they had ways of finding out. 'They may have heard a whisper.'

'But what about your trip to Portsmouth, my lady? Weren't you leaving today?'

I turned to him, stunned by what he seemed to be suggesting. 'Do you really believe I would leave the Island when John is in such danger?'

'I know some as would. But not you, my lady. You'd never do that.'

A remark that suddenly made it very clear why Mudd had been kidnapped, but I said nothing, for it would not have helped. Rising to my feet, I promised to let him know the minute I had any news. 'Try not to worry too much,' I urged softly.

After speaking to the constable, who immediately set about his own investigation, my uncle and I rode down to Dittistone Bay, where the grooms were already gathered. I was not surprised to learn they had found no sign of Mudd.

When I told them I believed Mudd had been kidnapped, they looked at me in amazement, as well they might, but before they began asking awkward questions I hurried on. 'I want you to ask every local farmer to search his outbuildings.' I gave each pair specific areas, telling them to return to Westfleet afterwards. I didn't believe Mudd would be found in such a place, but I could not discount it either.

Watching the men ride off, my uncle asked, 'Are you quite sure he's been kidnapped, Drusilla?'

'I am. Mudd's father said he knew I wouldn't go to Portsmouth while his son was missing. He was right. And the Fat Badgers knew that too.' Killing Mudd might not stop me crossing the Solent. Fear that his life was in jeopardy, would.

My uncle asked the question that had hammered in my mind ever since I'd left Mudd senior. 'Yes, but why would they want to stop you going to Portsmouth?'

'I don't know. It doesn't make sense to me either.' Yet there had to be a reason. And instinct told me that if I found the answer to that, everything else would become clear.

In the next few hours I called on everyone I knew in Dittistone, praying someone had seen something. But no-one had. I went back to Mudd senior, to learn his smuggling friends were equally unaware. They had promised to help, and if anyone could find Mudd, I thought, they would.

At this point my uncle insisted we went home, for we hadn't eaten since last night, and as he rightly said, my aunt would be worried too. In any case, I needed to work out where to look next. I accepted Mudd would be hard to find. Otherwise kidnapping him would be a waste of time. Riding home, absently watching the shipping in the Solent, I suddenly burst out, 'Uncle, he could be on a boat.'

'Of course. Why didn't I think of that.'

'After we've eaten, we'll go to Yarmouth.'

On approaching Westfleet church, we saw the parson coming towards us, and I said, 'I'll ask Mr. Upton to help. You go home and tell cook we are famished.' He rode off, exchanging no more than a greeting with the parson.

I reined in and had barely started to explain the situation to Mr. Upton, when he interrupted testily, 'Lady Drusilla, the whole village knows Mudd is missing.'

'Then you'll understand why I need every man to help find him. If you and Mr. Sims----'

'You expect *me* to help in this farce?' he burst out, his face turning puce. 'I'm sorry ma'am, but I have more important things to do than search for a mere servant sleeping it off under some bush.'

Gritting my teeth, I seethed, 'Mudd has never been drunk in his life. And I would remind you Mr. Upton, the Bible teaches us that everyone is equal in God's eyes, and that includes servants. You would do well to practise what you preach.' And blinded by fury I urged Orlando on towards Westfleet Manor.

When I walked into the drawing room, Julia was sitting with my aunt. She jumped up on seeing me and begged, 'Is there any news?'

I shook my head, and my aunt anxiously demanded, 'Where's Charles?'

'Here I am, my dear,' he announced cheerfully, coming into the room. 'I've spoken to cook, Drusilla. She promises us a splendid meal.' Explaining to Julia, 'Drusilla and I have been out since before breakfast.'

I related what we had done that morning, and when Julia said her grooms were eager to help, I suggested they checked farm buildings to the east of Westfleet. I thanked her with real gratitude and she hurried off to give them their orders.

Over nuncheon, we talked of where Mudd might be held. I hoped my aunt would think of something we hadn't, but regrettably she didn't, and after we had eaten, my uncle and I set off for Yarmouth. I soon realised this was an impossible task, however, for there were boats all around the Island. Checking them would take weeks, and instinct told me we were wasting our time.

Riding home I prayed Mudd had been found, or someone had discovered a clue that would lead us to him. But, again, no-one had. Not even the smugglers, Mudd's father having sent a boy with a message to that effect. If they couldn't find out, what chance did I have?

During dinner Aunt Thirza spoke of what we had originally planned to do that day. 'We would have been in Cowes now,' she said wistfully. 'And in Portsmouth tomorrow.'

'You wouldn't want to go while Mudd is in the hands of those murderers,' my uncle chided gently.

'No, of course not. It's just that I was so looking forward to the treat.'

After dinner I walked round the garden, thinking. This kidnapping had been carefully planned, and Mudd taken to a place where he would not easily be found. That much was obvious. But where?

I thought for a very long time, only it did no good at all, and having promised Julia I would keep her informed, I decided to ride over to see her. When I told my aunt where I was going, she ordered, 'Take a groom with you.' But the grooms were busy catching up on what they had not been able to do during the day, so I went alone. It was only a mile.

I was approaching the parsonage when a horseman suddenly shot out from the thick tree-lined drive, causing Orlando to whinny. On seeing who it was, I burst out, 'Good God, Mr. Sims, you startled me.'

'I do beg your pardon, ma'am. I was about to call on you, so I'm glad to see you here as I am in the deuce of a hurry.' I looked at him in surprise and he went on, 'I have been out all day and only heard about Mudd an hour ago.'

'You know something?' I asked eagerly.

'Well, it may be nothing, but I did see a light in an empty house late last night.'

'Where?' I burst out, suddenly feeling breathless.

'I'll show you, ma'am. I'm going that way, but I must be in Yarmouth in an hour. I'm sailing to Portsmouth with Mr. Young.'

'At night, Mr. Sims?'

'Mr. Young enjoys night sailing, ma'am.'

'A reminder of his smuggling days, perhaps.'

'Undoubtedly, ma'am.' And his face broke into a smile. 'Will you ride with me?'

I didn't hesitate, and we raced along the cliff top to Dittistone in the fading twilight, not slowing until we reached the first house. It was only when we turned into a dark narrow lane that I recalled my father's warning about not acting on impulse. That I should always stop and think first. But Mr. Sims was the only person to offer even a glimmer of hope, and I'd jumped at the chance. I saw now how foolish that was.

In the first place I didn't know if Mr. Sims was involved with the Fat Badgers. His excuse, when seen out late at night, was his interest in the stars. Which, frankly, I did not believe, and he'd also lied to the Uptons, about spending his evenings in Dittistone with an academic friend. The friend was real enough, but his time was mostly spent with Mr. Young. Illness had supposedly brought him to the island, yet he seemed perfectly healthy to me, and I began to fear his short, skinny appearance had led me to underestimate his intelligence.

Then I thought of my groom, perhaps tied up and gagged, and knew I would take any risk to free him. For, he had been as certain in my life as the morning light, and every bit as reliable. He had never let me down, and never would. When I'd warned him of the danger he could be in by assisting me, he'd shrugged it aside as being irrelevant. But it wasn't irrelevant to me. If I decided to do something dangerous, that was my choice. Mudd was only in this situation because I'd agreed to work for Mr. Pitt. I'd told him his duties did not include assisting me in this way, knowing what his answer would be.

Abducting Mudd was the perfect way to lure me to a quiet spot where it would easy to kill me. I believed I was safe while Mr. Hamerton was in Portsmouth. But what if I was wrong?

I knew the lane well, but I said, as if in doubt, 'Isn't this where Mr. Young lives?'

'Yes, his is the first house, and I was there last night with friends. When I left I noticed a light in the house at the top of the lane.' As I well knew, they were just two houses in that road. 'The light was only there for a few seconds, but I thought it odd, on account of the house being empty.'

'Yes. It's the house Mr. Hamerton bought.'

'Oh, really? I hadn't realised.' He sounded surprised, yet I wasn't convinced. 'Then there may be a perfectly reasonable explanation for what I saw. '

'What time did you see the light?'

'About eleven. Now I must beg you to excuse me. I should go with you, but if I do I'll be late.' I assured him with a calmness I was far from feeling, that it was quite unnecessary, and he cantered off.

If this was a trap, the two pistols I carried might not be enough; I could only fire one shot from each before they needed to be reloaded. But I was willing to take any chance to find Mudd. And an empty house was the ideal hiding place. Only this wasn't just any empty house. This was Mr. Hamerton's house. And there was no better place to hide Mudd. I told myself I had nothing to fear, not when Mr. Hamerton was in Portsmouth.

I dismounted some distance from the house, attached Orlando's reins to a strong branch of a tree, checked the pistols and, sticking to the shadows, crept quietly up to the house and forced myself to walk right round it.

It looked empty to me, but I decided it would be wise to check the stables at the back first. These were uninhabited too, then in the tack room I saw what I needed. A lantern, with a tinder box ready beside it. At least I would be able to see what I was doing. Once I managed to get the wretched thing alight, I saw a key inches from the lantern. My heart began to pound in alarm. Had the lantern and key been left there by the kidnappers to be handy when they came back? Or was it part of a trap, to make it easy for me to get into the house? Well, I thought, there was only one way to find out.

Creeping back to the house I heard nothing except the rustling of the breeze through the trees, and an owl hooting in the distance. Yet Mr. Sims said he'd seen a light for a few seconds. A reflection from moonlight, perhaps? Or had Mr. Sims lied, and lured me to this lonely spot, knowing someone was waiting for me to go inside?

Cursing my shaking hands, I tried the key on the nearest door, but it didn't fit. I tried a side door and this time the key turned the lock with ease. As I removed the key, a sudden noise made me swing round. But it was only a squirrel scuttling up a nearby tree, and patting my heart in relief, I slowly opened the door. It squeaked loudly enough to warn anyone hiding inside of my approach, and I took one of the pistols from my pocket.

As I did so I caught a glimpse, out of the corner of my eye, of a huge shadow right behind me, and I swung round to face it, pistol at the ready, convinced it was Mr. Silver.

CHAPTER 26

The huge shape bent in a sudden gust of wind, then I realised it was only the shadow of a particularly large tree, and I leant against the wall for a moment in sheer relief.

Stepping quietly into the stone flagged passageway, my heart began to race again. I stopped, listening for any sound, but heard nothing. The passageway took me into the hall, from where many doors led to other rooms. I looked into every one, and all were empty. Venturing up the creaking staircase I checked the bedchambers and then the servants' quarters, opening cupboards and wardrobes.

Going downstairs, I went into the big kitchen, where I came across a door that was locked and bolted. At first I assumed it led to the garden, until I realised the outside wall was much further back than this door. Its position not being easily judged in the dark with the aid of only one lantern. Believing there must be a room behind the door, I pulled back the bolts, and used the key hanging on the wall to open the door. Some rough stone steps led down to a cellar and in the light from the lantern I saw another door at the bottom.

I went down, my nose wrinkling at the mustiness of the air, but I soon forgot that when I heard a muffled shout. A key hanging on the wall in the same manner as the previous one, allowed me to unlock the door, and a moment later I was greeted by the familiar sight of Mudd's weatherbeaten face breaking into an astonished grin. 'My lady, how on earth did you find me?'

To see him alive and well again brought a lump into my throat, and made it difficult to speak, but after a moment I managed to say, 'It's a long story, John. Tell me what happened to you first.'

'Well, my lady, I'd just reached the Downs on my way home when four men appeared out of nowhere, pulled me off my horse, and hit me over the head,' he said, gingerly rubbing the bump. 'I managed to avoid the worst of the blow, but dropped to the ground like a stone, thinking that if they believed I was unconscious they wouldn't hit me again.'

I gave a rather watery smile. 'Very sensible.'

'Then they threw me over my horse and brought me here.'

The lantern cast enough light for me to see racks of wine, and I recalled Mr. Hamerton had bought the contents of the cellar with the house. 'Well, at least you weren't thirsty.'

'That I wasn't, my lady,' he agreed, grinning.

'You'll be hungry though.'

'Starving, my lady.'

'We'll soon remedy that. Come on, it won't do to hang about here. Your captors might return.'

'They won't do that, my lady. I heard them talking when they thought I was unconscious. They had orders to report to Mr. Brown in Portsmouth today.'

'What, all of them?'

'It sounded that way, my lady.'

Appalled at their callous unconcern for Mudd's life, I burst out, 'Do you mean they just left you here?'

'Yes, my lady. They said I had all the wine and beer I could drink.'

'Beer?'

272

'There are some casks over in the corner.'

'Did you see these men, John?'

'I managed to get a glimpse of them. Mr. Silver was in charge, but they used their false names all the time. There was Mr. Garnet, Mr. Pearl and Mr. Emerald.'

These were the names in Septimus's journal. 'No-one else?'

'No, my lady.'

'Did you know any of them?'

'No, but I'd recognise them if I saw them again.'

'They didn't tie you up then?'

'Mr. Silver said there was no need. No-one would ever find me, and I wouldn't be able to get out by myself. How did you know I was here, my lady?' I explained about Mr. Sims seeing a light in the house and he said, 'I'm very grateful to the gentleman.' A thought struck him. 'You didn't come alone, did you, my lady?'

I laughed. 'I did, I'm afraid.'

He shook his head at me. 'You shouldn't have done that, my lady.'

'I know, but all's well. Come on John, let's get out of here.'

I left the house exactly as I'd found it. I locked the doors, put the keys back on the wall, returning the lantern and the side door key to the stables. Then I sent Mudd off to see his father and get something to eat. It was only a quarter of a mile, and while father and son were enjoying their reunion, I called on Mrs. Woodford, my aunt's gossipy friend. Apologising for the lateness of the hour, I borrowed one of her carriage horses so that Mudd could ride home, promising to return the animal first thing in the morning. Aware too, that the worst gossip in Dittistone would spread the good news everywhere and save me a lot of time.

On our way home I told Mudd that, at long last, I had proof of Mr. Brown's identity, and explained where I'd left the reports I'd written. He instantly said he would be well enough to go to Portsmouth tomorrow, aware how vitally urgent it was for Mr. Dundas to see my report.

'Are you sure, John?' I asked in concern.' What about your head?'

'It's only a small lump and I wasn't knocked out.'

We reached Westfleet without incident, and I found my aunt and uncle anxiously waiting for me in the drawing room. My uncle leapt up, exclaiming in relief, 'Drusilla --- thank God. We were getting worried.'

'Have you been at Julia's all this time?' Aunt Thirza demanded. 'Do you realise it's nearly midnight?'

'Is it? It doesn't matter,' I said, beaming at them. 'I've found Mudd.'

I told them everything, which meant enduring a severe scold from my aunt for going off on my own. But she soon forgot that when I suggested we might still reach Portsmouth tomorrow if we made an early start.

In the event my aunt and uncle set off for Cowes in the carriage before nine. Mudd and I were to follow on horseback a little later, but the speed with which Mrs. Woodford circulated the good news brought such a flood of visitors to the Manor that we were delayed. Julia was first, rapidly followed by others who had helped with the search, all eager to hear how I'd found Mudd, and I could not, and would not, fob off these good people with a mere few minutes of my time. After all they had done they were entitled to know the truth. Or most of it. I did imply the reason for the kidnapping was that the villains meant to ask for a ransom.

Thus, it was early afternoon before we left Cowes, but we were fortunate enough to enjoy perfect sailing conditions, making a fast crossing to Portsmouth. As we approached the harbour, the sight of so many yachts and boats in the area left us spellbound. My uncle pointed out the "Queen Charlotte," Lord Howe's ship, and the Royal Barge. 'The King must be on the ship right now. What a wonderful day for Howe. He must be very proud.'

'I'm so glad we came,' my aunt said happily. 'Aren't you, Drusilla?'

'I am. I wouldn't have missed it for anything.' The French had taken a beating and there was no better reason for a celebration.

Arriving on dry land, my uncle soon organised a carriage to take us to the house we were to use, which was situated within sight of the Governor's House, where Mr. Reevers and Mr. East were staying. Excited crowds thronged the streets and our progress was slow. The people of Portsmouth were making the most of the King's visit, and clearly enjoying themselves. That would please His Majesty, I thought, for he loved to see happy smiling faces about him.

Our arrival at the house, a day late, was explained to the butler, who went off in unhurried, stately fashion to inform cook we were here at last. For, as I had smilingly told him, we were famished after the sea journey. He returned shortly with the housekeeper, who conducted us to our bedchambers, and when we came downstairs again, the butler brought some welcome tea and ratafia biscuits to keep us going until dinner. Mr. Hamerton and Richard, who were out when we arrived, had ordered a late meal, not wanting to miss any of the celebrations.

We were dressing for dinner when they returned, but later, over a delightful repast, we told them about Mudd's kidnapping. Mr. Hamerton appeared genuinely horrified that my groom had been kept prisoner in his new house.

'How could you have known?' I said. And assuring him Mudd was not seriously hurt, I begged him to tell us what we had missed that day.

'Well, it was most exciting,' he beamed. 'When the artillery fired the salute that told us the King and Queen had arrived at the Lion Gate a huge cheer went up. It's a sound I'll never forget. It was thrilling. Didn't you think so, Richard?'

'What?' Richard looked up with a start. 'Oh, the cheering. Yes, it was wonderful.' He spoke without enthusiasm and had clearly not been attending.

'The Gloucester regiment escorted the Royal party to the Dockyard,' Mr. Hamerton went on. 'Then we saw the Royal Barge heading out to Howe's ship. Imagine Howe's feelings, knowing the King had come expressly to celebrate his magnificent victory. I hear the King presented him with a jewelled sword.'

'It must have been the greatest moment in his life,' my uncle agreed heartily.

While we were talking about Howe, Richard suddenly interrupted, 'By the way, Drusilla, Mr. Reevers called yesterday. He assumed, as we did, that you were delayed by Mrs. Frère's cold, and----'

'Nonsense,' my aunt interjected in scathing tones. 'No cold would ever stop me enjoying such a treat as this.'

I asked if Mr. Reevers had left a message and Richard nodded. 'He said he couldn't see you today as he, Mr. East and Mr. Dundas would be engaged with the King until late evening. He promised to call tomorrow morning.'

I thanked him, but cursed inwardly. I wanted to see Mr. Dundas today and Mr. Reevers would arrange that. Still, I supposed another few hours wouldn't matter.

After dinner, I went out with my aunt and uncle. The streets were filled with jubilant crowds, and threading our way through them, I heard the same sentiments expressed everywhere, from the lowliest urchin to the most respectable gentleman. Sheer joy that we had finally given the Frenchies the whipping they deserved.

Street vendors, even at this late hour, were enjoying a roaring trade, the delicious smell of pies sharpening many an appetite. On our way back we bumped into Mr. Sims. He appeared particularly cheerful and actually broke into a grin when I told him Mudd had indeed been in Mr. Hamerton's empty house where he'd seen a light.

'I am delighted to hear it, Lady Drusilla.' I thanked him most sincerely for his assistance, to which he responded, 'Not at all, ma'am. I was glad to be of service. But, if you will allow me, I have some happy tidings of my own to impart. It didn't seem appropriate to mention it last night, but Miss Young has done me the great honour of accepting my offer of marriage.'

'That is good news, Mr. Sims,' I said, congratulating him.

'Miss Young?' my aunt inquired, a little puzzled. 'I don't think I---'

Mr. Sims proudly told her, 'She is the only child of Mr. Young of Dittistone, ma'am.'

'Mr. Young? But isn't he a-----'

Giving her a quick dig in the ribs, I said, 'He's the gentleman who owns that lovely house near to Mr. Hamerton's new residence. I believe he has an interest in politics.'

'Indeed he has, ma'am. Dittistone returns two members of parliament, as you know. One is retiring shortly, and Mr. Young has ensured my name will go forward in his place.'

Aunt Thirza remarked, 'Aren't you a little young to be a member of parliament, Mr. Sims?'

'Mr. Pitt has run the country since he was twenty-four,' my uncle reminded her. 'And George Canning is the member for Newtown.' Newtown being a constituency in the north of the Island. 'He must be about your age, Mr. Sims.'

'We were at university together, sir. In fact he told me about the vacancy.'

I said, 'Mr. Young is a Tory, I believe.'

'He is, ma'am. As am I.'

'Mr. Upton, if I remember rightly, favours the Whigs.'

'That is so, ma'am.'

'Is he aware of your good fortune?'

'I informed him of it yesterday.' He allowed himself a brief smile, which said much about Mr. Upton's reaction to the news. The parson's opinion of the Tory party, which he expressed at every opportunity, was that they were little better than rogues. 'I dare say he will become accustomed in time.'

Now I understood why Mr. Sims had come to the Island. He was an observant, if sober, young man, who knew exactly what he wanted. I had thought him rather self-centred, yet without his help I would never have found Mudd. Whether he had done so out of kindness, or because he thought I could influence the few who had the vote in Dittistone, I could only guess. Whatever the reason, his assistance removed any suspicion that he was connected with the Fat Badger Society.

I smiled to myself, realising precisely why he'd told the Uptons his evenings were spent with an academic friend. They would strongly disapprove of him marrying the daughter of a gambler, who'd made his money from smuggling, and worst of all, was a Tory.

When the light began to fade, we made our way to the Common, where special illuminations had the crowds gasping in delight. They were indeed beautiful and my aunt said she had not enjoyed herself as much in an age.

Eventually tiredness overcame us and returning to the house, everyone decided to retire early. Even Mr. Hamerton and Richard did so, saying the celebrations had tired them out too. No instinct warned me all was not as it appeared. Nor did I have any premonition of what was to come. My mind was too busy with other worries.

After two failed attempts on my life, and with August approaching fast, I knew I was in great danger. Nothing had been tried at Westfleet, but now I was in a strange house with servants who didn't know me, I was an easier target, and time was running out. When Mr. Hamerton went out, I knew I was safe. If we were both out, or both in the house, anything could happen. I'd made sure I was not alone, even for a minute. But I forgot about being alone at night until I was actually getting into bed. I got up again, locked the door, fixed a chair under the door knob, took a loaded pistol from the drawer and put it on the bedside table. I shut the windows, thinking if anyone broke the glass it would wake me. Having done all I could, I expected to fall asleep straightaway, but every creak in this old house sounded like someone creeping along the corridor, and that kept me awake for a long time.

Eventually I fell into a deep sleep, and woke up much later than usual. With the sun streaming into the room I felt a little foolish at the measures I'd taken. And I smiled to myself, imagining my maid's bewilderment if she had seen what I'd done. But fortunately, I'd left her at home, having decided my aunt's maid could do what little I needed.

There was no sign of Richard and Mr. Hamerton when I breakfasted with my aunt and uncle, and we assumed they had gone out early to enjoy the sunshine, for it was another glorious day. It also meant I was safe and could relax for a while.

I expected Mr. Reevers to call, as he had promised, but when we made our way to the upstairs room where we were to view the procession, he had still not arrived. And I wished he would hurry up. Once I'd seen Mr. Dundas I could enjoy the day, and not before.

I'd arranged for the servants to watch the procession from one of the other upstairs rooms, so I was a little surprised when the butler came in carrying a letter on a salver. I groaned inwardly, suspecting it was from Mr. Reevers informing me he couldn't call this morning after all. But, as I took the letter, the butler told me, 'Mr. Tanfield said I was to give you this, my lady, if he wasn't back by half past ten.'

In some relief that Mr. Reevers would still call, I thanked him, and asked casually, 'Did Mr. Tanfield say where he was going this morning?'

'No, my lady. But he and Mr. Hamerton left very early. Before breakfast, in fact.'

I frowned, wondering why they should do that, but I said nothing and the butler left the room. As I broke the wafer it struck me that perhaps they'd gone sailing, intending to be back in good time for the procession, and this note was to explain why they might be late.

I was quite wrong. Inside was another sealed letter inscribed, *"To be opened in the event of my death, or arrest.'*

CHAPTER 27

As I tore open the single sheet of paper, Aunt Thirza burst out anxiously, 'Whatever is it, Drusilla. You're as white as a sheet.'

I didn't answer at once but my uncle reassured her in his usual calm manner, 'When Drusilla has read the letter, my dear, I'm sure she will tell us.'

Richard had obviously written it in a hurry, his large handwriting covering the whole sheet.

My dear Drusilla,

I wish to God I could find some course other than the one I am taking today, but there is nothing else to be done. All my recent troubles have been caused by one man and today I mean to settle things once and for all. It is the only way I can change my life, and that of Julia, Edward and our unborn child, for the better.

If I do not return I beg you to make Julia understand I had no choice. That I preferred death to dishonour. Tell her Septimus was right when he said those who abuse their power should have it removed. That is why I must rid England of this tyrant, or die in the attempt.

Hamerton stands with me and I am determined to go through with it. I am, as you know, a good shot, and will take my chance.

Yours etc.

Richard.

My hand shook as I passed the letter to my uncle, and my aunt begged, 'What does he say? Tell me, for heaven's sake.'

I lifted my shoulders in despair. 'You had better see for yourself, Aunt.'

She barely waited for my uncle to finish reading before snatching it out of his hand. By now my mind was in turmoil. What was it that Richard meant to do? The conversation I'd overheard between him and Mr. Hamerton in the garden, concerned what would happen in August. And this was only the end of June. It seemed I had got it all horrifying wrong. And if Richard was dead, how could I face Julia?

'What does he mean by it, Drusilla?' my uncle demanded worriedly. 'Who is this tyrant he speaks of?' I saw the fear in his face, for he knew, as we all did, that was a word the French had often used to describe their King.

'I wish to God I knew,' I muttered. 'I was aware something was very wrong, but he would never tell me what it was. '

'Julia. She must---'

'He wouldn't tell her either. She has been dreadfully worried about him.'

'You must have some idea, Drusilla?' Aunt Thirza insisted agitatedly as she laid the letter on the table.

I shook my head, but before I could speak, the butler came in with another note. I took it from the salver, thanked him and as he left, feverishly broke the seal, certain the contents concerned Richard. I was wrong.

'It's from Mr. Reevers.' I saw their anxious faces relax a little and I went on, 'He meant to call this morning, but his duties have forced him to postpone his visit until tomorrow.'

I cursed under my breath. I had to see Mr. Dundas today. And I refused to wait another minute. Mr. Reevers could easily arrange it, and once he had done so, I need never see the wretched man again, I thought miserably.

Thus, without stopping to think, I blurted out, 'Uncle, would you escort me to Government House please? I must see Mr. Reevers at once.' I wanted to get this last meeting with him over with, before I weakened, before I gave way to my longing to give him a second chance.

He raised his brows in surprise, but before he could answer, Aunt Thirza warned, 'Drusilla, you should never be seen to chase after any man. It is not at all seemly.'

'I am not chasing after him,' I snapped. 'Will you come with me, Uncle? If not, I shall go by myself.'

'Go by yourself?' Aunt Thirza echoed in disbelief.

'Must you repeat everything I say, Aunt,' I muttered irritably.

My uncle came to sit beside me, and took my hand in his. 'This isn't like you, Drusilla.' And he reminded me they were as worried about Richard as I was.

His kindness, and all the pent-up unhappiness of the past week threatened to overset me, and as I fought to regain my composure, my aunt turned on me. 'Charles is right. You haven't been yourself ever since we left Windsor. You are a constant worry to us,' she fumed, shaking her finger at me. 'You were out alone when those robbers attacked you on the cliff, and when you rescued Mudd, and as if that wasn't bad enough, you called on Mr. Reevers without a chaperone----'

'That's why I want Uncle Charles to escort me now. I cannot walk into Government House on my own.'

'I should hope not,' Aunt Thirza retorted in shocked tones. 'But surely it can wait. If you both go, I will be alone.'

'It won't be for long, my dear,' my uncle promised. 'And you have the servants to look after you. I'll be back as soon as I can.'

But, as I stood up, the door burst open and Richard stormed into the room. I almost cried with relief. At least he was alive. He threw his hat onto a chair and spotting his letter on the table where my aunt had left it, he muttered, 'So you've read it then?'

'We all have,' I said, as Mr. Hamerton quietly followed him into the room and took a seat. Now I knew the truth about him, his presence made the hairs on the back of my neck stand on end. Whatever else happened, I had to make very sure I was never alone with him.

Richard said, 'Well, you can stop worrying. The whole wretched business was stopped, and we were warned what to expect if we tried again.' Pacing up and down the room, he suddenly slammed his right fist down onto the table. 'If I find out who laid information against us, I'll run him through.' He turned to Mr. Hamerton, his eyes smouldering, 'If it was you, I'll----'

'It wasn't. On my word as a gentleman.'

'Then it must be someone associated with Compton-Smythe. He didn't want to fight me in the first place and---'

I cut him short. 'Who is Compton-Smythe?'

'I told you in my letter.'

'No, you didn't. All you said was, you meant to rid England of some tyrant. You didn't mention his name.'

'Didn't I? Well, no matter. The duel was stopped anyway.'

'Duel?' I exclaimed in horror. 'Are you saying you called this man out?'

'Yes, of course. That's in my letter too,' he reiterated testily. Silently I handed him his note, which he read and threw back onto the table. 'Oh, all right, so I didn't actually mention a duel. I wrote it in a hurry. But you must have realised. I mean, what else could I have meant?' I shook my head at him, thinking of the anguish I'd suffered on his account. 'The thing is Drusilla, calling that blackguard out was the only way to---'

'Yes, but -- who is this Compton-Smythe?'

'He commands one of His Majesty's ships, and is the son of an influential and wealthy Admiral.' Richard sneered, 'But the man's a disgrace to the service. I had to strike him across the face with my glove before he would accept my challenge. That's the kind of weasel he is. And when the constables stopped the duel, he actually had the nerve to accuse me of being the one who informed the magistrate.' He stood looking out the window, his hands clenched.

'Why did you call him out, Richard?' I asked evenly.

'I – I can't say.'

Looking across at Mr. Hamerton I raised my brows in a questioning manner. He took the hint and going over to Richard, put a hand on his shoulder. 'It's my belief you should tell Lady Drusilla.'

Richard muttered, 'What good will that do?'

'You and I haven't been able to resolve this matter. Lady Drusilla has a sharp brain. She, or Mr. and Mrs. Frère might think of something we haven't.' Richard lifted his shoulders, but said nothing, utter despair written in every line of his face.

My uncle tried to reassure him. 'Anything you tell us will go no further than this room, Richard. If we can help, we will. And gladly.'

Richard slumped into a chair and put his head into his hands. After a moment he sat up and looked round at us all. 'Very well, I will do as Hamerton says, but I do not see how anyone can help. It began in the winter when our squadron was chasing the French fleet. We were caught in a storm and in that situation ships can become detached from the main force. As was my own ship, and Compton-Smythe's. Some way ahead of us a French ship of the line was likewise cut off. A ship comparable to Compton-Smythe's but twice the size of my own.'

We all nodded in understanding of the situation. 'Compton-Smythe, being the senior officer, ordered me to attack the French ship at once and capture it. He then promptly sailed off in the opposite direction and I realised he did not expect to see me again. At least, not alive. If I had attacked there and then, as ordered, my ship would have been blasted out of the water, as he well knew.'

My aunt asked in puzzled fashion, 'He wanted you dead?' Richard nodded. 'But why?'

Richard looked down at his hands, carefully studying his fingernails. 'I first met Compton-Smythe when I was given a ship soon after the outbreak of war. He did not like me, nor I him. He treated his men like dirt, considered their survival of little importance, and had them flogged for the slightest misdemeanours.

Foolishly, I did not keep my opinions to myself. My views got back to him, and ordering me to attack that ship was his way of dealing with the situation. But I had no intention of throwing my life away, or those of my men, in that senseless manner. Instead I followed the French ship and when it anchored in a bay – probably to repair damage caused by the storm, I kept out of sight and waited until it was dark. By then the sea had calmed a great deal, and soon after midnight I led a boarding party to take the ship. The Frenchies were all asleep, apart from the few on watch, and we captured it without losing a man.'

My uncle commented, 'A very sensible strategy.'

'I thought so, but Compton-Smythe was furious. He accused me of disobeying a direct order, and of – of – cowardice.' He spat the word out, as if the use of it somehow tainted his very being. 'He swore he'd have me court-martialled. I immediately asked to see Lord Howe, told him what had happened, and he sent me back to my ship. And then----'

'You slipped and fell down the gangway,' I put in.

'An hour before the fleet sailed,' he acknowledged with a groan. 'I was unconscious for two hours and laid up for several days. Compton-Smythe sailed with the fleet, but before he left he wrote to the Admiralty, accusing me of disobeying his order out of cowardice. One of my officers, a surly brute I'd had to discipline more than once, swore I'd had to drink a huge quantity of alcohol before I led that boarding party.' He gave a snort of utter disgust. 'As if any man in his right mind would slow down his reactions with drink just before a fight. He also said I had deliberately fallen down the gangway rather than meet the French in battle. Before they sent me home, I was summoned to the Admiralty to give my account---'

'That was the day we met,' Mr. Hamerton intervened. 'A friend persuaded me to go to a meeting of the London Corresponding Society, where I got talking to Richard. Neither of us expected to meet again.' And he urged Richard to tell us what had happened at the Admiralty.

'If I must,' he sighed. 'They said nothing could be decided until Howe and Compton-Smythe returned to port. So I still don't know if I'm to be court-martialled.'

'I wish you'd told me about it,' I said. 'You were so unlike your usual self, I thought you must be involved in something dreadful.'

'I'm sorry, Drusilla. I wasn't thinking sensibly. In the end I decided to settle Compton-Smythe myself. I had meant to wait for the Admiralty to make up their minds about a court-martial, but when we reached Portsmouth on Tuesday and I saw his ship at anchor, I sought him out and challenged him to a duel. He said he didn't accept challenges from his inferiors. That was when I struck him across the face with a glove. But that will count for nothing if I am court-martialled. He'll tell the court I had the duel stopped, to prove I'm a coward ----'

'How can he?' I broke in. 'You didn't do any such thing.'

'No, but he'll find a way. I know he will. He's already accused me of it. My only hope is to find out who really had the duel stopped. And how am I to come by such evidence?'

No-one spoke, for such a problem appeared insurmountable. I said, 'The magistrate who stopped the duel must know.'

Richard shook his head. 'I've already tried that. It took me a while to find him, which is why I've been out so long, but he refused to name the informant.'

Seeing how that might be overcome, I said, 'It may still be possible. Let me try, Richard, before the celebrations start.'

One glance at the clock told me I could not expect Mr. Dundas to see me now until after the celebrations. So I went into the library and wrote to Mr. Reevers, explaining what had happened to Richard, and asking if he could use his influence to find out what Richard needed to know. I added a postscript, heavily underlined, that I must see Mr. Dundas today, as I had some vital information for him. After which I sent for Mudd and told him to take the note to the Governor's House and hand it to Mr. Reevers personally.

Richard needed all the assistance he could get if he was to win his fight against those with influence in high places. If that didn't work, well I was acquainted with people of influence. The highest in the land, in fact. I didn't know if the King, or Mr. Pitt, would listen, but if Mr. Reevers couldn't help, I would do everything I could to stop Compton-Smythe using his power to threaten the life and career of such a fiercely loyal patriot as Richard.

There being nothing more I could do then I went back upstairs, joining my aunt and uncle, who had an excellent view of what was going on down in the street. The chairs were arranged by the window so we could watch in comfort, and the good-natured, jubilant throng, growing larger by the minute, raised a cheer every time someone of importance rode past on a horse, or in a carriage. The pie and muffin sellers were enjoying a brisk trade, and people gawped in wonder at acrobats and jugglers who entertained them. I was watching a sailor dancing the hornpipe, when Richard and Mr. Hamerton appeared and settled themselves in comfortable chairs. Not surprisingly Richard was still very downhearted.

It was nearly an hour before Mudd returned with Mr. Reevers' answer to my query. Breaking the seal, I read his reply, which said that he'd spoken to the magistrate in question, who was one of the local dignitaries gathered at Government House. The magistrate had sent a servant to his house nearby, to collect the written information he'd received, giving details of the duel. He'd enclosed this note and hoped it would prove of use. The information was written in a small hand, but was not signed. And my heart sank.

I handed both pieces of paper to Richard. He quickly perused Mr. Reevers' brief note, looked at the informant's letter and immediately spluttered, 'Well I'll be....' He looked up at me, his eyes alight with hope. 'I would recognise that spider's scrawl anywhere. It's Compton-Smythe's own handwriting. He laid the information himself.'

I couldn't help smiling at his exuberance. 'Well, he could hardly ask someone else to write it for him, could he. It would be bound to get out. Besides, the local magistrate wouldn't be familiar with his writing.'

'I hadn't thought of that,' he said, scarcely able to believe it himself. He leapt to his feet, put the note on the table and slammed his fist onto it. 'I've got him, Drusilla. I've got him.' Richard passed the note to Mr. Hamerton and almost did a jig around the room.

While my aunt and uncle read it, I said, 'I'm so pleased, Richard. What will you do now?'

'I'm going to show this to Howe.'

'What, now?' I asked.

'If I can. He'll be at the ceremony, and I might manage a word with him beforehand.' He grabbed my hands and squeezed them. 'I cannot thank you enough, Drusilla. This will finish Compton-Smythe. And he had the nerve to call *me* a coward.' Eagerly he turned to his friend. 'Come with me, Hamerton.'

I saw no reason why he should not go with Richard, indeed I would feel very much safer if he did. As they hurried off, my uncle said, 'That was very good of Mr. Reevers.'

'Yes,' I agreed. He'd assisted Richard at once, I thought darkly, but done nothing at all about my seeing Mr. Dundas. He hadn't even mentioned it in his reply. As if that was of no importance whatsoever. Telling my aunt and uncle it was only polite to thank Mr. Reevers, I stormed back to the library in such a fury at him ignoring my request, that I slammed the door behind me. I wrote thanking him for helping Richard, then informed him bluntly that unless he arranged for me to meet Mr. Dundas the instant the King left Government House, I would call on that gentleman myself. Without an introduction. After all, the Governor's House was only a three minute walk away.

Sealing the note, I went back upstairs and sent for Mudd. As I waited, I wandered over to the small window at the side, which offered an excellent view of the wide alley running beside the house, and enabled me to see much further along the street to my right. I was watching the people milling around in the alley below, thinking we would get our first glimpse of the procession from here, when Mudd came in. I was about to hand him the note for Mr. Reevers when I caught sight of Mr East. He was dressed in breeches and a dark brown coat, and standing in the shadow of a doorway in the alley below, talking to another man in the manner of people who knew each other well.

So, despite his duties, he'd found time to watch the procession after all. I'd suspected he would. The other man was hidden in the shadows and I didn't recognise him until he stepped into the sunlight and jabbed his finger several times in the direction of Government House. The sight of him made me gasp out loud.

Mudd said, 'I beg your pardon, my lady?'

I pointed out of the window. 'Look down there, John. Quickly.'

He did as I bid, and looked back at me with widening eyes. 'It's Mr East.'

'And the other man?'

I heard his sharp intake of breath. 'Mr Silver, my lady.'

CHAPTER 28

Mudd turned to look at me. 'So you were right, my lady,' he said, his voice tinged with sorrow. 'A fine gentleman like Mr. East too.'

It filled me with an immense sadness, for I'd met few people more likeable than Toby East. But he'd twice mentioned facts that were unknown to anyone on the Island, except Mr. Brown and his murderous Fat Badgers. Facts I had not known either, until I read Mrs. Jenkins's letter. Details which, not being significant in themselves, I had not spoken of to anyone. Yet Mr East clearly knew.

First, before he and Mr. Reevers went to Portsmouth, we had talked of the night George Jenkins overheard Mr. Silver discussing plans for assassination, and he'd said Mr. Jenkins might still be alive if he hadn't gone back into the inn to collect his gloves. Septimus, in his journal, did not say what his friend had left behind, but Mrs. Jenkins had mentioned it in her letter.

Then, when Julia was speaking to Mr. East, and expressed concern for the safety of Mrs. Jenkins, he said he was sure that lady would be quite safe with her brother in Wickham. I'd failed to discover where her brother had moved to, except that it was a place in Hampshire beginning with a W. But from the threats Mrs. Jenkins had suffered, it was obvious Mr. Brown had found out. And, again, Mr. East knew. And that too was in Mrs. Jenkins' letter.

I wished with all my heart that I had made a mistake, for I liked Toby East enormously. It did not seem possible he could be Mr. Brown, responsible for the deaths of Septimus and George Jenkins, and for trying to have me killed.

But Mrs. Jenkins, in her letter, could not have been clearer about her husband's gloves, or where her brother lived. With that knowledge, I had looked again at all the evidence I had, and realised there was no mistake. It had to be Mr. East. And I saw too why he'd tried to stop me investigating the Fat Badgers.

Mr East had only been on the Island a day or so when that Frenchman tried to push me over the cliff, but quite long enough for a French spy to discover my morning routine. When that failed he staged the highway robbery. And, later, Mudd's kidnap. I realised now it was the questions I'd asked, the doubts I'd shared with him and Mr. Reevers, rather than anything I actually knew, that made him fear I would find him out. As indeed I had.

The evidence, cleverly manipulated by Mr. East, came close to convincing me that Mr. Hamerton was Mr. Brown. Yet, I could not quite rid myself of a nagging doubt. For, as time went on, and I saw how well organised the Fat Badgers were, I could not believe that Mr. Brown would allow something as vital as a letter to Robespierre, hang on the chance of Blackgang smugglers being prepared to take it to Paris. It didn't make sense.

Doubts that grew as I became better acquainted with him. For, his character and general behaviour soon made it clear to me that, if this was an act, and he was a French agent, then he was the cleverest man I had ever met. Which I could not believe, for in all other ways his intelligence seemed no more than average.

In fact, as I saw now, he was exactly what he appeared to be. A good-natured, likeable gentleman, with an even temper, who was genuinely interested in moths and butterflies. He was also, unquestionably, a patriot. Despite his sister's close connections to Robespierre.

In the beginning I had puzzled over the attempt on the King's life at Windsor. I thought it poorly planned, almost as if it was meant to fail. And that seemed odd, especially when Mr. Brown took such meticulous care with everything else. In fact, as I eventually realised, Mr. East had deliberately sacrificed the lives of those two men, so that he could be seen apparently risking his life to save the King. For, who could doubt his loyalty to England then?

Thus when John Hamerton arrived late that day with some far-fetched story, no-one believed a word of it, and suspicion was planted in all our minds. But his story was the exact truth. Mr. East had organised that, just as he'd made sure it was always possible to blame Mr. Hamerton for the attempts on my life. Which was why I knew I was perfectly safe when Mr. Hamerton was out; and in danger when we were in the same house, or out at the same time.

As for Richard's behaviour, I could not believe he was involved with the Fat Badgers. All his life he had been intensely patriotic. Whatever his problems were, he would never betray England. Or so I thought until that afternoon I overheard him talking to Mr. Hamerton about "going ahead in August." That had thrown me into utter confusion. But, checking what was written on my charts, I saw another possible answer to that. And why Richard was willing to help him. But I still didn't yet know if I was right.

I had considered Mr. Sims, for he was exactly the kind of cold, calculating man I imagined would be a fanatic. He spent very little time at the parsonage, was supposedly out walking during the highwayman attack, and had been in the vicinity when Mr. Hamerton met Mr. Silver at the church. But all Francis Sims wanted was to become a Member of Parliament, and to keep his plans from the Uptons until everything was settled.

I looked down into the alley again, taking good care to keep back from the window, in case Mr East or Mr Silver happened to glance up. I wondered briefly why he'd chosen such a meeting place, until I remembered Mr. Reevers had promised the owner of this house to keep our arrangement quiet, and consequently had told no-one, not even Mr. East.

A steady stream of latecomers were hurrying through the alley, adding to the wildly excited throng waiting for the King to drive up to Government House. No-one took any notice of Mr. East and Mr. Silver, nor the two men who had now joined them. One, a bespectacled tradesman of about forty, I guessed was the Mr Garnet in Septimus's journal. He carried a bag, which he set down in the darkest corner of the doorway. The fourth man kept looking around nervously; short and slim with ginger hair, and rather more refined, he had to be the clerk, Mr Pearl. He, along with Mr Silver and Mr Garnet, wore bright red neckerchiefs, making themselves easily recognisable to each other in the crowd. Only Mr. East did not wear one.

This, I assumed, was all that remained of the Fat Badger Corresponding Society, for Mr East was already addressing them in the manner of someone issuing orders. He was no longer the cheerful, carefree Toby East we all knew; this man did not smile, and in place of his usual nonchalance was an intensity I had never seen before.

I assumed he'd brought them here to observe how the King was guarded, to study the faces of the ministers, in order to recognise them in August, when the assassinations were planned. It was a sensible precaution, and typical of how the society was organised.

Until Mr. East had made those two small slip-ups in conversation, it hadn't even entered my head that he could be Mr. Brown. For Mr. Reevers, Mr. Pitt and the King all had absolute trust in him. And I had actually watched him save the King's life in Windsor. Unfortunately this wasn't my only mistake. As I was about to discover.

Looking down at the alley I realised time had run out. And I saw exactly why Mr. East had tried to prevent me coming to Portsmouth. He had stopped speaking, and as the other three moved closer together making conversation, he carefully concealed himself behind them, opening the bag brought by Mr Garnet. He was virtually hidden from people walking past, but I could see precisely what he was doing.

He took out two identical objects wrapped in cloth, and from the shape of them I guessed they were pistols. Having slipped them into the two deep pockets of his coat, he thrust the cloths back into the bag, changed places with Mr Silver, who then collected his two pistols.

That was the moment I realised Mr East did not intend to wait until August. The assassination was to be here and now, on the twenty-seventh of June, amid these victory celebrations, where the King and most top ministers were assembled together in one place. I ought to have realised that such a gathering offered the Fat Badgers the perfect opportunity to send Britain sliding into revolution.

One glance at the clock told me that, within five minutes, the King would drive through the dockyard gates on his way to the ceremony at Government House. I wished I knew who else would be in the procession. Were Dundas, Chatham, Lord Howe and other important admirals already at Government House? Or were they helping to make a fine spectacle for the public by being part of the procession? It seemed to me that virtually the whole of Portsmouth had come out into the streets to cheer them. And among them were four men, each carrying two pistols.

If only Mr Reevers was here. I hated to admit it, but he was the man I needed in this situation. So where the devil was he? And why had he ignored my urgent demands to see Mr. Dundas? The last message I'd written no longer mattered, and I thanked heaven I hadn't sent Mudd to deliver it. I needed him here.

Looking out the window again I cursed under my breath, and my uncle said, 'Did you say something, Drusilla?' I shook my head but he walked over to my side. 'What is it? You look like you've seen a ghost.' I pointed out of the window and he declared, 'Good heavens, isn't that Mr East?' Watching Mr. Pearl take the last pistol from the bag and put it in his pocket, he looked at me in utter amazement. 'What on earth is Mr. East doing with that gang of cut-throats? I thought he said-----'

'Uncle, I don't have time to explain, but you must go to Government House this instant.' Already the Fat Badgers were dispersing, going off one at a time, mingling with the crowds. Even if we ran down the stairs and out into the alley, it would be too late to stop them.

I had to get word to Mr. Reevers, but he'd ignored my other notes, and if I sent a verbal message that the man he trusted with his life was actually a French agent, he would not believe me. But if my uncle urged him to read the information I'd prepared for Mr. Dundas, and told him he'd seen the pistols being handed out, he must believe it.

When he read my reasons for believing Mr. East to be Mr. Brown, he would see I was right. I rushed off to my bedchamber, grabbed a hat and put it on, snatched up my letter for Mr. Dundas, ran back to my uncle and thrust it into his hand.

'Give this to Mr Reevers and make sure he reads it. Tell him Mr East and three other men are in the crowd with pistols, and they mean to kill the King. Tell him each man has two firearms, and three of them are wearing bright red neckerchiefs. He'll understand.'

'What are you going to do?'

'Go after them, of course.' And giving him a tiny push towards the door, I urged, 'Go down the alley and round the back way. It will be quicker.'

As he clattered down the stairs I turned to my aunt, who was staring at me, dumb with shock. 'I'm sorry

Aunt, but I must go. You'll be quite safe here.' I didn't need to tell Mudd to follow me. He would not have stayed behind, even if I had ordered him to.

The Fat Badgers had gone now and running to the window at the front of the inn, I caught sight of a man in a red neckerchief pushing his way through the crowds towards Government House. Under normal circumstances it was a two or three minute walk, but it would take him much longer today, and I was exceedingly thankful that my uncle had gone the back way.

I slipped the two pistols I'd brought with me into the pockets of my gown, and made sure Mudd was also carrying two pistols. Hurrying down the stairs, we went out by the side door into the alley and onto the street, where we, too, were quickly swallowed up in the jostling crowds. For once my height proved useful, for within a few minutes, I caught a glimpse of Mr Garnet pushing his way to the front, and quickly pointed him out to Mudd.

With a brief nod, he barged through the happy throng, tapped Mr Garnet on the shoulder, and when the man turned round, delivered one almighty blow to his chin, dropping him like a stone. People stared in amazement, and such unexpected force from my gentle groom surprised me too, but I said in a loud and imperious voice, 'That man stole my reticule.' And, at once, the crowd parted to allow Mudd to drag him out of the crowd, for the celebrations had brought many notorious London pickpockets to Portsmouth, and I heard a man announce angrily that he had lost a watch. Quietly I told Mudd to remove Mr Garnet's pistols. 'We might need them.'

Mudd handed them to me, then dragged the unconscious man into an alleyway and left him there. Glancing round I saw Mr Pearl mopping his brow, his eyes wide with sheer terror, for quite by chance I was pointing the two pistols directly at him. In an instant he tore off his coat and red neckerchief, threw them on the ground and ran off as fast as he could go. If the situation had not been so serious, I would have laughed. But there was no time for that with Mr Silver and Mr East still at large. A single bullet could kill the King and there were still four loaded guns out there.

In the distance we could hear the crowds cheering, which told us the King was not far away, and it sent the people around us wild with excitement. While I searched this side of the street, I sent Mudd to the other side, telling him, 'Look for someone wearing a red neckerchief, or anyone not waving and cheering, or for Mr East himself.'

Louder cheers made the crowds surge forward in eager anticipation, giving me a little space at the back. Picking up my skirts a trifle, I ran along, frantically searching for the two men, and wishing Mr. Reevers would hurry up. I prayed my uncle had found him. And that he'd read the report immediately. The facts were clear and concise. But would he believe what I had written?

My uncle would confirm Mr. East, Mr. Silver, and two other armed men were mingling with the crowds. Whatever else I thought of Mr. Reevers, he didn't lack intelligence. But he had to act quickly. If he sent his men out onto the streets now, we might still find these assassins in time. If we didn't, the King would soon be dead.

The cheers grew ever closer, the crowds pressed forward, eager to catch the first glimpse of the King's carriage. A woman fainted, and as the people made a path for her to be carried out, I caught sight of Mr Silver.

He was standing at the front of the crowd, as near to Government House as he could get. So that's where they meant to assassinate the King. A carriage slowing to a halt, or the King stepping from that carriage, was an easier target than one moving down a street. Mr East had planned it all very carefully.

It was then I saw Mudd on the other side of the road, and as I waved my arms at him and tried to shout out over the tumult going on around us, a familiar voice spoke quite calmly into my ear, 'I shouldn't do that if I were you, ma'am.'

CHAPTER 29

I swung round to find Mr East composed but determined. We were at the back of the crowd, but as all eyes were fixed on the direction in which the King would first appear, no-one noticed the pistol he dug into my ribs.

Speaking closely into my ear, he said, 'Lady Drusilla, we are going to walk away from here and find a quiet spot where no-one will bother us. If you would take my arm, then everything will appear perfectly normal.' When I hesitated, he urged, 'Please do as I say, ma'am. I don't wish to shoot you, but I will if I have to.'

I had no choice but to obey; the noise of a shot would never be heard above the joyous acclamations of the crowd. I'd hoped that being bumped and pushed by so many exuberant people would offer a chance to escape, but he made me walk close to the houses, warding off anyone who barged into us with comparative ease. We were walking in the direction of the house where I was staying, and as we reached it, he pointed to the alley beside it. 'Down here, if you please.'

The alley that had been so busy, was empty now, and as he forced me along it, the only sign of life I saw was a grey cat curled up in a small patch of sunlight. The doorway, where he had met the other Fat Badgers such a short time ago, was in deep shadow, and he retreated into that darkness, still holding me at gunpoint.

When I asked how he'd found me he said, 'I came across Mr Garnet and knew you must be nearby. With you out of action, there's no-one capable of stopping Mr Silver. Your uncle is an old man, Mudd is only a servant, and Radleigh would never believe I am Mr. Brown.'

I said nothing, preferring to let him think I had no argument to offer. Mudd did not need an order from me to deal with Mr Silver, my uncle might not be young but that wouldn't stop him doing whatever was necessary, and when Mr Reevers read the clear, indisputable proof of guilt that I'd written down for Mr. Dundas, I was convinced he *would* believe me.

Mr East eyed me speculatively. 'So you worked it out?' I inclined my head in acknowledgement. 'May I ask how?'

I gave a shrug. 'You told Julia that Mrs. Jenkins was safe in Wickham with her brother, and she chanced to mention it to me. No-one else on the Island knew where her brother lived, except you and your villainous society. I only found out when Mrs. Jenkins wrote to me.'

'A slip of the tongue,' he grimaced.

'Indeed.'

'Is that all?'

'Not quite. If you remember, before you and Mr. Reevers left for Portsmouth, we went over the information we had. When we spoke about George Jenkins overhearing Mr. Silver's conversation at the inn, you said he'd still be alive if he hadn't gone back for his gloves.'

'But that is what happened,' he said, puzzled. 'Septimus said so in his journal.'

I shook my head at him. 'Septimus wrote that George Jenkins had forgotten something, but he didn't say what. In her letter, Mrs. Jenkins said he'd gone back for his gloves. When I thought it all out, I finally saw the reason behind the failed attempt on the King's life at Windsor. After that it was easy enough.'

'Well, it doesn't matter now. It will all be over when the King reaches Government House. Mr Silver will see to that. He's an even better shot than I am. And other groups in London will rise up the instant they hear the King is dead.'

I realised then that while he believed Mr Silver to be undetected by anyone but myself, he would remain here. But, if soldiers were sent onto the streets Mr East would kill me, and then the King, if he could. If I could keep him talking it might distract him a trifle.

So I asked, 'Did you set up the Fat Badgers society because of Miss Rotherton?' Deep pain flickered in his eyes, but he did not speak. 'What happened to her was abominable, but I don't see what you have to gain by assassinating the King.'

There was a hint of mockery in the faint smile that touched his lips, and convinced he'd realised I was simply trying to distract him, I was afraid he wouldn't answer. But the temptation to explain overwhelmed him. 'Don't you, Lady Drusilla? Then, I will tell you. In this country aristocrats do as they please. Even with their own children. Rotherton said I wasn't good enough for his daughter. I've spent years risking my life to keep people like him safe, yet he swore he'd have me killed if she didn't marry that pig. And she believed him. When I think of what she must have suffered at the hands of that – that - libertine—' He spat out the word with such anguished loathing I caught my breath. Then he stopped quite deliberately and composed himself again, clearly remembering his purpose for being here.

'You must know Mr. East, that I and a great many other of the rich aristocrats you despise, consider Lord Rotherton's behaviour to be beneath contempt.'

'I am aware. But there are too many of his kind in England. Revolution is the only way to change that.'

He was quiet for a moment or two, and I was about to ask another question when he said, 'I was in France when I got word of her death. I went into an inn with a French agent, now working for us, who had supposedly become disillusioned with their revolution. I drank too much and told him about Rotherton. He said many people in England were bitter about the nobility escaping justice, while ordinary people committing similar offences were hanged, sent to prison, or transported, and was I interested in doing something about it. I said I'd like nothing better, and he told me he was a double agent, loyal to France, ordered personally by Robespierre to recruit agents to infiltrate the English Corresponding Societies and bring about a revolution. That's how it began. And I don't regret it. Not one bit.'

'But - you had Septimus murdered. And George Jenkins. Weren't they as innocent as Miss Rotherton?'

He sighed, shaking his head in a manner that implied I couldn't possibly understand. 'I'm sorry for Septimus, but he should have stayed with us. Once he left, I couldn't save him. The same goes for Mr Jenkins.'

'Who----'

'Oh, it wasn't me. The others did it. They had no choice. I was still in Windsor then.'

The mention of Windsor filled me with such rage, I burst out, 'Jeffel would be alive but for you.'

'That wasn't meant to happen.'

He spoke as if what he'd planned had gone awry, and it made me realise something I hadn't considered before. 'That bullet was meant for me, wasn't it.' He gave a shrug. 'You wanted me out the way even then?'

'Having met you, and listened to Radleigh singing your praises, I knew you would be a danger to me if Pitt employed you. I was afraid you would see what Radleigh would not.'

'So when Mr. Silver and Mr. Ruby turned highwaymen, you waited in the woods, and removed the body after we'd gone. And it was you who had Mudd kidnapped.'

He inclined his head. 'I wanted you on the Island, not here in Portsmouth. You have too sharp a brain.' Not sharp enough, I thought. It had taken me too long to see through Toby East. But who would suspect a government agent? A man trusted by the highest in the land.

It was then my uncle turned into the far end of the alley on his way back from Government House. Mr East saw him too, and quickly stepping back into the shadows, he took a second pistol from his coat pocket and ordered me to stand where I could be seen. When my uncle saw me standing in the middle of the passageway he broke into a run, and despite the warning I tried to give with my eyes, he rushed straight up to me.

'What on earth are you doing here, Drusilla?' He was clearly bewildered, and in answer, I indicated the figure in the doorway.

In a sudden unaccustomed blaze of anger, my uncle took a step forward. 'Why, you-----'

'Stand still,' ordered Mr East. 'Or I will shoot Lady Drusilla.' My uncle, who would not have stopped on his own account, did so for mine, as Mr East had judged he would.

The cheers of the crowds were so deafening now the procession had to be very near. Still Mr East did not take his eyes off of us. Yet I could not just stand here. I had to do something. I glanced at my uncle, and saw he understood exactly what I was thinking. Regrettably, it was also obvious to Mr East. 'I wouldn't if I were you,' he warned. 'You would both be dead before you reached the street.' Recalling the fate of the two would-be assassins in Windsor, I knew he was right.

My uncle, who was looking in the direction of the street, said provokingly, 'Perhaps we would, but even you can't shoot three people at the same time, I fancy.' And I turned my head to see Richard walking into the alley.

He looked so cheerful I knew all had gone well with Lord Howe, and guessed he had come back to tell us the good news. But, as he took in the scene before him, his eyes widened in shock. Mr East did not hesitate; he levelled the pistols at us, and as he did so, Richard launched himself straight at Mr. East. At the same time, my uncle pulled me out of the firing line with such force that I fell to the ground. Richard's actions caused one pistol to fire high into the air, but the other bullet struck him and he dropped like a stone.

'Oh, no,' I whispered in despair, just as my uncle threw a punch at Mr East. He ducked, avoided the blow, struck my uncle over the head with the butt of a pistol, and ran off. As I got to my feet, my uncle staggered to the nearest wall, leant against it and slowly slumped to the ground, dazed but still conscious.

Richard lay face down, crumpled up on the ground, and did not move or speak. I longed to stop, but knew I must not.

'Uncle,' I begged in a choking voice, desperately trying not to think of Julia, 'please see to Richard.' If he was dead, I could do nothing. If he was still alive my uncle would deal with it better than I could. My job was to stop Mr. East, who only had to reload the pistols to take part in the assassination. But when I reached the street, he was nowhere in sight. In the time it had taken me to get to my feet and speak to my uncle, he had disappeared into the crowd.

A sudden tremendous roar told me the King's carriage was in sight. Cheers rang through the air all along the street, people surged forward in their hundreds, eager to catch a glimpse of him. Picking up my skirts I ran in the direction of Government House.

It was then I saw Mr Reevers. He came towards me, his face so grey with shock I did not need to ask if he had read the report I'd written for Mr. Dundas. He ran a hand distractedly through his thick black hair. 'I just can't believe it. Not Toby---'

I was genuinely sorry and told him so, then I briefly repeated what Mr. East had said about Miss Rotherton, and why it had driven him to revolution.

'I thought he was over that.' He spoke jerkily, still too stunned to take it all in. 'He hasn't spoken of her for ages. I was convinced he'd fallen for Miss Adams.'

'That was to throw us off the scent, I fear.'

He said, half to himself, 'I thought I knew him.'

There was no time to commiserate and I begged, 'Tell me, have you found Mr Silver?'

'Yes, he's at the front of the crowd near Government House.'

'You've left him there?' I spluttered in disbelief.

'It seemed the best thing to do.'

'The *best* thing------ '

'Don't worry, he can't harm the King now.'

'But, Mr. East can. You haven't found him?' He shook his head and looked away, as if he could not bear me to see his desolation.

Another huge cheer broke out, telling us the King had arrived at Government House. It was impossible to speak above the noise, which went on for what seemed an age, and while I understood why the King wanted to take his time acknowledging this wonderful welcome, I wished he would hurry up and go inside.

Looking at Mr Reevers I saw the strain in his eyes as we waited. 'I told them to get him into Government House quickly, but he can be very stubborn.' At long last the cheering subsided, which told us the King had finally gone inside, and Mr Reevers let out his breath in one long sigh of relief. 'He'll be safe there.'

'Yes,' I said thankfully. 'Why did you leave Mr Silver where he was?'

'He was in the perfect place to assassinate the King, and I hoped that when Toby-----' the word caught in his throat, the pain of his friend's betrayal clearly etched in every line of his face. But he took a deep breath and went on, 'I hoped Toby would entrust the actual shooting to Silver. So I sent in six men, cheering wildly like everyone else. Local men, people Toby wouldn't recognise, brought in to prevent the pickpocket gangs ruining the Royal visit. They closed round Mr Silver, and quietly disarmed him. I hope you approve, it was all I could think of at the time.'

I did approve of such quick thinking and told him so. 'Mr East will have seen Mr. Silver and thought all was well. It was an excellent notion.'

Mr Reevers bowed. 'I'm thankful to have done something that gained your approval.'

I ignored the inference and demanded, 'Where is Mr. Silver now?'

'Being carted off to prison. I told them to wait only until the King was inside. Which I hope will make Toby see how pointless it is to go on.'

I shook my head at him, remembering the fanatical light in Mr. East's eyes. 'Believe me, nothing will stop him now.' And I urged him to warn the King of the danger.

'That's easier said than done. The King hates being interrupted when he's carrying out his public duties, and there's no real risk when he's surrounded by so many people. I'll speak to him before he leaves.'

'It would be wiser if he returned to the dockyard by another route.'

'What, and disappoint the crowd? He would never agree to it.'

'He could be killed.'

'As you saw in Windsor, His Majesty doesn't lack courage.'

The crowds were still milling around, some making their way homewards, others waiting to catch another glimpse of the King when he left. It was then I saw a familiar figure threading his way towards me.

'Oh, there's Mudd,' I said, thankful he was safe.

'Actually it was Mudd who spotted Mr Silver. In fact he begged me to let him shoot the man out of hand.'

'Mudd said that?' I gasped, for generally my groom was the gentlest of men.

A faint smile hovered on his lips. 'I don't think he approved of Silver and his friend trying to kill you on the cliff top.' And Mr East had not been afraid of what Mudd might do.

'When does the King return to the dockyard?'

'At three. He's dining with the ministers, admirals and local dignitaries back at the Commissioner's House at four.'

I shivered, all too aware that Mr. East wouldn't give up now. When I told Mr. Reevers how Mr. East had held us at gunpoint in the alley, he closed his eyes.

'How could Toby do such a thing?' he whispered, unable to keep the anguish out of his voice.

'It was Richard who saved us. He literally threw himself at Mr. East. My uncle pulled me out of the line of fine, but Richard was hit — '

'Hit?' he echoed in alarm. 'Is -- is he--?'

I swallowed. 'I don't know.' A picture of Richard crumpled up on the ground flashed before my eyes, but I dare not allow myself to think of him now. 'My uncle is with him. Our job is to find Mr East.'

'Yes,' he said, his eyes filled with so much pain I had to look away. 'I have men out looking for him now. I'll post others outside Government House and all along the route.' He pulled out his pocket watch. 'Just over two hours before the King leaves. I pray it will be enough.' I didn't answer, for I could not rid myself of a feeling of unease, which must have shown in my face, for he demanded, 'What is it, Drusilla?'

I ignored his use of my name, indeed I barely noticed it. 'I keep thinking how Mr. East has fooled us all for weeks. How he cast suspicion on Mr. Hamerton----'

'I have been wrong all along, so if you have any alternative to suggest----'

I shook my head. 'I can't think of anything better.'

'Then I must set things in motion.' He turned to Mudd. 'I know I can rely on you to stay with Lady Drusilla.' And he hurried off towards Government House.

When I congratulated Mudd on his part in Mr Silver's arrest, he pointed out modestly, 'I was the only one who knew what he looked like, my lady.' And looking past me at the crowds, he went on, 'Oh, there's Mr Frère.'

I swung round on my heel to see my uncle coming towards us. 'Tell me at once,' I whispered, when he reached us. 'Is Richard alive?'

He nodded. 'The surgeon is removing the bullet from Richard's chest as we speak. But it's touch and go, I'm afraid. All we can do is pray.'

I stared at him, thinking of Julia. 'If he hadn't knocked Mr. East off balance we would both be dead.'

'What Richard did was the bravest thing I've ever seen.' And he put a hand on my arm in concern. 'You should sit down, my dear. You look positively ashen.'

'I can't. There's too much to do.' Richard was in good hands, I told myself sensibly. I must not think of him, or of Julia, not now.

My uncle asked, 'Have you seen Mr. Reevers?'

'A few minutes ago.'

'When he read your report, he was convinced you were mistaken. So I told him I'd seen Mr. East with those men, and that they all had firearms. His face went white,' he said, his voice full of compassion. 'So I left him then. A man betrayed by his closest friend needs a little time alone.' He paused for a moment. 'I always thought Mr. East a splendid fellow, but it seems he is every bit as dangerous as those fanatical sans-culottes.' And he sighed, 'Well, I must go back to Richard. Will you come with me?'

'I can't, uncle.'

'I was afraid you'd say that. Please be careful, my dear.'

As he strode off, Mudd and I turned towards Government House. This being the area where I was convinced Mr. East would be. As I said to Mudd, 'Firing at a moving target is not as easy as it seems. And injury won't suffice. In order to kill the King, he must get close to the carriage. That's the one thing we can be certain of.'

Unfortunately, I failed to remember that there are very few certainties in life.

CHAPTER 30

I believed Mr. East meant to assassinate the King when he got into the carriage, or during the few seconds before it moved off. Even a good marksman like Toby East couldn't be certain of killing the King when the carriage was moving, and people all around him were shouting and waving their arms about in excitement. If he only injured the King, and His Majesty recovered, all his efforts would have been for nothing. My reasoning was sensible and logical, yet still that feeling of unease refused to go away.

A band was playing on the green near Government House, for the King loved music. It was also very popular with the crowds, a large number of people having gathered to listen, and a great cheer went up when the band started to play "Rule Britannia." Mudd and I mingled with the crowd desperately searching for Mr East, for there was no better place to hide. But finding anyone in this good-natured throng was not easy with people coming and going all the time, hailing friends, and where children and dogs were running about.

Once Mudd chased after someone he saw hurrying off, but it wasn't our quarry, and I was standing on the edge of the crowd considering what to do next, when I noticed a man a considerable distance away, walking purposely towards a side door at Government House. His formal attire suggested he was invited to the levee, although I did wonder why he was using the side door. Guests generally entered through the doors at the front.

When I pointed this out to Mudd, he said, 'Perhaps he's an official, my lady.'

The man had his back to me, yet even from this distance there was something oddly familiar about the straightness of his bearing and the way he held his head. Then, just before he went through the archway towards the door he glanced over his shoulder. 'Good God, it's Mr. East.' And picking up my skirts a little, I ran after him, not caring what anyone thought.

Mudd reached the door before me, and on opening it, we were immediately presented with a flight of stairs. Running up these we reached a corridor, but saw no sign of life. I had been to Government House once before, with my father, and although I knew there were more than forty apartments here, I had not seen them, nor had I ventured into this part of the building on that occasion. In truth I had no idea where I was, but hearing the distant hum of people conversing, I headed in that direction.

We ran along the corridor, down some stairs, then Mudd opened a door, and quite suddenly, I could pick out actual voices. In front of me was the huge room I had seen when with my father, a most impressive lofty hall decorated with arms of the kind I had once admired at Windsor Castle. A great many people were there, all correctly dressed for the ceremony, as Mr. East now was. No-one would think it odd to see him here, but I dared not show myself, for I would be very much out of place at such a ceremony. In any case I had a better chance of preventing his revolution if he believed I was still outside looking for him. I left the door open a couple of inches while I decided what to do.

The gentlemen were standing in a circle, with the King walking round talking to each in turn. Mudd, peering through the gap, whispered in awe, 'They all look very proud, my lady.'

'So they should, John. Can you see Mr. East?'

After a moment he said, 'Yes, my lady, he's talking to another gentleman.'

'If he changed his clothes that quickly,' I murmured thoughtfully, 'he must have procured another room nearby.' A place where he could meet the other Fat Badgers and hide what he did not want to risk being seen in his room inside Government House. A man of great determination, Toby East. He must have seen Mr. Silver taken into custody, and knowing men would be scouring the streets for him, he'd changed his clothes, confident that no-one would think of looking for him inside Government House. Aware too that the King would not be surprised to see him there.

I turned to Mudd. 'John, find Mr Reevers. We need his men here.' He raced off down the corridor just as the King began the official ceremony of bestowing honours on officers from Lord Howe's fleet. Through the slightly open door I could see Mr. East watching the formalities, working out what to do next. With so many people around His Majesty, assassination would not be easy.

Mudd soon came hurrying back. 'Mr Reevers isn't in his office, my lady, and no-one knows where he is.'

I cursed under my breath. 'He'll be outside somewhere, John. You must find him.'

He rushed off again, and when I looked back to where Mr East had been standing, my heart starting thumping in alarm. He'd disappeared. In rising panic I hurriedly searched the faces near the King, but Mr East was not amongst them. Where the devil was he then? And where was Mr Reevers when I needed him?

Perspiration broke out on my forehead, and as I stood there, frantically looking round the room for Mr East, I saw something glinting in a shaft of sunlight in an open doorway on the opposite side of the hall. I stared for a moment, wondering what it was. Then I realised; it was the barrel of a pistol. And it was pointing directly at the King, who was now conferring a knighthood on one of the naval officers involved in our triumphant victory. Mr East was waiting to get a clear shot.

I had to stop him, had to get across the hall to the rooms on the far side. With all eyes now on the impressive ceremony, I picked up my skirts and quietly hurried down the length of the hall, keeping close to the wall, where it was darker. When I reached the corridor opposite, I burst into the first door on my right, and saw Mr East aiming the pistol at the King, as if about to fire. Hearing the door crash open, he instantly swung round. 'Lady Drusilla,' he murmured, with a resigned sigh. 'You are becoming an infernal nuisance.'

I tried to drag my pistol from my pocket, but in my haste it caught in the cloth. While he, aware he must not draw attention to himself by firing a shot, rushed straight at me, lifting the butt of the pistol high in the air before aiming it violently at my head. At the last second I raised my arm which, along with my substantial hat, took the force of the blow, but I still slumped to the ground in agony.

Instinct warned me not to move. For, if I tried to get up he would strike me again. He kicked me once, but I managed not to react or cry out, despite the intense pain. Which, thankfully, convinced him I was unconscious. I heard him lock the door leading into the hall, then he left the room by the other door, locking that too. Somehow I struggled to my feet, and leant against the wall until the room stopped spinning. I had to get out of here, but if I screamed and made a lot of fuss, I was afraid Mr. East would throw caution to the wind and kill the King at once, any way he could.

The doors were so solidly built I would need a battering ram to get out. Then a more logical thought entered my head. Feverishly I searched the drawers of the desk and, there, at the very bottom was what I'd prayed to find. A spare key. Within seconds I was out of the room and on reaching the huge hall again, I saw him standing watching the ceremony. I quickly realised, as Mr. East must have too, that the room we had been in was too far away to be sure of delivering a fatal shot. Even for a marksman like him.

I saw too that although he wanted to kill the King, he also meant to escape. He wanted to lead the revolution, to take Mr. Pitt's place in Downing Street, and rid England of its nobility, executing the good along with the bad, as France had done. And unconsciously I ran a hand along the back of my neck.

I had to get back to the other side of the hall again, but could not do so yet, in case Mr. East saw me. So, keeping well out of sight, I watched what he was doing. After a few minutes I saw him walk, with casual assurance, up to His Majesty, who was still conferring honours on the heroes of the hour. And I knew he had worked out how to murder him. I thought for one terrible heart-stopping moment that he meant to do it there and then. Instead he waited deferentially until the King turned to see what he wanted, when he took His Majesty to one side and spoke quietly. Mr. East had his back to me now, and I took the opportunity to cross the hall and get back to where Mudd expected to find me.

The King, having listened to Mr. East, shook his head adamantly. 'No, I will not leave,' he said loudly. 'Not until I have honoured these brave men as they deserve.' When Mr. East began to protest, the King insisted, 'I will carry out my duty first.'

He went on with the ceremony, talking to the officers as he had before, showing no sign of haste. I guessed Mr. East had warned him his life was in danger, and advised him to leave the hall at once. Not for the first time, I found myself admiring the King. He was not easily frightened, which his would-be assassin must have forgotten in the heat of the moment.

Mr. East stood waiting by a door in a dark area of the hall. Waiting to take the King to a quiet place and kill him. Unless I stopped him. But how was I do that? If I told the King that Toby East was a French spy, he wouldn't believe me. Nor would anyone else.

Government ministers like Mr. Dundas and Lord Chatham were in danger too, but I put them out of my mind. Only one life really mattered, and that was the sovereign's. For Mr. East had said other groups in London would rise up the instant they heard the King was dead.

Dizziness threatened to overcome me again, and I watched in a dazed state as the King finished the ceremony and walked towards Mr. East. I shook my head in an endeavour to clear my brain, and saw the

King walking off with Mr. East. They seemed to be going in the direction of the apartments, where one would have been put aside for the King's use.

But which one? I ran down the corridor, past closed doors, but there was nothing to tell me if I was even in the right place. Suddenly, a servant came out of a room and I stopped him, asking if this was his place of employment, for I needed someone who knew the house, not some visiting servant.

He stared at me, taken aback, before informing me loftily, 'It is, ma'am.'

I nodded. 'Good. I can see you are a sensible man. I have a message, of a private nature you understand, for a -- a-- gentleman. But I don't know which is his apartment. If you would be so good as to tell me who is using which apartment.....' I jingled some coins in my pocket, praying he wasn't above being bribed, uncaring of what he thought of me.

He smiled less loftily, pointed out the King's apartment, told me who was using the others, and which were empty. I thanked him and rewarded him generously. He went off on his duties and I waited in the doorway of an unused room, thankful I was in the right corridor.

Within seconds I heard the King loudly reprimanding Mr. East for having interrupted the ceremony earlier. 'I'm surprised at you, East,' he said, as they walked along the corridor. 'You know how I feel about such things. I don't care if there is an assassin in the building, my duty comes first. Besides, it's almost certainly a lot of fuss about nothing.''

'Not this time, sir. I assure you.' I was about ten yards away, and kept well out of sight until I heard Mr. East say, 'Here we are then, sir.'

I saw him open the door and wait for the King to pass through before taking a pistol from his coat pocket. I was about to confront Mr. East when Mr. Reevers ran into the corridor. Mr. East saw him too, and quickly shut the King's door. The two friends looked at each other, but neither spoke, not until Mr. Reevers reached the King's door.

'Get out of my way, Radleigh.'

'You'll have to shoot me first.'

'Don't imagine I won't.'

There was no fear in Mr. Reevers' eyes, only pain at the treachery of his friend. When that friend instantly raised the pistol and took aim, Mr. Reevers simply leant back against the King's door, and quite deliberately folded his arms in defiance.

I held my breath, not daring to move, fearing the slightest sound would cause Mr. East to fire. They stood glaring at each other for what seemed an eternity, before the pistol wavered and was then lowered. 'Damn you, Radleigh,' Mr. East hissed. 'But I won't let you stop me.'

At that moment the King opened the door, causing Mr. Reevers, who was still leaning against it, to fall backwards. 'What the devil's going on here?'

Jumping to his feet, Mr. Reevers urged, 'Get back inside, sir.'

The King looked from one gentleman to the other. 'Don't point that gun at me, East. It might go off.'

Mr. Reevers threw himself at Mr. East, who instantly knocked out his friend with the butt of his pistol. Barely glancing at the inert figure at his feet, he turned to face the King, who was staring at him open-mouthed.

'Inside, if you please, sir.'

I emerged from my doorway, knowing exactly what I was going to do. Mr. Silver was in custody, Mr. Garnet and Mr. Pearl soon would be, and they would lead us to any other Fat Badgers. Mr. East was a French spy who'd had Septimus murdered, causing Julia great suffering. George Jenkins, another honourable man, was dead too, and the Fat Badgers had terrified Mrs. Jenkins into fleeing from the Island. But, worst of all, in my eyes, he was responsible for Jeffel's death.

It was all over in the blink of an eye. Not wanting to make a mistake, I shouted his name, knowing he would turn and present me with the perfect target.

He swung round instantly, his eyes wide with a mixture of disbelief and horror. Even as I fired the shot he saw I meant to kill him. And he was right. He was dead before he hit the floor.

CHAPTER 31

Thankfully, Mr. Reevers recovered his senses quite quickly. Later, with the King's safety ensured, and Mr. East's body swiftly and quietly removed from the building, he insisted on taking me to his office. He placed a chair, urged me to sit down, took two glasses and a bottle of wine from a cupboard, put them on his desk and poured me a good measure. Setting the glass in front of me he advised, 'It will do you good.'

I felt no remorse at what I had done. I'd had no choice; if I hadn't acted quickly Mr. East would have killed the King. The action that would start a revolution. But the sight of Mr. East's lifeless body had left me feeling so shaky I had to hold the glass rather tightly. 'I didn't feel like this when I shot Mr. Ruby.'

'He was a villain and out to kill you.'

'Mr. East wanted me dead too.'

'Yes.' He closed his eyes momentarily as if his thoughts and feelings were too hard to bear. 'But you knew, and liked, Toby. And that is quite a different thing. You will notice I could not bring myself to use a gun.'

'And nor could he,' I pointed out.

'No.' He spoke so softly I barely heard him, and when he poured himself a glass of wine I saw it wasn't only my hands that were trembling. 'I still can't believe he was spying for the French. I thought I knew Toby.'

I drank a little more wine and set the glass down on the desk. 'Did he ever talk to you about Lord Rotherton?'

'Only when that monster put a stop to his romance.'

He was so overwhelmed by sadness that I longed to put my arms around him but, of course, that was out of the questions now. 'I believed he was over it. He even told me he was.'

'Well, he had to make you, of all people, believe that he was. If he'd acted differently, you might have guessed what he meant to do.'

Swallowing some of his wine, he gazed unseeingly into the distance. 'I wish he'd told me how he felt. If he'd talked to me I might have made him see sense.'

I thought that unlikely, but I said nothing, there being no point dwelling on what couldn't be changed. Instead I asked, 'Tell me, what happened to Mr Pearl and Mr Garnet?'

'They're in custody. ' Finishing his wine, he put his glass down. 'They've admitted to being involved in murdering Septimus and Mr Jenkins. And that will suffice to hang them.'

'Justice will be done then.' Julia would be grateful. And Mrs. Jenkins could return to the Island without fearing for the lives of her children. Justice for Jeffel too, although it was a poor recompense for the loss of a man I still missed every single day, and would for a long time yet.

When I asked if they would be charged with plotting to kill the King, he said. 'I doubt it. That's not so easy to prove. Besides a public trial of that nature would serve no useful purpose when they will hang anyway.' I couldn't help but agree.

A messenger came in at that moment with a sealed note for Mr. Reevers. Dismissing the messenger he opened the note, its contents making him chuckle. Putting it into his pocket he told me, 'The King insists on returning to the Dockyard in an open carriage so as not to disappoint the crowds, and Mr. Dundas wants me to dissuade him.' I smiled too. That was so like the King, and I could see no reason why he shouldn't do so, not now. The Fat Badgers were either dead, or in custody. 'His Majesty also wishes to see you before he leaves.'

'Me?' I exclaimed in surprise. 'But, why?'

'To thank you, I imagine.' Mr. Reevers rose to his feet and walked round to me. 'If I may be allowed to escort you?'

'But I did very little.'

'That is nonsense, as you know very well. You saved the King's life.'

'I was fortunate,' I told him truthfully as I stood up.

Mr. Reevers escorted me to the King's apartment, where we found Mr. Dundas and Lord Chatham with the King. As I'd learnt in Windsor, the King was a surprisingly ordinary man, with a strong sense of duty. I curtsied deeply and he invited me into an inner room, leaving Mr. Reevers to persuade the two government ministers that all danger had passed.

The King asked me to be seated and begged me to tell him plainly about the Fat Badgers. He listened very carefully, putting an occasional question, and when I reached the end, he asked, 'What turned Mr East into a revolutionary, Lady Drusilla? I liked the man, and I thought he quite liked me.'

A picture of Toby East's face in that moment before I fired the pistol flashed in front of my eyes. I would never forget that look, that moment when he knew he was about to die. And I prayed I would never have to do such a thing again. Pushing such thoughts from my mind I told him about Rotherton's daughter. 'When she died, Mr. East blamed Lord Rotherton. Quite rightly, in my opinion.'

The King gave a sigh. 'I heard about Rotherton, of course. A shocking business. The Queen and I both thought so. How could any man force his own child to marry someone of Troughton's stamp?'

'She did refuse at first, sir, until Rotherton threatened to have Mr. East murdered unless she married Troughton.' He stared at me in a mixture of horror, outrage, and utter disgust. 'Mr. East thought it wrong for the nobility to have such power over life and death, even with their own children. And he wanted to change that.'

He stood up and walked slowly round the room before saying, 'A very sad business, what? I suppose it turned East's mind. I wish there was something I could do about Rotherton, but unfortunately he has broken no law.' Then he thanked me profusely for what I had done.

Acutely embarrassed, I said, 'It wasn't just me, sir.' I told him how much we both owed Richard. 'When Mr. East held my uncle and I at gunpoint in that alley, Captain Tanfield tackled Mr. East without a thought for his own life. The bullet meant for me struck him.'

I watched him working it out. 'Yes, I see. If he hadn't got in the way of that bullet, you would not have been there to prevent Mr. East shooting me. A brave man, indeed.' And he asked quietly, 'Was he badly wounded?'

'The surgeon believes he will recover.'

'That is good news, what? I should like to meet him. There's no better man than a brave one, what? Where will I find him?' I gave him the address and he promised to call the next day.

Once the audience was over, he sent for Mudd to thank him for his part in ensuring Mr. Silver was arrested. For, as I'd explained to His Majesty, that villain had stood within a few yards of where the King's carriage had stopped. An easy target. And Mudd was one of the few people who could recognise Mr. Silver.

By the time Mudd returned, Mr. Reevers had gone, and Mudd escorted me to the house where we were staying. I fully expected Mr Reevers to call later that day, but I didn't see him again until the following morning. By then Richard was well on the mend. Aunt Thirza and I took it in turns to sit with him, with Mr. Hamerton looking in often too.

After breakfast the next morning, when he and I were both with Richard, Mr Hamerton told me about his sister. 'She managed to smuggle a letter out to me some weeks ago. She said her husband had become a monster like Robespierre, and she could not bear to think of those dreadful atrocities he's associated with. She's desperate to leave him and return to England.'

Doubtfully, I asked, 'Is that possible?'

'I trust so. Every August she visits her husband's cousin, a widow, who lives in Normandy. That's her one chance to escape. She was terrified her husband would decide to accompany her. Fortunately, Robespierre's plans for August won't allow him to join her. So I shall cross the channel then and bring her back to my new house at Dittistone,' he said, as if rescuing her from France in the middle of a war was the easiest thing in the world."She always wanted to live on this lovely Island,' he added. At last I understood why he'd come to the Island, bought a yacht and learnt to sail.

Richard insisted, 'We'll go together.'

'No. You have to recover from your bullet wound.'

'I'll be fine by August.'

Still Mr. Hamerton shook his head. 'If anything happened to you I would never forgive myself. You have too much to lose. No, I have made up my mind. I am going alone.'

Hearing a carriage stop outside I looked out the window, and saw the King stepping down, accompanied by Lord Howe and Mr. Reevers. When I told Richard he stared at me, his eyes as round as saucers. 'The King is coming to see me? But, why?'

I laughed. 'Think about it, Richard. If you hadn't saved my life, I could not have saved his. Now let anyone call you a coward.'

He gave a great shout of laughter. 'Drusilla, you are a woman in a million. But it was sheer chance that I came back past that alley, you know. Frankly I thought Mr. East had gone mad.' He stopped as the door opened and the butler announced the King and Lord Howe. I did wonder why Mr. Reevers hadn't come in with them, but did not dwell on it. Mr. Hamerton and I left Richard to enjoy his moment of glory, and as we walked back to the drawing room I asked him how he'd managed to let his sister know what he intended to do.

'I wrote a letter and an Island smuggler said he knew someone who would take it to her in Paris,' he said. 'Cost me a packet, but I don't mind. He brought her reply too.' And added, 'He was an odd fellow. Insisted on meeting me at the church at one in the morning.

And after I'd read her letter, he made me destroy it.'

'Did he say why?'

'He said he could be hanged for communicating with the enemy, and the letter was evidence.'

I didn't tell him the real reason. That the letter was evidence of his innocence, for it would have told me he wasn't Mr. Brown. Whereas, the fact that he'd actually met Mr. Silver, and in the middle of the night, seemed to be conclusive proof of his guilt. Just as Mr. East wanted.

Which made me wonder about the aristocrat who'd knocked down and killed Mrs. Hamerton. A week later he was found murdered, and as no-one had ever been arrested, it enabled Mr. East to cast suspicion on Mr. Hamerton, by presenting the facts in a manner that suggested he had become a French spy because an aristocrat had caused his wife's death.

As we reached the bottom of the stairs, the butler informed me Mr. Reevers was waiting for me in the library. 'In that case,' Mr. Hamerton said, 'I shall go out to take the air, and enjoy the celebrations.'

I stood for some seconds, watching him go, dreading this meeting with Mr. Reevers. For, this time I would have to tell him why I had been keeping him at arm's length. And I wished with all my heart that this ordeal was already over.

When I opened the library door, he took one look at my face and came striding across the room, his hands outstretched towards mine. I shook my head at him and grasped the back of a chair, stopping him in his tracks.

'Oh, my dearest girl,' he murmured softly, a distinct catch in his voice.

'Do I look that bad?' I asked shakily.

'You look all in.'

'You have such a way with words, Mr. Reevers,' I said with a watery smile. 'I'm afraid I had trouble sleeping last night.'

He muttered tersely, 'I should never have embroiled you in all this.'

'Nonsense. I wanted to do it,' I insisted. 'And I don't regret it, not one bit.' I indicated the chair by the empty fireplace. 'Do sit down,' I said. I spoke as if he was a stranger, but I couldn't help myself. This was not going to be easy, and I was determined not to shed a single tear in front of him. I sat in the chair on the other side of the fireplace, putting a sensible distance between us. Delaying the evil moment, I asked if anyone else was aware of the attempt on the King's life.

'No, thankfully. The King won't speak of it obviously, nor will Lord Chatham and Mr. Dundas. We're all of the opinion that, with so much unrest in the country, the suspension of Habeas Corpus, the arrests of reformers, and the fear of a revolution here, it would be better if it didn't get out.'

'One of those villains might say something in court.'

'Not now they won't.'

I looked at him, puzzled. 'Why not?'

He gave a slight shrug. 'Because they're dead.'

'Dead?' I gasped. 'What all of them?'

He nodded. 'Last night we were taking them to London, and when we stopped to change horses they made a run for it. We had no choice but to shoot.' So that was why he hadn't called. I doubted it had been quite as simple as he made out, but frankly I didn't care. I was glad they were all dead.

I saw him take a deep breath, and knowing what was coming next, I babbled, 'What about Mr. East. He will have to be buried.'

'That is in hand. Everything will be done properly. It's not the first time we've organised a quiet burial.'

'But doesn't he have a family?'

'No-one close. His parents are dead and he had no siblings.'

'What about his friends?'

'We'll let it be known he's gone back to France, and after a suitable time, announce he was killed in the line of duty.'

'Then it's all settled.' I rose to my feet, meaning to ring for the butler to see Mr. Reevers out, but he was there before me. 'Not quite everything. Sit down, Drusilla. You know why I came here this morning. And I have waited long enough, don't you think?'

It was useless to protest; and in any case, now the Fat Badgers were no more, it was better to get it over with.

'Very well,' I said, returning to my chair. 'What do you wish to say?'

'Good God, Drusilla,' he spluttered in disbelief, as he too sat down again. 'You know what I want to say. In heaven's name tell me why you have been giving me the cold shoulder.'

There was only one way to answer him; I told him the truth, repeating what my godmother had said in her letter. When he put his head in his hands and groaned, I whispered shakily, 'So, it's true.'

'I won't lie to you,' he said in a constrained voice. 'Yes, it is true.'

I felt as if he'd struck me. I jumped up and walked over to the window, keeping my back to him so that he couldn't see my face. And I realised that, all along, I had half hoped it was one of those stories that became exaggerated with the telling. Well, now I knew it wasn't. He'd admitted he was a fortune hunter.

I had been taken in as easily as a girl just out of the schoolroom. Choking back the tears, I squared my shoulders and calmly returned to my seat to face him, determined not to let him see what I really felt for him. But the tenderness in his eyes almost undid me, and the words I'd planned to say stuck in my throat. In the end he spoke first.

'Try to understand, Drusilla. I was twenty-nine and had never met anyone I wanted to marry, and I was beginning to think I never would. Sophie and I got on extremely well. I liked her enormously. I still do. For her that liking turned to love, for me it did not. But she's an intelligent, beautiful woman, and I thought I could make her happy.'

'And it solved your financial problems,' I burst out bitterly.

'Yes. It's not an uncommon arrangement.'

'So you made her an offer, and she accepted.' He inclined his head with obvious reluctance. 'Did you have no compunction?'

'Drusilla, she wanted to marry me.'

'No doubt she believed you returned her affection.'

He bit his lip, and agreed that she had. 'That I do regret.'

'So what went wrong?' Catching a glimpse of myself in the looking glass on the wall, I was shocked to see how white and strained my face was.

'If you will allow me to explain?' I shrugged with as much indifference as I could muster, and he carried on,

'In the beginning her whole family welcomed me into their midst. I liked and admired her father, adored her mother. My circumstances did not worry them. But when I asked Sophie's father for her hand in marriage, he saw what Sophie had not, and asked me if I really loved her. And I could not bring myself to lie.'

He stopped briefly, as if remembering that moment. 'Her father reminded me he'd made it plain from the outset that he wanted his daughter to have the kind of loving marriage he and his wife enjoyed. He'd seen too much unhappiness in arranged marriages to be willing to accept second best for his beloved daughter. Furthermore, he said, he was bitterly disappointed in me, for he had not thought me a fortune hunter. I hadn't thought that of myself either, merely that this might be the perfect compromise for me, and that I would probably come to love Sophie in time. But I hadn't considered the marriage from Sophie's point of view, and I should have done. She deserved to marry a man who truly adored her. '

'So you could lie to the woman you meant to marry, but not to her father.'

He flinched at the bitterness in my voice. 'It would seem so. I am not proud of it, Drusilla. Her father said I should have been honest with her, and he was right. Then, if she still wished to go ahead, there might not have been any objection. He asked me if I would have proposed marriage if she had not been an heiress, and I had to admit I would not have. I was asked to leave at once.'

He looked at me, waiting for me to speak, but I could only think of how he must have made himself agreeable to her, as he had to me. Teasing, occasionally flattering her, making her believe that he loved her, and that his life would have no purpose without her. And having failed with Sophie, he'd hoped to succeed with me. I glanced up at him and saw he was watching me intently. Still he said nothing and eventually I burst out, 'Aren't you going to tell me it's not the same with me?'

'No,' he said softly. 'You wouldn't believe me.'

'How very true.'

'I'm not a saint, Drusilla.' I brushed that aside with a gesture of indifference. 'Nor would you be happy with such a man.'

I looked up at that, conscious it was all too true. 'You should have told me about Sophie.'

He lifted his shoulders in helpless regret. 'Perhaps. But I knew what you would think. Still, it is of no importance now. I have been ordered back to London, and from there to France. And a government agent in France, if betrayed, is as easily guillotined as an aristocrat or a simple peasant. While this war lasts I refuse to inflict that kind of anxiety on my ---- on any woman.' And he immediately rose to his feet. 'I must go. I have a number of things to see to before----'

'When do you leave?' I heard myself ask.

'In an hour or two.'

'So soon?' The words were out before I could stop them.

'We must find this double agent Toby spoke of. The one who turned him into a French spy. Tell me, what did he actually say about this man? Did he describe him in any way?'

I thought for a moment. 'He didn't mention the man's appearance. Just that he was a Frenchman who had come over to our side, having supposedly become disillusioned with the revolution. Whereas, in fact, Robespierre had charged him with the task of infiltrating the corresponding societies.'

'No matter. I'll seek him out.' He took my hand in a formal gesture of parting, but held it much longer than was seemly. Somewhat hesitantly, he went on, 'It would be better to say nothing now, I know, but I might not return, and for that reason I must, and will, speak. Whatever you think of me at this moment, I want you to know you are the only woman I have ever truly loved. I beg you to believe me, my dearest girl, for it is the truth.'

I felt tears welling and cursed them, for they made it impossible for me to answer. Emotions, I thought, are the very devil.

Lifting my hand to his lips he slowly and ardently kissed the tips of my fingers, one by one, before whispering huskily, 'Goodbye, Drusilla.' Then he turned and strode out of the room without a backward glance, leaving me breathless and shaken by the intensity of my own feelings. From the window I watched him walk out into the street and down the road. He did not look back and I did not move until long after he had disappeared from sight.

If he had lied about Sophie, made excuses, or pleaded with me, I would have instantly cast him out of my life. But he had done none of those things. Instead, by quietly announcing he refused to inflict on any woman the kind of anxiety other agents' wives endured, he had removed the need for me to make a decision. As if, by doing so, it would extinguish all my fears for his safety. I had not thought him so foolish.

As for my own future, I had been certain, after Marguerite's letter, that it could not include Radleigh Reevers. Yet, when he told me what had happened between him and Sophie, and of his remorse at failing to consider her feelings as he ought to have done, I longed to believe him. Longed to ignore the tiny nagging doubts that persisted at the back of my mind.

A sensible woman, I told myself, would have nothing more to do with Mr. Reevers. And I'd always believed myself to be eminently sensible. But feelings had nothing to do with sense, and the truth was, I could not bear to think I would never see him again.

Yet I had no idea what I would do if we did meet again. In fact, right now, I was only certain of two things; that he would return to France, and I would go home to Westfleet. Back to the Island and the people I loved. A thought that lifted my spirits and brought the faintest of smiles to my lips.

Perhaps there I would see things more clearly. For, whatever the future brought, that was where I wanted to be.

THE END

HISTORICAL NOTE

"The Fat Badger Society" is, of course, a work of fiction. It is, however, based on fact. Corresponding Societies sprang up in many cities in Britain in the early 1790s, electoral reform being one of their aims. They corresponded with each other by letter and, although most were peaceful reformers, a few did correspond with revolutionary France.

William Pitt appointed a Secret Committee to look into their affairs and their report suggested some societies were preparing for revolution. This led to the suspension of Habeas Corpus in May 1794, when many leading reformers were arrested. But, after Hardy, Horne Tooke and Thelwall were acquitted in October of that year, charges against the others were scrapped. The suspension was lifted in June 1795. Corresponding Societies were banned in 1799.

In 1780, under 3% of the adult male population had the vote. Reform acts of 1832, 1867 and 1884 very slowly improved on that figure, but it wasn't until 1918 that all men over 21 were able to vote. In 1918, some women over 30 got the vote, but the rest had to wait until 1928.

George 111 reigned for 59 years and several attempts were made on his life.

In late June 1794, the King, Queen and six Princesses went to Portsmouth to attend the celebrations for Admiral Howe's great victory, known as "The Glorious First of June." The King did present Howe with a jewelled sword, and the following day he held a levee at Government House where the heroes of the battle were suitably honoured.